BUILD ME A CITY

With best wishes to Cindy

BUILD ME A CITY

Secrets, Lies and Love
In Baron Haussmann's Paris

Nancy Joaquim

A Novel by
Nancy Joaquim

**MONTROSE
HALL**

This book is dedicated to my husband,

Richard, and our daughter Vanessa with loving

appreciation for sharing so fully in this journey.

ACKNOWLEDGEMENTS

I am grateful to those writers, historians, biographers, and photographers who pointed the way to developments and events relevant to aspects of my own research and study on Baron Haussmann and his Paris Project. **Build Me a City** is a historical novel based on true events. As such, the story of Charles Fabron and Daniel Lazare is set against the very real background of the extraordinary but largely forgotten Haussmann years and it is those seventeen years upon which my research and study have centered.

The loss of thousands of Haussmann-Era related documents in the disastrous 1871 fire at the Hotel de Ville (City Hall) has left a great void in the Haussmann archive. Baron Haussmann's vast complex of offices and sumptuous apartment in the magnificent Right Bank building which also headquartered the city's many public works departments as well as scores of municipal agencies contained a treasure trove of invaluable records including original drawings, notes, maps, letters, and files which of and by themselves would have formed a compelling portrait not only of Baron Haussmann and his moment but also of the role played by Second Empire politics in the often controversial modernization of an ancient city. Fortunately, years later, when he had retired to his Bordeaux estate, Baron Haussmann wrote three volumes of Memoirs which exist today. They have served as an important guide to my understanding of the man and the dynamic period in which he lived and worked.

I wish to express deepest thanks to my husband, Richard, whose opinions and viewpoints contributed immeasurably to my work on the manuscript, his background in architecture and land planning of particular value in my approach to the development of characters significant to the Haussmannization of Paris.

I thank our daughter Vanessa whose observations and impressions in reading the manuscript as it progressed made her an invaluable editor. Her thoughtful comments contributed greatly to the shaping of **Build Me a City.**

I am grateful to Tom Wallace, friend and agent, for his advice and counsel. His unfailing encouragement and attention have continued to inspire and motivate me.

The poet is a kinsman in the clouds
Who scoffs at archers, loves a stormy day;
But on the ground among the hooting crowds,
He cannot walk, his wings are in the way.

Charles Baudelaire
Les Fleurs Du Mal

PREFECT OF THE SEINE
MASTER BUILDER OF PARIS

The Baron Georges Eugene Haussmann (1809-1891)

Pierre Petit (French, 1832 - 1909)

[Baron Georges Eugene] Haussmann (1809 - 1891), about 1865,
Albumen silver print
84.XD.379.72

The J. Paul Getty Museum, Los Angeles

As a gifted young architect left his home in Rouen to take part in the great transformation of Paris, an infant male child was placed in an orphanage.

The architect and the child lived many miles apart, but their narrative had begun, and later, as the orphan grew and became a man, the architect unraveled a secret that in its devious abstraction would bind them together forever.

CIRCUMSTANCES

Paris 1863

THE SUMMER HEAT had been relentless that year. There seemed to be no end to it. Day after day, through late August and into mid-September when temperatures normally began to fall, the sun had blazed hot and dry. There was not a drop of rain. The incessant noise and endless clouds of dust emanating from every corner only added to the discomfort, but we were building a city and discomfort and inconvenience were everywhere. We were transforming Paris, the cultural center of the world. The massive transformation of the legendary City by the Seine had been in progress since 1853. Understandably, given existing conditions ten years later, citizen patience was at a low point.

Every night, Parisians fell asleep longing for the brisk chill of autumn and the return of midnight silence to a city calmed and cooled. When they awakened to another graceless day and found nothing changed, some fell to their knees and prayed. Others wept. Still others lingered in their beds for an hour or two of dreaming. Their dreams were wrapped in aching images of the untroubled past. In surges of vivid memory they caught tender glimpses of childhood, they saw familiar faces they loved, and they remembered when no one in the house was angry or afraid or pervasively bitter. It was as if they were living through a war, which I suppose in many ways they were.

In houses crowded close together along age-old lanes and passageways, men dressed in the dark. They kissed their sleepy wives and children good-bye and set out for another day's work, making their way onto narrow streets and alleyways they had known all their lives and now hardly recognized. Even in the pale blue light of breaking dawn it was impossible to avoid the piles of rubble lying everywhere. Some of the men walked over the refuse without hesitating. Some tripped and fell. Here and there a cast-off chair stood like a shadowed throne awaiting the arrival of a foolish king, and as the sun rose and shone down upon the changing world that was Old Paris, the deafening drumbeat of progress in a city being wrenched out of its past was heard, and so began another day in my chaotic world.

I hired the men who dressed in the dark. I watched and waited as they took up hammers and axes and destroyed untold numbers of houses and shops to make way for the long blocks of new buildings and miles of wide avenues and boulevards being built under the leadership of a dynamic forty-five-year-old Baron named Georges Haussmann. My supervisory role in this ambitious undertaking was significant, but as the following pages will reveal, my daily responsibilities were seldom cause for rejoicing. People were displaced. Families were fragmented. Of course there were soaring triumphs and countless occasions of speechless awe as Baron Haussmann's New Paris emerged in the magnificent torrent of buildings, parks, and monuments that today define the beautiful City of Light, but by their destructive nature my daily responsibilities in making that magnificence possible felt neither triumphant nor awe-inspiring. There were times when I wondered why I should continue on. Over time I wrote four letters of resignation. I never submitted them. By the summer of 1863 I was tired and emotionally drained, but on a day in mid-September I found myself re-evaluating my role in the revitalization of Paris. It was a Saturday. I had just completed appraisals on buildings scheduled for demolition along a section of Boulevard Saint-Germain and was making final notes in my ledger when a loud voice called out, "Bonjour Monsieur Fabron!"

Looking up when I heard my name, I remember watching what I thought was a workman coming toward me with an impossible to fill request or more likely, a well-rehearsed complaint. Tall and lean, he walked in long, confident strides, the way an experienced workman walks when he has a specific purpose in mind. In the clear morning light the first thing I noticed about him was his hair. It was impossible to ignore. Long and blonde, with every turn of his head it caught glimmers of sun as it brushed against the frayed collar of his gray shirt. When I asked who he was and why he was interrupting my work, he said, "My name is Daniel Lazare. I am eleven years old and I am your new Runner. Marie Duclos sent me."

"My Runner? I'm not expecting a new Runner," I quickly snapped. "And how do you know I am the person Marie Duclos sent you to see? There are many people here on the boulevard today! You must be mistaken!"

"No, Monsieur Fabron, I am not mistaken," came the immediate, surprisingly calm response. "You are the person I was sent to see. "Marie Duclos told me at breakfast this morning that I was to meet you today. When I asked where I was to go and how I would recognize you, she said I was to come to Saint-Germain, to the blue doors of the Abbey, and from there I was to look across the boulevard for a tall man holding an important looking black book. You are tall, Monsieur, you are holding an important-looking black book, and you looked up when I called out your name."

This was my introduction to Daniel Lazare.

———※———

I had been at work on the Paris Project from the beginning, making every attempt, as the city was being torn apart and put back together, to maintain a reasonable sense of order in fulfilling my daily responsibilities which dealt with appraisals, evictions, demolition schedules, and clearing of land. On this particular morning nothing was going according to plan. My carefully calculated agenda was proving worthless. Boulevard Saint-Germaine was in total disarray. Wagonloads of demolition equipment were late, teams of waiting laborers were threatening to leave, and a profusion of pushcarts, carriages, horses, vendors and pedestrians crowded the boulevard making expected deliveries impossible. Daniel Lazare was one more irritation. Had it not been that I needed help sending messages requesting prompt assistance in clearing the area, I would have sent him on his way, but having dismissed my former Runner a few days before and conditions being what they were, I handed him two quickly written notes and gave him directions. I wasn't expecting to see him again. Despite his height, he looked thin and frail. There were beads of perspiration across his forehead. Dark circles had settled under his blue eyes, but as if to compensate for his obvious fatigue there was an admirable air of self-certainty about him as he assured me my messages would not only be delivered promptly but answered as well. "Monsieur Fabron, do not worry," he stated with a firm nod as he set off along the boulevard. "I will return with replies as soon as possible."

Looking back, I remember it was with a rare feeling of admiration that I watched this young stranger disappear into the confusing spectacle on Boulevard Saint-Germain, his understanding that my messages required replies providing a welcome touch of logic on a morning completely void of any shred of logic. When in a surprisingly short time he returned with replies assuring me of rapid solutions to my dilemma, I knew I had acquired a dependable Runner. Daniel Lazare had not been assigned to me with advance notice as was the customary procedure in the Runner Program, but formalities aside, with his quick grasp of my problem he had managed to impress me and I immediately approved him.

From the start I saw Daniel as an unusual boy. He was serious about his responsibilities and not at all like other Runners I had apprenticed in the past, those orphaned boys and runaways between the ages of nine and fourteen who, for a few centimes each week, carried messages as a means of communication between construction and demolition sites. Daniel smiled often, even when there was little to smile about, which was most of the time. I liked that about him. I also liked the fact that with a maturity well beyond his years he didn't carry the burden of resentment I saw all too often in the hostile eyes of similarly abandoned boys who went about their tasks with little more than mute resignation. Daniel was different. He was observant and interested in everything happening around him. Of course he had his childish moments. He was just a boy, but much to his credit, he never complained; not about the long hours and not once about the weather, the clouds of dust, or the mountains of debris we lived with every day. In no time at all he became the best of the Haussmann Runners, fast and reliable. I can close my eyes and see him exactly as he was in those years: a tall, slender boy moving like the wind as he carried his messages, his cheeks flushed, his flaxen hair a ready foil for the glints of sun that seemed so eager to follow him. Many who toiled to create the new City by the Seine came to know and love Daniel. By the time he disappeared he was affectionately known as the boy with yellow hair.

Daniel Lazare became my Runner during a pivotal period in the French Capital City. From the beginning and in his own way, I believe he understood that. He was hardly a student of history, but it was common knowledge even among the youngest Runners that Paris was emerging from the inertia of centuries, every dramatic aspect of its transformation driven by a highly motivated leader. In December of 1852, Louis Napoleon the Third had become Emperor of France. His arrival had stirred national curiosity to a near fever pitch, and understandably so. He was a Bonaparte, a nephew of Napoleon I, son of Napoleon's brother Louis, King of Holland and Josephine's daughter, Hortense. The lineage was great fodder for the Paris café crowd. They couldn't get enough, intrigued by the fact that as a result of his fascinating Bonaparte affiliation, Louis Napoleon had lived in exile all his adult life and yet here he was, another Emperor of France named Bonaparte. More important to the true state of affairs was the further fact that on a cold December morning a very serious Louis Napoleon had come through the gates of Paris as Emperor with great ceremony and a highly ambitious agenda. Details of his regal carriage, its eight plumed horses, and the extraordinary length of his entourage became the stuff of local legend and a story which in increasingly exaggerated detail was repeated from one end of Paris to the other. What was not repeated or as widely known was that although eager to proceed with matters of state and quickly display his administrative abilities, the new Emperor was far from happy with the Paris he found. Coming into the city through the monumental Gate of Saint-Denis and continuing on to the Tuileries Palace he had looked out from his carriage window in shock. This was not the Paris he had expected. It was dirty. It was littered with garbage. It was muddy and foul-smelling. It may have had its impressive history and glamorous culture but it was not beautiful. It was not clean. It did not set a suitable stage for the glorious Second Empire he envisioned as the envy of all Europe. Something had to be done. And it was. In the course of the next seventeen years Louis Napoleon would re-establish French international prominence by appointing an ambitious and highly capable municipal administrator named Baron Georges-Eugene Haussmann to change the face of venerable old Paris in an extraordinary period of construction and redevelopment devoted to breathing new life into the aging City by the Seine.

These then, were the circumstances in which I found myself when in 1853, at the age of thirty, I too arrived in the French Capital with an ambitious agenda, mine accompanied by neither title or crown nor the myth of an uncle named Bonaparte, but of a nature that by the scope of its spectacular productivity would place me at the forefront of all Emperor Louis Napoleon demanded of his dazzling Second Empire. In all its dereliction and promise this was the same Paris in which Daniel Lazare also found himself when in 1863, at the tender age of eleven, he appeared at my chaotic Boulevard Saint-Germain worksite unannounced and unprepared, but eager to become my Runner and participate in the great re-development of The City by the Seine. As we became acquainted, working together and witnessing the miracle of a city coming into its golden age, neither of us could have imagined the magnitude of what lay ahead, but I will admit I have sometimes wondered what would have happened if I had lived a simpler, less complicated life, perhaps as a banker or better yet, as a beloved civil servant known for his good deeds. Of course, having pursued neither of these professions, suffice it to say that I am Charles Fabron, French citizen and University-trained architect. I was born and raised in Rouen and was enjoying a respectable degree of professional success in my home city when seven short months after Louis Napoleon assumed his empirical duties, I received a letter from a Paris official close to His Imperial Majesty. It conveyed a simple but compelling message, one that prompted me to turn away from everything I cared about: my home, my family, and my career. The persuasive communication awaited me on one of those idyllic mid-summer afternoons when sunshine immerses the French countryside in its notorious light and a glance to the flawless blue sky suggests all is right with the world even if it really isn't.

Blonde, blue-eyed Daniel Lazare was eighteen months old and resident of an orphanage in the village of La Bouille. We lived 12 miles apart.

PART I

WITH FEAR AND FAVOR

CHAPTER ONE

The Letter

Rouen,
July 30, 1853

I HAD LEFT MY HOUSE on Seine-Maritime Hill early that morning, intent on reviewing proposals and contracts at my architectural offices in Rouen's central district. There were final details to be worked out on structural restoration of the city's oldest medieval square and a new road south to Evreux had been proposed by the City Council, this a major fifty-kilometer project requiring the technical expertise of a surveyor, an occupation for which in addition to my profession as an architect, I was also qualified. Having been away from the office for several days I was looking forward to meeting with my staff. They were a group of six talented designers, draftsmen, and assistants and they shared my enthusiasm for projects focused on restoration of historic sections of Rouen and its centuries-old half-timbered buildings, many dating back to the fourteenth century. Arriving at the doors to my own recently restored half-timbered building at Number 4 Rue de Vicomte, I stepped out of my carriage eager to begin the workday.

I did all the right things. I went through the motions of meeting with designers and their assistants. I glanced through documents on the Evreux project. I signed letters to city officials. I smiled and joked and made every effort to study drawings and plans, but by early afternoon I had left for home; unproductive, dissatisfied, and unable to make sense of anything at all. It was the same old problem. I couldn't concentrate. I wanted nothing more than to be left alone. Outside, on Rue de Vicomte, I hailed a for-hire carriage.

As time has passed, I have often wished I could return to the handsome, half-timbered building at Number Four Rue de Vicomte on that July day. I would change everything. I would handle people and situations like the purposeful man I am today and not like the disquieted human being I was then. I would be decisive and disciplined, true to myself and kinder to others. I remember how in the carriage, returning home to Seine-Maritime Hill that afternoon, I sat slumped into a corner of the brown leather seat, disgusted with myself for once again failing to accomplish much of anything, yet at the same time oddly comforted by the prospect of another uneventful evening alone at home. Passing Rouen's towering Cathedral and the confrontational architecture of the bank building across the square which never failed to annoy me, it pleased me to think about the approaching dimness of twilight and the fall of night at the house on the hill. There were no demands, no obligations, and the routine seldom varied.

I liked spending the late afternoon hours walking the dogs. If the day was sunny and clear we went as far as the abandoned old mill at Jacotin Pond where Zoe and Fleur ran along the water's edge barking, chasing frogs, and fetching the sticks I threw out toward the willows. Zoe and Fleur understood the routine. They understood me. Most remarkable of all, they understood when I was ready to return home. To this day when I look back on those afternoons I wonder if their signal to put an end to our outings had something to do with my change of mood; something they instinctively sensed when they knew I had tired of our play, but in an instant they would leave the water's edge and turn onto the path leading home, jumping playfully over fallen branches as they went, tails wagging as they ran past familiar old stands of oak and pine trees, always circling back to be sure I was keeping up. As the familiar white house at the top of the hill came into view they raced ahead, running faster and faster, two brown and white spaniels scampering under the rose arbor to the garden door and the water bowls waiting in a corner of the kitchen while I made my way to the study to pour myself a cognac, light a pipe, and take comfort in my own thoughts or turn to whatever book I might have started reading the night before. At six o'clock the chimes rang out from the clock on the mantel. With the sixth chime it was time to leave pipe, thoughts, and book and climb the stairs to my room at the end of the upstairs hall where I spent twenty minutes bathing in the warm water of the alcove tub. Ablutions complete, I would dry off, dress, pour myself another glass of cognac downstairs, and read through the mail before my solitary dinner at seven. It wasn't a terrible routine. It was just the way life was.

On this particular July day the routine changed. It would never be the same. In a very short time there would be no further meetings with assistants and staff, no failures of concentration, and no long walks with Zoe and Fleur to Jacotin Pond. I had barely stepped through the front door when Pauline, my housekeeper, announced with great excitement that a letter from Paris had been delivered earlier that afternoon by special courier. I could see the oversized envelope on the hall table. It was propped up like a trophy against a vase of freshly cut roses which I assumed Pauline had clipped from the garden to mark what she believed, or more likely hoped, was an announcement inviting me to something. But that was Pauline, a kindly, patient soul who invariably chose to look on the bright side of things. Given my circumstances I was fortunate to have her. Before taking on responsibilities in my home Pauline had worked for my parents. She had come to them as a girl and I cannot think back to my childhood without her being there to see me through the normal boyhood proliferations of scraped knees, bruised elbows, and hurt feelings. "Ah, mon petit monsieur Charles," she would say in her sing-song voice, shaking her head as she applied compresses to my assortment of minor injuries, "you must be more careful! You don't want to grow up with ugly scars all over yourself, do you? You are a fine young gentleman and your parents want you to look like one, cared for and in one perfect piece. And always remember," she wisely advised when I poured out my troubles, upset over an argument with a classmate, "disagreements with others are part of life. You will always have them but you mustn't make enemies over them."

By the time she took over care of my household, Pauline was beloved by my entire family of uncles, aunts, and cousins, and she knew me as well as anyone. She also knew it was highly unusual for me to receive courier-delivered letters from Paris at Seine-Maritime Hill. Despite Pauline's best intentions, however, and quite thoroughly in keeping with what in recent months had become my typical approach to surprises, I was absolutely certain that the communication so prominently displayed on my hall table carried bad news. Someone had died or I was being sued.

"The courier was such a nice young man," Pauline said with her shy smile as I took the pristine envelope in hand, "and I must say, Monsieur Charles, he was very complimentary about this house. He said he had enjoyed the beautiful walk up the hill. Of course I told him how everyone enjoys that walk and that this house is a landmark in Rouen. It was such a warm day I thought it would be nice to offer him a glass of cool lemon tea. I hope you don't mind. I know how you feel about strangers in the house. Everyone is so curious about this place, especially now that you live here alone, but the young man looked a bit tired so I took him into the kitchen and we chatted over our tea while he took a little rest. He told me that big changes were coming to Paris, something about new buildings and parks. It sounded as if the city was going to be completely made over. Do you think such a thing could really happen Monsieur Charles? My sister in Paris hasn't said a thing about it in her letters."

Thanking Pauline, I assured her that despite my aversion to admitting strangers into the house, she had done the right thing in offering tea to the courier on a hot summer day and I added that yes, I had heard something about the Emperor intending to make a few changes to Paris. I also said I would be sure to let her know as soon as possible what news the letter had brought. Pauline smiled a relieved smile and excused herself while along with my own mounting curiosity I took the now rather foreboding hand-delivered message into my study. Seated at my desk, I carefully lifted the red wax seal from the back of the envelope. I slowly removed the folded sheet of ivory vellum from inside and proceeded to read and re-read every remarkable word written on the page. Citing my professional experience as an experienced architect and surveyor in the City of Rouen, the newly appointed Mayor of Paris was offering me a supervisory position in his Offices of City Planning. Of course I was immensely flattered, but I couldn't imagine why the Mayor of Paris would have contacted me. We lived miles apart and had never met. There were dozens of well-qualified French architects and surveyors he could have called on, many older and more experienced than I, most living closer to Paris.

More than thirty years have passed since that July day. Events have played themselves out and history itself has revealed the power of masterful delusion, but in that summer of 1853 my small world was turned upside down, for the author of my letter was no ordinary Mayor and his were no ordinary mayoral duties. My letter had come from Baron Georges Haussmann and only weeks before, Emperor Louis Napoleon had appointed him not only Mayor of Paris, or Prefect of the Seine, as he was to be officially known, but after a brief meeting on June 29th the Emperor had also appointed forty-five-year-old Haussmann to the immense task of directing the transformation of the City of Paris. He was to demolish thousands of centuries-old houses, hovels, and shops on narrow, garbage-littered lanes and replace them with wide new streets, fine new buildings, and landscaped parks and squares. He was to clean the River Seine, eliminate its foulness, and create a system for sending sewage out of the city. Overnight, Prefect Baron Georges-Eugene Haussmann had become the city's Municipal Administrator, its Master Builder, and the Emperor's favorite citizen.

Throughout the next seventeen years, I worked at Baron Haussmann's side as with carte blanche from our Emperor he performed miracle after miracle, successfully transforming Paris from a medieval walled city languishing by the polluted River Seine into the sanitized, soul-stirring urban masterpiece the world knows and loves today. I was there as The Baron's lavish parks, magnificent gardens, grand monuments, and uniform blocks of elegant residential structures rose one after the other, year after year, along a vast network of wide avenues and boulevards lined with the glittering array of cafes, restaurants, apartment buildings, and hotels which would define the mercurial Haussmann years, bringing pride to its citizens, fame to Baron Georges-Eugene Haussmann, and as was intended from the start, glorious prestige to Emperor Louis Napoleon's ambitious Second Empire. I was there when Queen Victoria and Prince Albert came to admire the wonders of the New Paris. I was there when plans for the Bois de Boulogne, the great two-thousand-acre Park of Paris, were nothing more than sketches on paper. I was there when the Arc de Triomphe, long isolated in an overgrown field, became the iconic centerpiece of its now famous radius of twelve avenues, and I was there when imperial medals, citations, and accolades came with jealousy, obstruction, and accusations of every ugly sort.

We can look back in wonder as I do now, at the conditions and events which have shaped our lives, often unaware until too late that their greatest potentials were disguised and governed in one way or another by uncontrollable circumstances and the state of our own emotions. Today, from my own self-imposed exile in the Bordeaux where I live in a country cottage with young versions of Zoe and Fleur and tend to what often seems too large a garden, I remain grateful for the opportunities granted me during an extraordinary time, but those years were not always kind. My assignments were difficult. Historic old cities are not transformed with champagne and chamber music. As Paris was torn apart, re-built, and re-defined there were hardships and tragedies. There was disagreement, animosity and loss, and in the course of it all, there was no shortage of human suffering. I blame no one person, certainly not The Baron, for the difficulties and disappointments I faced day after day in the midst of remarkable triumph. For good or ill, I made my own decisions, but I do harbor one personal regret. It concerns Daniel. My best hope is that the years ahead will provide opportunities fulfilling enough to erase the pain lodged in his childhood memories of life in an orphanage, but he is a grown man now. The damage is done, and at the end there may be no forgiveness. I must be prepared for that. For the time being, though, and for purposes of this Memoir which I dedicate to Daniel, I will do my best to accurately relate facts and describe events as I knew them and lived them. There are sets of circumstances concerning the nature and progress of the Haussmann Project that must be understood from their earliest beginnings, and not only by Daniel, but by others who cared and tried. It was a critical period in Paris. I cannot over-emphasize this point. People from all walks of life had good intentions, but like me they were living through a transformative time in an imprudent world. I hope to make that clear in the course of the following pages and perhaps by recalling, and in some cases re-living the intertwining of events and relationships during the early Haussmann years as I do in Part One, and by relating the nature of their powerful impact on a young orphan as I do in Part Two, that flaxen-haired boy who appeared one day at my worksite on a Paris boulevard and is now a celebrated citizen of the world will at last find answers to questions he has asked all his life.

CHAPTER TWO

The Journey

IT WAS 1853, SATURDAY, August 27th, when I stepped off the afternoon train from Rouen, a thirty-year-old architect and surveyor wearing his best suit, pulling nervously at his sleeves, glancing every which way in the bustling crowd at the Paris station, not knowing what to expect of Paris or himself, but with every intention of grasping an opportunity and adjusting to the demands of a new life. And a new life was exactly what was needed by the disillusioned malcontent I had become. I had been widowed for more than a year and remained deeply bereaved. Grief dominated my life. It drove my every thought and action and no matter what I did or how hard I tried, I couldn't shake it off; not at my offices, not at Seine-Maritime Hill, and not in long walks with Zoe and Fleur to bucolic Jacotin Pond.

At the age of twenty-two, my beautiful wife, Louisa, had died in childbirth along with the infant twin sons she had struggled to bring into the world. Their loss had come as a terrible shock, mainly because as Louisa's labor had progressed through a long December night, the doctor had kept appearing to reassure me that everything was advancing "absolutely as normal." When morning came and I was told what had happened, I couldn't make sense of the words. I had to hear them over and over again. I had to repeat them to myself. My wife and infant sons dead? No, it couldn't be. It was a dreadful mistake. Christmas was coming. Louisa had bought presents. The nursery was freshly painted. It was furnished and ready. Everything had been going so well. How could this have happened?

Waiting all that night in the downstairs hall, I had crossed and uncrossed my arms dozens of times. I paced. I sat. I stood. I prayed, anxious but delighted to imagine what it would be like in coming years to hear the sound of childish laughter echoing through the lovely house on Seine-Maritime Hill I had bought for Louisa shortly before our wedding. I had intended to design and build a house for her eventually. I had drawn up preliminary plans, but several weeks before we were married, the house on Seine-Maritime Hill came on the market. It was a property I had admired as a boy, often fantasizing about what it would be like to live there on the outskirts of the thriving city of Rouen in a beautiful, spacious house at the top of a hill where the surrounding land bordered the woodlands of the rolling countryside. When I was told the owners had decided to sell, I hoped Louisa would fall in love with the house and its grounds as I had. I was not disappointed. "Darling, its wonderful here," she said when I took her to see the property for the first time. "There's lots of room and a big lawn. This is a place for a family, for parents and children and their children. Those trees look as if they're just waiting for swings and climbing. Do you really think all this could be ours?"

I would have sold my soul to buy that house for Louisa. From the first moment I saw her I wanted her to share my life. I wanted her to have everything I was capable of giving. We met at a Sunday luncheon party, one of those weekly events Paris was famous for in those days. It was April. She was chatting with a group in the garden. She smiled and laughed as she talked. I watched her, riveted. She was the most beautiful girl I had ever seen. Andre Rousseau, a friend of mine, must have noticed me staring. He came up beside me and handed me a glass of champagne. "Charles, you look as if you need this," he said. "Are you nervous about something?"

"Who's that pretty blonde girl over there?" I asked, doing my best to sound only mildly interested as I took the champagne. "I've never seen her before."

"Ah, Charles, I might have known you'd notice her," Andre said, feigning annoyance as he took an impatient breath. "That's my cousin Louisa. She and her family moved from Dijon to Rouen a few weeks ago and I've been assigned the happy task of escorting her to dreadful affairs like this and seeing to it that she meets some nice people, which does not include tall, good-looking rogues like you!"

He laughed. "Beautiful, isn't she? That hair. That smile, and have you ever seen such a tiny little waist? And she's so nice. Not too flirty, not too unapproachable. Pity we're related. I could get serious about a girl like that. All the women I know are pushy and dying to get married. They're also fat. Not that I'm such a great a catch, but I really prefer slim, graceful women and I've noticed there's a real shortage of that type in Rouen these days. You know how it is: the beautiful tray of eclairs at Madame Algarde's one afternoon, the delicious pots de crème at Monsieur Barre's on another, and that's while they're still young. Over time it all adds up. Can you imagine what will happen when they get as old as Madame Gauthier over there? Now there's a case of too many eclairs and pots de crème allowed to thrive and multiply. Look at her stuffing herself with chocolates! If she gets any bigger, she'll have to be carried around in a sedan chair!"

It was rude of Andre to make fun of Madame Gauthier who was a good friend of my parents, but I laughed out loud. I couldn't help myself. Andre was witty and clever and in this case he was right. Madame Gauthier really was large. Andre laughed too as he looked away to survey the groups gathered in the garden and I continued in my admiration of the beautiful girl from Dijon.

"Charles, it's against my better judgement," he announced, turning back to me as if he read my mind, "but alright. Come with me. I'll introduce you to beautiful Cousin Louisa. You haven't been able to take your eyes off her. I hope I don't live to regret this, but I do wish I had time to warn her about you. On the other hand, I'm beginning to feel sorry for you. Louisa has enormous charm. Poor Charles, the most eligible bachelor in Rouen could soon be out of circulation! Such a pity!"

I remember hearing Andre speak her name, Louisa Dietrich, and I remember the slight tilt of her head when she smiled at me and said hello, but I remember nothing else about Andre's introduction. Whatever he may have said didn't matter. They were only words. I would have been happy to stand there all afternoon and all night in complete silence, just gazing into those beautiful blue eyes, my stomach in knots, a strange elation sweeping over every inch of me. The next day we had lunch together in a small neighborhood restaurant. I had left the office early and called for her at her home where I met her parents. The Dietrichs seemed to like me well enough and didn't object at all to the idea of Louisa and I having lunch alone together. In those days, unattached young ladies of a particular status were not allowed to leave their homes without a chaperone, usually a stern old aunt who had been carefully trained never to smile. I later learned that weeks before, the Dietrichs had met my parents at one of those Sunday luncheons Andre detested and that I had been discussed in highly favorable terms. I never did return to the office that afternoon. After lunch I hired a carriage. We talked and rode around Rouen for hours. Knowing Louisa was new to the city, at first I assumed the role of tour guide. I may have pointed out Rouen's old buildings and its beautiful cathedral. I really don't remember. All I wanted to do was gaze at this heavenly creature named Louisa and hold her attention for as long as possible.

She told me she was twenty and that there was no one special in her life. I was relieved. I told her I was twenty-seven and that there was no one special in my life either. She smiled that smile of hers and glanced away. The next night we had dinner at La Couronne. We were there again the next night and the night after that. Dinner, lunch, a carriage ride, a moment, an hour, an afternoon, anything would do, any excuse to be with her. I had never felt like this. I couldn't get enough of her smile, her nearness, the way she tilted her head when she spoke to me and how easily she talked about the things that interested me: my work, my family, her family, her friends. When we were apart I thought of her constantly. I sent flowers and notes. When we were together I didn't recognize myself. Ordinarily I was calm and confident with women, but with Louisa it was different. I was clumsy and shy the first time I took her in my arms. My hands shook and my face felt hot. She laughed softly and pressed her cool cheek against mine. She looked up and I kissed her. It was a soft, uncertain kiss at first, but it quickly became sure and passionate. Whenever I think about her as I do now, I can feel her warm hand at the back of my neck, her yielding lips telling me everything I wanted to know. That first kiss opened a world of oneness and wholeness for us. It was the beginning of a love affair that blazed throughout our brief engagement, beyond our wedding day, and in my own heart and mind well beyond the night Louisa died and left me alone in the lovely house on Seine-Maritime Hill.

For months I struggled to come to grips with my loss. I was wild with resentment. I couldn't understand why death had targeted us. Louisa and I were good people. We loved each other deeply. We wanted children. We wanted to care for them and create a good home for them. Louisa was healthy and energetic. There was no reason to worry. All through her pregnancy she had been feeling so well. She was more beautiful than ever, the picture of good health. Her blue eyes sparkled, her blonde hair was thick and gleaming. I was so proud. Everything felt so right, so perfectly normal, but we didn't know we were having twins. For some unexplained reason, Doctor Mercier had not heard two heartbeats. After Louisa died, on at least three occasions I stormed into his office, shouting angry accusations and demanding he tell me exactly what had gone so horribly wrong. Why had he not heard two heartbeats? Why had he not prepared himself for any emergency? Surely he had considered the possibility of twins. How could he call himself a doctor? Each time, Doctor Mercier calmly expressed his great sadness and extended his sympathies and each time I was left more bereft and more furious than ever.

"These things happen," he said repeatedly. "We physicians do everything we can. We use all the skills we have at our command, but Charles, there are those times when we are powerless to prevent a tragedy like this. Now and then, nature has a way of taking over. Louisa's babies were in an abnormal position. I tried everything. I'm so very sorry."

Sorry? Sorry wasn't enough. Sorry was for stupidity and weakness. Sorry was for the ravages of illness and old age, not for a beautiful young woman in the prime of her life, not for two babies struggling to breathe the air of their very good mother's world. My rage was unrelenting. Every night I paced up and down in the bedroom where my wife and children had died. Again and again I pictured how it must have been for them. I would sit at the edge of the bed and see Louisa there, smiling at me through the first signs of labor. I would hear her telling me it was time to leave the room and not to worry; that Doctor Mercier was on his way, that everything would soon be over and she would be just fine. Lying where she died I could see her damp, blonde hair on the pillow, her beautiful lips slightly parted, the dreaded covered basket beside her, our two lifeless babies in it. I would lie there all night, beating my fists against the pillow, eventually falling into a tortured sleep until another dawn arrived to torment and paralyze me with its emptiness. My once flourishing career suffered. I isolated myself from friends. My parents were beside themselves with worry. I was their only child and when Baron Haussmann's letter arrived offering me a position and the chance for a new life in Paris, they saw a fine opportunity for me. I, on the other hand, flattered as I was by the offer, hesitated not for moments, but for days. I wasn't ready for change. I wanted nothing to do with the future. I wanted my past back.

"Another offer like this will not come along," my Father warned again and again. "Charles, you're a young man. You must think ahead and carve out a secure, settled new life. The Paris experience Baron Haussmann is offering would be ideal for you. You must take it."

Father was a practical-minded lawyer in control of every aspect of his life. He valued order and stability and as the head of his household he expected these same qualities to prevail in those closest to him. As a diversion from his well-organized daily routine, every evening after dinner he played the piano in our drawing room. Moving through memorized Bach preludes and Schumann's ethereal piano pieces as effortlessly as he did, it was not difficult to imagine that for a time in his youth he had seriously considered a concert career. Encouraged by his parents who, for the sake of his future in music had moved the family from Strasbourg to Paris, at the age of seventeen he was accepted for private study at the Paris Conservatory with the renowned concert pianist, Jacques Villet. He made virtuoso progress with Villet, and after only a year he was signed for a concert tour with appearances in Vienna, Berlin, Salzburg, and Milan, but before the tour had ended he had concluded that the unknowns of a concert career presented too great a risk. He decided that a study of the law was better suited to the solid future security he had in mind. Before his parents could voice a dissenting opinion or remind him of their sacrifice, he had bid a fond farewell to the concert stage and to Jacques Villet and had enrolled himself in the Law and Economics Department at the University of Lille, passing the admittance examinations with high scores. He had met Mother during a visit to a fellow student's family in Rouen. They had lived in Rouen since the day of their marriage and it was there that Father had joined his father-in-law's legal practice, later establishing his own law offices. A child had been born before me, a girl named Anna. She had died of a fever at the age of four, two years before I had come along.

Mother was a very different person. I have often wondered how she and Father tolerated each other. There was no intensity about Mother, no rush to complete tasks or schedule a long list of daily responsibilities and fulfill every one. No matter what the day held, she always made time for me. I loved everything about her. On any given day, wearing one of her big hats she would spontaneously leave everything to take me for an afternoon walk in the nearby Parc Verdrei. In summer we would admire the flowers and try to name them. In winter we would trudge playfully through the snow. At any time of year, on stormy, gray afternoons we would sit and read to one another by the fireplace in the sitting room. Mother's life centered on her home, her church, and father and me, but she found time to write poetry. Most of it was about the people she knew and thoughts that came to her when she was sitting quietly in one of the yellow flowered chairs in the sitting room. When I married Louisa she accepted her as the daughter she had lost, telling me that I was a very lucky man to have found and fallen in love with such a fine young woman. Louisa returned Mother's regard and affection and the two had quickly established a close relationship.

"Your father is right. Louisa would want you to go on and be happy," Mother said to me repeatedly in the weeks and months that followed the December night that had broken my heart and changed me, tears glistening in her eyes. "Charles, you can't go on this way. You have so many years ahead of you. You must live them. Louisa would want you to. I want you to. Please."

From the day of her death, both my parents had mourned Louisa's loss in the same disbelieving way that I had, but the arrival of Baron Haussmann's letter helped to heal them in a way it did not heal me. That letter gave them hope for my future and they became relentless in their effort to convince me to accept his offer and move ahead with my life. They were, as always, kind and loving of course, but their urging was constant. I had never seen them this way. I argued and fought them off for as long as I could. Finally, exhausted by my own ragged emotions and worn down by the endless stream of lectures, I agreed to try, but my concession was half-hearted. The last thing I wanted was to leave Rouen. A move away from all that mattered to me would change everything. It would rob me of my precious daily visits to the cemetery where Louisa and our sons were buried and I would be selling, or at the very least renting, the house Louisa and I had loved. I was confused and indecisive and my father was having none of it.

"Charles, I know how difficult these past months have been for you," he said to me one evening after one of my mother's dinners which once again, in an attempt to tempt my flagging appetite, was comprised of my favorite foods, "but you cannot go on this way; seeing none of your friends, losing touch with your career, spending every morning in a cemetery. What happened to you is terrible. It is a tragedy no young man should be expected to bear, but enough time has passed and I refuse to stand by any longer and watch you destroy yourself. I respect your feelings and of course your mother and I admire your loyalty, but the time for mourning is over. If Louisa were here with us right now, you know she would be encouraging the move to Paris. She would have begun packing and organizing things. She would be excited and happy, chattering on and on about living in a big, sophisticated city, going to the theater and the opera, all the while reminding you of your talents and the bright future ahead of you. Charles, you must accept this position with Baron Haussmann, and soon. He won't wait forever. His offer could go to someone else. And what architect or even mildly dissatisfied municipal surveyor wouldn't jump at the chance to be part of the renovation of a city like Paris? It promises to be a fantastic period in our French history! You could be part of that! Wake up! Put the past behind you! Here is your train ticket. It's valid for three weeks. Now get busy! You have a house to dispose of, an architectural office to close, and some packing to do! And take off that black armband once and for all!"

The next day I responded to Baron Haussmann's offer in the affirmative. By the end of the week a signed confirmation letter complete with a date and time for our first appointment had arrived from Paris, once again by special courier, and it was done. Within the next two weeks everything fell into place. I leased both my house and offices to an architect who had been with me for three years. He and his wife were the parents of a young son and a baby girl. In an odd way, it satisfied me to know that my house would be lived in by a family much like the one I had expected to have. Providing further comfort, it was arranged that Pauline would stay on at Seine-Maritime Hill.

"This is my home too," she said when I told her how pleased I was that she was agreeable to the arrangements. "I wouldn't want to leave Seine-Maritime Hill for any reason, and don't worry, Monsieur Charles, I'll take care of everything the way I always have. The new family is very nice and I'm sure they'll be good caretakers, but I know how you've felt about this place. It just won't be the same without you. I'll miss you every day. Please write to me."

Much to my delight, the young family taking over my home agreed to look after Zoe and Fleur. I told them about our walks to Jacotin Pond and they assured me they would continue the habit, including the ritual of water bowls waiting in a corner of the kitchen once they returned home. A few days before my departure, Andre Rousseau said he wanted to arrange for a bon voyage dinner with a group of our friends at the Café Ulysses, one of our old haunts on the outskirts of Rouen. I said I wasn't in the mood to celebrate with a lot of people. "Fine!" he said. "Then it will be just the two of us and a bottle or two of acceptable wine. Seven o'clock. Don't be late! And Charles, please comb your hair!"

Andre was my closest friend. We were the same age and had known each other since our school days at Saint Cecelia's. We had indulged in our share of pranks and had laughed our way through the silly, mischievous things young boys do. We put mice and frogs in nuns' desk drawers, we put our fathers' best hats on our horses, we collected grasshoppers in jars, and one afternoon for lack of anything better to do, we decided to swallow a few worms to see who would throw up first. We waited. Neither of us threw up, but all that summer we worried. By September when it was time to start back to school, not the slightest trace of a worm had been coughed up and we wondered where, in the mystery that was our bodies, they had landed. "They're going to live inside us forever!" Andre stoically decided, walking beside me in my mother's garden one afternoon. "Until the day we die they'll be nibbling at our brains or wiggling around down there in our underpants."

No sign of a worm ever appeared in our underpants or was seen to be affecting our ability to learn and reason, but as we grew up, whenever something went wrong or one of us got sick, we said, "It's the worms!"

Summer was the best of times. Every day, if the weather was good, we swam stark naked with neighborhood boys in Jacotin Pond. On the hottest afternoons the water was cold as ice. We continued those group plunges into the Jacotin well into our twenties, even in winter. One day when we were about eighteen, Andre and I made a pact to meet there once a year for the rest of our lives. We promised we would shed our clothes and jump into the Jacotin just as before, no matter how old and fat we grew or where life took us, which at the time we didn't expect to be very far away from Rouen. I laugh to myself when I remember that when we were about thirteen and discovered girls, we wondered what kissing was like. And what was that situation we had heard that girls were in every month? When we were a little older and kissing and the monthlies were no longer a mystery, we talked about how far beyond kissing certain girls we knew would allow us to go. We agreed that well-developed Jacqueline Remi was the number one candidate for testing the limits of our curiosity. A few days later, Andre smugly reported that we had been absolutely correct in our assessment of Jacqueline. "She touched me right down there," he said, pointing to his crotch. "She wouldn't let go, so I touched her right back in that girl place and I wouldn't let go. Charles, cross my heart, it was as if fireworks had been set off! You have to try it!"

We reached maturity none the worse for wear, both of us well-educated and more like brothers than friends by the time he introduced me to his cousin, Louisa. By then, Andre had become a banker and investment counsellor in Rouen. He was very good with money and handled mine. When Louisa died, he could not have been more supportive. Along with both sets of parents, mine and Louisa's, he saw me through the ordeal of the funeral and he was at my side in the terrible days and nights that followed. He did his best to reassure me during my long bouts of swearing and drinking and breaking things. Carrying flowers, he came to the cemetery with me dozens of times and on more than one occasion he put me to bed as if I was a small child. I treasured his friendship and I knew I would miss him. Two days before I left for Paris, there he was, at the Café Ulysses, as punctual and reliable as ever, a bottle of wine and two glasses waiting on the table.

"You look much better," he said, greeting me with his typical snicker. "Charles, dark circles under the eyes don't suit you at all. They distract from your hatefully thick head of hair which, I must say, you have combed quite nicely for this occasion!"

It was so good to see Andre. I could share my fears about Paris with him in ways I couldn't with anyone else, not even my parents.

"Charles, my friend, you've been through hell this past year," he said, pouring wine into our glasses with the exaggerated flair of a seasoned waiter. "I've hated watching you fall apart, but now you have a chance to put yourself back together. I'm glad. I'll miss you, though. A lot of people will, but Paris will be just the right thing for you, and the offer you have sounds exciting. Believe me, if I had the chance for even a modest position in a Paris bank, I'd take it in the blink of an eye."

"I just hope I'm doing the right thing," I said. "I like it here in Rouen. My life is here."

"Nonsense! Andre remarked, leaning forward and casually running his finger around the rim of his wine glass. "Charles, life is where you're happy and you're not happy here. In a city like Paris you'll learn more about life than you could anywhere else in the world, and your attitude, which I must say could use improvement, might change. Imagine that! Sometimes I think we can be our own worst enemy and you certainly have been yours. Charles, you're a gifted architect and a smart, thoughtful man. Take this chance. You can make it work. I know you can."

"What if Baron Haussmann doesn't like me? What if after meeting me he regrets having offered me a position?"

"Please, Charles. Don't play the part of helpless victim with me. It doesn't suit you. Everyone who meets you likes you. You have a talent for befriending people. Even when we were schoolboys you had that edge. Our teachers always forgave you for every nasty thing you did and when we grew up and you became so damnably good-looking I would watch you come into a room with that swagger of yours and that stare, and it was all over for the rest of us." Who is he?" the women would ask in their sweet voices. "Why is he here again, the men would moan?" Charles, you always got the prettiest girls and invitations to the fanciest parties. I was never jealous, not really. I guess I just wanted to be you."

"Well, you wouldn't want to be me now. Who would? Not so long ago I had everything I wanted. Now look at me. Indecisive, alone, and chronically angry. If it weren't for you and your way of setting me straight I don't know where I'd be in this sorry head of mine. What will I do without you? I don't know a soul in Paris."

"That's good. You start with a fresh page! Forget all this. Forget me. Forget all of us. Make new friends. Go to parties again. Bring back that stare and swagger. Just get on with things. And please remember to comb that mop of brown matter you call your hair!"

Departure morning arrived too soon. I was dressed and packed early, but I wasn't ready to leave Rouen. Inside, I was in turmoil. I brought flowers and said a long, painful good-bye at the cemetery. I sat on the bench by the fountain and talked to Louisa. I promised her I would come back as often as I could. I told her how much I loved her and how I hated to leave. As I walked away I kept looking back at the three grave markers that were all I had left of the young family that had almost been mine. My parents and

Pauline were at the station to see me off, my mother wordless and forcing a smile as she hugged me one last time before I boarded the train and took my seat by a window where I sat watching her wipe away tears, Pauline standing beside her, stoic as ever, my father looking oddly triumphant as in shrieks of whistles and puffs of steam the train bound for Paris began its slow departure from Rouen and he waved and smiled approvingly.

All the way to Paris I fidgeted and worried and kept asking myself the same questions. Was I doing the right thing? Had I made my decision too impulsively? Should I have listened to my well-meaning parents at all? Wasn't I a grown man with a mind of my own? What if my work failed to please Baron Haussmann? What if I didn't like him? What if I couldn't take myself in hand, adjust to new surroundings, and find satisfaction in the so-called Paris experience of which my father had spoken so highly? By the time the train pulled into the Gare du Nord I was regretting the whole business of Paris and Baron Haussmann and leaving Rouen. I hadn't been to Paris since I was ten and visited my grandparents. It was twenty years later. My grandparents were dead, I didn't know anyone, and I wouldn't know my way around. What had I been thinking? Deciding to catch the next train back to the safety of my familiar world, I stepped into the crowd, intending to check the posted departure schedule, find a ticket booth, and buy a return ticket to Rouen when I was confronted by a middle-aged woman with a broad smile on her face.

"You must be Charles Fabron!" she said as I nodded, my eyes searching frantically for the nearest ticket booth. "Your mother wrote and asked me to meet you," she went on, raising her voice to attract my full attention as I continued to scan the walls and kiosks. "She said I should look for a tall young man traveling alone, very likely looking lost and arriving on the 2:15 train from Rouen. You fit the description perfectly, especially the looking lost part."

In my unsettled state, I had completely forgotten that my mother had arranged for me to stay with Claire Villard, a Paris friend of hers, until I found an apartment. At the last minute she had told me that Madame

Villard would meet me at the station. I didn't want to appear ungrateful, but this friend of mother's was annoying. She pulled at my arm and faced me squarely, forcing me to look directly into her brown eyes.

"I'm Claire Villard," she said slowly and deliberately. "You'll be staying in rooms at my house. I think you'll like it there. Charles, I've known your mother for years. She must have told you we were neighbors as girls growing up on Rue de la Huchette. Whenever your parents come to Paris, which I'm sorry to say is not so often anymore, we have a nice visit. Your mother and I haven't seen each other in a while now, but we do exchange letters. Hers are always filled with news about you. She loves you very much, you know. I have children myself, so I understand all about being a mother. Well now, welcome to Paris! Let's collect your luggage and move out of this crowd. My husband has a carriage waiting."

Claire Villard, despite her persistence, was as charming a woman as I had ever met, quite like my mother. She talked louder and walked faster and under different circumstances I would have admired her singlemindedness, but I was feeling single-minded myself and as we sped through the station I tried to stop her and say that I would not be staying on in Paris but returning to Rouen on the very next train. Taking ever faster and longer steps, she gave me absolutely no opportunity to explain my change of heart. The porter carting my luggage could hardly keep up with the pace she set. I could hardly keep up with her non-stop talking. The station was "too hot," the crowd was "too noisy," posted train schedules were becoming "so unreliable," and "wasn't I lucky that my train had come in on time?" When she launched into her opinions of Baron Haussmann and what she had heard about his proposals for the renovation of Paris, my interest was piqued and for a few minutes Claire Villard had my full attention.

"Paris needs a lot of work!" she said, maintaining her swift pace as we reached the station's south exit and she pointed out the waiting carriage across the street. "Some people say we're just a bit frayed around the edges. Frayed indeed!" she added, looking back to be sure the porter was keeping up. "Charles, I understand from what your mother told me in her letter that you have a few free days before you begin your position with Baron Haussmann. Good! That will give you time to see for yourself exactly how things are here, just as the Emperor did when he arrived from England last December. I only hope Monsieur Haussmann will do everything I hear he wants to, even if he is a Protestant!" she continued, holding on to her feathered hat as the warm summer breeze whipped up. "Well, whatever his religious beliefs may or may not be, I like a man who believes in something! And I do like his idea of eliminating the filthy slums and re-directing the smelly sewage away from the Seine and out of the city. Those two accomplishments alone would be enough for me, and of course with the Emperor solidly behind him, he's in charge of everything now: the roads, the bridges, the water supply, everything. You could be in for a very busy time, Charles."

"But Madame Villard," I finally interrupted, taking full advantage of a momentary pause, "you don't understand. I am not staying in Paris!"

"This city has very bad habits," she said, ignoring me completely while directing the porter's loading of my luggage onto the rack at the rear of the carriage, her complaints continuing on in an endless stream. "Someone has to do something!" she announced with a flourish of hands, "and soon! "Do you know that every day hundreds of people dump their pots of personal waste into the Seine? You can see all that filth floating by. Can you believe it? It's no wonder we have epidemics of cholera. People should have more self-respect. You'd think we were still living in the middle ages! Why, just yesterday I saw the carcass of a huge pig rotting in the sun on a pile of garbage. In the middle of Place Saint-Michel if you please! Don't be shocked by scenes like that, Charles. They're everywhere. Well, don't worry. We have none of that in my neighborhood!"

Helpless in the company of this indefatigable dynamo I reluctantly followed her into the waiting carriage. I had barely seated myself, prepared at last to calmly and politely make my position crystal clear when my head suddenly jerked backward and we were rolling away from the train station into the clamoring Paris jumble of omnibuses, milk wagons, and a myriad of carriages and horses. Introduced to Madame Villard's husband, Henri, I maintained my composure and made polite conversation, all the while telling myself that I must find a way to escape this folly which had begun to feel like a kidnapping. And of course I wasn't at all sure how to react to Claire Villard's remarks regarding conditions in the city I had been planning to call home. My father had insisted that Paris was wonderful, but if Claire Villard was to be believed, it needed plenty of work to maintain that lofty image. Once again I felt myself caught up in waves of doubt and conflict. If I stayed, I could be closely involved in the transformation of a major city, an active participant in improving its lifestyle and appearance, even its health. If I left and Baron Haussmann's massive project was successful, I would always wonder what would have happened if I had stayed. As Claire Villard waxed on mercilessly about smelly animal carcasses rotting in the sun, the stench from the Seine, and neglected rows of dirty hovels, I decided I must see all this for myself. Perhaps I would stay for a week. Yes, perhaps I would walk around, take a look at Paris, and meet with Baron Haussmann as had been arranged. After that I would evaluate. Until then, it seemed I had no choice but to accept the Villards' hospitality. It would be only a week and they seemed nice enough. The time would fly and if and when it was time to leave, I would do so in good conscience.

How fortunate I was in those uncertain hours, and how terribly childish and fragile I must have appeared to the Villards, a grown man lost in his own forlorn world, unsure of himself and headed for a breakdown. What they must have thought of me, pale and thin, wearing the once perfectly fitted gray suit that in a year's time had become too large for my scrawny frame, under my arm the brand new, completely empty leather briefcase my mother had presented to me a few days before. Entirely dependent on these new friends, I had no idea what the week ahead would hold, but I had left Rouen and had arrived in Paris. It was a momentous step.

Daniel was now 73 miles away. He was a favorite of the nuns at the orphanage.

———— ◆ ————

The Villards were a family of booksellers. They sold everything from volumes on French history to textbooks, newspapers, and the latest tawdry novels. The University of Paris, the Sorbonne, and the Ecole des Beaux-Arts were in the immediate area, the close proximity of these institutions creating a reputable and loyal clientele. Henri Villard was a pleasant, outgoing man with persistently rosy cheeks, a deep voice, and a hearty laugh. He clearly

enjoyed life and he just as clearly adored his wife of twenty years. The two
Villard daughters, Lily, aged twelve, and Simone, aged nineteen, were as
observant as their mother. Henri and Claire doted on them. Lily attended
the nearby Catholic girls school. Simone was engaged to be married and
worked with her parents at the book store which was just a short walk away
on Rue du Jardinet. Rounding out the household were a yellow cat named
Mimi and a small black dog named Sou-Sou.

The home of this congenial family was located on the Left Bank of
Paris, in the Rohan Courtyards, a self-contained and charming compound
comprised of three connecting yards approached through an iron gate at the
end of cobblestoned Rue du Jardinet. The Villard house was in the second
yard. The sizes of the houses in the three yards varied, but all the exterior
walls were swathed in an impessive summer blaze of purple and pink
flowering vines. When I voiced admiration for the appearance of the houses,
Henri told me that originally The Yards had been owned and occupied by
the Bishops of Rouen during their trips to Paris, thus the Courtyards' name
which over time and due to an unintended error in spelling had evolved
from Rouen to Rohan.

Showing me to my rooms after a short conversation and cups of cool
tea in the intimate drawing room, Claire confided to me in hushed tones
as we climbed the stairs that in spite of clerical opposition, King Henri II
had built a large house in the third yard for his mistress, Diane de Poitiers.
I feigned absolute shock at the very idea of such behavior on the part of one
of our French kings. "And in a neighborhood of Bishops!" I said.

Claire laughed and stopped to turn on one of the steps. "Why Charles
Fabron! Is that a smile I see on your face? You really should do that more
often!"

My rooms were on the third floor. It was a climb of two flights of stairs
and thirty-six steps plus a landing, which left me breathless at the top, but
I appreciated the privacy. There was a sitting room, a bedroom, and what I
was sure must be the tiniest lavatory in Paris. All the walls were painted pale
blue and reminding me of my mother's house, the air smelled of lavender
soap and freshly washed curtains. Clearly, considerable thought had been
taken in preparing the third floor for me. The small details impressed me

most. Along with a bowl of fresh pears and grapes, there was a vase of yellow flowers on a round table. Everything was immaculate and well-tended and despite the noticeable warmth of the top floor on a sunny summer day, the open windows let in a constant breeze. The one difficulty I noticed was the positioning of the sitting room, part of which was directly under the steeply pitched roof, making it impossible for me to stand completely upright under the sloping ceiling.

"Watch yourself there, Charles," my hostess warned. "You're a tall man and I wouldn't want you meeting Baron Haussmann with a big lump on your head! Do take care. Henri and Lily will bring up your luggage."

Claire made the household routine very clear as she welcomed me. "We sit down to dinner every evening at seven," she informed me. "Please come down a few minutes early. We like to talk for a while about the day's activities. In the morning, breakfast is on the sideboard from seven until nine. Everyone helps themselves. A woman named Evelina comes in every day but Sunday to look after things and tidy up while we're at the store. Charles, it is a pleasure to have you with us. Ah, one more thing. Do remember to write your mother and let her know that all is well. She'll want to know you arrived safely. I left you some letter paper and pens and there's a well of ink on the desk in the bedroom."

Dinner that night was delicious and for the first time in months I was hungry. I couldn't remember the last time I had eaten with such appetite, a detail I told myself I would be sure not to include in the letter I was planning to write to my mother who through the past year had fretted constantly about my weight loss, doing all she could to prepare my favorite foods at the dinners to which she had invited me with unfailing regularity.

"Charles, tonight we celebrate your arrival in Paris!" Claire announced, as from a large tureen she ladled consommé into five bowls. "Good things are ahead of you. I feel it!"

"May you enjoy many happy days here in Paris!" Henri added, pouring wine into what Lily whispered from her chair next to mine were the family's best glasses.

The consommé was followed by a platter of roasted chicken served with potatoes and a ring of sliced carrots. In what appeared to be a well-practiced routine, Henri carved the chicken, Claire served the vegetables, and Simone passed a basked piled high with warm rolls. Lily was in charge of the butter which she made abundantly clear to me was from Monsieur Michaud's specialty shop on Rue de l'Eperon, a highly respected establishment patronized, as she put it, by men of letters from the Sorbonne for so many years that the butter, famous for its delicious rich flavor, became known as Sorbonne Butter.

"When you are settled in Paris, Monsieur, you must buy your butter from Monsieur Michaud. I will take you to meet him," she concluded with a firm tug at one her braids. "Will you be living in a house or an apartment?" she asked with a pensive glance up to the ceiling. "I think a house is best," she concluded, turning to me with another tug at her braid.

At the age of twelve, Lily was at a plump stage in life. She was also a fountain of information, not all of it important or interesting. A spray of freckles crossed her upturned nose and her dark hair, which was parted straight down the middle was combed into a pair of braids, one of which she idly twirled around her fingers when she was stating her opinions or making her comments. Lily was curious about everything and everyone, and like her mother she was full of advice and perfectly in tune with the dynamics of her world. It was not difficult to imagine that as a child, Claire had been exactly like her. Once the dinner plates were cleared, Simone, who was the quieter of the two sisters, presented a crystal bowl filled with a crème caramel. "She made it as soon as she came home from the store," Lily announced. "My sister makes delicious desserts. Tomorrow we're having a gateau of some kind. She hasn't decided yet what flavor it will be. I hope its chocolate, don't you?"

During the meal there was a constant flow of conversation concerning the day's activity, all of it mundane to me, but every detail important to the Villards. Simone, who had tended the store that afternoon while her parents came to the station to meet me, said she had sold several books to Leon Fournier, a regular customer and her future brother-in-law. Sitting across from me at the table, she said that Leon was an accounts clerk at the Commodities Exchange. I tried to look interested.

"He sells wheat," Lily chimed in. "Not real sheaves of wheat, of course, but orders for wheat. He has customers all over Europe," she added with great authority, ignoring her sister's glare, "mostly in England," she emphasized, insistent upon having the last word. "I think Simone should be marrying him, not his boring brother!"

Simone's face turned scarlet and although she made no comment, I had the definite feeling that before the night was over the jousting sisters would be exchanging a few heated words. To her credit, Simone immediately changed the subject, stating that she had sold several Paris guidebooks to a group of German tourists and that a newspaper had been purchased by the woman next door.

"The woman next door has no husband," dear Lily added, turning to me. "She lives alone with her three dogs. They are very old dogs and every day she buys a newspaper for them. They can't read, of course, but you know what I mean."

I had done all I could to hide my amusement with Lily's commentaries, but at that point I could no longer hold back my laughter.

"Lily is right," Henri said, laughing himself. "Those old dogs may be losing a bit of control over themselves, but they do have their saving graces. They never bark!"

"And they have no teeth, Papa!" Lily announced, concluding her description of the canines next door with a final tug of braids. "They must eat soup!"

That dinner, my first in Paris, touched me deeply. It was magnificently ordinary and uncontrived, its simplicity in perfect harmony with a contented family's daily routine. I never could remember what, if anything, I contributed, probably nothing, but I do remember observing that the Villards were comfortably sharing the day's news and a little sibling rivalry over a meal with a guest, their charming home and its secluded courtyard the background against which they obviously thrived. After dinner we sat together in the drawing room where Claire served tall glasses of sweet citron presse, the delicious freshly prepared lemon water served in every French household during the warm summer months. This was how I had envisioned my own family living in the house at Seine-Maritime Hill:

beautiful children growing into their lives, a sweet dog being patted by their contented father after dinner, the family cat nestled into a window sill, a loving wife and mother guiding the conversation, needlework in hand, the simple pleasures of security and peace under her roof a condition she expected to live with every day of her life.

———◆———

I did my best to settle into the Villards' welcoming environment. They were warm and inclusive, but in spite of their every effort I was lonely. For the first two nights I didn't sleep well at all, images speeding through my mind in the dark not unlike those I had been living with in Rouen. It was always the same. Louisa smiling, Louisa walking toward me, Louisa's hand circling my neck as I kissed her and held her close, Louisa's body pressed against mine, her lips soft and yielding, the warmth of her entire being dissolving into mine, the passion flaming up between us as fresh and new as it had been the first time we made love. She was so real in my dreams, so alive, that by morning, in my half-asleep haze I was sure she would be there, lying beside me, reaching out to me. When I saw she wasn't, the old throbbing pain returned, invading every fiber of my body like a fire. I would begin to perspire and worry. Had I done enough to make her happy? Had I told her often enough how much I loved her? Had my work occupied too much of my time? A terrible dryness scorched my mouth. My eyes burned. I felt desolate and torn and when I awakened on my second morning in Paris I realized I was killing myself.

I may have had a death wish. I had certainly thought about dying. What did I have to live for? Memories? Disappointments? What was left for me? Darkness? Despair? A sad, friendless life of isolation in a strange city? And why was that? I was an intelligent, well-educated man from a good family. I had established a successful career. Awards and citations covered the walls of my architectural office. I had been popular with my friends and before Louisa I had known my share of attractive women. I was still young. Negative conditions had been forced on me, but a fine opportunity for a new life had been set before me in my country's capital city. Yes, I missed Louisa terribly and yes, I wished with all my heart that she and our sons had lived.

I would never stop loving them and wanting them with me, but somehow I had to face the reality that they were dead and I was alive. I had to let go. Perhaps someday, in some other life, I would see them. I prayed for that, but for now, in this life, I would surely die or lose my mind if I didn't find a way to come to terms with their loss and squarely face whatever might lie ahead without them. Until I did that, nothing about me and nothing about my world would make sense. On my third day in Paris I started to find my way.

I began the night before, by making a promise to myself. For the time left to me before I was to meet with Baron Haussmann, I would force myself to remember only the good things, the happy untarnished months Louisa and I had shared. I would do all I could to avoid the troubling images of her death. Somehow, I would find a way to use my best memories of our time together as a foundation for the construction of a brighter outlook. To start, I would think about our wedding trip to balmy, beautiful Nice. I would remember our long, romantic walks hand in hand along the beach and I would see the view of the Mediterranean's clear blue waters from the terrace of our hotel. I would remember the palm trees waving in the sea breezes and the flowers lining the boardwalk for as far as the eye could see. Yes, that was a good beginning, simple and uncontrived, and that was how the architect in me decided it would be. I would set about building something new. I would draw up a mental blueprint of only what I chose to remember. It would demand discipline and planning and it would be all about determination. I would start slowly, by beginning every day in as orderly a fashion as possible, first and foremost by bounding out of bed as soon as I opened my eyes, which was usually by six o'clock. There would be no further lingering in paralyzing reveries at dawn. Beginning with paying attention to my appearance. I would carefully indulge in the morning rituals of bathing and shaving. I would trim my beard and brush my hair. I would dress with care, check myself in the mirror, and I would make my way to breakfast downstairs. I would serve myself from the sideboard in the dining room. I would make conversation with Henri or Claire or one of the girls who might happen to be at the table, and finally, I would force myself out of the door and into the world that was Paris.

Monday morning didn't go well. I was out of bed at six but I couldn't find anything. My brushes, shirts, and underclothes were in a terrible jumble in the drawers of the bedroom chest. I had just thrown them in when I arrived. My trousers and jackets were still in my suitcase. It took forever to find a necktie and handkerchief and forgetting Claire's clear warning, I bumped my head on the low-pitched ceiling in the sitting room. By the time I had bathed and dressed and gulped down some coffee downstairs, it was after nine o'clock and I had a big red bulge on my forehead. Intending to walk quickly and begin my exploration of Paris, I went only as far as the street sign on Rue du Jardinet. The bump on my forehead began to throb and suddenly feeling exhausted I returned to my third floor rooms. The next day was better. Claire had given me an ointment for the bump, the throbbing had stopped, and I was out of the house by eight. I still had the red bulge on my forehead, but I had organized myself. Socks and underwear in the top drawer, shirts neatly folded in the second, sweaters and caps in the third, trousers and jackets hanging in the armoire. By Wednesday I was out again exploring Paris by eight, but I walked only along nearby streets. I kept looking back, intent on maintaining my bearings. Despite my surveyor background and a well-developed sense of direction, I had a great fear of getting lost. I told myself it was the people. There were too many. They were everywhere. There was incessant human movement and too much noise. For months in Rouen I had lived in a quiet, solitary world. I seldom went anywhere but to my office or to visit my parents or Louisa's family. My own house harbored only silence and contemplation. Every Monday evening Andre came for a visit, but in the daily scheme of things there was no one to talk to except for Pauline who went about her tasks with the reliable efficiency I had come to expect. I could have engaged her more often. I should have. I could have told her how much I appreciated her fastidious attention to every room in my house. I could have thanked her for all she had done for Louisa and me when life had been bright and happy. I could have shown my gratitude when things changed and she took complete charge of the household without being asked. I could have inquired about her family, thanked her for the food she prepared that went uneaten, and I could have complimented her on how well she washed and starched my shirts and kept the rose garden. I did none of those things. I chose to be distant and reclusive. Now, this constant human activity in Paris, this constant coming and going, was too much, too unsettling. Something was wrong with me and I knew I had to do something. Once again I negotiated with myself. I told myself I needed an objective, a very good reason to leave the borders of the Rohan Courtyards without fear of crowds or getting lost. I decided to find the best walking route to Baron Haussmann's offices at the Paris City Hall, the building known as the Hotel de Ville. I was due there at nine o'clock on Friday morning and I could not get lost or be late.

"You will not have far to go. The Hotel de Ville is easily recognized," Claire Villard assured me as early on Thursday morning she walked with me to the Rohan Courtyards entrance gate at Rue du Jardinet and handed me a sheet of paper on which she had written a set of clear directions.

"The Hotel de Ville is the very large building across from the Ile de la Cite on the Right Bank," I recall she said to me. "Now, be careful," she was quick to warn. "You must remember that the Ile de la Cite is a narrow natural island that separates our Left Bank from the Right Bank, so from where we stand now you will first follow the streets and turns I have marked. Once you reach the river, which is also marked, you will cross a footbridge. It will lead you directly onto the Ile de la Cite and the grounds of Notre Dame. You will then walk straight across the island and onto a second footbridge which will take you directly onto the Right Bank and the Hotel de Ville. The building is outstanding, Charles. You won't miss it. It's very grand, very opulent and old, and it has a long history, not all of it pleasant I'm sorry to say. Centuries ago, the public gathered on the grounds to witness executions. Use of the old guillotine was restored during the Revolution. I don't like to think about that. I prefer to imagine what it must be like to work in the beautiful Hotel de Ville of today. I have never had reason to go there, but Henri has told me it is as regal as Versailles. He presents himself there every January to renew our licenses and pay the fees for our permits. A customer of mine told me that Baron Haussmann will be living in one of the big apartments. It's to be his official residence. Imagine, living and working in all that splendor! Charles, you're a lucky man. I hope the Baron gives you a nice office."

My curiosity piqued, the architect in me eager to behold this spectacular edifice that was the Hotel de Ville, I set out following the directions I had been given, concentrating on looking straight ahead and not at the human activity around me. By some miracle it was easier than I had imagined it would be to walk along in the midst of fellow pedestrians. Those walking in groups chatted and laughed and those walking alone had things on their minds. No one paid the slightest bit of attention to me. It was wonderful. I was just one of the people; anonymous, alone, and with thoughts of my own.

Following Claire's directions, I found it was a pleasant twenty minute walk to my destination. From Rue du Jardinet I turned onto narrow Rue du Barre which connected to Rue de l'Eperon. I soon reached Rue de l'Arche and exactly as Claire had said, I came to a footbridge crossing the river from the Left Bank to the Ile de la Cite. Once on the island, I passed the grounds of Notre Dame Cathedral. A short distance ahead, I crossed a second footbridge which placed me on the Right Bank of the Seine where I had my highly anticipated first view of Baron Haussmann's world, a view which, before I had even crossed the bridge, left me frozen in my tracks.

My home city of Rouen had its claims to fame. Joan of Arc, the young Maid of Orleans, was burned at the stake in the Rouen Square in 1431. Our splendid Gothic Cathedral, burial site of Richard the First of England, was consecrated in 1063 in the presence of William the Conqueror. We were proud of our distinguished place in French history, but we had nothing to compare with the Hotel de Ville. Claire Villard had not exaggerated. The building was indeed a spectacular edifice. Built by Francis the First in the grand Renaissance Chateau Style, it was an unending series of imposing arches, pillars, courtyards, massive windows and pavilions, its romantic grandeur prompting me to think more of the glitter and glory of fairy tale castles than to consider the Hotel's practical purpose of serving as headquarters for the city's municipal administration and seat of the Paris City Council. I did not enter the building, but satisfied with having successfully fulfilled my objective in simply finding it while at the same time becoming part of the pedestrian scene, I smugly returned to Rue du Jardinet and the Left Bank, promptly turned around, and made the same twenty-minute journey back to the Hotel de Ville all over again. So pleased was I with myself in having successfully ventured into the smallest fragment of Paris life as at the same time I came to understand the positioning of the Right and Left Banks and the Ile de la Cite between, that the day would remain etched in my memory as a turning point. Through the passing years there would be other turning points, many far more important, but it was on that day that I felt the City of Paris had placed a benevolent hand on my shoulder.

Near noon that same day, emboldened by my success, I left the Courtyards, deciding to remain on the Left Bank but to walk in the direction opposite to the route I had taken earlier. Minutes away, on the Rue Fosses Saint-Germain-des-Pres, I found a series of shops and the Café Le Procope, a restaurant which, according to its sign, had been in continuous operation since 1686. I went in, admired the classic red and gold decor, and since it was mid-day, I proceeded to enjoy a fine lunch of coq au vin and summer vegetables. My congenial waiter, proud of Le Procope's longevity and eager to be helpful once I told him I was new to the area, informed me that in their day the likes of Hugo, Voltaire, Rousseau, and the Americans, Benjamin Franklin and Thomas Jefferson, were among Le Procope's most loyal customers.

"I'm told that Monsieur Franklin always had beautiful ladies with him and that he favored the private room in the back," he informed me, raising his eyebrows as he poured wine into my glass, also pointing out that adding further to area's distinction were the nearby University of Paris as well as The Sorbonne, the Ecole des Beaux-Arts, and the legendary Comedie-francais, the distinguished French national theater on nearby Rue de Richelieu, its roots dating back to Moliere and the seventeenth century. Following my history lesson and a delicious dessert of strawberries in cream, I decided to venture a bit farther away from the Left Bank's impressive landmarks and establish my bearings. It wasn't long before I realized that there were four distinct locales in the city, all related to the River Seine, each possessed of its own distinct personality. The Right and Left Banks were clear enough to me, but the Ile de la Cite was not the only island. There were several, the Ile Saint-Louis being the second largest and most residential. Variations in the demographics of Paris became increasingly clear as I grew more courageous in my walk. The Left Bank, where the Villard house was located, was the artistic, educational area of Paris. The Right held the city's administrative and financial centers, while the Ile de la Cite, considered to be the center of Paris, was the site of the Cathedral of Notre Dame as well as the Hotel-Dieu Hospital and the Palace of Justice. Understanding this general layout which I felt would prove essential to my work, I decided that in the next days I would continue to explore and venture away from my now somewhat comfortable familiarity with the areas closest to the Courtyards.

As my confidence grew and I walked father and farther and took in the passing scene, I saw that Paris was, exactly as Claire Villard had said, showing its great age. The decline was clearly visible on every narrow street and in every crowded neighborhood. The city was, after all, more than a thousand years old. It had faced the repeated ravages of war, revolution, and pestilence and under the worst possible circumstances had refused to die, but now, despite its noble courage there was an unmistakable aura of decay hovering around every corner and always, the stench from the river. Of course the city had its great palaces and elegant mansions. They stood as tributes to a valiant, fascinating past, but as I saw it, the Paris of 1853 was in terrible straits. Right Bank, Left Bank, Ile de la Cite, it didn't matter. The city's municipal maintenance everywhere was not only poor, but for the most part non-existent. Henri Villard had told me that over the years a few improvement programs had been attempted, some of the more significant in Napoleon Bonaparte's time, but they had not gone far enough. Several new major roads and buildings had been added to the city's profile, a number of bridges had been built across the Seine, and attempts had been made to lay out a ceremonial approach to the city at the Champs Elysees, but the dirt and decay had not been eradicated, cholera epidemics were commonplace, and the inconsistencies were maddening. Charming old cobblestoned streets lined with mature trees and well-maintained houses suddenly became garbage-littered alleyways. Rows of dilapidated shacks cropped up out of nowhere and endless labyrinths of rat-infested slums had been allowed to take over what I was certain must at one time have been lovely medieval squares and quarters.

As I now walked without regard for my whereabouts and tried to imagine the centuries-old past I began to wonder what international visitors must think of all this squalor lying in the shadows of the majestic Louvre, the beloved Tuileries Gardens, and the popular Palais Royal, its elegant shops specializing in the expensive luxuries of fashionable hats, shawls, walking sticks, and wigs. I also began to understand what had surely been Louis Napoleon's embarrassment when having resided in sophisticated London and an admirer of its elegant parks and buildings, he was confronted by far from acceptable conditions in his capital city as he took up his position as Emperor. Seeing the city through his eyes I began to admire him for addressing its pressing needs. Even then, during my earliest days spent exploring Paris, I somehow knew that Emperor Louis Napoleon expected nothing short of miracles, but no one, not even the powerful Emperor himself could predict how or when those miracles would come about or if indeed Baron Haussmann was the man capable of performing them. Looking back as I do now, it does appear that prayer could have played a role in the proceedings.

In my student days at the University of Lille I had studied the required Eighteenth-Century works of Voltaire. In a popular essay, he had lamented the filth and decay of Paris and famously prayed for its deliverance. As I best remember, in his plea to The Almighty, he asked for "a man zealous enough to undertake such demanding projects as will be required to liberate our city from its medieval stranglehold, a man possessed of a soul firm enough to follow through with his plans, and one spirited enough and accredited enough to make them succeed." A hundred years later Voltaire would have had no trouble recognizing the decaying Paris he had lamented, but now there was hope. Out of nowhere, a Baron named Haussmann had exploded on the scene. Later, when results of his vision emerged, it did not go unnoticed that this Baron seemed remarkably possessed of the same zeal, soul, and spirit for which Voltaire had solemnly prayed.

Throughout the years, I have remembered the city I found in 1853 to be not only the dreary, muddy city of Voltaire's day, but one of dramatic contrasts. It did not take long to see that miles of poverty-stricken quarters were the haunts of thugs, thieves, and prostitutes and that nearby well-guarded neighboring palaces, elegant houses, and gated private parks were the sublime refuges of the wealthy and highborn. The River Seine remained the city's common denominator, promoting equality by serving as the community sewer and disposal plant. It made no class distinction and judged no person. It favored no riverbank and preferred no island. It made itself available to all and accommodated all without prejudice. Claire Villard had not exaggerated the river's powerful grip on the city. Night and day its odorous cloud hung over Paris, its watery rancor fueled by chunks of human waste floating by in tandem with discarded mounds of unidentifiable garbage often topped by a perfectly rounded orange peel. The rankness was truly overwhelming. I couldn't imagine what it was like to live anywhere close to such foulness. Indeed, for all its rich history and culture and the charm of an occasional gated courtyard, to me this Paris of 1853 was beyond redemption. It was too needy. It was too late, and I honestly could not imagine why any sane man would attempt its rescue. I was to meet with Baron Haussmann the next day and I was worried. What would I say to him about his city? Surely he would ask my opinion. Would I lie just to be polite, or should I be brutally honest in my assessment and be done with it?

I continued to walk and think. Perhaps instead of meeting with The Baron and running the risk of being embarrassed by my own outspoken candor, I would send a note explaining my doubts and my intention to return to Rouen. As I considered every possible explanation I could offer, I was aware that for the first time since my arrival I didn't care about getting lost. The corner vendors and street musicians were friendly. They would provide directions whenever I needed them, but by the time I had safely returned to the Courtyards I had made up my mind. I would write my note to The Baron and prepare to return to Rouen.

I cannot say why I didn't write that note. I could have offered any number of appropriate excuses. I could have expressed polite words of gratitude and it would have been over. I could have delivered the note to a receptionist at the Hotel de Ville and returned to Rouen with exciting plans to re-establish my career. I did nothing of the kind. Perhaps it was the disappointment I knew I would find in my parents' eyes or the excuses I would feel required to make at Louisa's grave, but apart from any personal consideration, I firmly believe it was Paris itself that in a very short time had found and claimed me. Despite the neglect of centuries the city was heroically managing to hold up its head every day and maintain its great dignity. I felt it. You didn't read about it in guidebooks or travel journals. You didn't see it, you couldn't touch it, but pride and stamina were permanent fixtures everywhere. They were in the daily jumble of carriages, pushcarts, omnibuses, and milkwagons; in the urgency of barking dogs, in the spirited shouts of children and street vendors on dusty roads and at entrances to the darkest alleyways. Nothing deterred it. Nothing interfered. There was joy in the noise, assurance in the boldness of human activity, and always touches of humor in the fearless confusion. It was a powerful allure. My appointment with Baron Haussmann was scheduled for nine o'clock the next day. I arrived a half hour early.

Sister Angelica was teaching Daniel to catch and toss a ball in the play yard at the orphanage. The ball was red. He liked running after it more than he liked trying to catch it.

CHAPTER THREE

Resonance

I WALKED THROUGH the Hotel de Ville's heavily carved entrance doors at eight-thirty. The exterior of the building was impressive enough but its interiors went far beyond anything I could have imagined. It was a world of outright opulence and flagrant intimidation which, of course, was the point of all those soaring marble columns and allegorical ceiling paintings, their glorious colors and themes of supplication reaching directly up to the heavens. I was struck by the collection of life-sized Greek marble sculptures exhibited along the walls in the poses for which they were famous. I thought back to my student days at the University of Lille and how proud mythology-loving Professor Caron would have been to see me in this distinguished setting, able to identify Apollo with his laurel wreath and his brother Hermes, the messenger, bearing his snake encrusted staff. I must confess that for a moment or two I reveled in my own academic grasp, but as I stood taking in the full impact of the Hotel de Ville's vast spaces, the architect in me became more interested in the mammoth scale of the building which in its masterful design succeeded in making even the tallest people look small.

Since I was early for my appointment I thought I would spend time admiring the grandeur of my surroundings, but at every turn the flurry of activity was distracting. Once again, as in the small neighborhoods and crowded thoroughfares I had explored, people were everywhere, coming and going and moving like practiced players on the stage in the Hotel de Ville that was the endless flow of black and white blocks of marble underfoot. I decided to save my admiration for another time and although I was still early, I approached the desk of the solemn-faced receptionist just inside the entrance doorway. He took my card and entered my name in his register. He paused and slowly looked me up and down, adjusting his spectacles with great ceremony as he carefully scanned his appointment book. Satisfied that I looked presentable enough and that I did indeed have a nine o'clock appointment with Baron Haussmann, he made a note in the register and with a grand flourish of his hand he signaled to an usher in formal morning dress who escorted me past one of the imposing red-carpeted staircases, along a paneled hallway, and through double doors into a large reception room filled with several seating arrangements. On one wall there was an enormous marble fireplace, over it a large painting of the Emperor in military uniform mounted on a black horse. A man I took to be a secretary or administrative assistant sat at a desk near to yet another pair of double doors. He too paused when I approached, and he too looked me up and down and scanned his register to confirm my nine o'clock appointment. Looking up from his desk he then smiled pleasantly and introduced himself as Charles Merruau, Baron Haussmann's Secretary-General. He handed me his engraved card and invited me to be seated. As I waited, I heard music. It was beautiful. Someone was playing a stringed instrument, a viola or a cello. The melodic phrases soared, accompanying in an odd way, the constant parade of men who came and went through the double doors, each solemn faced figure carrying stacks of paper which were deposited on the long table to one side of the Secretary's desk.

"The Prefect will see you now," Secretary Merruau announced promptly at nine, leading me into Baron Haussmann's private world and the powerful center from which he administered not only the re-invention of Paris, but also the city's ongoing municipal matters, everything from public works, to public education, mines and quarries, military matters, taxation, and the Emperor's many charities.

I remember entering the lion's den with my heart pounding. I came from a distinguished Rouen family of lawyers and physicians. They practiced their professions in well-maintained historic buildings, but this man functioned in an elaborate, empirical world with which I had no experience. It was one thing to arrive at the Hotel de Ville for a meeting confident of my professional credentials. It was quite another to consider being part of this rarified enclave where both the business of matters affecting thousands of lives and the fate of a city were conducted in an environment of unrestricted opulence.

I would later learn that there were more than a hundred rooms in the Hotel de Ville. Eventually, I would see all of them. There were immense, lavishly decorated reception halls, ballrooms, apartments, and a spectacular Throne Room on the second floor where, for the eighteen years of the Second Empire, Emperor Louis Napoleon received official visitors and frequently hosted splendid balls and dinners for thousands of guests. Baron Haussmann lived and kept offices in two large adjoining squares of the luxurious quadrangle on the first floor, his receptions and dinners, like those of The Emperor, often held in the Throne Room. Also like The Emperor's fetes, The Baron's social gatherings were always on a grand scale. There were long, beautifully arranged buffet tables, masses of flowers, and an orchestra. Nothing was too lavish, too exuberant, or too costly. I would soon come to the conclusion that Louis Napoleon's Second Empire and Baron Haussmann were made for each other.

Entering The Baron's private offices, Secretary Merruau announced me from the door and immediately left. I then received a warm welcome from the Prefect of the Seine who for the next half hour conducted himself in a surprisingly informal manner, chatting on and on and addressing me as if we were old friends enjoying a long overdue visit. I was relieved by his skillful attempts to put me at ease, but this characteristic of The Baron's, this abundance of charm, I was to observe over the following years, served him very well and he knew it. Baron Haussmann was not an insincere man, but he understood his natural gifts and he used them to satisfy his objectives with the pinpointed skill of a celebrated fencing master.

"Ah, Charles Fabron! I have looked forward to this moment!" he said, coming toward me with a broad smile. "It is a pleasure to meet you at last," he said as we shook hands. "We have a great deal to talk about, but first we should sit down with a cognac and become acquainted. When did you leave Rouen? I hope you've had time to explore a little of Paris. What do you think of our city?" He gestured toward a grouping of chairs in the center of the room and as I seated myself he poured two glasses of cognac from the decanter on a nearby table. Trying to relax into the weighty environment, I took notice of the elaborate paneling on the walls and the immense Savonnerie carpet underfoot. When I also noticed a cello leaning against a chair by one of the windows I realized that the beautiful music I had heard in the outer reception room had been played by this Master Builder of Paris himself. "While I was waiting to see you I heard the cello music," I said. "It was beautiful."

"Ah, thank you. I'm working on the first of Bach's six suites for the cello. For now I'm just playing the notes. I'll get the music out soon. It's in there waiting for me."

I had formed a picture in my mind of what the Prefect of the Seine might look like. I had envisioned him as an overfed man of sophisticated city habits, frequenter of the finest tables and most discriminating receptions and soirees in Paris, likely a lover of beautiful women, perhaps with a secret mistress or two, certainly a man seduced by power and influence. Now that I was in his presence I saw that as was the case with the impressive vastness of the Hotel de Ville itself, nothing could have prepared me for this vastly impressive man.

He was tall, noticeably long limbed, and more striking than handsome in appearance. Of medium build and to my surprise not at all overfed, his impeccably fitted black morning suit and gleaming black boots were worn with the flair and confidence of a well-groomed man long accustomed to the services of the best tailors, bootmakers, and barbers. His dark hair was thinning and his beard, which covered only the lower outline of his jaw, was clipped very short. A stiff, sharply pointed white collar and crisp black silk bow tie emphasized his unusually thick neck, above it the most prominent, clean-shaven chin I had ever seen. I took him to be in his mid-forties.

"Following the compulsory: "It is my great pleasure to meet you, Monsieur Prefect," and "Paris is a marvel," were all I could think of saying in response to his first question. Concentrating on avoiding mention of the city's obvious flaws at the start of our conversation I seated myself as directed and did my best not to appear as nervous as I really was.

"I arrived four days ago," I continued, taking the cognac offered me while trying to sound perfectly at ease in the company of the most powerful man in Paris other than the Emperor, "and as I'm sure you know, Monsieur Prefect, Paris can be somewhat confusing to a newcomer. In the few days since I arrived I have had time only to familiarize myself with areas on the Left Bank, mostly in those surrounding the Rohan Courtyards where I am staying with family friends until I find an apartment. Now, though, I am eager to see a detailed map of the city to determine the exact location of its most important features."

I thought a remark on the map of Paris would make me appear forward thinking and highly professional.

He sat cross-legged in the chair across from mine, sipping his cognac. He studied me closely and said not a word. I felt he was judging me, assessing me. He studied my face and body structure like a physician, taking what seemed an interminably long time to reach his diagnosis. The heavy silence made me uncomfortable. It gave me the same blanching feeling I remembered from my first meeting with the stern-faced Directeur of the strict Lycee Henri-IV where I was enrolled at the age of fourteen. I sipped at my cognac, not really enjoying it or wanting it, but grateful for something to do with my hands. At the same time I struggled desperately not to stare at the remarkably large chin just a short distance away.

"How did you come by that bump on your head?" I was finally asked. "Is the Left Bank so difficult to maneuver?"

He broke into laughter. I laughed too and explained the circumstances, grateful for the moment of levity which ended all too abruptly. I can still see the sudden poignancy in his facial expression as I described the sloping ceiling at one end of my sitting room on the third floor of the Villard house. I can also see the strange shadow that crossed his face and the touch of sadness that came into his brown eyes as I briefly described leaving Rouen and adjusting as best I could to new conditions in a new environment. I didn't understand his manner then, but I do now. I saw that same shadow crossing his face when at the end and it was over, we stood together watching dawn breaking over the Seine as we had hundreds of times before. He looked up to the sky streaked brilliant yellow and red, then he gazed across the glistening river to the endless stream of Haussmann buildings, each structure standing as a testament to his vision. There were tears in his eyes. "People live there now, Charles," he said. "They have a new way of life. Do you think they miss the old Paris, the old ways? I hope we've done the right thing. I want to be known for doing the right thing."

The Baron was never nostalgic. He was incapable of sentimentality, but his deep respect for what Paris meant to those who loved it could never be denied. In his offices and as Prefect he was always about the serious administrative business of Paris, but during our first meeting and at our last, he displayed a degree of personal sensitivity I saw only on those two occasions.

"Well, I do hope you soon find accommodations more suitable to your height!" he said with a change of mood and another hearty laugh. "I myself stand at six feet, three inches tall, so I know there are height challenges now and then. But Charles, your observation on Paris strikes a sensitive chord, and you're right. The city is confusing. I know Paris well, and sometimes it confuses me. But I intend to change all that. The Emperor has appointed me to make sense of what presently is an impossible difficult city to maneuver. He wants to provide the people of Paris with a sensible, well-organized living environment, one with great ease of access from one area to another. Eventually, that ease will extend to a fine system of new roadways as well as a much improved railroad system which will allow for inexpensive public travel in and out of Paris and to points well beyond its present boundaries.

It's an exciting prospect, but the first key to unlocking the city's potential lies in addressing the problem of our many miles of dilapidated medieval buildings and what may or may not lie under them. Charles, according to your dossier, I see that you know a good deal about medieval buildings. Your record of experience in the historic sections of Rouen bears this out. I want to hear more about it, but first tell me a little about your education."

"I studied architecture, engineering, and mechanics at the University of Lille," I quickly answered, pleased to have the opportunity to discuss the university background in which I took great pride, "and I took an additional year of advanced studies with Professor Johann Walther," I added. Professor Walther, as I'm sure you know, Monsieur Prefect, is a renowned architectural history scholar from Vienna. At Lille, his classes focused on Antonio Palladio's principals and Four Books of Architecture. The independent work the Professor assigned was quite challenging. He was a kind, patient man and he was well-liked, but he had very high standards. Not everyone did well in his classes, but I studied hard, earned high grades on my examinations, and graduated first in my class as is recorded in my dossier."

And so our amicable conversation went on, The Baron guiding its direction in order to learn as much as possible about me, I assumed, an approach which seemed entirely normal for an employer conducting an interview with a potential employee. I enjoyed telling him that after leaving Lille I had traveled for a month in Spain and Italy with my father and that upon returning to Rouen my first professional assignment as an architect had placed me at the forefront of the ambitious restoration of Rouen's historic half-timbered buildings along the medieval Rue du Gro Horloge, a project which, along with a variety of additional design and construction contracts in and around Rouen, had continued to occupy my time and interest and advance my career. I said nothing about Louisa but concentrated on the matter at hand.

"It was a privilege to be working on houses and municipal buildings standing stalwartly around the famous Rouen clock tower since the Crusades," I said, detailing what had become the very necessary and delicate work of restoration before years of decay had effectively destroyed all evidence of Rouen's extensive medieval history. I also mentioned that I had been especially careful not to destroy the many richly carved old supporting oak corbels which were unique to Rouen's structures. I had placed their restoration in the hands of a team of craftsmen who labored diligently to maintain their character while at the same time making repairs so artfully that when completed, they were undetectable to the naked eye.

The Baron was a good listener, attentive and interjecting comments as I proceeded to outline a profile of my work. He was also a good talker, equally attentive and focused when it came to talking about himself and his own professional accomplishments which he described to me at some length. I learned that he had been in municipal service all his adult life and that his twenty-three years of service as Deputy Prefect or full Prefect at various locations in the provinces had included posts at Yssingeaux, at Var, Lot-et-Garonne, Giron, Nerac, and Yonne, and finally at Bordeaux where his appointment as full Prefect provided him the position he had coveted for years.

"The Bordeaux holds a special place in my heart," he told me. "It always will. I had served in some of the most beautiful provinces in France, but for me Bordeaux was the prize. My wife is from the Bordeaux and through each of my appointments she very much hoped that one day we would return to the area where she had been born and where her family has lived for generations. We have a country house there and many friends. I can honestly say that I would have been happy to remain Prefect of Bordeaux for the rest of my life, but the opportunity here in Paris was irresistible."

As he reviewed aspects of his life and work, I was aware of a distinct arrogance. It was very real and very deliberate and it did not offend me at all. The pride The Baron so obviously took in himself was exactly what I would have expected of a man appointed to an important post by the Emperor of France, his self-assuredness delivered firmly but with enough grace to admire and enough information to establish the solid understanding that he knew exactly who he was and what he was about.

To say that Baron Haussmann enjoyed talking about himself would be an understatement. I would learn through the course of our many encounters that he was his favorite subject. He was wordy and he loved presenting detailed descriptions, but he was an excellent story teller. He used his deep voice to advantage, making dramatic pauses in his speech, avoiding the commonality of clichés, and always using his hands to emphasize a point. Watching and listening to him, I thought he would have made a good lawyer, a profession he later told me his family had encouraged. "Too dull! Much too dull for me!" he said. "I could never see myself defending or prosecuting criminals and poring over boring documents day after day. I cannot deny that I like a good argument, but I like what I am doing here much more. I'm better suited to it."

I understood perfectly how during our first meeting The Baron would have wanted me to grasp the extent of his background and I must admit that his experiences were interesting, but I was anxious to get on to the matter of my responsibilities. That was, after all, the point of our meeting. I wanted to hear details pertaining to what I would be doing as an architect and surveyor in his Paris Project. Would I be designing houses and public buildings? Were there people I should meet who administered particular agencies? Where was the focus of my attention to be? I had a hundred questions. Unfortunately, my patience would be stretched yet further. The Baron had a philosophical message to convey. He launched into a lecture of sorts, a statement of beliefs regarding the human personality and a clear recognition that his years of administrative experiences had presented him with examples of every type of human being God had ever created and perhaps some He hadn't even thought of. Clever as this remark sounded to me at the time, I later realized it had been tossed out into the air for my benefit. I have never forgotten the impact of the words or the words themselves, and I have never forgotten the troubling feeling that came over me when I understood what had really been said.

"People live their lives in one of only six or seven categories," he stated, uncrossing his legs as he leaned forward, "and Charles, in the business of employing hundreds of people as I have for years, I have met examples of all of them. Now I find them easy to identify. First, there are the politely reserved but calculating. They know what they want and they have the talent and drive to achieve their goals. What they seek is opportunity. Next are the conscientious and kind but easily intimidated. They follow orders beautifully and are the most loyal. Their creativity and originality can be limited, but their dedication and honesty are impeccable. Perhaps the most interesting fall into the predictable last group of four who I believe are as closely related as brothers. First are the self-appointed realists who are convinced they see everything for exactly what it is. Their egos are inflated and their bravura exceeds the reach of their intellect. Second and linked to them are the pseudo idealists who are convinced they know everything. They put on a good show but fail to accomplish much of anything in life. Third, and closely linked to the realists and idealists are the outspoken and angry who find fault with everything and spend their lives arguing and searching for answers that never come. Finally, lurking around every corner are the easily corrupted who simply cannot suppress their greed. They take and steal with pleasure and at the end they have wealth but little left of themselves."

There was more to The Baron's philosophical observations, but by then I had tired of his expounding, so much so that I didn't even care into which category I had fallen. Thankfully, he eventually said, "Now, Charles, let's get on with things."

At last. The initiation ceremony was over. I had passed some kind of test. I hadn't been asked to leave, I had listened politely, and we had reached the moment I had been waiting for. My heart was racing. I remember telling myself I was about to become an active participant in Baron Haussmann's emerging plan for Paris. What more could an architect ask for? I still had my doubts regarding the likelihood of his or anyone's ability to create a New Paris, but in the quiet privacy of his inner sanctum nothing seemed impossible and I allowed myself the fantasy of looking ahead. Could it really be that one day in the City of Paris, buildings and houses would be erected according to my design and plan? Would they stand as testaments to my abilities? Would people live and work for years in environments of my creation? I would not disappoint. I would make everything I touched come to beautiful life. I would succeed beyond all expectations.

"Charles, first let me say that your architect's eye for classicism as evidenced by your Rouen work on medieval structures is well-developed," began the message that interrupted my reverie and nudged me back into the moment, "but your experience in related engineering techniques is evident as well. I also like your study of Palladio. With considerable enhancements, a Neo-Classic tone closely related to what we know of Palladio and his followers will dominate the classic architecture of the New Paris and, as you must understand, in order to set that tone and prepare the way, virtually anything; any building, any house, any business or shop standing in the path of progress must be destroyed, occupants relocated, the land cleared and readied for construction. Charles, with these important requirements in mind, I am assigning you to supervise the demolition and removal of structures in those sections of Paris designated for re-construction. You will have all the laborers and equipment you need and you will report directly to me. Supervisor of Demolition is an important position. Congratulations!"

I was stunned. I didn't know what to say. Had I heard correctly? Demolition? Removal? What was happening? I had not left Rouen and everything I cared about to tear anything down. I was an architect. I had come to Paris to design and build. What was Haussmann talking about? I didn't understand. My education, my experience, my life's greatest interest had led me to a love of design and construction, yet I was being told I was not to be involved in architectural design or construction at all. Instead, I was to supervise the destruction of great swaths of old Paris and arrange for the relocation of residents forcibly removed from their dwellings and places of business.

"Your demolition work will be critical to execution of the orderly urban plan the Paris Project demands," Haussmann reaffirmed with a broad smile.

I could feel every muscle in my body stiffening. "But Monsieur Prefect, I have never supervised demolition work!" I heard myself say in a voice I didn't recognize. "In each of my projects such work, when necessary, was completed by a team of hired laborers supervised by a duly appointed municipal administrator with experience in these areas. In your letter you led me to believe I would be involved in urban planning and architecture. You cited my experience in such projects. Monsieur, I have improved and re-modeled existing buildings. I have built new ones. I have designed new houses and roads for which I have surveyed and analyzed vacant, available land, not occupied land. Do I understand correctly that I am being asked to tear down neighborhoods and destroy people's homes and places of business? In the process, am I also to requisition people's possessions and property? Where will these people go? What will happen to their belongings? Are there no laws prohibiting such activity?"

With that last statement I knew I had crossed a line, but I couldn't help myself. I felt all the air being pulled out of me.

"Of course there are such laws! Decrees have been set forth by the Council of State and the French Senate," The Baron emphasized, clearly annoyed by my response. "The Emperor has been meeting with Council and Senate members for weeks. Properties destined for demolition are to be designated as existent in the public domain, their confiscation legally deemed essential to benefit the municipal good. Property owners will be justly compensated. The issue of public health will be a major factor in determining areas applicable to decrees of public domain. We must stop these outbreaks of disease! Charles, all this has been carefully thought through. Your path is clear. You will be in a privileged position. The French Senate has given me full authority to expropriate or confiscate as I see fit all land and all buildings on both sides of any street in Paris. You will be working with great authority and with my full support as well as the support and approval of the Emperor. And it will be an orderly process. Exact locations, names and ages of owners and occupants, value of contents, and numbers of occupants at each location will be recorded on appropriate forms which are being prepared as we speak. Transfer of dislocated persons to appropriate locations, most of them to newly created suburban areas west of the city, will also be conducted in an orderly fashion and will, of course, be entirely voluntary. People will be free to make whatever personal arrangements they wish, but Charles, you will be in a position to offer opportunities for healthier lives, for employment offering good wages, for greater dignity and decent educations for hundreds if not thousands of children. By expanding areas beyond the city to include new suburbs, the size of greater Paris will be increased by hundreds of kilometers. There will be countless opportunities for the development of housing, industry, and manufacturing. The path ahead is one of pure gold for our beloved Paris."

I could listen no longer. "Monsieur, I do apologize most sincerely, but I am not comfortable with the assignment you describe," I said. "There is no need for us to discuss this further. I will return to Rouen and pursue my architectural career there. Please understand. I am grateful for this opportunity and for your time in meeting with me, but I am an architect and surveyor. I have no heart for demolition and appropriation. The position as you describe it is wrong for me. Once again, I sincerely apologize."

"No heart for demolition and appropriation?" he thundered at me, rising to his feet. "Ridiculous! Charles, no one has the heart for demolition! No one is born to specialize in appropriation! "Don't you think I know that? Removal of citizens from homes and businesses and destruction of neighborhoods people have known all their lives isn't something that fits into you! You fit into it! You grow yourself into it and train yourself into it, and if I didn't think you had the temperament and discipline to do exactly that, you wouldn't be here! I've written to people who know you, individuals who have worked with you, and they all say the same thing: that you are at all times a refined gentleman, but that you are also a solid, strong-willed man who lives and works in an orderly, disciplined world. These are qualities perfectly suited to the work I'm assigning to you. If you don't wrap yourself in the dangerous web of compassion, you will adapt and succeed beyond expectations!"

He stared into my eyes for what seemed an eternity. I wanted to run but I felt frozen to my chair. He neither smiled nor frowned, and there was that silence between us again. "Do not make a decision right now, Charles," he finally said slowly with a purse of his lips and a thrust of his boxy chin. "Come back and meet with me tomorrow. Two o'clock. Make your decision after that and not a moment before. I insist. I shall be expecting you. Two o'clock."

I left the Baron's office and the Hotel de Ville in a blind daze, having neither agreed nor disagreed to meet with him again the following afternoon. All my anticipation. All my worry. What had it been for? I raced back to the Villard house in the Courtyards, my head pounding. I climbed the stairs to the third floor. I took two steps at a time, yearning for a solitary cave to hide in, a lonely hollowed out cavern where I could become an angry

Haussmann-hater and love every minute of my hate and anger. I don't know how much time passed as my outrage festered, but a knock at the door interfered with my grim assessment of the Master Builder of Paris. It was Claire. Her dog, Sou-sou was at her side.

"I thought we might have a cup of tea while you tell me all about your meeting with Baron Haussmann," she announced brightly. "I can't wait to hear about it. What did you think of the Hotel de Ville? Isn't it wonderful? Do you have a nice office?"

I clenched my fists and said nothing as the tea tray complete with embroidered napkins and a plate of galettes was placed on the sitting room table and Claire seated herself in one of the chairs. She poured the tea. Sou-sou came to lick my hand. Evoking no response, she sulked off and curled up on the floor under the window.

"Come, sit here with me, Charles," Claire went on, the happy expectation in her voice more than I could bear. "This is so exciting! I left the shop earlier than I usually do at midday. I've been thinking about you all morning," she waxed on. "Simone made these galettes. They're very good. The girl really does have a talent for baking. Tell me what you think of them."

"I don't think anything, Claire!" I shouted out, unable to contain myself any longer. "I don't think I care for tea! I don't think I care for Simone's galettes and I certainly don't think I will sit with you or stay in this damnable city! I'm going back to Rouen! Haussmann is a fraud. He's a liar. He convinced me to come to Paris under false pretenses. He wants me to demolish houses and businesses and relocate their occupants to God knows where and only he knows how so that he can get on with the pleasure of building a glorious new Paris. Supervisor of Demolition is the title he expects me to assume! Destruction is to be my responsibility! I am to be a villain, not an architect! I am to be a monster to people who have no control over their lives. Do you know that Haussmann has the power to confiscate any property on any street in Paris? He is a puppet of the Emperor! The whole situation is insane. And he had the arrogance to tell me, yes tell me, not ask me, to put off a decision on his proposal until we meet again tomorrow. "I insist!" he said to me. "Claire, before today I was doing so well.

I was actually taking kindly to the idea of making my way in this overblown hell-hole called Paris!"

Claire slowly put down the teapot. She stood and came up close to me exactly as she had in the train station four days before. The same determined look was on her face.

"Charles, you are absolutely right to be upset," she said calmly. "I'm so sorry about what happened. I didn't expect to hear anything like this. The Baron should have made your responsibilities crystal-clear in his letter to you, but you cannot let yourself be defeated. The meeting wasn't what you expected, but don't be foolish! Keep the appointment tomorrow afternoon. Difficult as it may be to listen, let Baron Haussmann do the talking. And I believe he will. He could have been expecting you to react exactly as you did, but he has left the door wide open by insisting you return tomorrow. Don't you see? He knows you left the Hotel de Ville disappointed and angry. He also knows how capable you are. He wants you with him, and just as you will be thinking about how best to handle him tomorrow, he'll be thinking about how best to handle you."

It was difficult to listen to Claire. My blood was boiling. I didn't want her reassurance or advice. I wanted her to be just as angry and upset as I was, but she went on.

"I can't imagine that too many people say no to Baron Haussmann," she said, seating herself at the table once again. "Charles, you have thrown a bit of dust into the Prefect's air, haven't you? I must say, you showed great courage! Not too many people would have stood up to the Prefect of Paris the way you did. Of course when all is said and done you must make the decision that is right for you, and you will. But Charles, it's important to remember this: right now no one knows how the New Paris will turn out, not even Baron Haussmann. It could be a complete failure, but I've been talking to people at the store. Most of my customers are well-educated, thinking men and women. They're respected professors and assistants at the University, the Ecole, and the Sorbonne. Students come to me too. They're serious and smart, but they are also deeply involved in everyday Paris life, especially on this Left Bank. I learn a lot from them and as you surely know, everybody likes to talk in a bookstore. Thankfully, they like to talk to me, and the most popular topic these days is Baron Georges Haussmann. The impression I'm getting is that he's a brilliant city planner and administrator. I understand he isn't an architect himself or even much of an intellectual, but I'm also told he plays the cello and likes the opera. Those are good things. Most important of all, from what I'm told he isn't a newcomer to municipal administration, which also means he isn't new to the business of hiring the right people and putting them in the right places. I think some people just have an inborn talent for that sort of thing. Maybe Monsieur Haussmann is one of them. Charles, please give this another chance. You have nothing to lose. Rouen will always be there for you. Don't you see? You have that security."

I dropped down into a chair at the table, bitterly disappointed and still boiling over with rage. What a waste of time this foray into Paris had been! I hadn't wanted to come and I really hadn't wanted to be part of any renovation of Paris! I had wanted to stay in Rouen. I couldn't stop my ranting. Claire pulled her chair closer to mine. She said nothing, but now and then she patted my hand as she let me rage on. Between my continuing outbursts and her patient understanding we finished off the pot of tea and ate every last one of Simone's galettes which were delicious. Later that evening, when I had calmed down, I realized how fortunate I was to have someone like Claire Villard in my life. Common sense ruled her world and somehow I now understood I had to learn to allow it to rule mine.

That night I fell into an exhausted sleep. I dreamed of Louisa, but it was different this time. There was no pain, no anguish, no longing. We were walking hand in hand along a green ribbon of grass. Her blonde hair glinted in the sun. Her face was bright with happiness. She kissed my cheek and disappeared.

——◦◉◦——

The next day I was at the Hotel de Ville at one thirty. Once again, I wore the gray suit, but this time I added a blue silk cravat to the freshly starched white collar Claire had brought up to me. "Be patient," she said as she handed it to me. "And when your meeting is over, come to the bookstore.

Just come along Rue du Jardinet. It's high time you visited our little treasure house. You'll see our sign. I'll be waiting for you."

It was a breezy midsummer afternoon. I thought about flagging down a carriage, but it was such a nice day that I decided to walk. I reached the now familiar footbridge crossing the Seine to the Right Bank and I considered what I would say to The Baron, finally deciding, as Claire had advised, that I would concentrate more on listening than on talking. My attitude toward the ideas of demolition and expropriation had not changed, but I needed to be sure I was clear on what could lie ahead. Perhaps, at some point my responsibilities would change and The Baron would offer me the architectural opportunities I craved.

Of course everything was the same in the sumptuous municipal palace. The reception hall's vast marble floor still gleamed like a mirror and the impressive parade of Greek gods still empowered the gilded spaces. The same receptionist took my name, adjusted his spectacles, looked me up and down, and checked his register to be sure I had an appointment with The Baron. Once again, an usher led me along the first floor hall and into the inner sanctum. This time there was no waiting and no time to admire the Emperor's painting over the fireplace. Instead, there was an immediate greeting from Secretary Merruau.

"Ah yes, Monsieur Fabron. Good afternoon. I am happy to see you. Baron Haussmann requests that you join him in the Throne Room. Please follow me."

The Throne Room? Why would The Baron want to meet with me in the Throne Room? Certainly The Emperor himself wouldn't be there, or would he? Just the thought of meeting the Emperor made me nervous. I must address him as Your Majesty, I quickly considered. Or was it Your Imperial Highness? I prayed I would say the right thing and bow the proper way. But what was the proper way? Someone would introduce me; probably The Baron. I would watch him and listen to the way he addressed the Emperor. That was it. I felt better as I was led up one of the elaborate red-carpeted staircases and to another wide reception hall on the second floor. At its end Secretary Merruau opened a pair of doors and led me into yet one more magnificent room of the Hotel de Ville. Against the far wall directly ahead and under a red velvet canopy stood a heavily gilded throne chair. The chair was unoccupied but a large rectangular table had been set into the center of the room. Seated around it were The Baron and seven men.

"Ah, yes, Charles Fabron!" came the cheerful greeting as Baron Haussmann rose from his chair. "I'm very happy to see you this afternoon. Welcome! We have saved a chair for you. Charles, this is the staff I have assembled to attack work on the New Paris. Today we are in discussions which should interest you. Please be seated."

He pointed to the empty chair directly next to his. I nodded politely to those around the table and seated myself, utterly mystified.

"Gentlemen, this is the young man I have been telling you about: Charles Fabron, accomplished architect and surveyor from Rouen with valuable experience in medieval structures. Since he is new to our project please try not to frighten him away with too many of your own distinguished talents. Charles, this morning, we are discussing The Plan and now that you're here, I shall continue.

I was unsettled by the unexpected nature of this gathering, even more by the forgone conclusion that I would arrive and willingly occupy the only available vacant seat. Confounding me further was a document, or what I took at first glance to be an official statement waiting at each place at the table, including mine. Quickly glancing down at the heading, I understood it to be a directive authored by The Baron. It was exactly that. Each man had been given a copy of the first document Baron Haussmann was presenting to his staff. I have kept mine along with other documents significant to my work in Paris. It is a clear outline of The Baron's initial plan of action and leaves no doubt of his intention to create an international legend and a city for the ages. When I visit Paris today and admire all I see, the document highlights even more clearly than it did that afternoon, his great skill in organizing the earliest approaches to fulfilling Emperor Louis Napoleon's charge. The Document was titled The Plan and I include a general overview here as testament to his vision. The Baron introduced its subject and his purpose in a series of remarks which left no doubt of his leadership ability or the level of his expectations.

"You have before you the initial planning document concerning conditions related to the work ahead. Transforming Paris will require long hours of planning and years of demanding work, so understanding what we will refer to as The Plan at each and every stage of that planning and those demands must become our way of life," he began. "It is a simple title for a complicated project, but simplification had always been my goal when initiating municipal projects and as we proceed on the work ahead I shall make every effort to simplify your work as well as my own. I do not intend to waver in this objective and make no mistake about my position in all this. Because I have the privilege of our Emperor's favor and confidence I do not delude myself into believing I am a god. I am but a man, but I know my own talents and abilities. I am an expert administrator and organizer. I will be your leader and advocate, but I will not be your father or teacher. I shall rely on your expertise at every step of the way, but I will be making all final decisions, and I emphasize the word, 'final.' I shall ask for your advice at every turn. I will not always take it but I shall insist on your best judgments and finest work. Do not present anything to me, not any drawing, outline, or proposal, that is not signed by you as representing your very best, most highly polished effort, and do not attempt to engage in proposal discussions with me unless you have your material well prepared. Each project will maintain a daily schedule and an intended completion date. You will follow these schedules and intended completion dates on the large Calendar pages which will be on continuous display along the second floor hallway leading to your suite of offices. For now we have a six-month Calendar which will allow us to track our scheduled progress from day to day until this same date in February of the New Year. The Calendar is not intended as a mere guide. It is the life blood of our endeavor. Keep that in mind. Due to unforeseen circumstances such as storms or miscalculations on delivery dates of required materials not by you, but by contractors, the schedule posted on The Calendar may not always conform to expectation, but maintaining its intended time frame as closely as possible should remain your most important consideration as work proceeds. As work begins, please remember that the Emperor is not a patient man. He expects rapid results and I intend to present the first example of those results as quickly and efficiently as humanly possible. As to procedure on project design and execution, most of the time you will work independently. At other times collaboration will be required as projects demand. I expect you to cooperate with one another. Of course, at times you will clash, but I do not expect you to turn on one another. You are grown men. I expect you to debate and question freely and at the end to solve your differences and present your best solutions to me. After hearing all considerations, I will be the final judge. Please understand that while I am watching over the forest, you will be planting the trees. Should there be any question in anyone's mind about the cost of those trees, know that I am fully in charge of finances. I intend to succeed in fulfilling my Emperor's charge that I build him a city and I thank you in advance for your shared faith and patriotism."

With his presentation of The Plan and its related Calendar, The Baron had set a rigid path. Looking back on that afternoon as I do now, I think of the Paris that lives today: its miles of beautiful structures, its lyrical landscape, its lively tree-lined boulevards. Most of all, though, I think of the magnificent city that on a summer afternoon in 1853 existed nowhere but in the minds and hearts of one impatient Emperor and one courageous man.

As expected, in practice and over the years The Baron and his Plan made little room for flexibility. He had a mission, and when the unavoidable delay did occur and the dreaded Request for Extension was filed, it was indeed a dark day at the Hotel de Ville. The Plan reigned supreme. The Calendar to which it gave birth became a divinity.

Of course, on that remarkable mid-summer afternoon Baron Haussmann had included me in a meeting of his inner circle. And it was an effective ploy, a brilliant way really, to ensnare me, but the seduction went much further when in the meeting's next phase I was introduced to the seven immensely gifted members of that inner circle who would breathe life into the Haussmann dream. Before making these introductions, The Baron detailed initial requirements of the agenda. I will quote him and at times in my own words relate his instructions as I remember them, but clearly, it was here and with these words that for the first time the basic foundations of his intended alterations to Paris were set as if in stone.

"Now, how and where to begin with our agenda," he announced with the firmness to which we would soon become accustomed. "We shall advance in stages of no more than three to five projects at one time. Should I see this pattern proving successful, I may increase our forward view to include a greater number of projects in simultaneous progress throughout the city. I fully expect this increase to take place, but right now, as we begin our work, our Emperor has made his three most pressing wishes known. First, and in order to begin facilitating public movement from one part of the city to another as is His Majesty's overall demand, we will create an East to West extended central thoroughfare. This will begin as a cut directly through the Right Bank of the Seine along Rue de Rivoli which, as a result will be extended by some considerable length. Secondly, an additional cut from north to south will be made at Rue de Rivoli's absolute center, thus forming a great cross. This second cut will create two new major arteries which, in advance of their completion, have been named Avenues Strasbourg and Sebastopol. These two major projects will require the elimination of surrounding neighborhood slums as well as the elimination of a number of higher quality structures standing in the way. These hundreds of buildings will be torn down methodically and under current laws of appropriation their occupants will be compensated, removed, and relocated to suburbs west of the city where with their needs in mind, new factory and housing complexes are being developed as I speak. A new system of inexpensive and efficient railway lines will connect these suburbs with the city, making it possible for people to move from place to place with as much ease as possible. I must emphasize that the displaced will not be required to relocate to these new suburban areas. Although by law they must surrender their property, they are free to make relocation arrangements of their own and to take their possessions with them, but those who do relocate to areas outside of Paris and according to municipal plans will enjoy opportunities for employment, inexpensive housing, and a better way of life. Third, and also close to the Emperor's heart will be the re-design and dramatic enlargement of the Bois de Boulogne, the old hunting preserve which presently stands as a derelict haven for vagrants and thugs. When completed, the Bois de

Boulogne will be a safe, public park of unmatched beauty. Its maintenance will be systematically supervised by teams of expert gardeners, its seasonal planting and growth patterns controlled and maintained accordingly. It is the Emperor's wish that in addition to improved housing and transportation, our citizens enjoy unfettered access to beautifully landscaped areas open to all and planned for the public's pleasure. The Bois will serve as the hallmark of his desire to offer citizens free access to the joys and grandeurs of nature. Now, on a more personal note let me move on to your individual assignments. I have met privately with each of you, and let me say that you have been chosen because you are experienced, recognized leaders in your professions as architects, engineers, landscape designers, geologists, and surveyors. In the past I have worked with several of you at my various posts. You know me and you know what I expect. Others among you are meeting your colleagues for the first time. I would like now for each of you to introduce yourselves and briefly describe your assignments. I introduced you to Charles Fabron earlier and since he is new to our group and as yet has not reviewed an assignment, we shall anticipate hearing from him at a later date. Thank you all for your dedication."

What followed was an experience unlike any other of my lifetime. By the time I had heard the last of the seven speakers, I was fully convinced that Paris had only to sit back like a cherished saint and enjoy the happy transformative blessings about to begin swirling around her. In reality it would take thousands of workers laboring twenty-four hours every day for seventeen years to satisfy Baron Haussmann's demands, but along with his clarity of his vision, it was the creative genius of the seven individuals who introduced themselves in the Throne Room of the Hotel De Ville that day who would plan and execute the brilliant facets of the jewel Paris was ultimately to become. The air absolutely crackled with expectation as each man stood and made his statements, describing his background and explaining the range of his proposed assignments. By the time it was over, I knew I had stepped into a rarified world.

First to rise from his seat and introduce himself was Adolphe Alphand. He was 36. An experienced engineer and designer of parks, The Baron had appointed him Head of the Service of Promenades and Plantations, a sober and entirely appropriate title for a man with Alphand's impressive understanding of nature's many moods.

"At the present time, Paris contains only four public parks, all in the center of the city, and all neglected," he began. "Those will be scraped to the bare ground, re-designed and re-planted. The re-design of the very large ancient royal hunting preserve at the western edge of the city is being planned as the great wooded park of Paris. This is, as Baron Haussmann has indicated, The Bois de Boulogne which dates all the way back to the thirteenth century and Phillip the Fourth. In its re-design the Bois will cover over two-thousand acres requiring the planting of thousands of trees, and the creation of numerous ponds, ornamental lakes, fountains, monuments, and cascades. At Petit-Bry we are growing the necessary trees, and at Vincennes an appropriately large area has been set aside for the cultivation of required ornamental plants and shrubbery. The fountains, monuments, lakes and ponds will be left up to those among you assigned to their design and construction."

In the final analysis, Alphand's ambitious work would not end with his masterful re-design of the Bois. Many attractions would be added to the Bois in the course of the next five years, these including collaborations with fellow architects and landscape designers for the creation of the Longchamps Racetrack and the Restaurant of the Grand Cascade. Alphand was tireless. He was devoted to his creative work and he poured over it for hours every day, many of those hours spent walking for miles as with an ever watchful eye he supervised the spectacular evolution of the Paris landscape not only in the Bois, but in park after park and garden after garden. In the wake of his work on the Bois, and at times simultaneously, would eventually come the popular Parc Monceau, the Gardens at the Champs-de-Mar, a controversial but highly successful re-design of the Luxembourg Gardens, and many informative books on the Promenades of Paris. Here I will digress for a paragraph or two, for I feel it is important to reveal that alterations to the Luxembourg Gardens proved trying for both Alphand and Baron Haussmann. It was an early controversy, the first of many, but it taught me an important lesson and made me eternally grateful that due to Alphand's role as Head of Parks and Promenades with an army of landscapers at his command, I had absolutely no involvement.

The Luxembourg Plan required destruction of a twenty-six-acre section of the very old and beloved Luxembourg Gardens. A series of connecting new streets would replace this section. The centerpiece of the entire garden complex was the grand Sixteenth-Century Luxembourg Palace, forerunner of The Louvre and through its many years of existence the home first of its builder, Catherine of Medici and later, home of Napoleon Bonaparte. Although by the time the gardens were placed in Alphand's hands and numbers of his new, larger gardens had been created throughout Paris to great acclaim, when it came to touching an inch of the adored Luxembourg Gardens, the public outcry was deafening. So vocal were the complaints by local citizens and tourists alike, that intense criticism stalked The Baron for weeks. Adolphe Alphand's name was not well known to the public, so except for a few unflattering comments in newspapers, he was spared embarrassment. Haussmann's name, however, was by then ingrained into the Paris vocabulary and in every neighborhood café and corner patisserie, his judgment was being questioned as was his capability to lead the ambitious renovation of Paris at all. Unsavory cartoons and caricatures of him appeared in pamphlets, decrying his role in the desecration of the Luxembourg Gardens, their entertainment value a high priority for those who despised the very idea of the entire Haussmann project. For a man with the Baron's self-confidence and love of the limelight I thought the negativity would surely pose considerable, possibly lasting difficulties for him. The fact is he didn't care; not about the destruction of twenty-six acres of an old garden and not about the caricatures or variances in public opinion. Although he respected the public's demonstrable affection for the centuries-old Luxembourg and its history, he respected his vision of urban progress more. Eventually, the Luxembourg storm died down and the without fanfare or publicity the Luxembourg Gardens remained untouched as more interesting new storms came along to alarm and cause even greater outcry, but the experience vividly illustrated to me the fact that no matter how grand or glorious Haussmann's Paris might turn out to be in appearance, the rock-like fiber of the devoted residents of the City by the Seine would never allow the dramatic transformation of human attitudes he and the Emperor had in mind. New boulevards and picturesque public gardens were one thing, but not all the old ways and not all the old places would be casually tossed aside in their favor. The cityscape might change but the humanity alive within it would not. Parisians had their voices. They had their opinions and their resolve and they were quick to battle for their traditions and beliefs. Above all, and as I had witnessed myself, they loved their city emotionally and intellectually and at the end I was not the only observer who knew in his heart that regardless of the extent of Haussmann-induced glory and grandeur, Paris would always be a large city made up of small neighborhoods.

One major element that did successfully unite urban voices was the matter of cleanliness and sanitation. Fortunately, The River Seine and its foulness had met its match in the person of Eugene Belgrand. He introduced himself at our meeting with humor and confident expertise. From the beginning he impressed me as a savant, a naturally gifted scientist who had found his calling and had no experience with failure. Belgrand was 43, a civil engineer and a graduate in Geology of the Ecole Polytechnique. His background in earth science would hold him in particularly good stead as he attacked the problem of re-directing the city's water system and at the same time faced the most unglamorous of all jobs: the building of new sewers. "Yes, strange as it may seem," the elegantly groomed Belgrand stated, "I am competing with the Seine for the distasteful collection of human waste. I plan to be greedy and uncompromising in my theft and in the process I intend to create the most efficient, most beautiful sewers in the world. Eventually I will invite you to visit me underground. I predict you will love it there. One day what lies beneath our new boulevards and avenues will be as splendid as what rises above them. The foulness of the Seine will be forgotten and the great river of France will become the source of pride it should be."

Belgrand had designed a complex system of fountains at Avallon, a community in the Department of Yonne where Haussmann had served for several years as Deputy Prefect. The Baron saw enormous potential in the unique water engineering technique Belgrand had employed and engaged him at the start of the Paris Project. Belgrand was to supervise the Paris Water Service, bringing to bear on his assignment his expertise not only as a geologist, but as a topographer, an invaluable additional asset as the underbelly of Paris was gradually revealed and seen from the first days to present a wealth of major problems. For all his studious work and unfailing clinical approach, it did not go unnoticed that under the most trying circumstances Belgrand managed to maintain his sense of humor. The same could not be said of Jacques Ignace Hittorff, an engineer born in Cologne and at 61 years of age the oldest and most experienced member of the group.

A serious, somewhat remote individual who, much to The Baron's delight, worshipped at the altar of strict scheduling, Hittorff had developed expertise in the structural use of cast iron, a new material he was to apply to the railroads, first among them the Gare du Nord, the train station he had designed for Baron Rothschild's railroad and the station at which I had arrived in Paris, its strategic location offering a rather fine view of the intimidating Saint-Lazare prison. Later, Hittorff would apply his considerable talents to the innovative glass and iron design of the Pavilions of Les Halles, forever changing the profile of the marketplace of Paris and its immediate environs where, until his time, as many as 400 people lived on an acre of land in Central Halles and an absence of health and food handling regulations resulted in frequent outbreaks of disease. Hittorff held himself somewhat above his Paris colleagues, having prior to his arrival in Paris, enjoyed enormous popularity as celebrity architect to a long list of well-heeled patrons in England, Germany, and Italy. He made no secret of the fact that he had come to the Haussmann Project with impressive credentials and that he had distinguished himself as a prominent Paris architect long before The Baron and Louis Napoleon had arrived on the scene, having designed many fine private Paris houses, and between 1833 and 1846 having made alterations to the Place de la Concorde where he had supervised placement of the Obelisk of Luxor and erected the two spectacular Fountains de la Concorde, one depicting river navigation, the other navigation of the oceans.

As one of the first associates hired by The Baron, Hittorff had designed the cafes and restaurants on the Champs-Elysees as well as the Eugene

Napoleon Orphanage on Rue du Faubourg Saint-Antoine. Much to the chagrin of his fellow designers, Hittorff was part of the team assigned to the design of The Grand Hotel du Louvre which, despite his outspoken disdain for working "on a committee," was opened to great acclaim and in time to house Emperor Louis Napoleon's distinguished guests on the occasion of the World Exhibition of 1855. Hittorff died unexpectedly in 1867 and I have never been able to walk along the Place de la Concorde without thinking of him and his elegant German accent, his unparalleled industriousness, and above all, his unfailing demand for maintaining the schedule.

Victor Baltard was 48 and architect of what he proposed as the Twelve Pavilions of Les Halles. Baltard and The Baron had known each other for some time. They were close in age and had been classmates at the Lycee Henri-IV. As practicing Protestants, both men also attended The Calvanist Temple in the Marais. Their friendship continues to this day. Baltard continues to be a frequent guest at The Baron's country house in Bordeaux, and has designed its numerous renovations. The collaboration between Baltard as chief architect of Les Halles, and Hittorff as innovative designer of its glass and iron Pavilions, did not always go smoothly. It was a long, complicated project and there were many arguments between the two men overheard in the Hotel de Ville staff hallways. Fortunately, both handled their differences with deference to The Baron, his ultimate power over Les Halles and all projects for the New Paris providing a reliably convenient outlet for arbitration between opposing parties.

Twenty-nine-year-old Jean-Pierre Barillet-Deschamps was the engineer in charge of The Plan, which meant he maintained The Calendar. The Baron regarded the hand-written information on The Calendar's enormous pages as central to success. Barillet-Deschamps was The Calendar's dedicated guardian. He was a plain man, a bit sloppy in appearance, but meticulous in his work. If Hittorff worshipped at the altar of strict scheduling, Deschamps worshipped at the altar of accuracy. He had been transferred from the Surveyor Department and placed at the head of the Planning Section where he remained throughout all seventeen of the Haussmann years. With steely attention to every detail, he tracked and charted progress and development, setting the pace along with The Baron for where streets were to be cut, when construction was to begin, when the next demolitions would take place, when and in which direction the city boundaries were being extended, and what the new streets and boulevards were to be named. As if these responsibilities were not enough, Barillet-Deschamps became known as the great gardener of the Second Empire. Gardens were his first love and he used his unerring eye to great advantage in suggesting the artistic gradation of plants and flowers in the newly designed parks and squares, his attention to color and its impact against a variation of tall shrubs and background greenery leading Alphand to select him as the first Chief Gardener of Paris. He worked with Belgrand as water systems for the new parks were created and at the same time he coordinated with the designer of all park structures, Gabriel Davioud.

Alphand had a gritty, piercing voice and an intense love of color. "Perhaps a bit of bright red here, more white here, and yes, two long lines of elegant lime trees there, maintaining the walkway between," I remember hearing him say in his inimitable vocal style to Deschamps as they reviewed the charted progress of planting for the Luxembourg. Together with the gifted Barillet-Deschamps, Adolphe Alphand found time to lay out the great gardens of the Bois de Boulogne, those of the Bois de Vincennes, of the Parc des Buttes-Chaumont, and it was he who with Alphand completed plans for the remaking of the Luxembourg Gardens with yes, the planting of its now famous long lines of lime trees, the romantic walkway maintained between.

Joseph-Louis Duc was 51, an architect born in Paris and educated at the Ecole des Beaux-Arts. He had been awarded the Prix de Rome in 1825 for a design of a proposed Paris City Hall. Later he spent several years at the Villa de Medici in Rome. Returning to Paris, he created the decorations for The July Column which stands in the Place de la Bastille and commemorates the three days of the 1830 Revolution. A Knight of the Legion of Honor, later elevated to Commander, Duc would spend the last forty years of his life renovating the Palace de Justice.

Twenty-nine years of age and born in Paris, Gabriel Davioud had also studied at the Ecole des Beaux-Arts. Highly enthusiastic and another tireless creative talent, The Baron had appointed him Chief Architect for Parks and Public Spaces as well as Designer of Theaters, most famous among his theatrical masterpieces the Theatre du Chatelet. Davioud designed monuments and fountains and brought the distinctive concept of Street Furniture to the Haussmann Plan, the imaginative street lamps, benches, bandstands, signposts, balustrades, kiosks, and public lavatories which would emerge as what writers and journalists around the world would call "the most original features of the Haussmann years." Davioud designed the monumental gates of the Parc Monceau and essentially all structures in the parks. In 1868 he left the Paris Project for Houlgate, a village not far from Deauville where he built a beautiful villa by the sea he called La Brise.

When Davioud concluded his brief speech detailing his plans for the design of what would become the most beautiful of world-renowned Paris landmarks, there was no sound, no coughing or clearing of throats. It was one of those moments when silence is everything and a collection of significant faces is forever engraved on the soul. Looking back, I am completely enamored by the idea that I can close my eyes and re-live that moment and see those seven faces whenever I choose. They are etched into my brain as a crystal-clear symbol of what Paris was and what it would become. Enhancing the assembled richness of talent around me, the greatest wonder of all to me that day was Baron Haussmann himself, his calm, steady voice and deliberate assurances making me startlingly aware of the fact that he had been carefully planning, diligently interviewing, and that now, on this pivotal day, he was taking pleasure in the knowledge that the choices he had made in his staff were nothing short of brilliant. I would soon learn that his approach to staffing had been remarkably simple. He had looked for people who could do things he could not.

Over time, additional support staff would be added to the elite circle, much of it on a temporary basis, a vast number of architects, engineers, and surveyors called on to assist in various individual projects. In the course of seventeen years I never asked where the money for all this manpower and round-the-clock labor was coming from, but on more than one occasion The Baron made it clear to us that he alone was in charge of finances. At the beginning it was rumored that 95 million francs had been set aside for his project. At the end that figure would be found to have multiplied many times over.

Of course, by now you know how I reacted to the events of that day and you also know that I became the eighth member of the inner circle. What you cannot know is that following this meeting, Baron Haussmann invited me into his offices. "I have something to show you," he said with a secretive smile as the meeting was adjourned.

The lion's den felt very differently from what I remembered of the previous day. It could have been my own elevated sense of potential for a project in which earlier I had no faith. It could have been my new-found respect for The Baron as a leader that made his sumptuous inner office seem perfectly comfortable. Whatever the reason, I do know that in the presence of the newly formed inner circle, I had been left with no doubt in my mind that Paris was about to become an international treasure house of beauty and urban efficiency and that I wanted to be part of it. I would demolish or remove, shatter or crush as required, and I would find it somewhere in me to supervise the demolitions of Old Paris with a clear conscience.

Elizabethan bards and a few noble warriors of The Crusades wrote that man's courage of conviction if tied to a sincere and purposeful heart can provide a coat of armor impervious to slings and arrows. Their writings remind us that in its simplest form courage is faith and that faith in one's own strength opens to avenues of determination where anything is possible. Little did I realize on that momentous afternoon how often in the future I would be required to remind myself of this revelation.

The Baron opened a long drawer in one of the many cabinets lining his inner office. From it he removed two rolls of thick paper. He said they were plans, hand-drawn maps of the city as it was known to exist in the late eighteenth-century. He took them to a long table and slowly unrolled them, placing a pair of bronze weights at each end to hold them down.

"The Emperor and I reviewed these plans for Paris on the day he appointed me at Saint-Cloud," he said. "They were created by his uncle, Napoleon Bonaparte, and are enhanced by our present Emperor who has added his own markings. I treasure these documents and I treasure the

Emperor's trust in me to preserve them here. When he arrived in Paris to assume his duties as Emperor last December, he brought these plans in his luggage along with his Uncle Napoleon's famous gray overcoat. As you can see from the hand-applied colored markings, Napoleon's intention was to create a much more accessible Paris. His wish was to begin by extending Rue de Rivoli, establishing it as the most strategic thoroughfare in the city, and this is exactly how the Emperor wishes to proceed. Of course, these plans and the detailed markings in Napoleon Bonaparte's own hand, make it clear that the future growth of Paris was very much on his mind. The Emperor calls his uncle's plans the Artist's Plans. He intends that they serve as a guide to the new city's growth and future development. Charles, during our meeting yesterday you said you were eager to see a map of Paris. I'm sorry to say that there is no accurate map of today's Paris. There are old renderings showing the ancient Roman walls, city gates, and locations of aqueducts. Cartographers have drawn up several modern, hand-drawn street maps and area surveys, but the city's overall boundaries have never been clearly defined and street names have changed countless times over the centuries. By the time we finish our work, Paris will have a reliable map for the ages. For the present, these drawings originally made by Napoleon Bonaparte are invaluable assets."

Green, blue, and yellow colored markings in the hand of the legendary Napoleon Bonaparte had been set before me. They took my breath away. I couldn't help but smile and look up at The Baron with admiration. Prominent Paris landmarks likely drawn out at least thirty years before were clearly labeled: The Palais Royal, The Madeleine, Notre Dame, and the Champ de Mars inside the city gates. The margins held the present Emperor's signed, hand-written notes on ideas for the landscape. The importance of trees was emphasized, as was the need for more natural light beaming into the city. I marveled aloud. "These are wonderful documents," I said, "and to have a tangible look into Napoleon Bonaparte's thinking is remarkable. Thank you for sharing these with me, Monsieur Prefect. They have added to my many good impressions of this day."

A few minutes later we sat across from one another as we had the day before, and once again The Baron poured two glasses of cognac. He smiled and said he was pleased I had been present at the afternoon meeting. He did not ask about my impressions and he did not seek compliments for himself or those he had chosen to form his inner circle. He did not ask me if I had made a decision to stay or go. Our meeting ended with a firm handshake when he said, "Charles, I shall have Secretary-General Merruau arrange for your office. See him on Monday morning when you arrive to begin your work. And one more thing: in the weeks and months ahead you will be receiving invitations to receptions and dinners. Secretary Merruau will present your invitations and advise you on the nature of the event and the manner of dress. Socializing with the influential people of Paris is important to our work."

This then, was the world into which I was plunged, and as set forth by The Baron these were the requirements with which I would live for the next seventeen years. The men of the inner circle were those I would work with, take issue with, eat, drink, and worry with. They became my Paris family as the great wheel of Haussmannization began to turn and together we watched it rotate twenty-four hours each and every day, regardless of the season or the weather. Nothing stood in its way, not houses, not shops, not the rich or the poor, and not people who struggled to maintain some semblance of the only lives they had ever known. The human upheavals were never pleasant. The well-heeled did better than the poor. Many escaped to country houses with plans to return to the city when the worst was over. When they did return, some moved into luxurious new Haussmann apartments in the heart of a modernized Paris. Some of the less fortunate never did return. Others disappeared, while still others took full advantage of the Haussmann project. They made fresh starts with an eye to advancement, at first finding steady employment as laborers, stonemasons, and painters, the more stalwart and creative soon rewarded for their tenacity and rapidly developed skills, acquiring experience, earning promotions, and ever-higher wages. Some of the cleverest developed entrepreneurial skills, exceeding their own wildest expectations while becoming rich tar merchants, maintenance managers, and wealthy owners of hauling and tool companies. Many of the less scrupulous kept close track of progress, buying up houses and shops known to be standing in the way of scheduled demolitions at low prices and quickly selling them at higher prices to the even less scrupulous who quickly applied fresh coats of paint, cleaned the windows, and awaited the official assessment which was always set at a higher rate for visible property improvements. Some of the less ambitious found there was money to be made in piles of stone, broken glass, and sticks of furniture abandoned on the street by the expropriated and displaced but ideally suited to land fill. The night workers earned more than the day workers so there was great competition for those assignments, especially in the heat of summer when dayworkers were sweaty and sunburned. Although all along electricity was available and could easily have illuminated the dark nights, The Baron insisted on gas lighting, and so it was that night after night across Paris, strings of gas lighting illuminated the way of armies of night labor. Regardless of the season or the hour, circling clouds of dust, mountains of dirt, and immense deposits of rubble were the companions of all. Resonant sounds of pickaxes, hammers, and scrapers set the cadence of daily life and echoed their high notes across every sector of the city, but for seventeen years unemployment was unknown and any man who wanted work could find it. There were frequent protests. There were pockets of bitterness and anger, but none of it affected The Baron. He had the Emperor and the Emperor had him. It was a match made in heaven.

———⚫———

Leaving the Hotel de Ville with an exhilarated sense of anticipation for what lay ahead, I returned to the Left Bank with great confidence in my ability to adapt to my new responsibilities. I headed for Rue du Jardinet and the Villard Bookstore as Claire had suggested. I was eager to tell her how much I appreciated her good advice. She was at the counter, chatting with a young man.

"Ah, Charles! I was hoping you would come by. From the look of you, things must have gone well. I'm glad. I want to hear about it, every little detail. This is Bernard Fournier, Simone's fiancé. He's coming to dinner tonight."

I shook hands with Bernard, remembering that Lily had called him "Boring Bernard." I had to admit he was the serious-looking, no nonsense type. He didn't smile as he shook my hand and he didn't appear interested in engaging me. He seemed completely focused on continuing his conversation with Claire without interruption and I was apparently intruding. I decided to wait until he left to talk with Claire myself. "Claire, since it's my first visit to the store, I'd like to browse for a while," I said. "I'll look forward to seeing you at dinner tonight, Bernard."

Claire understood my meaning. In minutes I heard her say good-bye to Bernard. "Seven o'clock," she called out to him at the door. She found me in one of the aisles idly leafing through a volume of Alfred de Musset's poems. "I like Bernard, but I couldn't wait to hear your news," she whispered. "Take Monsieur Musset's book with you if you like, but let's go upstairs where we can sit by ourselves and chat."

We climbed the winding stairs to the loft where shelves teeming with books of every size and color lined the walls and a pair of overstuffed green chairs waited in an inviting alcove. Comfortably seated and enjoying the surroundings, I related details of my afternoon at the Hotel de Ville. Even with Claire, though, who I trusted implicitly, I held back, somehow aware of the need to maintain a certain confidentiality about what had transpired. The mood of the afternoon meeting had not conveyed a strict demand for secrecy, but I had come away with the distinct feeling that the less said about inner circle conversations and activities the better. Fortunately, Claire seemed much more interested in my decision than she was in its whys and wherefores.

"How wonderful!" she said, with a clap of her hands when I told her I'd accepted Baron Haussmann's proposal. "That means we'll have you here with us in Paris for a long time. I'm so happy!"

"Claire, I'll be starting to look for an apartment," I said to her. "I've imposed on you and your family long enough."

"No, no! You haven't imposed at all!" came Claire's immediate reaction. "Don't be ridiculous! Charles, you've quickly become like a son to us! We love having you. I know you'll want to settle into a home of your own eventually and have things your own way, but there's no need to rush. Stay with us a while longer. I'm just so happy you've made the decision to work on Baron Haussmann's project. I have a good feeling about it."

That evening, Bernard arrived promptly at seven. Over a glass of dubonnet I did all I could to engage him, but he was noticeably guarded in his conversation, revealing nothing to me about his work or his interests and asking nothing about mine. I tried talking about the inviting mood of the Villard bookstore, a topic I thought would surely appeal to him. "There are bookstores exactly like it all over Paris," was Bernard's caustic remark. When Simone entered the room and he walked toward her, I was relieved to turn my attention to Lily.

"Isn't he awful?" she whispered, coming up close to me. "Rude! I saw the way he just walked away from you, and may I say that our Villard Bookstore is considered one of the best in Paris? Ask anyone who knows about books. And I have the honor of sitting next to the creature at dinner. Simone shouldn't be marrying him. Promise me you'll say clever, witty things and make me laugh."

I smiled, nodded, said I'd try to make her laugh, and asked about her day at school, delighted when as I expected, she launched into a lengthy review of events covering the day's entire scholastic schedule, adding, just as Claire announced that dinner was served, the recitation of a poem she had memorized on the walk home.

Claire's dinner that night was, once again, delicious. She presented a fine boeuf bourguignon and Simone had outdone herself with a Tarte Tatin for dessert.

"The apples for the tarte came from Madame Lepin's tree. Lily informed us. "She's the lady next door, the one with the old dogs. Simone left the store early so she could prepare Bernard's favorite dessert. Isn't it your favorite, Bernard?"

"Lily, a gentleman is entitled to enjoy his favorite dessert when it's made by his fiancé," Bernard replied. "You would do well to follow your sister's example when your turn comes to be a fiancé!"

"Bernard, I don't think I want to be a fiancé," Lily fired back. "It's a lot of trouble, especially if you're making desserts all the time!"

"Lily, one day you will change your mind," Henri said shaking his head. "When you find someone to care about, you want to do special things for them."

In the drawing room after dinner, compliments for Simone's culinary talents took over the conversation, but once again I was left with the distinct impression that the Villard sisters would remain at odds for the remainder of the night and perhaps through the following days. Something was wrong between them, and Bernard's presence didn't help. I had noticed he took no opportunity to openly admire Simone's abilities, culinary or otherwise. I couldn't understand it. Simone was a capable, pretty young woman; intelligent and well-spoken. There was always a pleasant greeting to me, an inquiry into my day's activities, or a positive comment on something she had heard in the store about Baron Haussmann. However brief our encounters were, I had come to appreciate Simone's attempts to make me feel comfortable in her family's home. Bernard Fournier was marrying a fine young woman and his reluctance to display at least some demonstrable affection for her was baffling. I had formed the opinion that he was as wooden and dull as Lily had said he was, that is until Henri mentioned my new position with Baron Haussmann.

"Haussmann will create nothing but instability!" came Bernard's sudden response when told of my Haussmann association. "We do not need the renovations he plans! The charm of old Paris is part of its great legend and I am not alone in believing that things should be left as they are. What he is planning is a travesty!"

"Now Bernard," Claire interrupted in her reliably gentle tone. "You must admit that some things in the city are not as they should be. Of course we have our long history, but we cannot continue to ignore the neglect many of our old neighborhoods have endured. Surely you notice the blight. It gets worse by the day. Baron Haussmann will make the changes we need. He has the Emperor's complete confidence and at the end we may find ourselves living in a cleaner, healthier city. I pray that happens."

"No! You are wrong! Baron Haussmann and the Emperor have no interest in perfecting Paris," Bernard went on. "They have grasped an opportunity to enrich themselves. They conspire to make us think they are paving the way for a splendid new Paris. They do very well at their conniving, but their only interest is in making money on every new road and every new building, and this man you have living under your roof will help them to do that! He is an outsider! He knows nothing of Paris! He is part of the treachery and should go back to wherever he came from! I don't know why you would invite him here to live under your roof!"

"Bernard!" Simone exclaimed. "Charles Fabron is a guest in this house!"

"Simone, thank you, but you needn't defend me," I immediately said, doing my best to remain calm and ignore the shocked faces around me, "and Bernard, you are misinformed. The aims of both Baron Haussmann and our Emperor are clear. They intend to beautify and sanitize Paris for the people. There will be public parks and public gardens created for the public's pleasure. New roads, railways, and thoroughfares will make it easier to move about. Improvements will be obvious everywhere. Do you approve of the Seine as the community sewer? Perhaps we should keep that as it is. You must love the stench hanging in the air night and day. Do you frequent the homes of friends living in the hovel-riddled slums? Aren't the hundreds of dark, garbage-littered alleys filled with rats a delight? Let me take you to experience the joys of old Paris. I've been here for a short time, but I know where they are. Bernard, I would think twice about spreading the venom which obviously fills you. I have no idea where your anger comes from, but it is misplaced. You should hold your tongue until you see for yourself what great benefits are in store for Paris. And one more thing. I am proud to be part of the Haussmann project and I intend to do my best as I work on it."

"And exactly what is your work on the Haussmann Project to be? Simone tells me you're an architect."

"I am Supervisor of Demolition!" I stated without reservation. "I will be removing the old slums of Paris, those unhealthy clusters of mud and slime of which you seem so fond."

"Demolition! I might have guessed it. A professional destroyer! I didn't know that was a profession to be proud of. I repeat! Fabron, you're an outsider! Go back where you came from!"

He laughed the wretched, snarling laugh of the terminally angry of whom The Baron had so aptly spoken at our meeting the morning before. "Are you being well paid?" he asked, "and are you headquartered in the palatial Hotel de Ville?" He laughed his surly laugh once again. "Fabron, you have not heard the last of this!" he said to me, a glaring cloud of hate filling his eyes as Simone burst into tears and with Lily at her side, ran out of the room. With this last threatening remark, Bernard stormed out of the Villard house. Henri went after him. Claire's face was flushed. Like Simone, she too broke into tears. "Charles, I'm so very sorry," she sobbed. "I don't know what happened to Bernard. I don't understand. He has never been like this." She came to me and I put my arms around her. She was shaking. "It's alright, Claire" I said, "but I'm obviously a problem for Bernard and as a result, for all of you in this family. I'm the one who is sorry. I had no idea these feelings were in the air. I've disturbed everything. I'll begin searching for an apartment tomorrow. I just hope Simone will be alright."

"Simone will be fine," Henri said, coming through the doorway. "I'm sure she is hurt and embarrassed, just as her mother and I are. She will cry her eyes out for a few days, but she'll recover. I have broken her engagement to Bernard. I will not have a man capable of such anger in my house or marrying my daughter. He is dangerous. Marriage to Bernard Fournier is out of the question. Claire, go upstairs and tell Simone what I have done. Bring handkerchiefs. And be sure to tell her she is not to see Fournier again, not under any circumstances. Now, I will sit down with a nice glass of the Genepy my brother brought to us from the Alps this winter. Will you join me, Charles?"

The Genepy was old and tart. It gave two annoyed men the chance to sit back, breathe deeply, and take pride in their actions. For all its rancor, I would look back on the evening as another milestone in my rapidly changing world. I had stood up for my beliefs. I had been firm and I had felt the liberating joy of loyalty.

The next morning, Simone was at breakfast, her eyes red and swollen. I had expected her to remain secluded in her room at least for the day, but she said she was planning to be at the store as usual. When I tried to tell her how sorry I was about the night before, she shook her head with a vague smile. "Thank you Charles, but it's for the best," she said. "Bernard and I have very different views of life. Our marriage would have soured very quickly. I suppose I've known that for some time. As sure as I am, though, that my father did the right thing in breaking my engagement, I need to be away for a while. My mother agrees that a change of scenery will do me good. She's arranging for me to visit with her sister in Brussels. I like my Aunt Nicoline very much. She's very outgoing and has interesting friends. It will be good to spend time with her."

A week later, we were at the door waving good-bye to Simone. It would be six months before she returned from Brussels. In that time my life would take on very new dimensions. Not only did I begin my work with Baron Haussmann, I also found a Paris home of my own.

CHAPTER FOUR

We Shared a Field

October 1853

MY INTENTION was to find an apartment, quickly buy furniture, and settle in, but before I could even begin my search, meetings for initial stages of work on Rue de Rivoli became so time consuming that I was left with only one free day each week and that was Sunday. What with church attendance and the popular Sunday ritual of long afternoon family gatherings, few Paris landlords made themselves available on Sundays, so I took to conducting my search in the evening. It was a discouraging task, usually conducted by candlelight. Everything I saw through flickering, dull shadows needed renovation. My schedule being what it was, I had no time to engage and supervise carpenters and painters. Once again, the Villards came to my rescue.

"A house in the first courtyard is for sale," Henri informed me at breakfast one morning as I gulped down my coffee, in a rush to get to a meeting at the Hotel de Ville. "It's a nice property, Charles. You should see it. I know the owners. We can go at any time. Just let me know."

I hadn't thought of buying a house in Paris. I owned a house. It was miles away, on Rouen's Seine-Maritime Hill. Owning a house in Paris would make a statement I wasn't ready for. It would meant permanence. I had made the solid decision to remain in Paris to work with The Baron, but I wasn't ready for the responsibility of a house, not yet. Besides, there were always matters of maintenance to consider. There were gardens to tend and something always needed painting or repairing. I didn't have time for such things. In an attempt to be courteous I told Henri that sometime within the week I would be happy to look at the house in the first courtyard, but under my agreeability I was convinced that a conveniently located rented apartment in a well-maintained building was my best choice. That same afternoon my meetings were concluded early. With a few free hours on my hands, my curiosity got the best of me. I decided I would see Henri at the store and ask if we could look at the house he had told me about. What harm could there be in just looking? I was an architect. I liked looking at houses. Telling Claire he would return in about an hour, Henri and I set out together on Rue du Jardinet. We passed the shops and the friendly people sitting outside. Henri knew everyone. Reaching the gate opening onto the Courtyards I imagined how pleasant it would be to call this secluded neighborhood home, not just temporarily as was now the case, but permanently. I quickly changed my mind and told myself I was considering such a ridiculous idea only because I was becoming familiar with the surrounding Left Bank areas.

The first yard had fewer houses than the other two. Mature linden and chestnut trees framed and shaded each of the four stucco houses. The house Henri pointed out to me as the one we were about to visit was nestled into a slight recess at the end of the cobblestone yard. Its pale yellow walls were covered with deep purple flowering vines. Potted plants lined the walkway and there were fanciful blue balconies at the second floor windows. The shutters needed repair as well as a fresh coat of the blue-gray paint which appeared to be the color of preference for all the Rohan Courtyard shutters and balconies, but overall, the exterior of the property looked to be in good condition. The owners were Claude and Deanna Girard. They welcomed us warmly and invited us to come in and freely explore their home. I fell in love at the door.

"All the furniture will stay," Madame Girard announced in the hall, "and all the china and curtains. Monsieur Fabron, I must tell you that my husband and I have loved this house, but we are no longer young and now it is too much for us to maintain. We are moving into a small cottage on our son's property at Caen. It has everything we need and we will be near our grandchildren which is the most important thing."

It was too good to be true. I had dreaded the thought of having to go through the ordeal of buying furniture and curtains and all the necessities required of a home, but here was a house ready to move into. It was in a familiar area and everything was in perfect condition. There were no cracks on the walls and I saw no chipped paint anywhere. I had loved living in the Seine-Maritime house. Its ceilings were high. Its marble fireplaces were beautifully carved, but here the mood was very different. Informality prevailed. Ceilings were low and beamed. On the first floor a massive stone fireplace dominated the long central room which opened into a dining room followed to one side by a sitting room and a small study with yet another fireplace. There were three bedrooms and a lavatory on the second floor, a spacious attic above. The price was more than I had imagined it would be, but I had maintained a respectable personal account at my friend Andre Rousseau's Rouen bank and with a line of credit which would offer me peace of mind I quickly calculated that based on my current income and with a little discipline, I could manage. It could also be that I would be able to negotiate a lower price with the owners. Perhaps my friendship with the Villards would carry some weight. It did. With very little negotiation, the Girards agreed to a lower price, the preliminary documents were signed, and in ten days' time Andre had approved my draft for release of personal funds and their transfer from Rouen to the Bank of Paris where I opened a new account and was approved for a generous line of credit. Within two weeks' time a notaire was drawing up the final documents.

"So pleased to hear you are settling into Paris life," Andre wrote. "You deserve to be happy. Save one of the bedrooms in your new house for my visits. Remember that I like simple wallpaper and easy access to a lavatory. By the way, I've met a lady I like. Now that you've left Rouen, men like me have a fighting chance. Thank you."

I became an official Paris homeowner in mid-October. It didn't take long to settle in. I walked into an immaculate house where all the furniture was in place. Dishes and linens were in cupboards, and other than my clothes and the books Claire had given me, I had very little to carry away from the Villards' third floor. It was a blessing. By the time autumn's chill was in the air, the City Planning Offices at the Hotel de Ville were buzzing with activity and I had little time to fuss over equipping a new home. The first official Calendar had been completed and approved, every member of the inner circle was at work, and I was preparing for my role as Supervisor of Demolition by visiting the areas Deschamps had marked for destruction. I was determined to be thorough and efficient. I drew up my own maps of the first areas to be demolished. Day after day I studied them. I found the Baron's foresight concerning procedures of enormous help as I confronted a myriad of organizational demands. Well in advance of any commencement of work, mine or that of any other staff member, he had organized a series of essential allocation systems and storage locations, each supervised. These included vast supply and wagon yards as well as barns for hundreds of horses, complete with feeding and watering stations. There were tool houses, paint centers, and areas set aside for the exclusive use of stone masons, carpenters, gardeners, and tar merchants. By forming these agencies, projects were set into motion systematically, gaining a life of their own with substantive ease.

Through a new, fully staffed Excision Office I was able to arrange for removal of all discarded structural material and debris as required. Through the only slightly older Procurement Office I was able to order thousands of hammers, hand saws, wheelbarrows, shovels, and dig bars. I was allocated funds adequate enough to purchase horses, carts, and wagons, these promptly delivered and stored in newly constructed and staffed stables and barns on land adjacent to the Hotel de Ville. Through the Central Stowage Office I arranged for storage and distribution of all deconstruction materials and tools such as broken glass, re-usable wood and stone, sledge hammers, crowbars, and picks. At proposed locations I made notes regarding the widths and lengths of existing streets. My experience as a surveyor served me well. I prepared graphs and ground plans. I studied alinements and centerlines likely to affect demolition and new structural foundations. I spent hours in preparation. It was tiring, but when I walked through my own door at night, it was with satisfaction and an appreciation for my pleasant home surroundings. Unfortunately, cooking was not a high propriety.

I usually ate dinner at the Café Procope or another of the nearby cafes. Claire and Henri extended frequent invitations and although I appreciated their thoughtfulness, I was reluctant to take advantage of their generosity more than I already had. In the morning, on my way to the Hotel de Ville, I frequented a patisserie where the coffee was fresh, the croissants were just coming out of the oven, and the jam was my favorite strawberry. It was a pleasant morning habit until worksites became active and I began arriving at dawn to notify property owners, assess values, and assign laborers to begin their onslaughts. Luckily, one morning just as this intensified schedule began, I happened on a street vendor who had decided to station herself at the convenient corner of Boulevard Saint-Germaine and Rue l'Eperon before sunrise. In a short time and in what became a well-timed daily routine, she had my coffee and whatever pastry she had baked the night before ready for me. I paid her, we chatted for a few minutes, and I sipped my coffee and nibbled on my pastry as I continued on my way. Conditions improved when Claire arranged for a housekeeper.

"Charles, you cannot go on living like this, depending on strangers for your meals, "she said to me over one of her Sunday luncheons. "It's fine to enjoy a café or restaurant meal now and then, but after a long day's work you should be eating nourishing meals at home and enjoying that charming house of yours. I will arrange for a housekeeper."

Natalia was a Godsend. She took to my house and to me with a gentle but decisive touch. She made no secret of loving the Courtyards and although devoutly Catholic and a loyal congregant of Saint-Sulpice, cleanliness was her true religion. Not only did she dust and sweep every day, she kept stacks of soap in a pantry cupboard and paid particular attention to my shirts which often required a good deal of scrubbing since dust and dirt were becoming my daily companions. Adding to her household talents, Natalia was a wonderful cook. Claire had seen to that. A fine dinner awaited me every evening. Natalia bought the freshest meat, fish, bread, and vegetables in the shops where I opened accounts for her, she made and preserved the strawberry jam I loved, and thanks to young Lily Villard, she frequented Monsieur Michaud's shop where she bought delicious cheeses and the famous Sorbonne butter. Natalia also made time to tend the potted plants at the front door and the rose garden at the back of the house. On any given summer evening I would come home to find a colorful bouquet at the center of the dining room table or waiting for me by my favorite chair in the sitting room. Natalia was with me throughout all the years I lived in Paris. She lived in the spacious sunny room behind the kitchen, adjacent to the thriving rose garden which eventually became her pride and joy. Her presence as well as her ability to create an inviting home provided me with a level of stability I hadn't really known I craved.

In a matter of weeks I found myself well settled and ready to assume my new responsibilities as Supervisor of Demolition. My colleagues were likewise moving forward, preliminary planning was completed, and the Haussmann Project was underway. The litter-strewn slums surrounding the Rue de Rivoli, were my first challenge. I have them to thank for introducing me to the disparate worlds of impoverished families, angry shop owners, vagrants, and prostitutes victimized by the marvels of Haussmannization.

"In the eyes of the public, the Rue de Rivoli project and its extension will set the standard for all that is to come," The Baron reminded me the day before I was to begin, "and Charles, I cannot emphasize to you strongly enough the wish of the Emperor that its renewal and improvements be completed as quickly as possible. He wants to see results as quickly as I do. As you know, this central artery extending through the heart of Paris, east to west along the Right Bank and all the way from the Louvre to the Bastille, will necessitate the creation of two new north-south avenues. Vital to the final outcome of this important cross section project is the efficient demolition of whatever stands in the way, in particular the removal of all structures in full view of the grand buildings now standing parallel to the Louvre. Their destruction must be swift, for with the prompt completion of the Rivoli extension we will be signaling to the public in the most obvious way possible and exactly as the Emperor wishes, the beginning of a new era marked by an unparalleled level of civic pride. I know you will not disappoint."

I came to admire The Baron for many reasons, but as Emperor Louis Napoleon's Good Will Ambassador, he had no equal. So contagious and articulate were his expressions of loyalty and devotion to Imperial intentions, that many who worked at his side frequently felt the rush of national pride capable of motivating extraordinary achievement. Unfortunately, I was the slowest member of the staff to feel that rush. The work of my associates was creative and rewarding. I envied them. My work was focused on destruction and at the beginning I had developed no emotional weaponry strong enough to steel myself against the human dread I was sure I would encounter. Starting out, I didn't know what to expect and despite all my hours of preparation, I really didn't know how best to proceed. I had formed plans and had done valuable advance work, but except for The Baron's clearly expressed sense of urgency, I had been left completely on my own. The Baron was an excellent leader, but he expected his chosen staff to take the professional initiative. Early on I saw that it was exactly as he had mapped out in his Planning Speech. He provided the opportunity, set the rules and the pace, but the staff was responsible for setting the stage, playing the music, and of course meeting Haussmann approval. This, then, was the climate in which I approached my first day of work in the field. I was on Rue Carrelle.

It was early November. I arrived just as the sun flashed up in a burst of gold and pink. A covey of blackbirds circled twice against the rush of color before perching on the long corridor of soot-blackened roofs, their reluctance a suitable match for my own. The air was rank with a rancid mix of decay, chimney smoke, and human waste. One after another I could hear doors being slammed shut. Word had travelled fast. People knew I was coming. I knew they were afraid. This was the Rue Carrelle I would destroy methodically and completely, and this was the Rue Carrelle I would sulk over and ache over for years after, its collection of wretched shacks, shops, brothels, and seedy taverns my initiation into what it really meant to be a 'demolisseur.'

I knocked at the door of the first house, my stomach churning. I waited. No one came. I knocked again. My throat was dry. I had promised myself I would handle my responsibilities professionally and with arms-length neutrality, but in those anxious moments I hated my assignment. The door opened. A woman stepped out. She held a baby in her arms. Two small children clung to her skirt. I had rehearsed my speech a hundred times. I had recited it aloud, making every attempt to make it sound as convincing as possible, and now, looking down at those two small faces, I couldn't remember a word. I had to clear my throat. "Madame," I finally announced with great effort, "I come with official orders to ...." She didn't let me finish. The children began to cry. Fear was stamped all over the woman's face but her eyes blazed with fury.

"I know why you are here!" she shouted. "We all know why you are here! Go away!"

A litany of profanity followed. My mother was called a whore. My father was grossly maligned, his private parts bearing insults of the most heinous sort. My own genitalia was accused of being grotesquely undersized, thus lacking in its ability to function normally and produce progeny. Of course I gave off the impression of ignoring the woman's attacks, but under my show of composure I understood her outrage.

"Madame, I'm sorry, but my orders are clear," I stated flatly.

"Take your orders and go away!" she cried out, hot anguish continuing to spill over in her voice. "You will not take my house! I have nowhere to go! Is it not enough that I cannot feed these children? Is it not enough that we live in this filth? Leave us alone!"

"But Madame, I am also authorized by French law to move you and your children to a new area west of Paris," I said to her as if I offered some wonderful, benevolent gift. "If you have nowhere else to go, you will be taken to a temporary new home there. You will be compensated for the value of this property. That money should last until you find work. Every day, women are being hired to make dresses and coats in the new factories at Neuilly-sur-Seine, at Argenteuil, Chatou, and Levallois-Perret. They are able to pay rent and buy food. You could be one of them. It would be a better, healthier life for you and your children."

"And what of him?" she asked, turning as a silver bearded man came up behind her. "This is my father. He is old and lame. Will there be factory work, compensation, and a better life for him? Will the bread and wine be free?"

"The compensation amount applies to the owner of one household, regardless of the number of occupants in a house," I said as directly as I could. "You have two days to prepare. A wagon will arrive on Thursday morning to transport you and your family with others from Rue Carrelle. Keep in mind that although you must leave this house, you are not being forced to board Thursday's wagon. If you can make your own arrangements for a home elsewhere, do so as soon as possible. Now, I must evaluate the contents of this house and prepare a report. Do you have jewels or gold?"

I was immediately humiliated by my mistake. I had asked a question intended for the well-to-do with whom I would also eventually deal, but I had been absolutely stupid in the presence of this distraught woman. I could feel my face flaming up red with embarrassment. The woman laughed, her eyes filled with disgust.

"Ah yes, Monsieur Demolisseur!" the old man called out. "We have many beautiful rubies and pearls and my daughter has trunks full of fine dresses and furs! Do come in and see for yourself!"

Their laughter rang in my ears as I stepped into the house to fulfill my duties and take an inventory of contents. The strong smell of urine filled my nostrils. I took short breaths and held them for as long as I could as I quickly went about my tasks. The few pieces of furniture in the two rooms were worthless and covered in layers of dust. There were no items of clothing, no books or children's toys. A fire pit against one wall in the first room sufficed for cooking and heat whenever firewood was either scavenged or stolen. The room was damp and cold, firewood apparently in short supply. Near to the fire pit a few empty kettles were strewn on the floor. "What are your names and who is the owner of the property?" I asked, the required forms and a pencil in my hand.

"I am Comtesse Aguillard," came the response with a scowl. "My dear father here is Comte Vallier. He is the owner of the property and these are my three beautiful children, all girls, all titled of course. I am so sorry their father, the great swordsman, Baron Aguillard, cannot be here to meet with you, Monsieur Demolisseur, but he has been away on important business.......... for several years." Again, the two adults laughed heartily.

"In addition to the compensation you receive, if you wish I will do what I can to see that you are re-located to an area where your children can attend a school," I said, ignoring the mockery and wanting to offer this desperate woman a glimmer of hope. "I cannot make promises, but I shall try," I added. "Now, what are your real names? Please be aware that I am conducting the business of the Emperor. Under penalty of law you are required to tell me the truth."

"I am Marie Levesque Dubois and this is my father, Claude Levesque," came the weak reply. "He owns the house. The children are Marie, Yvonne, and Emilia Dubois. I do not know their father's whereabouts," came the terse response with the sharp tone of resentment I would hear again and again during the course of that terrible first day.

I left Marie Dubois and her family with a pounding headache, my stomach in knots. I asked myself how I could have been so wrong to think I could assume this loathsome task. How could I have been so foolish as to believe that after one stimulating meeting in the grandeur of the Hotel de Villet I could join a staff of talented engineers, designers, and architects who would deal with future grandeurs while I would inflict harm and generate hatred?

I trudged along the dusty path to the door of my next victim. She was Yvette Bernier, an eleven-year-old girl whose parents had died within hours of each other in the most recent cholera epidemic, an event which had left her completely alone for two months. "Do you have a neighbor or relatives I could take you to, a grandmother, an aunt? What about the Levesque woman next door?" I asked. "No, I have no one," the girl answered, "and the Levesque woman doesn't like me. She doesn't speak to me. She doesn't want me near her children. She says I have the sickness that killed my mother and that I will infect her children. What will happen to me? Monsieur, please do not send me to the convent. The nuns are cruel. My mother always said so. Please take me to live with you! I will serve your house. I am strong. I will not steal. Please Monsieur!"

This young girl, like so many young females of her Paris, would do all she could to find a man to save her, a man who would provide a home and food in return for household service and perhaps by the grace of God not ask too much of her in the dark of night when doors were quietly closed and silence hid the price of shelter and sustenance. More than likely, though, in this miserable world of want, if a girl was pretty enough, which under her pale, disheveled look, this eleven-year-old appeared to have the potential to be, she would find herself eligible for life in a house of pleasure. In some cases, such girls could achieve great notoriety, demand large fees for their services, and through their roster of rich clients accumulate money enough to buy houses in the city and chateaux in the country complete with large staffs of servants. To live in this dangerous half-world between survival and self-sacrifice was the aim of scores of poverty-stricken, lonely young girls like Yvette who had nowhere to turn. They started out by roaming the streets, praying with every step for deliverance from a brothel owner or 'maquereau' (pimp) with whom they might find favor. Before long and as the result of a play by Alexander Dumas, that half-world became known as the demi-monde, growing into an integral part of the Paris legend, as well-known and in many cases as beloved as the city's most famous landmarks.

Later that same day on Rue Carrelle I encountered an old woman who did not know her name. I was required to record some form of identification for everyone so I listed her as Madame des Italiens. Answering my knock almost immediately, she invited me in to join her at luncheon. She made a great ceremony of setting a non-existent table and serving trays of non-existent food. "Will we go to Rome today?" she asked, sipping from her imaginary cup, an imaginary saucer in her hand. "I love it there. My husband was Italian. Did you know him? You must have known him. He was a famous sculptor. Do have one of these macaroons. I have been saving them for a long time, hoping for a visitor exactly like you. Are you Italian, Monsieur?"

I made it a point to be at Rue Carelle on Thursday when the wagons came to carry off its displaced residents. I lifted frail Madame des Italiens onto the first wagon and asked young Yvette to look after her as best she could. I had listed each of them as owners of the houses in which I had found them. They received a small compensation. I never saw either of them again. Marie Dubois and her family were nowhere to be seen that day and as the wagons drove away, I could only hope that they had found decent housing somewhere.

In the days and weeks that followed, situations like these repeated themselves with merciless regularity. Names and faces changed, but to one degree or another all the houses and shops I inventoried and assessed sheltered the similarly poverty-stricken and angry. With the exception of the hopelessly bewildered like Madame des Italiens, the only security known to these people was the daily routine, and whether begging, stealing, or simply existing, survival was the goal. Clearly, these needy souls had no interest in a New Paris. They felt they would never be a part of it and they said so. To them, the New Paris was being built for the rich and royal. Were it not for the Emperor's widely publicized insistence that new housing and beautiful outdoor spaces were being created for the good of the general public from every walk of life, be they parks, sidewalks, public markets, halls, or public conveniences such as street lavatories, gas lights, and a clean water supply, this alienation and sense of betrayal might very well have persisted as was exactly the case until the first signs of a cosmopolitan, inclusive city became evident in accessible transportation, vast expanses of equally accessible green space, and a sensibly organized system of roads. Not too surprisingly, over time and even as one success followed another, the naysayers remained stubbornly locked in the grip of their own beliefs. The doubters were always eager to pounce, citing sympathy for the poor and disdain for the destruction of charming old Paris, but by the time Haussmannization was well underway, many of those doubting minds and hearts eagerly supported the objective of the New Paris which, as work progressed, was seen more and more as a project intended to beautify a city open to all and serving the common good. The prospect of newly created wide avenues and boulevards, however, raised serious questions regarding the sincerity of both the Emperor and The Baron. Early on, many saw these thoroughfares not as part of a beautification program at all, but as aids to the military in the event of civil unrest. The most historic and violent social uprisings of the past had been launched by angry mobs assembled on the narrowest of Paris streets. When the military had appeared to quell these mobs as they did on Rue Lantern des Arcis during the Revolution, they were effectively confronted by impassable barricades quickly formed in the tight space by immense piles of furniture, animal carcasses, and garbage, the armed French citizens behind and on top of them prepared to defend their ideals. In many cases, full military battalions found themselves ready and able but unsuccessful in piercing incidents of resistance confined to these spaces.

Here it must be said, and with all credit to The Baron, that following the first dramatic slice into strategically located Rue de Rivoli, an action which was met with howls of indignation, it was the quickly completed and highly successful work on Rue Rivoli's Pavilions of The Louvre which began to turn the tide of public opinion. This obvious improvement at the center of traditional and historic Paris life showed that perhaps Baron Haussmann and Louis Napoleon had not made empty promises after all. Proof of their intentions was there on Rue de Rivoli for every eye to see.

I stroll along these areas whenever I am in Paris, recalling my peculiar role in preparing for the impressive appearance they make today. I think of long vanished Rue Carrelle, I remember the old Rue Tirechamp, Rue Constantine, and Rue de Seine, and I remember Madame des Italiens, young Yvette Bernier, Madame Dubois, and the countless human beings I faced and suffered with so that this popular public area of Paris could develop its own legend.

Clearly, none of these souls, not the Dubois, not Yvette Bernier, no one from my deconstructed world felt compassion for me. Why would they? I was the destroyer, the smasher and crusher, and I spared so little. Even many fine houses and beautiful gardens of the well-to-do, including the house where Baron Haussmann himself was born, eventually fell to the deafening invasion of my ruthless armies wielding hundreds of axes, sledgehammers, and shovels, swarms of waiting horse-drawn sleds and wagons ready to drive away the rubble of vanished times and forgotten lives to fill the deep caverns being dug in preparation for the solid foundations of all that was newest and best. And as I forged ahead with my deletion of anything and everything that stood in the way, at my heels a New Paris was being unfurled along both sides of the Seine. It was a time filled with remarkable energy and extraordinary accomplishment. I marveled at the level of achievement. One after the other, each and every day, great plans and greater ideas were brought to life as the once bleak canvas of a neglected city was framed and shaped and painted over with the brilliance of new color, new light, and new life.

One by one I could take the time to review my old documents and describe to you here in some detail a profile of the thirty-thousand buildings I was responsible for demolishing. I could describe many of the hundred or so assisting demolition agents I eventually employed to complete that task. I could characterize the sounds of breaking glass and cracking wood, and I could complain about the cries of those forcibly removed from the only homes they had every known, but the review would be an exercise in repetition and too painful a return to the darker side of good intentions. On the brighter side, I watched more than fifty-thousand new structures replace those thirty-thousand and by now you must be wondering how I managed it, how I emotionally equipped myself for so destructive a role.

It is not enough to simply say that my employment as Baron Haussmann's Supervisor of Demolition became a routine for which I was despised and well paid. The truth is that I was ill-suited to the work of demolition and expropriation. I wanted to be a practicing architect, but I was determined not to fail at the assignments I had been given. I had needed a new life and I had depended on the activity in Paris to provide it. As a result, every day I made every effort to present as positive a picture as possible. I gained strength from the few souls I met who without looking back, courageously left everything behind. I still marvel at their stoicism. Some of my displacements separated families when older, grown children took matters into their own hands, said good-bye to their parents and siblings, and left the city for brighter horizons. I believe I offered people as much assistance as I could under existing laws. Over time I developed a suit of armor that served me fairly well. I cannot say exactly when the steeliness in me appeared, but it did. I do know that there were several people who came into my life and diverted my attention successfully enough to allow me to carry on until I began to see for myself the magnificent results of my violent labors.

The members of the inner circle were among the most supportive. I was unaware of it at the time, but word circulated early on that I might be too emotionally affected by my work. Every day, several of my colleagues, in particular Alphand and Belgrand, checked the Calendar in the Planning Department hallway every day to see what I was tearing down and every day, one of them would stand in my office doorway and offer an encouraging comment or two. They knew as well as I did, that demolition was absolutely necessary. Their work depended on it, but they also knew that the human factor was taking its toll on me. It was in this supportive atmosphere that the camaraderie in the circle began and it was at this time that I began to feel I had a group of supportive friends. It was Alphand who first suggested we start meeting regularly at a location away from the Hotel de Ville.

"I'm asking everyone to meet at Cardon's when we finish here tonight," he said to me on my return to our offices one day shortly after my first month or so at work. "I know Michel, the head waiter. He'll take care of us. We're all so busy, but we should get to know one another, don't you think? Belgrand and Davioud like the idea. I wish you could have seen the ethereal look on Belgrand's face when I suggested we could talk about beautiful gardens and disgusting sewers and all the splendor in Paris' future while feasting on whatever Michel recommends."

Cardon's was a good choice. It was noisy and busy. It made me feel part of the city as at a table against the mirrored wall were able to be ourselves and enjoy getting acquainted. In the late afternoon when I wearily returned to my office in the Hotel de Ville, the thought of a leisurely hour or two over dinner with friends encouraged me to plod on for the next hour with required reports and I appreciated the always stimulating company. Gabriel Davioud was especially encouraging, at least that was his intention.

He called me The Surgeon. Davioud loved the theater and took great pleasure in dramatizing the emotions related to my destructive role. Many of his attempts at amusement although not always welcome or appropriate, occasionally provided a welcome light touch, but Gabriel spent long hours at his drafting tables, pursuing his creative work and enjoying his imaginative forays into his designs for park structures and the proposed new theaters. At first he didn't grasp the reality or depth of human plight I dealt with, but my own struggles seemed worthwhile when I saw the stunning results of his work. Once I understood the brilliance of his reach and grasp, it did not surprise me that Gabriel Davioud would go on to design the Theatre du Chalet with great flair and a theater lover's understanding of the dramatic arts. He loved Moliere and Shakespeare and could recite long passages he thought relevant to my work. I must have heard Hamlet's "Is this a dagger I see before me?" speech more than a hundred times. It was usually followed by Portia's definition of mercy as she observes In Merchant of Venice that "the quality of mercy is not strained."

In the early days he would greet me with "Ah, the distinguished surgeon returns from the operating theater," these words recited in his best melodramatic stage actor voice, his hands clasped over his heart as late in the afternoon I walked into the office we shared to prepare my reports. "How goes it today, Monsieur Docteur?" he would ask. "Will the patient survive the night? I hear there is objection to the procedure. Perhaps the new medicines from the chemist in Vienna will arrive in time to perform the miracles you hope for and I will not die! But if they fail, my children will have no father! Please think of them! I beg you!"

I appreciated Gabriel's attempts at levity, but he didn't understand that by late afternoon cleverness eluded me. The best I could do in responding was to cite examples of the serious wretchedness I found on Rue Tirechamp and Rue de l'Arch and countless other locations across Paris. For all his lightheartedness, though, Gabriel always listened to me with great interest, frequently taking notes as I related details of the day's activity. At one point he said, "Charles, I try to lift your spirits when you come trudging into the office, but difficult as your work may be, you are meeting the real people of Paris. Do you realize that they have been the builders? They know the blood and sweat of it. You are living through a great drama."

So interested did Gabriel become in the great real life drama of the Paris I dealt with, that on several occasions he accompanied me on my missions. It was in his company that on Rue Tirechamp I found the rare man eager for change. I have never forgotten him.

Jean Florante was forty-five years old. He said he cleaned chimneys in summer and chopped firewood in winter. Quite obviously, these were not successful ventures. He lived in one small room of a dilapidated house with his pregnant wife and nine children. All nine were painfully thin, yet as the family spokesman he was highly optimistic.

"We have lived here for five years," he said, "but we can be ready to leave at any time. You say the wagons will come for us in three days? Monsieur, can you take us today? Please, I want the child who is coming soon to be born far away from all this. And will it be all right to take the cat? The children love her. She will cause no trouble."

The cat in question was clearly as fertile as Madame Florante. What could I say as nine wide-eyed children awaited my answer?

On Rue de l'Arche Marion, Gabriel and I met red-haired Lilou Edanne. I judged her to about fifty. She had very likely been a great beauty once, but time had not been kind to her. Neither had her nocturnal companions. Lilou carried a long black scar on her left cheek and walked with a cane. "Ah, come in," she said warmly at the door. "Such handsome young gentlemen have not come to me in a long time. What may I suggest to you today, Messieurs? An hour? A night? I have friends."

"I am here to inform you that by order of the Emperor you must leave this house in one week's time," I announced in the monochromatic voice I had learned to adapt. "If you are the legal property owner, you will be compensated. Today I must evaluate the property and make a list of its contents. Please step aside."

"Of course, my handsome Monsieur Demolisseur," Lilou quickly agreed. "Would you like to see all my treasures?" She laughed. "I can make them available to you at a moment's notice," she added, striking what was intended as an inviting, provocative pose, but one which in fact was the embarrassing attempt of an aging woman to survive for one more day in the only way she knew. Gabriel coughed and said he would wait for me outside. "Yes, I somehow knew you would," I replied.

As would be the case with situations like Lilou's, I went about my tasks quickly, filled out my interminable forms, and made my way out of the door, but not without feeling a blast of spit at my back followed by a loud burst of profanity, this the type of doubly offensive occurrence to which I would reluctantly become well-accustomed.

"Ah, my dear Charles, these experiences will expand your vocabulary," Gabriel said with a laugh. "I heard curses today that even my drunken Uncle Theo never uses. Charles, it is but one of the benefits of your position. I must check on the definitions of 'fils de pute' and 'conard.' They have such a nice ring to them."

"I had no idea it was like this," he said to me on a more serious note as we approached the next row of houses. "I know Paris needs us, but the smell, the filth, the hate you encounter out here every day! It's terrible! Charles, I've been too hard on you with my silly remarks. I apologize. I hope The Baron is paying you well. And you really should have an office all to yourself. You deserve that. I'll speak to him."

<hr>

In the space of several hectic weeks, demolition projects multiplied so quickly at Rue de Rivoli sites and progress was so rapid, that in slightly more than two months' time I had more than ten demolition agents assisting and reporting to me. It had become impossible for one man to handle the rapidly advancing work load alone. In the early weeks I had been out every day, appropriating properties, estimating values, and supervising progress on one project as I organized the next, but all too soon scheduling became my greatest concern. Although the agents assigned to me helped to relieve the chaos of any given day by organizing teams of laborers, assigning them locations, and controlling street traffic, they were not qualified to appropriate or estimate values. That responsibility remained mine. To complicate matters, I was inundated by the volume of daily reports, compensation forms, and inventories the Baron required for presentation and discussion at our weekly meetings. In a very short time I became one of the men I had seen on my first day at the Hotel de Ville, one of those solemn-faced beings who crossed the marble surface of the second floor every day and deposited his stacks of paper on the table to one side of Secretary Merruau's desk. I also had a frequent companion to think about.

The Baron had engaged Charles Marville, to photograph old streets and neighborhoods before their destruction and again after they had been re-developed. I learned a great deal about Paris from Marville and we got on well together. He was a solidly built, handsome man with a curling mustache and a long goatee. He was not part of the inner circle, but I have always felt he should have been. In over 400 fine photographs, he managed to reach deep into the heart of old Paris, his subject matter infused with honesty and the unvarnished reality that only the newly popular onset of photography could provide. He often shared my carriage, a genuine luxury provided to me after several months, complete with driver. Lest you be raising your eyebrows right now, thinking me to be unduly showered with favor, I must tell you that the carriage, although quite adequate for my needs, was not at all like the fleet of gleaming black broughams The Baron had at his disposal. Mine was a modest brown carriage drawn by a pair of dapple grays and it carried more than a few scratches, dents too, from its history with former owners. In the course of its time with me, my carriage acquired a great many additional scratches and dents, emblems of honor I like to think, of its many days contending with the batter and bruising of daily passage along narrow streets and the frequent barrage of rocks thrown at it by the dispossessed and consistently and chronically angry. Marville photographed the carriage on more than one occasion. I wish I had those pictures now. They somehow disappeared at the end.

Marville kept a studio on Boulevard Saint-Jacques. For a time he also stored equipment in a corner of the office Davioud and I shared at the Hotel de Ville. Davioud never complained about Marville's intrusion or the growing accumulation of my stacks of paper and charts, but between his drafting tables, my ledgers and scheduling graphs, and Marville's bulky equipment, the once generous space we had initially been delighted to share quickly became cramped. The Baron understood our needs perfectly. He assigned our briefly shared office to Davioud and his drafting assistant, Marc Basse, for their exclusive use. Charles Marville was given the spacious room under one of the grand red-carpeted staircases, and in short order I not only had a private office on the first floor of the Hotel de Ville, I had an administrative assistant, a keeper of records, and a certified appraiser. I had also gained The Baron's confidence.

"Charles, you are handling things very well," he said to me when the subject of our crowded office arose. "Your grasp of our needs is impressive and you meet the demands of the schedule with unfailing success. Even Hittorff has complimented you, and you know how he is about maintaining the schedule."

The knowledge that I was proving myself helped to solidify my personal loyalty to both The Baron's vision for the New Paris and my own role in that vision. I did not have the gratifying architectural position I had expected and wanted. I had no assurances that I ever would, but I was handling the difficult work I did have very well, and it was beginning to feel as if I was turning my life around. I had purpose. There was a steady pace to my daily routine. I had a fine home and a good reason to get out of bed every morning. I knew my overall attitude had improved and I liked my new friends at the Hotel de Ville. It helped that I was extremely busy and that I often worked on reports late into the night. My work mattered. I knew that, but there were times when the past came back to haunt me. It had been almost two years since Louisa's death and I still missed her. The nightmares had stopped, probably because I fell into such an exhausted sleep every night, but in the middle of a conversation, on my way to a destination, or whenever I saw a blonde woman in a café or restaurant, I would suddenly think of her and our children. Had they lived, the twins would be very active now. They would be running and laughing and tossing balls across the lawn at Seine-Maritime Hill. I tried to picture what they would look like. Surely they would be beautiful children. They would look like Louisa. They would have her blue eyes and blonde hair. I also imagined what the future might have held for them. In weak moments I longed for the opportunity I'd once had to be a father watching his children grow, planning with their mother for their educations, celebrating birthdays and Christmas with grandparents and cousins in Rouen, but my relapses into whatever might have been made absolutely no sense. What was past was past, I repeatedly told myself. Paris would be my home throughout the foreseeable future. I was establishing a life here, and I really was, as Andre Rousseau had advised on my last night in Rouen, "getting on with it."

Daniel had been ill. Sister Angelica had nursed him through three days of fever.

CHAPTER FIVE

And Then There Was Adele

November 1853

ONE AFTERNOON in early November of 1853, my preliminary work on the Rue de Rivoli project well underway, I was in my office organizing schedules when The Baron sent word through Secretary Merruau that he had arranged for my invitation to a reception in his honor. It was being hosted by Adele Alessandri, an Italian opera singer who made her home in Paris. Although I had occasionally enjoyed the opera, I had not attended a performance in quite some time and I must have been one of the very few people in all Europe who had never heard of Adele Alessandri.

"Madame Alessandri is famous for both her beautiful soprano voice and her parties," Secretary Merruau informed me as he handed me the invitation and provided a bit of background. "I'm surprised you don't know about her. She has appeared all over Europe. Audiences absolutely love her. I heard her last year in Meyerbeer's Les Huguenots. She was magnificent! Five curtain calls! Bouquets of flowers! She was married to the Marquis de

Courtivron. What a splendid couple they were; she beautiful and famous, he a handsome nobleman from an old French family. They were one of the most popular couples in Paris; very rich, very elegant, but about four years ago the Marquis died in a boating accident at Etretat. I understand he was an experienced sailor, but it's been said he misjudged the tide. His body was found floating below the rugged twin cliffs. Can you imagine such a tragedy? Of course Madame Alessandri took it all very badly. She had to identify her husband's remains and what was left of his boat. God only knows what condition he must have been in. After that she didn't sing for months, but once she recovered she not only returned to the stage and her adoring audiences, she also decided to open the doors of her beautiful house whenever she was in Paris. Her parties are wonderful. There is always an orchestra for dancing, and the most attractive people. Everyone is lively and interesting and The Baron thought you deserved a special evening out. Madame Alessandri's mansion on Place des Vosges is one of the loveliest in the Marais. I know you will enjoy being there. I was there once. I wish I were going again."

Secretary Merruau smiled an unusually friendly smile and leaned in close to me, lowering his voice. "Monsieur Fabron, it will be a formal evening," he said in a near whisper. "One would want to wear a black tailcoat and trousers with a white waistcoat, a white bow tie or cravat and of course, a freshly starched white shirt and collar. A white scarf with a long fringe is always a handsome touch when one arrives at the door, don't you think? Butlers look at you differently when you just slide it off and fling it away to them as if you have ten more at home in the armoire. And I always think a top hat, white gloves and a cloak complete a gentleman's evening attire quite nicely, don't you? This year, Baron Haussmann's cloak has a deep blue satin lining. Perhaps you will choose red, or perhaps white? The Baron and most of the gentlemen here use Monsieur Lambert's tailor shop on Rue Allard. If you like I will prepare a note of introduction."

Agreeing to Merruau's offer to write a note to Monsieur Lambert in my behalf, I quickly wrote a note of my own to thank the Baron for his consideration, indicating that I would be honored to accept Madame Alessandri's invitation. Once I reached home at the end of the day, I went to my bedroom armoire to inspect and try on the evening clothes my mother had insisted I bring from Rouen. In seconds I knew I would have done better to have left them in the trunk I had stored in her basement. Everything was too large. The coat tails were too long and my whole body looked swallowed up in the trousers. I had neither white scarf nor white gloves and the expense of a cloak and top hat added to what would surely turn out to be a budget-breaking expense for a new set of evening clothes was out of the question. Madame Alessandri's reception was three weeks away; not much time for a tailor to fit me for a new set of clothes and barely enough time to re-organize my budget and consider the value of dipping into my line of credit.

The next day, late in the afternoon, I went to Monsieur Lambert's tailor shop on Rue Allard. Setting the concern of expense aside, I presented the envelope with the note Merruau had prepared. Monsieur Lambert opened the envelope, read the note, and in less than an hour he had guided my choice of fabrics, every inch of me had been measured, and I had made a friend. Lambert was a great fan of Baron Haussmann and made no secret of his enthusiasm for the Paris Project. He even understood my role as Supervisor of Demolition and the difficulty of my responsibilities.

"All the good things in life require a little sacrifice," he said. "People should understand that. In this establishment, when we see that seams and stitches are not going the way they should, we tear things apart and start over. Some of our customers become impatient with the time this can take, but I tell them our reputation and their appearance depend on superior work. It is the same with you, no?"

I left Monsieur Lambert's with an appointment for a fitting in a week's time. To my surprise, he had not handed me a billing statement. At the door, when I hesitantly asked what the total cost of my evening finery might be, he said I was not to worry and that we would discuss it at my fitting. In a week's time, when I returned for my fitting and again inquired about costs, I was told that Baron Haussmann had taken care of everything. I didn't know whether to be pleased or embarrassed. I decided I would not pursue the issue with Monsieur Lambert but that Secretary Merruau would be the person to explain this unexpected gift. The next day, when I inquired, Merruau informed me that as occasions arose, Baron Haussmann made similar gifts to each member of the inner circle. I was told I was not to thank him or make mention of the gift to anyone.

On the appointed evening I arrived just after nine at Maison Courtivron on Place des Vosges which was the most fashionable address in the Marais. I was apprehensive. This was, after all, a new world to me, but I stepped out of the carriage I had hired rather pleased with myself and my elegant evening attire, and as Secretary Merruau had suggested, I did rather enjoy being greeted at the door by the butler and handing off my new white fringed scarf as if I had ten more at home in the armoire.

I had chosen a white satin lining for my cloak. It was all very dramatic, very correct. My white collar was appropriately starched, my tie startlingly white, my vest made of white brocade. Entering the high-ceilinged reception hall, I almost felt like the same man I had been before Louisa's death; confident, composed, and yes, possessed of the stare and swagger Andre Rousseau identified with me. I have never been sure why he connected those characteristics to me. I certainly hadn't worked at creating them, but as I arrived at Adele Alessandri's prestigious address, it was reassuring to know that somewhere deep inside I had held on to some vestige of my old self.

As Secretary Merruau had pointed out, Adele Alessandri's reception was indeed the first formal soiree I would attend in Paris. Many followed, but none remain more memorable. The house itself was a treasure. It was the grandest residence I had ever seen and just as gracious and glittering a home as one might expect of a successful international opera star accustomed to the limelight. As soon as my carriage made its way through the gates I heard music being played by an orchestra. Romantic and lyrical, it spilled out onto the drive and continued inside without pause during the entire evening.

Madame Alessandri greeted her guests in the reception hall where the view was to the opulent ballroom behind her. The scene was like a painting; a color-filled depiction of private Paris caught socializing in evening grandeur and it was as elegant a canvas as Secretary Merruau had led me to expect. Tall silver urns were filled with masses of fragrant white lilies. Candlelight blazed from a parade of candelabra. The women graced the setting in an array of glittering jewels and pastel colored gowns. The men were resplendent either in red military tunics or formal evening attire similar to mine. The red tunics were ablaze with medals and bright blue, gold, or green sashes reflecting affiliations with noble French families or rankings in military regiments, academies, and historic institutions. Many of the men attired in white tie and tails also wore sashes and displayed medals, their obvious ease and familiarity with a collection of friends lending a light-heartedness to what I might otherwise have interpreted as a stiff, labored occasion. I would soon learn that this was the secret of the wealthy and well-connected in Paris. Wary of outsiders, they gravitated toward one another, their circles exclusive and small, their lives lived out in a constantly revolving series of comfortable encounters and predictable circumstances. A novice to all this, I was fascinated by their interaction. Many of the men posed handsomely in their finery and made idle conversation with people they had known all their lives. Some of the women flirted openly with handsome officers in heavily decorated red military tunics. Other ladies remained aloof, content to quietly admire and observe the proceedings from behind their fluttering fans. Overall as a group, I have remembered the women as lovely. Some were truly beautiful, but none compared to Adele Alessandri. Waiting to be announced, I was unprepared for her striking appearance.

She was dark-haired and surprisingly slim for an opera singer. Drawing closer I saw that her almond-shaped eyes were a vivid shade of green, their extraordinary color accentuated by dark eyebrows and thick fringes of eyelashes. Standing in the flattering candlelight I couldn't help but notice the dramatic bone structure of her oval-shaped face, her cheekbones classically high, slight hollows beneath, her full lips and the small cleft in her chin completing a thoroughly exotic picture.

"Ah, yes, Charles Fabron! Baron Haussmann has told me all about you!" she said, smiling as I was announced and kissed her hand. "I understand you've come to Paris from Rouen, the City of a Hundred Bell Towers! As a young singer I gave a concert in the hall at the Lycee Pierre Corneille. You must know the building. I remember how the bells rang out at least four times during the performance, and of course never in places where they would have made the greatest impact!" She laughed in light, brilliantly melodious tones I can hear as clearly today as I did then. "I am very happy to meet you, Monsieur Fabron," she said, looking directly into my eyes.

"The champagne is especially good tonight. It is from the vineyards at Verzenay. You must let me know what you think of it. I will be waiting for your opinion."

That was how Adele did things. That was how she drew people in. It was her way. If she decided she wanted to pursue a conversation with you, she would create a reason to engage you later, when she was ready. In the meantime, you would think about what she had said and how she had said it. You would tell yourself it would be unforgiveable to look into those green eyes later on and find you were unprepared to voice an opinion or make a suitable comment regarding the champagne from the vineyards at Verzenay. And in the days and weeks ahead you would tell yourself you should have had nothing at all to say about the orchestra, the lilies, her dress, or her hypnotic gaze.

I walked into the ballroom and chatted politely with a few guests. Making light, meaningless conversation with strangers was not one of my talents, but if I was to be attending these receptions as The Baron had made clear I would, I realized it would be necessary to perfect my delivery of nuances surrounding current weather conditions, the likelihood of rain, and the past summer's splendid crop of peaches from the Brie, conversational distinctions which people around me appeared to have mastered with enviable expertise.

I was standing at the foot of the staircase when Baron Haussmann was announced. He paused and stood tall and proud in the middle of the gleaming marble-floored hall. I had looked forward to his arrival, more than mildly interested in what his demeanor might be in a social setting away from the Hotel de Ville. I was not disappointed. No one could have been. He was in full formal regalia, the distinguished Medallion of the Prefect of Paris attached to a blue satin ribbon crossing the pleated bib of his white silk shirt, the intricate silver embroidery on his black velvet jacket truly spectacular and entirely reminiscent of eighteenth-century court dress. Even in those early days there was something about him; something heroic and memorable about the way he looked, the way he moved. That great things lay ahead of him seemed perfectly clear. That he was about to become the most talked about human being in Paris was, as the American Minister to France, John Mason, put it that night in his introductory remarks and in perfect French, "as certain as the daily sunrise."

The Baron kissed Adele's hand, clicked his heels, and together they entered the crowded ballroom to a loud burst of applause followed by a flourish of trumpets, an orchestral introduction, and Adele's singing of Partant Pour La Syrie, the French National Hymn which had been written by the Emperor's mother, Hortense de Beauharnais.

Selected by the Emperor shortly after his arrival in Paris as the French National Anthem, this was the first time I had heard the new French Hymn. As the years passed, I would hear it many times over, but until 1870, when The Marseilles, made famous during the Revolution was officially restored, Partant Pour La Syrie would distinguish all events related to Louis Napoleon's Second Empire and no one sang it more beautifully than Adele Alessandri. Secretary Merruau had not exaggerated the beauty of her voice. Even in the somewhat militaristic hymn, her phrasing and expression were mesmerizing, the impression she made as a seasoned performer nothing short of triumphant. It was not difficult to understand why she enjoyed the adulation of audiences around the world. She had been born to be seen and heard. As the music for dancing began, The Baron took her hand, led her onto the dance floor, and smiled the vague, secretive smile I would soon come to recognize as his public expression of satisfaction. As together they circled the room, chatting and occasionally laughing, every eye was fixed on them, and why not? They were dazzling. Their poise, their beautiful clothes, even their posture exuded the elite courtliness which I was discovering were requirements of the upper echelons of Paris life to which I was being introduced but into which even then I knew I would never feel accepted. Baron Haussmann was a superb administrator, as talented in his career as Adele Alesandri was in hers, but he was not inclusive when it came to social relationships either as Prefect of the Seine or as Master Builder of Paris. Over time, those of us who were part of his inner Hotel de Ville circle attended many prestigious social events, including several to which we were invited by The Emperor. There was, however, always a line to be drawn and The Baron drew it masterfully, to the extent that in later years and with rare exception, few people would remember the names of those of us who contributed to the re-invention of Paris. We worked diligently and with great dedication, but our names and deeds quickly vanished into the shadows of history while Baron Haussmann's name alone was prominently linked to the successful transformation of Paris. I cannot identify a single man among us who actively sought recognition, and of course since it never came, we were not disappointed. Early on, The Baron had made it clear that our primary responsibilities and commitments were to our work and our specific assignments. I would hasten to add, however, that in the early days and within the strict working environment he established at the beginning, he made a great effort to be considerate. At times he went so far as to be overly complimentary and overly friendly. As the Paris Project grew into its massive self, however, he changed. He could become insulting and demanding and cuttingly dismissive of those he felt stood in his way or established a position contrary to his own. Essentially he became a man resolutely determined to fulfill his Emperor's requirements no matter the toll it took on those closest and most helpful to him.

Considering the nature of my responsibilities, I gladly shrank away from brushes with the fame The Baron was eager to grasp. I had another, less awe-inspiring type of recognition to contend with and for the most part I preferred to leave its impact buried in the streets of Old Paris. I do understand though, how Baron Hussmann's rapid rise was in keeping with the spirit of the times. It was the age of the aristocracy. The grandeur and royal formalities of Empire were powerful, and he was closely related to them. Now, in 1885, life in France is very different. The age of aristocracy has lost its singular power to influence, but for all the years of our collaboration I recall quite clearly that like the Emperor himself, Baron Haussmann knew exactly who he was and what he wanted. His confidence never wavered in the elevated settings through which he lived and worked, and he understood better than most court followers that as much as Louis Napoleon and Empress Eugenie wished to contemporize the look and feel of an all-inclusive Paris, that at the same time they were eager to restore the royal trappings of the past. Together they succeeded in creating an empirical environment of extravagance and splendor. Throughout the years of the Second Republic they expanded its richness, their influence on public taste reaching an incomparable degree of public fervor. Eugenie's hairstyle was copied not only by Parisian women but by thousands of women across Europe. When the Waltz King, Johann Strauss, came to Paris, he waltzed with Eugenie and overnight the waltz became wildly popular. The Empress was Louis Napoleon's greatest asset.

From his earliest days as Emperor it was commonly known that Louis Napoleon had set two major goals, the first being to marry a suitable wife who would share the burdens of his Empire and provide him with a Bonaparte heir, the second being the appointment of a Prefect who would administer the transformation of Paris. Quickly addressing the matter of marriage, the bachelor Emperor who famously enjoyed the company of a long list of mistresses and considered a number of marriageable candidates, finally chose the twenty-six-year-old widowed Spanish Countess of Teba and Sixteenth Marchioness of Ardeles, the extraordinarily beautiful and stylish Eugenie de Montijo who even in France was rumored to be madly in love with the dashing Spanish Duke of Alba. It was a brief engagement, but there was no need for an extended betrothal. Eugenie and Louis had known each other for several years and had played the game of cat and mouse with skill and daring. Eugenie liked Louis Napoleon's Bonaparte lineage, but when he became Emperor of France she liked the idea of advancing herself from Countess and Marchioness to Empress of France even more. She was not, however, about to fall into the French Emperor's magnificent bed before a proper marriage had been sanctified in the Church which, until the wedding day, was impatient Louis Napoleon's fondest and most persistent wish. The elaborate civil marriage ceremony took place at the Tuileries Palace on January 22, 1853, the solidifying religious ceremony at the Cathedral of Notre Dame on January 29th, one month following the Emperor's arrival in France.

In short order, Eugenie became every inch an Empress, gathering around her a luxurious circle of servants as well as a staff of jewelers, dress designers, milliners, and artists. Franz Winterhalter painted her portrait not once, but several times. She went so far as to engage a young trunk maker and packer who was responsible for creating and packing the custom made containers into which her clothes, accessories, and personal items were placed and transported to whichever palace, estate, or spa she was travelling. The young trunk maker and packer to the Empress was Louis Vuitton, and with her royal endorsement, the praise and patronage of her influential friends, and an address at Number One Rue Scribe, he soon developed a successful business as a designer and maker of high quality trunks and traveling cases of every conceivable variety.

Safely married and establishing between them the mutual desire to live their lives with a return to the most formal of French royal traditions, after their wedding the Emperor and his Empress promptly set standards for the high style of the Second Empire which included restoration of a long list of seventeenth and eighteenth century court formalities. In rapid succession, palace guards, valets, grooms, footmen, and butlers were costumed in the elaborately ruffled and gold-embellished velvet, lace, and brocade livery that any Bourbon king would have recognized. Curtsies, bows, and the clicking of heels were interminable and members of the Court, regardless of title, were expected to meet a long list of ceremonial requirements while extravagantly dressed and bejeweled, at the same time deporting themselves with great shows of formal deference to superiors. Court life and its regimented formalities may have offered status and access but it also made exhausting and expensive demands. I don't wonder that many close to the Emperor sought frequent refuge in country houses and chateaux far from Paris. Thankfully, I was not involved in court life and its complicated procedures but I did have a front row seat to its effects. The Baron, however, was heavily involved, and I had further reason to admire him when I saw with what ease he handled the demands of his own status, especially his easy access to the Emperor. And here I will digress once again for a paragraph or two. The relationship between The Baron and The Emperor was much too unique to be passed over in a few sentences.

They met every morning. Even with so well-scheduled a personal association, I am not sure that over the course of years they ever became true friends, or that their frequent interaction ever defined much more than a high degree of mutual respect. Even in private and with those closest to him, The Emperor was known to be a haughty, self-promoting man, and of course he held all the cards, but he trusted Baron Haussmann, and I believe that at least for a time, The Baron returned the favor. In their daily meetings which took place at The Tuileries Palace, the Elysees Palace, or the Chateau of Saint-Cloud, they reviewed progress on the city's transformation projects and planned ahead, but they also met frequently with Ministers and Council Members whose approvals for designated improvements and budgetary allowances were legally required. A good deal of negotiation and debate took place at these meetings, Ministers and Council members at times patiently allowed to have their lengthy say and only occasionally their way, the terms of these predictably unpredictable conditions usually determined by The Emperor's mood on any given day.

At Adele Alessandri's reception, I was not yet aware of the existence of these intricate empirical dealings, but I was becoming very much aware of the formality which defined the Second Empire. Although beautiful to observe, at first this behavior was difficult for me to grasp, particularly as I observed the hostess and the honoree who circulated among the guests with a great to-do over each and every one. Fortunately and as happened, the gentleman who came to stand beside me took it upon himself to guide me through the ways of this new formal world with blessed informality, thus lessening my general discomfort by some considerable measure.

"It's like watching a ritual dance, isn't it," the resonant voice beside me stated without benefit of introduction, "something tribal, full of secret movements and a strange, dark mystery," came the further comment as I turned and was met by the smile of a silver-haired gentleman in a red military tunic decorated in a blaze of gold medals, sword at his side, champagne glass in hand.

"I hope those two don't collide with one another in this overdressed crowed," he added, watching the hostess and the honoree with a wry smile, "but I suppose this is the way it will be at these dreadful affairs now: competition for the brightest light, endless self-absorption under the chandeliers, all those things I thought went out with the Bourbons and their endless fleurs de lis. Well, hopefully, when the City of Paris is the way the Emperor and Baron Haussmann want it, we will all be the better for it. The Baron certainly is good at all this hand-kissing and heel clicking! Look at him out there!"

"Allow me to introduce myself. I am Count Andre Leclerc," he announced with his own grand clicking of heels. "Madame Alessandri has asked me to make you feel comfortable in this ridiculous atmosphere. I'm sure it has everything to do with my advanced age and abundant charm which I gladly spread throughout Paris as often as I can and completely free of charge. I know everyone here, so I'll steer you away from the dragons, and be advised, there are plenty of them here tonight. I've been hearing about your position with The Baron. Your title sounds fascinating: Charles Fabron, Supervisor of Demolition."

"You know my name, Monsieur," I said, unable to suppress my surprise, at the same time delighted by the Count's approach. "You also know the nature of my assignment with Baron Haussmann. News travels quickly in Paris. Is it always like this?'

"No, not always. Sometimes it can take as long as half an hour for the powers-that-be to spread their information. In this case, Haussmann himself was responsible for getting the latest Rue de Rivoli news out to this crowd, and exactly as he intended, it has spread like wildfire. It's exactly what he wants: to stir things up and get people talking. Young man, you must understand that most of the people you see here have nothing of any real importance to do. They're bored and boring. They thrive on the latest flashes of news and love to consider its impact on their privileged lives. They can go on and on about it for hours with anyone who will listen and that's also what Haussmann wants. Countess Langlois standing over there by the champagne fountain lives to make judgments on Paris life. This Haussmann project should hold her for a while. I pray it does. She's been far too busy complaining about the decline in the city's morality. Isn't that a joke? As if her opinions and pleas to the Bishop will affect the debauchery and whoring we've been enjoying for centuries! But, I suppose cities do live by their reputations. And speaking of reputations, life may never be the same for Georges Haussmann, or for you, Charles Fabron. I went past the north side of The Louvre yesterday and saw you had begun pulling things apart. You're making quite a mess out there, young man! People are taking notice. Not everyone likes it."

"Yes, I suppose you might say that," I said with a chuckle. "I know the upheaval is unpleasant, but it's essential to what will eventually come. This is an exciting time for Paris. The Baron has planned very well. So much lies ahead. He is pleased."

"Is he now?" Well, we'll see if he remains pleased for long," the adroit Leclerc slowly remarked, between sips of champagne, smiling and nodding pleasantly to every person who walked past. "But there is always The Emperor," he added in a near whisper while looking straight ahead. "His Majesty may be enthusiastic about the Paris project now, but experience has taught me that his attention is easily diverted. I've known him for many years and I'm not telling you anything I haven't told him. I was with him at Boulogne-Sur-Mer and although I know I don't look it, thank you very much, I'm old enough to have been at his Uncle Napoleon's side toward the end of the glory days. I was appointed to his general staff just a month before the British decided to rearrange our lives at Waterloo. That was the saddest day of my life. Oh well, it was another time and it's over. I lived through it. In any case, in your planning and demolition forays, stay away from the houses here on Place des Vosges. Members of my family have lived here for four generations. Of course, this lovely residence of Madame Alessandri's will undoubtedly stand untouched, and due to that happy circumstance I'm reasonably confident that I will die peacefully in my bed just a few doors away. It does pay to be on, shall we say, favorable terms with the Emperor. Charles, you're new to this ridiculous circus world of ours, so let me give you a word of fatherly advice. Don't be fooled by things you see at affairs like this. We love our glamour and our excess and we're very good at flaunting our grandeur, but it's all a big show. What isn't part of that show is the Emperor's sincere affection for our hostess. He lavishes attention on women like Adele Alessandri. He loves beautiful women. What man doesn't? In this case, however, Louis Napoleon does have the advantage. He is after all, the Emperor, but titles aside, I understand that he and Adele are engaged in a few of their own little projects together. Frankly, I'm not too clear on what they are. Something about designing private gardens at small estates no one knows a thing about. Sounds intriguing doesn't it? Ah, to be an Emperor in possession of small estates and secret gardens! And as I think about it, I should point out that George Sand may not be the only woman in Paris known to wear men's trousers. It seems to me that any female gardener worth her salt, including our beautiful hostess, would dress the part, especially an opera singer accustomed to an endless choice of costumes. And one more thing for you to digest before I conclude my informative lecture: Madame Alessandri is older than she looks. Be careful. She has a penchant for good-looking young men like you. Welcome to our greenhouse, Charles Fabron, and good luck in this world of glass."

I was at a loss for words. Of course it was quite true, as Count Leclerc had pointed out, that I was new to the ways of the Paris upper echelons but it was also true that I really had no desire to participate in its show or to reside in its world of glass. Oddly enough, between endless meetings with The Baron, attending to the business of expropriation, and familiarizing myself with the City of Paris, I had found absolutely no time to study the daily workings of the upper classes, but the aging chevalier's reference to the female novelist, George Sand, who I did know had created quite a stir in Paris by wearing men's clothing in public, struck me as interesting. I had read two of Sand's novels. I liked Consuelo, but A Winter in Majorca had left me yawning. It centered on the author's love affair with Frederic Chopin and the few months they had spent on the island of Majorca during the final stages of the composer's illness. Like the entire evening at Madame Alessandri's, their lives were also terribly complicated. Returning home that night to the Rohan Courtyards, I welcomed the simplicity of my private world. There was something wonderful about closing the Rue du Jardinet gate behind me and hearing the latch fall securely into place.

Over the course of the following weeks I caught glimpses of Adele Alessandri at Hotel de Ville receptions and a number of dinners hosted by The Baron which were becoming more frequent and considerably less intimidating. From across the room she would smile to me and nod her head in recognition. I would smile back and promptly disappear into one of the card rooms. A glass of brandy in hand, I would join a table for an hour or two before leaving for home. On one such evening, Count Leclerc invited me to join his table. He signaled me with a flourish of his long cigarette holder, continuing to expound on the failures of childhood education in Paris as I approached. I had no sooner taken my seat when Adele came to stand behind the Count's chair, his lecture on the pitfalls of French education quickly terminated as he turned to her with a smile and fresh cards were dealt.

"Ah, such serious faces in this room! How gloomy you all are! Adele said to him with a pout, "and out there, the music is so lovely for dancing. Count Leclerc, we have not danced together in ages. Come now, is a dance with me not more appealing than that very poor hand of cards I can see you have been dealt?"

The Count glanced around the table, rose from his chair and kissed Adele's hand. "My dear, you are irresistible," he said. "Gentlemen, as it does appear that this evening my cards, like our public education, leave much to be desired, I believe I shall be occupied in some dancing for the remainder of the evening. I wish you good fortune and bid you good-night."

"If Adele Alessandri had asked me to dance, I would have left all of you too," Christian Leroy said to those of us remaining at the table. "That beautiful woman is one of a kind. I don't know how Leclerc does it. He must be twice her age. Rumor has it that they've been involved for years. I can't decide whether to believe it or not."

"Why don't you ask the Countess Langois?" Didier Alains remarked with a chuckle. "She's in there standing by the champagne fountain again. The woman knows everything about everyone, including you, Christian."

I had watched the Count and Adele leave the card room, curious myself about the nature of their relationship, even more curious about the Count's ability to dance. In recent weeks I had noticed his limp. On this particular evening it was clearly hindering his ability to walk.

In the next half hour I was dealt good cards and won hand after hand. I had just decided to say good-night and leave for home when I saw Leclerc standing in the doorway. "I need a word with you, Charles," he called out, leaning against the door frame. "Thank God you haven't left!" he said in a breathless whisper as I reached his side. "Charles, you must dance with Adele Alessandri. My knee feels as if it is about to burst and fall out of my leg. It's an old injury that kicks up now and then, all thanks to Uncle

Napoleon's last battle with that haughty Englishman. Adele knows all about it, but she insists on continuing to dance with me! She has refused three perfectly charming young men who know about my injury and have tried to cut in. I'm sure she won't refuse you and I want her to enjoy the evening. Adele is very dear to me. I'll explain all that to you some day. Now, Charles, please do this for me."

I liked Andre Leclerc. I held him in high esteem, but I didn't attend these receptions because I wanted a social life. I was obligated to attend. None of us who worked with The Baron refused his invitations which were issued in a carefully organized rotating system. According to Secretary Merruau, serious illness or a death in the family were the two acceptable excuses. Of course I knew it was an honor to be invited, but I never felt obligated to dance with anyone at the Baron's fetes, least of all with intimidating Adele Alessandri.

"Count Leclerc, I am so sorry," I said to the clearly ailing man as sympathetically as I could, "but it's late and I have a very early start in the morning. The work of demolishing Old Paris begins at dawn. I really must be leaving."

"Charles, don't be silly. So what if you're a little late tomorrow. I'll put in a good word for you with the Baron. He likes you. He has told me so. Besides, you're young. When I was your age I hardly slept at all. Life was too exciting. There were too many beautiful women, too many fetes, and too much wine. It was a waste of time to rest. It still is. Why do you think I appear at all these events? It's an old habit I cannot break! Think of an assignment like this as part of your work, which it is."

Andre Leclerc had undoubtedly lived his life fully and well. Amused as I was by his levity, I couldn't help but admire him. Even in advancing years it was clear that he valued a good time and would to the end. "Charles, by now you've seen what these affairs hosted by The Baron are all about," he continued. "We dress ourselves up and turn ourselves out because we are assistants, not only to him, but to the Emperor. We come to promote the interests of the Empire and the progress of the New Paris. People like Adele Alessandri are influential. They know what we're doing and what you're doing and they're on our side. We need them. They know everyone who's anyone and they're either entertaining in their homes or out at crowded soirees every night of the week talking about exactly what you and I care about which is a new and improved Paris. Our influence can only go so far, but a positive word or two from someone as well-known and charismatic as Adele is essential. It will come as no surprise to you that we need the approval of as many people as possible, especially now, and you must also realize that not everyone approves of this idea of a modernized Paris. The Emperor can take refuge behind the guarded doors of his palaces, but Haussmann' neck is out there. I feel sorry for him. He has a good life, luxuries by the wagonload, but he's taking the brunt of the criticism. I hope it doesn't hurt him. I, for one, want to do all I can to help, but there's a growing sentiment out there that he will destroy the city's history, spend too much money, and hurt too many innocent people. Nonsense, I say! The work is barely started and there are already complaints about the dust and dirt, the noise and congestion. Why do people hate change when it is so obviously for the best? Fortunately, Haussmann is strong and can take it all with the proverbial grain of salt, but have you seen that terrible pamphlet being circulated about him? It describes his love affairs, names his mistresses, and calls him entirely unqualified to be Prefect of the Seine. Sounds to me like there's an attempt being made to destroy him. Why would anyone want him to fail? Dreadful business!"

I had heard about the gossip. I cared nothing at all about it. True or not, The Baron's private life, his mistresses and love affairs, were none of my business. I had work to do and it demanded my full attention. As for my immediate dilemma concerning the Count's request that I dance with Adele Alessandri, I told him I never danced at these affairs.

"Well then Charles, it's high time you started," he said to me with a decisive nod. "A whirl or two around the dance floor gets a man's blood moving, especially when his partner looks like Adele Alessandri. Charles, stop being such a prude and go over there!"

I hadn't danced with anyone since Louisa and I had danced at her sister's wedding. It was the last celebration we had attended. By then Louisa's condition was becoming obvious and modest as she was, after the wedding we agreed that for the remaining weeks of her pregnancy we would attend only family gatherings. Until Count Leclerc made his plea, I hadn't given the slightest thought to dancing or dancing partners. Besides, the orchestra was playing music for a quadrille and I was out of practice.

Adele was chatting with a group in a corner. I squared my shoulders and walked toward her. She saw me coming and extended her hand. Without a word I led her onto the dance floor, held her at arm's length, and joined the group in the quadrille, performing the required chasses and entrechats. I didn't do the intricate entrechats very well at all. "Why, Charles Fabron, surely you can dance better than this," she said bowing and making her turns with a pout. "I've watched you walk across a room. You have a rhythmic ease about you. Isn't this as good a time as any to show it off?'

"Madame Alessandri, I haven't danced the quadrille in quite a while," I said, struggling on, "but if the orchestra plays a waltz, I may surprise you. In fact, I hope you will be up to it. In Rouen, long before Monsieur Strauss came to Paris, I was known to be rather good at waltzing."

The orchestra played another quadrille. I continued to struggle, which amused my cynical partner enormously, but when I heard a melody being played in three-quarter time I decided I would show Madame Alessandri a thing or two. I pulled her close to me, pushed her hand up into the air, and started out with the waltz steps I remembered. It all came back in a flash. I suddenly felt so confident that I really didn't care if she kept up. I would drag her around the dance floor and leave her breathless and panting in a corner if necessary. Who did this brazen Adele Alessandri think she was, placing me in a compromising situation and criticizing my dancing? Much to my chagrin, I didn't have the chance to drag Madame Alessandri around the ballroom of the Hotel de Ville and pile her into a corner. She was very good at following my lead, excellent really. We whirled and turned and spun around the room again and again. I became more confident with every step. She was a feather in my arms. It was as if we were flying. I knew I was smiling. Our eyes met and we both laughed.

"I knew you'd be like this," she said, as the orchestra played its final chords and we left the dance floor. "You just needed a little prodding and the company of a fascinating woman like me to pull you out of that shell you wear like a turtle. You are a turtle, you know; head kept down, everything kept safely inside. I've watched you. You're very handsome but too correct. Do you ever let yourself go and have fun?"

A waiter passed with a tray of champagne. She took two glasses. "This helps loosen the limbs of men like you," she said, placing one of the glasses in my hand. "Enjoy, my turtle! A la belle France!"

"A la belle France!" I returned slowly, raising my glass, strangely intrigued by this audacious woman. Turtle indeed!

"I'm giving a small dinner tomorrow evening," she said. "Eight o'clock. You know the address. I'll expect you."

"I'm sorry Madame," I quickly responded, "but I have an engagement."

"Cancel it!" she said. "Eight o'clock. Don't be late."

With that, she walked away, champagne glass in hand, the train of her white satin gown flaring out behind her in a cloud. I watched her disappear, convinced that I would not be attending any dinner to which the likes of Adele Alessandri had invited me.

———— ✦ ————

It was well after eight o'clock when I rang the bell at Maison Courtivron on Place des Vosges. Contrary to the clear directive that I not be late, I was quite late. I was deliberately late. I was so late that I was enjoying my lateness. This Adele Alessandri wasn't about to dictate the use of my time. She had annoyed me and I wanted nothing more than to return the annoyance to this over-privileged huntress and be done with her.

"Ah, my handsome turtle! I had a feeling you would be late!" she announced, coming toward me with a bright, cheerful smile as the butler took my coat and I handed off my white fringed scarf with practiced flair. "I know how busy you must be and what long days you must be enduring. Don't worry, Charles dear. You're forgiven!" she added, taking my arm. "And, you will be pleased to know that I have advanced our dinner hour. Guests are still arriving and dinner is still being prepared, so you needn't feel embarrassed at all. Come, let me introduce you to a few of my friends."

It would be like this between us: the jousting, the maneuvering, the fight for the upper hand, the challenging clash of wits, and until late

December at one event after another always the dancing, the laughter, and the conversations late into the night in her beautiful drawing room. I knew I was walking into a dangerous world. My first instincts told me to stop spending time with this famous, well-connected woman. I felt disloyal to Louisa's memory and I worried that I could be jeopardizing my position with The Baron. He and others could be noticing my attention to Adele and hers to me, but since as far as I was concerned there was nothing more than companionship between us, I convinced myself to stop worrying. Adele was a delightful companion and I enjoyed spending time with an interesting, accomplished woman. It was when she suggested a holiday at her country house in Bordeaux that I knew things were going too far. I told her I couldn't foresee a time when I'd be able to be away from Paris long enough for a holiday in Bordeaux or anywhere else. Adele being Adele, she wouldn't drop the idea.

"But I want you to see my precious little house," she insisted. "As an architect you should see it," she urged repeatedly. "It's a jewel! The trees and garden are beautiful and there's a meadow. Charles, of course I understand you can't be away from Paris right now, but we'll go in the spring. We'll wear old shoes and floppy old hats and we'll pick the wild daisies in the meadow. I'll plan everything. The house is comfortable and intimate. You'll love it. It sits like a picture at the edge of a beautiful pond. It was in my late husband, Didier's family for years, but after his mother died, no one wanted it. Didier knew I loved it. The year before his accident he gave me the deed of ownership on my birthday."

I was drawn to Adele. I cannot deny the attraction. She was beautiful and desirable and I enjoyed her company, but I was intimidated by her stardom and wealth. At first I found it disturbing that she was not only wealthy and famous, but that she could also be outspoken and argumentative. It was the strangest thing, but when I was with her I became just as outspoken and argumentative. Thinking about it now, perhaps those opportunities to argue back to someone I saw as worth the effort were good for me just then. Whatever it was, the frequent friction between us had its allure. Nonetheless, there was no avoiding the fact that Adele Alessandri lived in a world vastly different from mine. She was a famous opera singer who as a result of her marriage also happened to be a Marquessa. She was a larger than life figure who lived in a privileged world. I should have discouraged our friendship, but in my own way I managed to convince myself that a few pleasant hours in her challenging company were harmless. She distracted me from the stress of my work. I also convinced myself that friendship was all there was between us. Deep inside, though, I knew exactly what was preventing me from pursuing her as something more than a friend. I was in love with a dead woman named Louisa and Adele Alessandri was nothing at all like her. She had none of Louisa's gentility or natural grace and of course that contrast eventually became the attraction. She was everything Louisa wasn't. Adele was a diva in every sense of the word: demanding, unpredictable, and temperamental. She embarrassed me at times by saying and doing anything she wanted to at any time she wanted to say or do it. She cursed and made crude gestures. She taunted and bullied but there I would be, feeling it was my responsibility to calm her down, point out the error of her ways, and find a rational approach to understanding whatever had caused her to explode. For some mysterious reason she was always satisfied with my role as her sounding board, protector, and appeaser.

"Charles, you know how to handle yourself," she said one night as we sat on the long curving sofa in her drawing room. "You also know how to handle me. I admire that. You make living look so easy," she added, a shadow crossing her lovely face, "the good manners, the kindness, the patience. You're not like other men I've known. You're a good influence on me, perhaps the only man who is, or has ever been. Didier didn't pay much attention to me. He liked me well enough physically, but he disapproved of my behavior. He preferred well-bred ladies who had never heard curse words and practiced their posture by walking with books on their heads. I suppose he married me because I was talented and famous and he could show me off to his friends, but he had his distractions. He had his boats and his horses and his mistress in Etretat. I saw her once. It was after a performance of La Favorita. People were crowding around me with flowers and congratulatory remarks, but through the flowers and faces I could see my husband with my competitor. She was young and beautiful and I could tell she was madly in love with the man I called my husband. And why not?

He was very handsome, very rich, and he ushered her into a life of luxury. There, in the opera house, for everyone to see, he was looking at her in a way he had never looked at me and she looked back at him as if he was a god. I changed after that night. I knew that neither of us could risk the scandal of divorce, so I took my revenge by ignoring Didier and concentrating on becoming the very best at what I knew best, which was singing. Didier didn't seem to mind. I drove myself relentlessly. Performing and preparing for performances across Europe were all I thought about. It was a hectic world of new roles, new costumes, new itineraries, and a collection of new adoring men in my life; conductors, composers, bankers, industrialists. I filled every day with the goal of improving, constantly bettering myself, perfecting my talent and professional connections, but I also enjoyed myself. When I wasn't performing, I filled the nights with a succession of lovers. I admit to more than a few indiscretions, but I wasn't distracted from my goal. My singing came first. I vocalized tirelessly. I rehearsed endlessly, and my efforts resulted in exactly what I wanted: a career filled with honor and glory and above all, a coveted place at the top of the international roster of opera singers. Unfortunately, I found that honor and glory are only words. They haven't turned out to be as fulfilling as I had expected. Oh, there are the post-performance parties and the gala receptions in my honor. I love them and I love the people who host and attend them, but for the most part when the velvet curtain comes down and the adoring audience has disappeared into the night, I'm left absolutely alone. If there is no special man in my life, I leave the concert hall or opera house and arrive at the doors to my hotel suite anticipating nothing more than a robe and supper on a tray. Of course, here in Paris I have my wonderful house. My life is different here, but I can't be here all the time. Away from Paris and on stages across Europe, I'm doing what I love, and I do it well, but away from the theatrical glimmer and gloss I live a cold, lonely life. I suppose I could re-arrange the schedule and spend more time in Paris, but it would be no different. Odd, isn't it? Wherever I go, even here in this welcoming city, I'm surrounded by people. They say nice things and do nice things, yet there are very few connections that last and matter. Many famous musicians like that sort of life. It doesn't work for me."

"But Adele," I quickly responded, watching her walk toward the fireplace and turn to me, "that's the life of a successful professional. Surely you have faced that. You do your work and enjoy the accolades and when it ends for the night or the season, you resume your personal life and the routine that goes with it. Isn't that what you do by coming back to Paris and this house at every opportunity?"

"It isn't enough, Charles," she said. "I might as well tell you now: I'll be giving a concert just before Christmas. It will be my farewell. I'll sing the things I'm known for: Rossini, Donizetti, and maybe two or three Schubert songs to close. It won't be difficult to prepare and I want to enjoy it. David Lasserre and I have already begun to rehearse. He's making all the arrangements."

Lasserre was Adele's manager and had guided her mercurial career. He was also her rehearsal pianist and concert accompanist. Naturally, they had a close relationship and although I had wondered about the extent of that closeness, I never observed a sign of intimacy between them. Whenever I saw them together it seemed to be all about the music.

"David must be devastated," I said, trying to absorb the impact of this renowned singer's decision to abandon her career. "He's been so important to you, and you to him. What will he do? What will you do?"

"David Lasserre is a fine musician and he's well-connected in the operatic world. I owe him a great deal, but he'll find another singer to nurture and manage. Once the news is out, it won't take long. A pianist-manager of his caliber is always in demand. And David is a splendid accompanist. He understands the human voice and the singer's temperament. He knows we sing only as well as we feel. Beyond that, his knowledge of the repertoire is staggering. He'll be at the piano on my farewell evening. He knows everything I've ever sung inside and out. I hope you'll be there for my good-bye. I'll have a ticket waiting for you."

"But why, Adele?" I asked. "Why are you turning your back on such a successful career? Loneliness can easily be remedied. You're a dynamic, beautiful woman! I don't understand. You've reached the pinnacle you've yearned for."

"I'm tired, Charles, tired of being alone and tired of constantly relying on this thing inside me called a voice. That voice is tired too. Singing is a very physical thing. It's part of who and what you are. It's always there, like another being, and when you ask it to come out and make itself heard, you hope you've done all the right things to make things happen exactly the way you want them to. It's a lot of pressure until you learn to trust the instrument inside you and believe it will always be there, ready to do whatever you demand of it at any given moment. I've been lucky. My voice has never disappointed me. A tenor I thought I was in love with once told me that to him singing was a celestial experience, a rapture for which there was no rational explanation. In many ways I believe that to be true, but right now, for me, the magic isn't quite there the way I want it to be, not the way it used to be. Oh, it doesn't show much right now and I know I'm a terrible perfectionist, but I've reached my own zenith. There's no further to go. I hear it. I feel it. Whatever I've yearned for in terms of my own artistry has been achieved and I want to leave before tremolos and singing out of tune become a way of life and audiences begin to shrink."

"Adele, are you sure you're making the right decision?" I ventured again, frankly shocked and saddened by what I was hearing. "You could be retiring too soon. I think you are. After a well-deserved rest you could regret your decision. Singing has been your life. You seem too young to give it all up. How old are you? Nothing about you appears old enough to retire."

"Ah, my dear turtle, my age will remain my little secret," she said with a laugh, "but Charles darling, if you think of me as being too young to leave the stage, then I shall be very happy knowing that."

She stared at me for a sad, poignant moment, her lovely green eyes shining with tears. I immediately regretted having questioned her decision. I left the sofa where we had spent so many hours talking, arguing and coming to terms with each other and I walked toward her. I put my arms around her. "I'm so terribly sorry," I said. "You must make your own decisions and handle them in your own way. It's really none of my business. Forgive me."

She rested her head against my chest. She stayed there, breathing softly against me. When she looked up, she smiled and slowly stroked my cheeks with her long fingers.

"Stay with me tonight," she whispered, her lips brushing against my cheek. "I want you to stay. Don't leave me here like this, not tonight."

"Adele, no. If I stay, it will change everything between us. I should go."

"Let it change," she said, her lips brushing mine. "Let everything change. Let this night change you and me. Let it change everything about the frightening worlds you and I live in."

Her bedroom at the top of the stairs was bathed in candlelight. That night, for the first time in almost two years, I knew the beauty of a woman's softness. I knew the inviting contours of her body, the miracle of her accepting warmth, and the soaring passion I thought I had left hidden somewhere in a house on a faraway hill. The aching loneliness, the hunger for stability, all the old anxieties vanished in the magic of a winter night when two insecure people found each other and became lovers.

———————

December 18th. On farewell night Adele looked like a girl, vivacious and clearly thrilled to be doing what she knew she did very well. I needed no ticket for the performance. I was with her, waiting in her dressing room for the onstage call and I was in the wings when she walked onto the stage with David Lasserre. I stood there for the entire performance. There was not a single empty seat in the concert hall of the Paris Conservatory. It held a thousand people. Baron Haussmann was one of them.

I listened for the slightest lapse in Adele's singing. I was no connoisseur of singers, but I did know when intonations were poor and when notes were not pitch perfect. I heard nothing to make me believe that this gifted Adele Alessandri had no further to go. She was a glorious force of nature standing there alone before her audience, a gifted artist perfectly comfortable on an elegant stage, singing magnificently in a long blue satin dress for the first half of her concert, in a green silk gown for the second half, its train the longest I had ever seen or ever would see a female performer wear as she stepped onto a stage. Walking from the wings, the length of the iridescent green train trailed behind her on and on endlessly until she reached the piano where she paused and slowly pulled the gentle gleam of green silk all the way toward herself from the wings, smiling and bowing to an applauding audience on its feet, wild with delight. She spoke briefly before nodding to Lasserre to continue with the program. I saved the handwritten message she had prepared and memorized before handing it to me in her dressing room.

"It is a privilege for me to sing for you tonight," she said in a clear and steady voice, "especially here in my adopted home city of Paris, and I thank each and every one of you for your love and loyalty. I am ending my career with this concert. It is my hope you will remember that on this night the length of the train on my dress was symbolic of my long career which hopefully, I am leaving like its color........... fresh and green."

There was thundering applause and loud cheering. There were shouts of "Brava! Brava! and "Encore! Encore!" For her encore Adele sang the French National Hymn. There was not a dry eye in the house.

Many of her admirers had wanted to plan celebration dinners and late night suppers, but Adele declined all invitations. When the congratulations were over and her streams of admirers had left the concert hall, we returned to Maison Courtivron and had a late supper alone by the fireplace in the drawing room. Adele seemed satisfied but tired. Over our meal we reviewed the high points of her program. My compliments pleased her, and when she said she wanted to get to bed and rest I understood perfectly. I kissed her on the cheek, said good-night, and in the next few minutes the tirade began.

"Charles, before you go there is something I must tell you," she said. "I'll be spending Christmas in Florence with my family. I'm leaving Paris tomorrow."

I was caught completely off guard. "Oh," I responded with no little hesitation. "I was hoping we could spend Christmas together. I had things planned; Christmas Eve dinner and perhaps Midnight Mass at Notre Dame. When will you be back?"

"I don't know," came the slow reply. "I haven't decided. Perhaps a few weeks or a few months, perhaps longer, but I have nothing to worry about. While I'm away this house will be well cared for by the staff and I'll come back to it when I'm ready. Write to me."

"Write to you?" I could barely form the words. "Is that all you have to say to me? Adele, something is wrong. You're talking to me as I'm a stranger, someone you've just met at the stage door. Is it that this farewell concert has been too much for you?"

"Too much?" she laughed. "Charles, you should know by now that nothing is too much for me! I've made a decision. I'll be in Italy for a while. That's all there is to it!"

I was overwhelmed. Why was this woman I had grown so fond of and thought I knew so well treating me this way? She was more concerned about the care of her house than she was about me. I didn't understand. I wanted an explanation. This was not the same Adele Alessandri I had known and made love to. I stood in a state of complete awe as I watched her calmly seat herself at her desk, take up her pen, and quickly write an address on one of her calling cards.

"Charles dear, you look surprised," she said, coming toward me with a hollow laugh, the card in her hand. "It isn't as if we're madly in love or committed to each other in any way, but I've had a wonderful time with you these past weeks. You've shown me what a true gentleman is. We can try to renew acquaintance when I get back. In the meantime, here is my mailing address in Florence." Her eyes looked into mine. The beautiful green eyes I knew so well were as dark as a forest at midnight.

"Try to renew acquaintance?" I blurted out, "after the relationship we've had? Adele, I'd say we've been more than acquaintances. And now you're telling me that you've had a wonderful time and good-bye Charles Fabron? There has to be more to this. Tell me what it is, Adele. You owe that to me!"

"Owe? Charles Fabron, I don't owe you a thing!" she shouted. "It is you who owe me! You were a turtle in a shell when I found you and invited you into my life. You were interesting and handsome, intelligent too, but you were a shadow of a real man, lost and needy. Now look at you! Out and about in Paris every night, wearing hand-tailored evening clothes, dining in the best houses and restaurants, meeting the best people, dancing, exposed to the best of Paris! We have nothing more to discuss! I'm going away and that's the end of it. Now go back to your dusty world of axes and hammers and leave me alone! Go!"

"What kind of disturbed person are you?" I shouted back as I tore the card she handed me to shreds and quickly walked toward the door.

"I am Adele Alessandri!" she shrieked as the butler stood in the hall holding my coat open, my white fringed scarf draped over his arm. "I do what I please whenever I please!"

I left Place des Vosges completely baffled. I walked for hours until finally coming to the conclusion that I had been a complete fool. The famous opera star, Adele Alessandri had invited me into her rarified world and I had been seduced, not only by her beauty, style, and high spirits, but by her acceptance of me.

Adele had succeeded in making me feel I was essential to her life, but we had absolutely nothing in common except for dancing, laughing, and having a good time. I suppose I needed to dance and laugh and have a good time with a woman. I had wallowed in layers of lonely, desperate grief for so long, but how very easy it had been to become the willing victim of an experienced, well-schooled temptress. "Yes Adele. Of course, Adele." They were phrases I had relied on too often and too readily. I may have been a sad, lost turtle struggling in his new glass house but I had advised and supported Adele Alessandri with sincerity and sound advice and I had become her lover. That was her final triumph.

"Stay with me. Don't leave me like this, not tonight," she had pleaded, kissing me again and again, stroking my face with her long slim fingers, whispering into my ear and bewitching every pulsating fiber of me until with flagrant immodesty she slowly reached down to caress and inflame a carnal desire more intense than any I had ever known. It was an intimate performance she would repeat over and over again and it was one I relished and reacted to with the lust of a man whose entire being had succumbed to his need for physical satisfaction with a woman who took the initiative and held nothing back.

Adele had, in a word, enchanted me, but each time, when the lovemaking was over and we were lying exhausted across her bed, pangs of guilt would sweep over me. I thought not of Adele, not of the exquisite passion we had shared, not of the long surging moments of sheer ecstasy we had known free of barriers. I thought of Louisa. I saw her face. I felt her tender warmth in my arms. I remembered what it was like to kiss her lips, to untie her robe, to let it fall to the floor and know every part of her in a passionate rush of need.

I was being disloyal. I knew it and I couldn't stop myself. But Louisa was dead, I argued with myself again and again. She was lying in a cold grave in a Rouen cemetery. Our life together was over. I had to forget what loving her was like. This woman beside me was real. She was warm and alive. I could touch her body. I could hear her voice. I needed her and I believed she needed me, but I should have understood what was happening. I was a diversion. I was caught up in a reckless affair, readily available for nothing more than a fleeting set of entertaining hours, the willing victim of a woman who knew what it was like to have any man she wanted. And it had all been managed so well. The great diva had made herself available with brazen drama and challenging wit. We had jousted disparagingly, quarreled loudly, apologized endlessly, and on a cold December night I had been drawn into her complicated web with nothing more than a whisper. How delighted this Marquessa de Courtivron must have been to watch me tumble headlong into her game. She had played it many times before and by the time she had sung her last farewell concert and left the stage, she had grown tired of the game and tired of me.

So this was Paris. So this was how the rich and well-connected handled themselves, their lives too precious, too far beyond the understanding of the common crowd, too gilded and gleaming to be tarnished by a flirtation with an ordinary man like Charles Fabron. By the time I reached Rue du Jardinet I had convinced myself that I was the biggest dolt in Paris. I opened a bottle of wine and sat on my sitting room sofa, nursing glass after glass, wondering how many times Adele had done this; wondering how many unsuspecting men she had tempted and stomped on as she had tempted and stomped on me.

"Welcome to our greenhouse," Andre Leclerc had said to me the month before, "and good luck in this world of glass."

CHAPTER SIX

On Dangerous Ground

CHRISTMAS EVE came with snow that year. I joined the Villards for Midnight Mass at the Church of Saint Sulpice. I recited the prayers and heard the music but I wasn't there. My pride and I were miles away. As voices of the choir filled the vaulted spaces and organ music soared across the apse my pride kept telling me how foolish I had been to indulge my hunger for a woman's love and acceptance in a city where love and acceptance wore a hundred disguises. My self-assurance dwindled further as the smell of candle wax and incense filled my nostrils and my thoughts turned once again to Count Andre Leclerc. "We love our glamour and our excess and we're very good at flaunting our grandeur," he had said in Adele's very grand house, "but it's all a big show."

A big show? Glamour? Excess? Grandeur? They were the supporting pillars of Adele's life. They defined her hostile selfishness. They nourished her irresponsible behavior. I knew all that. I objected to it all, yet I missed her. I missed her touch, her laugh, her green eyes staring into mine, and more than anything, I missed my damnable, wonderful place in her life. The Mass was ending. I heard the Agnus Dei being sung. I bowed my head and fell to my knees, praying for deliverance from my cavern of emptiness.

Returning to the Villard house I was grateful to be included in the Reveillon, the traditional Christmas Eve dinner. Claire and Lily had worked on it for days. Complete with rabbit terrine, roasted stuffed goose, and all the delicious accompaniments, it was an elaborate feast. I did my best to put on a celebratory face and join wholeheartedly in the festivities, but under my attempts I was far from happy. It was the third Christmas I had spent without Louisa and now as I nursed my bruised ego I missed her more than ever. I thought of the one Christmas we had spent together at Seine-Maritime Hill. It had been celebrated with true joy. Now the month of December, for all its festivity, was turning out to be a dismal month of the year.

I said nothing to Henri or Claire about Adele. I had never talked to them about her, but I believe Claire was aware that something painful had happened to me. She never asked, but for several weeks after Christmas whenever she passed my chair at lunch or dinner, she would pat my shoulder, and when she greeted me at her door she would hug me and look into my eyes in exactly that same riveting way she had in the train station the day I arrived in Paris. It took time for me to understand Claire's unusual sensitivity, but once I did, I came to know her as a gentle, calming influence who never demanded explanations from the people she cared about. I appreciated everything she stood for. In her generous way, she took the time to help me select books as Christmas gifts for my parents and along with a silk shawl for my mother and a new pipe for my father, I sent them off to Rouen with a loving Christmas message. I had thought about spending Christmas with them in Rouen, but I was afraid of what a return home could mean. I would be tempted to stay and any progress I had made in healing and creating a new life would be wasted. I did miss seeing my parents, but through frequent letters I had kept them apprised of my work with Baron Haussmann. I wrote about the Villards and the exciting developments in Paris while avoiding much mention of the human difficulties I faced every day. Their letters back to me were filled with neighborhood news, encouragement, and countless expressions of pride. According to my father, Baron Haussmann's name and the extent of the Paris project were becoming well known in Rouen. He wrote that he and mother were enjoying telling their friends about my involvement. I could imagine the satisfied expression on my father's face as he proudly shared the nature of my experiences with his office associates. That I had bought a house was both a surprise and another source of parental pride. I invited them to visit with me at any time, but no specific date had been set. My close proximity to the Villards was particularly pleasing to my mother, especially at Christmas, and although I may have been preoccupied by the recent turn of events in my personal life, on Christmas Eve I found I was missing my family in Rouen just as much as Simone Villard was missing hers in Paris. Since her arrival in Brussels, Simone had written weekly letters to her family. At the Reveillon, Claire opened the satin-lined box of Belgian chocolates Simone had sent as well as the Christmas letter she had written. She read it aloud. It remains among the things Claire wanted me to have.

"I am sending all my love to you at Christmas, my dear family," Claire read with a frequent catch in her voice. "I think of how you will be preparing for the Reveillon and I wish I could be there to help. I would have made a croquembouche for our dessert. I remember how much Papa liked the one I made last year. I promise to make one next Christmas when we are all together again and it will be even better and more beautiful than ever before. In the meantime, I hope you enjoy these chocolates. They come from a lovely little shop in the main square of Brussels. I miss you all very much, especially at this time of year, but Aunt Nicoline is very good to me and keeps me busy. Her friends join us for dinner almost every evening and in the afternoons we visit at one house or another. All the activity is tiring sometimes, but I have met some very nice people. Everything is festive here in Brussels right now. The squares are decorated with garlands of pine and there are manger scenes of the Christ Child, Mary, and Joseph. People bring flowers and in the evening candles are lighted around the mangers. I wish you could be here to see it all with me. You will be interested to know that I have been invited to a New Year's Eve Ball. Since I have never been to a ball, when the invitation arrived I was nervous, but Aunt Nicoline was invited too, so I shall just do whatever she does. She insisted on buying me a new dress for the occasion, also a pair of satin shoes. We met with her dressmaker yesterday and chose a beautiful white brocade fabric embroidered with small gold flowers. Once the dress is finished, I know I will like it very much and of course when I come home I shall bring it with me. Dear ones, you are in my prayers every night and on Christmas Eve I shall light a candle for each of you. Thank you for your love and remember me to Monsieur Fabron and all our friends in the Courtyards."

"She is having a wonderful time with my sister!" Claire said, tears in her eyes. "I'm very glad of that. Simone is meeting new people and making new friends, as she should right now, and isn't it wonderful that she has been invited to a New Year's Eve Ball? I knew Nicoline would take good care of her."

"Simone will be the prettiest girl at the ball!" Lily affirmed with a nod of her head. "I wish I could see her in her new dress. I hope she wears her hair swept up and all wavy at the top. I think the ball will be like one of the prince and princess stories I like to read. Charles, you have been to balls at the Hotel de Ville. Are they as exciting as I think they are? Are the ladies very beautiful?"

"Oh, yes," I answered, quickly recalling a few occasions I was trying to forget. "The balls are very exciting indeed and Lily, the ladies are as beautiful as you imagine, but I'm sure that on this New Year's Eve, Simone will be the most beautiful young lady in all Brussels."

Lily paused for a moment before she said, "Charles, I think you should take Simone to one of the Hotel de Ville balls when she comes home. By then she will know what to do at a ball and she will have a very nice dress to wear."

Henri came to my rescue with typical aplomb. "Lily, it will be weeks, perhaps months before Simone comes home. And who knows? By then she may have met a nice young man in Brussels who will occupy all her time. Besides, Charles is perfectly capable of deciding on who he wishes to invite to Hotel de Ville events. Now, help your mother clear the table."

"Well, I hope Simone doesn't marry anyone from Brussels!" Lily called out over her shoulder as she removed a vegetable platter. "She'll be living over there in Belgium and making desserts every day and we won't see her anymore!"

Daniel received a little hand-carved wooden horse that Christmas. The initials DL had been carved into it. It had been delivered to Sacred Heart along with a rocking horse.

———◉———

I spent New Year's Day of 1854 with Gabriel Davioud and a group of his friends. We met at the Ledoyon, and in keeping with the long standing French tradition of eating oysters and drinking champagne on New Year's Day, we feasted for the entire afternoon on the irresistible morsels which came into the city from Arachon, where new oyster farms had been created by decree of the Emperor.

"I may be partly responsible for the shortage of wild oysters Louis Napoleon found when he came to France," Gabriel remarked, raising yet another glistening shell to his lips. "I was weaned on them. They were favorites of my parents. Thank God the Emperor had the good judgment to save the species. Can you imagine life in France without them?"

I don't recall how many oysters we consumed or how many champagne toasts were proposed throughout the course of that afternoon, but I do remember looking back on the old year, grateful to have it gone. My sense of gratitude was promptly set aside on the second day of the New Year when I arrived at my office and learned that 1854 was about to become a hectic period. Secretary Merruau circulated an announcement to the staff that Victoria, Queen of England, had invited The Emperor Louis Napoleon and Empress Eugenie to London. The dates were set for April of 1855. That seemed a long way off and the state visit in London had no effect on the Haussmann project, or so we thought until we were told what was to follow. Eager to return the Queen's hospitality as soon as possible, the Emperor and Empress planned to invite Queen Victoria, Prince Albert, their children, and the full royal entourage to the Paris Universal Exhibition of 1855, their visit scheduled for August of 1855 and the highlight of an event during which Paris could show itself off to the world as a developing industrial and commercial power as dynamic and competitive as any in Europe. This eight-day tour de force was to take place in just over eighteen months. We had been at work in Paris for barely six months but so encouraged was Louis Napoleon by the progress he saw that he had exercised what seemed an unrealistic sense of optimism. I was not the only staff member convinced that the city could not possibly be ready to show itself off in eighteen months. So palpable were the elements of doubt and misgiving in the Hotel de Ville, that on the second afternoon of January The Baron ignored the daily schedule and called a meeting. Once again the inner circle gathered at the table in the Throne Room.

"You must be thinking what most of Paris will be thinking, including the Council and the entire French Senate," he began following the announcement made to us for a second time by the ever meticulous Secretary-General Merruau. "Once the news is circulated, which because this is Paris should take all of fifteen minutes, everyone will be talking. "How ridiculous!" they will say. "The city will still be in a shambles! We will look like fools not only to the Queen of England, but to the whole world!"

It was at times such as this that I took a deep breath and prepared myself for the assurances I was certain were coming. The Baron never faltered in justifying his decisions or actions, and it was this level of confidence pulsating in every fiber of him that made much of what I confronted on a daily basis more tolerable. He was at his best under pressure and every day I did my best to emulate that same characteristic.

Glancing around the table he pulled his shoulders back and stood to his full height. "Mark these words, gentlemen," he said, his eyes slowly circling the table. "We will be ready for the Queen of England, the Czar of Russia, the American President, or any other world leader who wishes to come to Paris for the Universal Exhibition of 1855! As a world capital we shall look grand and we shall be grand. To begin with, we will have completed enough of the Rue de Rivoli project to reflect on the greatness that lies ahead for Paris. By the time the Queen of England's carriage brings her through the monumental arched gate of Saint-Denis and into the city, at least a mile of Rue de Rivoli and its landscaped pedestrian walks will be ready. Surfaces will be well-finished, a number of new buildings will be erected, and the intersecting Boulevards of Sebastopol and Strasbourg will be close to completion. A luxurious new hotel already named the Grand Hotel du Louvre will be ready for the Emperor's distinguished guests. Not a trace of debris will be seen. Hundreds of trees and thousands of flowers will be planted throughout the city. Several wide promenades in the Bois de Boulogne will be completed, along with statuary, fountains, and ponds. All this will take a coordinated effort the likes of which has never been seen in Paris or anywhere else in the world, but I have no doubt whatsoever that once our Emperor greets the Queen at Dunkirk he will be in a position to meet her with pride and the satisfaction that we have created the nexus of Europe's most beautiful, most important city. One last thing: the Queen's visit will conclude with a formal ball here at the Hotel de Ville to which each of you is invited. The Emperor is inviting a thousand guests. I am inviting that same number."

We returned to our offices staring at one another in astonishment but fully confident that it would be exactly as The Baron had predicted. Somehow, some way, we would be ready for Queen Victoria in eighteen months. In a matter of minutes the infant Paris Project had reached maturity. It was no longer an idea in exploratory stages. It was a fully formed, fully viable concept of reality, its intended impact well understood.

Within the next weeks the acceleration was palpable. The brilliance of the balancing act was astounding, every detail coordinated by The Baron. I don't know when he slept. He cared about everything: the placement, the look, the quality of construction materials, the length and width of a boulevard, the numbers and species of trees to be planted, the colors, the air flow, and always the light and the Schedule. Before ending the day and returning to his private apartments he had reviewed every document, every request, every message from the Emperor's ministers and every proposal and inventory we had placed on the ever-present table beside Secretary Merruau's desk. Every afternoon he met with members of the team who had left the field and returned to the Hotel de Ville.

Throughout the months that followed, we lived in a constant swirl of smashing and crushing and a world of dust and debris. In the midst of unprecedented upheaval, the gradual rise of elegant new structures became a way of life for all Parisians as the Haussmann style began to shape the

City by the Seine, its profile irrevocably defined not only by the introduction of the growing network of glamorous avenues and boulevards, but also by gradually emerging blocks of distinctive pale stone residential buildings each between five to seven stories high, roofs at a distinct 45-degree pitch to allow daylight to reach pedestrian sidewalks, all structures neo-classic in design, their rectilinear uniformity creating a standardization never before seen in a European city.

The plan for construction of these buildings with the essential of enough space around them to allow light onto pavements and to be seen and admired from a distance did not evolve over time. Their basic design was determined from the very beginning and building exteriors remained adamantly neo-classic in architectural concept for the life of the Haussmann Project. Their interior designs likewise remained uniformly classic.

First, in each new structure there was typically a ground floor planned for commerce, for shops or galleries, a basement beneath. Above the ground floor came what was known as the first floor, this primarily a utilitarian space with its own entrance, load bearing walls, and an imposing staircase leading to the second floor, the second floor and its grand, light-flooded principal residential rooms designed with elaborate wrought iron exterior balconies often continuing the entire length of the building. Fanciful carved stonework cornices framed second-floor window exteriors. Interior graciousness was enhanced by high ceilings, marble fireplaces, parquet de Versailles floors, and elaborately detailed moldings in every room. Above this grandeur, third and fourth floor rooms designed for use as bedrooms and personal spaces were also enhanced by parquet floors and marble fireplaces, these floors designed with less ornate exterior stonework and window surrounds and often without balconies. In some cases, as when a spacious apartment was being custom built by special arrangement with a specific purchasing individual, a ballroom occupied the entire expanse of the third or fourth floor and was complete with chandeliers, ornately carved overdoors, and romantic balconies. The fifth floor exterior was often lined with highly decorative balconies and contained a warren of small servant rooms exposed to light through some of the loveliest dormer windows in the world. The numbers of small attic rooms highlighted by these architectural gems were at times extended by two additional floors and additional dormers, these low-ceiling rooms located just under the hallmark zinc-clad mansard roofs which in their blue-gray color were shown to great advantage along the banks of the River Seine, their emergence further defining the architectural splendor of Haussmann's Paris.

The seasons of 1854 passed, one into the other in a steady rhythm. I was so busy assimilating myself into my work and preparations for the Queen's visit that were it not for the flurry of planting in the Tuileries Gardens I would not have noticed the way seasonal color changed the Paris landscape, giving it fresh appeal in the flowering of spring and delighting the eye as in turn temperatures cooled and autumn produced its annual show. By the time New Year' Day of 1855 was being celebrated my personal life had once again taken on new dimensions. My house was a refuge as well as a pleasant distraction. I was enjoying its location and privacy. I had added pieces of furniture to those in place when I purchased the house and I had made a few improvements. The shutters and iron balconies had been painted in the gray-blue color prevalent in the Courtyards, leaks in the tile roof had been repaired, and the rose garden close to the back door was thriving. I had met my neighbors. A few had kept their distance, disapproving, I could only assume, of my destructive assignments in Paris. By contrast, a few of the ladies were eager to introduce me to their daughters, granddaughters, and visiting nieces. I nobly resisted with a convincing series of practiced excuses related to my professional obligations, thus remaining quite content in my bachelor existence. I do confess, however, to several dalliances with ladies I met at the endless rounds of receptions and balls I attended. To say I enjoyed their company would be an understatement. Experience had taught me that in Paris there was no shortage of beautiful women who, married or not, openly invited the attention of men they found attractive or interesting or both, and my illuminating experience with Adele Alessandri had taught me that in the long conducive shadows of the City by the Seine it was no sin to charm such women with a little stare and swagger and engage in casual, brief affairs.

I met Denise Barrand at one of Count Leclerc's dinner parties that winter. She was the wife of a naval officer who spent long months at sea. Denise had the look of a porcelain-faced doll. Her beautifully proportioned features were framed by a mass of dark lustrous hair and the first time I took her hand and led her onto the dance floor I knew I wanted to fill her lonely evening hours. Denise soon proved agreeable to my advances and we began an affair, one abruptly, and I must add sadly terminated by Colonel Barrand's unexpected return to Paris and his assignment as Commander Emile Justaine's Chief of Staff, a position which, although demanding, kept the Colonel conveniently headquartered in Paris and close to home, thus able to fill his wife's lonely hours with the close attention she craved.

Baron Haussmann introduced me to Estelle LeBlanc. I came close to marrying her. We liked the same things: books, music, dogs, and houses. With her easy manner and lively sense of humor, Estelle distracted me from the serious implications of my work. When we were together we laughed at silly things and enjoyed our silliness. We attended the opera and the theater. We dined in restaurants and cafes. On Sundays we strolled in the Bois and admired the new fountains, and no matter where we were I loved looking at Estelle. I loved the way she walked, the way she dressed, the way she gazed into my eyes and spoke volumes without saying a word. Estelle made no secret of wanting to marry me. We talked about it time and time again. She wanted a husband and children to love. It wasn't that I was opposed to the idea of marrying Estelle. She was everything I could have asked for in a wife. More importantly, she was the only woman I had met who I didn't compare to Louisa. No one would ever replace Louisa. I would never forget her, but Estelle had a way of filling the empty places in my heart. She made me feel glad to be alive. Intelligent and sensitive, she made me believe I deserved a happy life with a woman I could love for the rest of my life. I really don't know why I was slow to act on the idea of marrying this lovely young woman. Whatever the reason for my hesitancy, by the time I had decided to propose, Estelle had tired of waiting and was seeing someone else. Within a few months after we had parted ways she married a successful investment banker with offices at the Bourse.

Daniel was three years old. His favorite game was tag. His favorite toy was the little hand-carved wooden dog he had received at Christmas. It was always with him.

———————◦《◦》◦———————

I had been in Paris for just over a year. In that time I had come to regard the Villards as my family. Claire and Henri treated me like a son and Simone and Lily had drawn me into the family circle as if they were my sisters. We visited together often, shared dinners and Sunday luncheons, and kept up with neighborhood news. The bookstore was doing well and outspoken Lily was quickly growing into a charming but talkative young lady. Surprising us all, after an absence not merely of six months as had been the original plan but almost a year, in the autumn of 1854 Simone had returned from Brussels as a very new Simone.

"I knew she would come home a little different after going to all those fancy parties, but I didn't expect this!" Lily said to me a few days after Simone's return. "What do you think happened to her in Brussels? I don't recognize my own sister!"

Simone had indeed become a new and improved version of herself. She looked differently. She behaved differently. She wore fashionable dresses and hats, her hair was always swept back from her face, and she had a fresh, lighthearted way about her. She laughed and conversed easily, and by some miracle Lily's blunt assessments and personal remarks no longer unsettled her which meant, thankfully, that there were fewer of them. Under the guidance of a loving, well-connected aunt, she had, as Lily carefully noted to me, become a sophisticated individual and at the age of twenty-one had learned to make the most of herself.

"Charles, I think you should marry Simone," Lily whispered to me at a Sunday luncheon. "I see the way she looks at you. You must see it too. I think you make a nice couple."

I almost choked on my croissant, informing Lily once luncheon was over and I could take her aside, that at the moment I had no intention of marrying anyone, not even the beautifully transformed Simone. I further added that my bachelor status suited me very well. Besides, I said I had come to think of Simone as a sister, not as a woman I could or should be interested in. She was a Villard. She was family. All my rational protest was put into somewhat different perspective when I came home early one summer afternoon to find Simone in the rose garden with my housekeeper, Natalia. They had been arranging flowers for the altar at Saint-Sulpice and it was clear that Simone had pricked a finger rather badly on rose thorns. Natalia was applying a wet compress to the bleeding wound.

"It's nothing, Natalia, really nothing," I overheard Simone say through the open back door. "One would think I had never cut a few roses for the church! But thank you. You are very kind. Monsieur Fabron is fortunate to have you."

"Mademoiselle, it is I who am the fortunate one," I heard Natalia remark. "Monsieur Fabron is a fine man. He is very fond of your family. I just wish he had a family of his own. Things would be so much better for him if he had a wife and children. Of course he gives off the impression that he's perfectly content with his life as it is, but I don't think he's content at all. He gets dressed up and attends those grand receptions and balls at the Hotel de Ville. He knows important people and he has new friends including a few ladies, but he works hard. He keeps long hours and usually comes home well after dark. He's lonely living here by himself. I see it. At night, after dinner, he reads and smokes his pipe, then sometimes he just sits there in his chair, staring out into space. When that happens I know what he's thinking. He's thinking about her, about them. Pity about his wife dying so young. And those two little babies. Things would be so different for him if they had all lived."

"I knew his wife had died," Simone said, "but I didn't know there were children. What happened?"

"Mademoiselle, things can go very wrong when twin babies are struggling to come into the world. Everybody suffers. But I really shouldn't say more. It's not my place. There now, the bleeding has stopped. Next time, you must remember to wear gloves!"

I could see Simone as she thanked Natalia and turned toward the path leading to the outer courtyard, her profile etched against the opaque light. I watched her until she disappeared. I thought about what Natalia had said.

"He gives off the impression he's content with his life as it is, but I don't think he's content at all. He's lonely living here by himself."

It was true. All of it. I was satisfied with my living arrangements but I really was lonely living by myself. I enjoyed my occasional dalliances with women, but except for Estelle, no one had touched me in a meaningful way. I was still that solitary creature of habit who had left his office in Rouen looking forward to the dimness of twilight and the onset of evening; that same man who had waited for a clock to chime six times before he climbed the stairs to his bedroom at the end of the hall; that same solitary individual who had bathed, dressed, read through the day's mail, and promptly at seven dined alone. I thought about what Lily had said. "I think you should marry Simone. I've seen the way she looks at you. I think you've seen it too."

I invited Simone to The Baron's February Reception of 1855. She wore the brocade dress her Aunt Nicoline had given her in Brussels, an embroidered ivory-colored satin cloak over it. Her hair was swept away from her face. Her cheeks were flushed with excitement. She looked beautiful. When we arrived at the de Ville, she took my arm and walked beside me as if we had done this together hundreds of times. I couldn't help but smile. The relationship that developed between us following that evening was free of drama and filled with a quiet contentment I welcomed. In the months that followed we saw each other often. I developed a great fondness for Simone. She was kind and gentle. She was attentive and supportive. By spring we had become lovers. We arrived at that intimate stage in our relationship one night following a walk in the Jardin des Belles Plaisir.

I have never known whether it was the romantic lantern-lined walkway or the garden's sweet April air, but somehow a few tender kisses in the moonlight turned into soaring heated passion and we returned to the seclusion of my house desperate to be locked in one another's arms. I couldn't close the door behind us quickly enough or hold Simone closely enough. In my bedroom at the top of the stairs she gave of herself completely, without hesitation, her soft body pressed against mine, her desire arousing a new need, a new certainty in me. Simone was not Adele. She was not Estelle or Denise or any other woman I had known since Louisa's death, and that was her gift to me. Simone was uncomplicated and approachable. She was not made of contrivances or desperate need. She was a woman meant to be loved and to love in return. As early summer bloomed we talked about marriage, but somehow the weeks passed and we never acted on the idea. It was something for the future, a 'someday' or 'sometime' sort of thing. It could be that we were so comfortable with one another and so genuinely happy in our relationship that the formality of marriage seemed unnecessary. Time, however, was racing by. Simone was twenty-one. I was thirty-two. We often joked about not being young anymore. In early June, Claire took matters into her own hands.

"Charles, what are you waiting for? You and Simone have become more than friends. It's clear to everyone who knows you. When you're not working, you on the Paris Project and Simone at the bookstore, you spend every waking hour and I suspect many nightly hours, together. You take Simone to events at the Hotel de Ville. You have introduced her to your friends. She tells me the two of you are planning a visit to your parents in Rouen. Charles, I know you love Simone and I know she loves you. I see your eyes light up when she comes into a room. I hear the compliments she pays you. Charles, you and Simone are ready for marriage and as someone who loves you both, I'm tired of waiting! Let's plan a wedding! And soon!"

That night I talked to Henri. I declared my intentions and asked for his blessing. "Claire and I have hoped for this," he said. "All the signs have been there for a long time, so I'm not too surprised. Charles, you not only have my blessing, you have my admiration. You've been searching for happiness and last you've found it. I know you and Simone will have a wonderful life together."

That same night I wrote to my parents. I told them I was about to ask Simone Villard to marry me. I asked my mother to send me my grandmother's opal and diamond ring as soon as possible and I began to plan. I received the ring four days later. I decided I would ask Simone to marry me the following Saturday evening. I would suggest a wedding date for late June which would give us almost a full month to plan. I thought through every detail of my proposal. First, I would hire one of the new elegantly paneled carriages to take us to Le Grand Vefour where we would have a romantic candlelit dinner. I would arrange for a bottle of champagne to be waiting at our table. As we sipped our champagne and when we weren't gazing into one another's eyes, we would admire the gilded mirrors and red plush seating. Dinner would be a leisurely affair. We would begin with scallops and caviar, then proceed to duckling and foie gras. For dessert, our waiter would serve an apricot mousse with cognac cream. After dinner we would return to the Courtyards and there, in the small sitting room that was Simone's favorite room in my house, I would propose. I would make a great ceremony of taking my grandmother's ring out of my vest pocket and placing it on her finger. We would kiss and hold each other tightly and we would promise to forget all the disappointments and losses of the past. There would be laughter and joy in our lives. There would be the devotion of our friends and the love of our families and there would be children, as many as we could have.

She was at the store as usual that Saturday morning. She had unpacked a shipment of text books and was carrying several large volumes up to the reading loft when she fell. She tumbled from the top step all the way down to the bottom of the stairway. Every attempt to revive her failed. At the age of twenty-one Simone Villard was dead.

I was at home at the time. Henri delivered the news. I don't remember much of what happened in the next hours or days. My world became a blur. I do remember seeing Simone in her coffin. I had never seen her look more beautiful. Her face and hands were translucent. She was wearing a rose-colored dress with lace around the collar. I remember Lily clinging to me and sobbing outside the Church of Saint-Sulpice. I remember my parents were there. Pauline was with them. I don't remember seeing Henri or Claire at all. Of course they were there, but whenever I think back to that time I can't see their faces. Later, Gabriel Davioud told me he had attended the funeral, Alphand and Deschamps too, and my Rouen friend, Andre Rousseau. He had come with my parents and Pauline, but I couldn't remember having seen any of them. I can't now. I was told that The Baron sent a magnificent basket of white flowers along with a note of sympathy. I don't remember seeing the flowers, but I have his note.

What can I say here to adequately convey my feelings? That my life had taken another ugly turn? That I was hollowed out by Simone's death? That

I felt victimized by some terrible contaminated cloud hanging over me? All are true, but having been through the loss of Louisa and our children I knew what to expect. I was a seasoned griever. The claim was hardly noble but it was sustaining, and in the weeks that followed as I forced myself to accept the fact that I would never see Simone again, I was grateful for the overwhelming nature of my thankless work and every day I was happy to be inundated by one more distracting dilemma, one more angry voice, one more nasty threat.

For Henri, Claire, and Lily the next weeks and months were dark with overwhelming pain. The store was closed for two weeks as they secluded themselves in their home and went through the motions of living. Lily did not attend school for a while, and for the first time I saw her not as a frivolous child, but in a new role as her parents' guide and advisor. Dealing with her own grief, she was at the same time kind and loving as she made suggestions and assisted Henri and Claire through the daily routine, such as it was. She assumed complete responsibility for running the household and with a new sense of maturity she purchased food, checked on the store, and gathered mail and messages. She also found time to help me through my grief. In the course of long conversations she dwelled not so much on her own tears and pain, but on the happiness I had brought to Simone and the love she had seen grow between us.

"I knew it would happen," she reminded me more than once as she thought back to her earliest predictions. "From the beginning, I thought you were perfect for each other. You were Simone's true love. She said so. Charles, be happy about that. I am. "

Lily's willingness to talk openly and without hesitation about my loss of not one but two beloved women, forged a path to healing which although never entirely complete, strengthened my resolve. In those next months, her reliably unabashed candor allowed me to look ahead. It did me a world of good not to turn away from negative thoughts, but to face them squarely and talk about them honestly.

For weeks after Simone's funeral thoughtful customers and friends left notes and bouquets of flowers at the gate. Every day I gathered them and shared in their expressions of sympathy as Henri read each and every message to us aloud. I felt a great responsibility to help these dear friends through their mourning and I admit I didn't always know quite what to do. "Just be here," Lily said. "You don't have to say anything. We only need to see you."

Strange as it seems to me now, announcement of the British Queen's arrival in Paris could not have come at a better time. As much as Simone's loss had hurt me, preparations for the Queen's ten-day State Visit diverted my attention and compelled me into accepting what I was powerless to change. As the arrival day grew closer, the entire Hotel de Ville staff was under pressure. Nothing interfered with preparations, not even an assassination attempt on the Emperor.

On July 30th of 1855, on the Champs Elysees, quite near the Chateau de Fleurs, Giovanni Pianeri fired a pistol at Louis Napoleon as he passed through a crowd in an open carriage. He missed his target. Quickly apprehended, Pianeri was found to be carrying not one, but three pistols. His shot wounded an onlooker who was promptly attended to and recovered. Serious as it was, the incident was swept aside. There were more important things to consider. The British Queen was coming.

———※◆※———

In his final years, Emperor Louis Napoleon referred to Queen Victoria's 1855 visit to Paris as one of the highlights of his life, but of course the carefully staged event had been meticulously planned, no detail, no event for an hour, a day or an evening overlooked, the Emperor's plan in promoting his city's progress and its most outstanding accomplishments intended to ease the long-standing friction between France and England and to establish a new friendship between the two nations. Preparations were ambitious, expensive, and time-consuming, but when the Queen and her party arrived, they were greeted by a sea of colorful bunting, flags, and elaborate royal emblems of France and England decorating the city's streets and signposts. Davioud had designed the emblems in an afternoon. Paris was glowing. Every day, large crowds turned out to catch a glimpse of the royal party in their opulent open carriages as they toured Paris. The schedule, although hectic, was brilliantly carried out. Most mornings there were elaborate outings in the Bois de Boulogne, complete with heralding trumpeters, color guards, and drummers. The crowds cheered, applauded, and waved flags. The Universal Exhibition was attended twice. Held in a vast hall built on the Champs Elysees soon known as the Palace of Industry, the royals attended the Exhibition with great ceremony and in the company of the distinguished and high born. Everyone in attendance was in formal dress and at each and every formal event, The Baron took his place at the side of the Emperor, resplendent in full military uniform and Ribbons of the Prefect, visibly pleased, and rightly so. Conditions in Paris could not have been better. Remarkably, the area surrounding the Louvre was finished, new roads had been cut around the Hotel de Ville, the recently completed Boulevard de Strasbourg led into the center of the city, and a grand triumphal arch had been erected in Rue de Richelieu. The Exhibition was reflective of the latest scientific and industrial developments of the time. The Queen and Prince Albert admired displays on photography, gas heating, the use of electricity, and the powering of machinery, but the royal visit overall and exactly as Louis Napoleon had hoped, led to significant changes of attitude toward Paris as an international city with a newly emerging personality.

Beginning with the State Visit of the British Monarch, the spirit of the Second Empire was seen to be rising and at its heart the legend of 'Gay Paris' was born. It was as if word was being sent out to the entire world that life in the French Capital City was changing; that its new beauty was to be enjoyed openly, without hesitation, and that the frequent gloom and pessimism of the past was disappearing, never to return. Overall, the royal party was kept too busy to pay much attention to such subtle changes, but the young Queen herself was a highly perceptive woman. She had developed a reputation for being alert to innuendo and detail, and during her visit she was given many opportunities to exercise these talents. Every day there were serious meetings with ministers and members of the Senate. There were private consultations with the Emperor, but there were also shooting parties in the company of accomplished, amusing people who remained in touch with the times and easily shared feelings and opinions on their city. There were long, leisurely luncheons under vast tents where the conversation flowed as freely as the wine. Theater and opera productions followed by gala late night supper parties were particular favorites of the Queen, each carefully planned extravaganza providing yet one more opportunity for the spirited conversational exchanges at which she excelled.

The most opulent of the balls was held at the Hotel de Ville on August 23rd, three thousand guests in attendance. This event was placed in the hands of The Baron, the Hotel de Ville as his official Prefect residence, making him the evening's official host. The magnificent structure dominating the Right Bank had seen prestigious events throughout its long history. The splendor of its extraordinary balls and the glories of French hospitality extended in its palatial rooms were known across Europe, but prior to this occasion few people outside Paris had witnessed the stage-loving talents of a Baron named Haussmann.

An immense red and gold canopy had been erected at the main entrance. Upon their arrival, members of the royal party led by the Queen and the Emperor were greeted there by the formally attired Baron himself. Invited guests followed in a dazzle of jewels, military uniforms, ribbons and medals. Under the glass-roofed Louis XI Courtyard where an orchestra played Mozart and Haydn, the visual effects were extraordinary. At every turn, banks of flowers and fountains set into immense crystal urns were illuminated by gas-powered lantern lights circling tall gilded columns, their heavy bases wrapped in acanthus leaves symbolizing long life and regal white roses representing elegance and beauty. Into the ceremonial hall, red velvet draperies fringed in gold hung from every window, the initials of Queen Victoria and Prince Albert intertwined with those of Louis Napoleon and Eugenie. Although masterful vision and the burning desire to impress had driven The Baron's plans for the event, the Emperor would choose to record as most imminent his visit with the British Monarch to the tomb of Napoleon Bonaparte at Les Invalides where beside the lustrous red quartzite of Napoleon's final resting place, with a handshake and a smile, an Emperor and a Queen set aside the animosity of their two countries which to one degree or another had lingered for 400 years.

Today, when I'm at work in my Bordeaux garden, I like to pause and reach for a few of those precious souvenirs of the past, recalling with considerable pride that by the time Emperor Louis Napleon had met Queen

Victoria at Dunkirk and with appropriate ceremony had accompanied the royal train into Paris, the regal visitor was nothing short of 'enchanted,' as The Baron put it. I remember his telling me at a later dinner that the Queen had engaged him in flawless French, describing her entrance into Paris as overwhelming, the great crowds lining the fine new streets and the 50,000 uniformed troops accompanying her entourage all the way from beautiful Boulevard Strasbourg into the center of Paris and on to the Chateau of Saint-Cloud where the British royal party was installed, "the most extraordinary sight imaginable"

In terms of the city's readiness, the scope of achievement in a relatively brief period of time was beyond all expectation. The balancing act led by The Baron consisting of simultaneous destruction and construction at multiple sites had created an agenda at times overwhelming, at times barely manageable, but he did not waver, not once. His grip on the steady beat of progress was unflinching. The days were long and hectic. Work pressed on for twenty-four hours every day. I myself often worked at demolition sites from the early morning of one day into the early morning hours of the next, but by August of 1855, all efforts had shown impressive results and exactly as predicted, more than a mile of Rue de Rivoli was completed and landscaped. Dramatic improvements surrounded The Louvre. On the Right Bank new roads surrounding the Hotel de Ville had been cut. Renovations to the railway station known as the Gare du Nord were nearing completion, and like a relentless pounding drum, work continued without interruption as a medieval city was jolted into modern times. It would be years before Baron Haussmann's Paris endeavors would come to an end, but as a result of diplomacy and sheer had work, in the space of a ten day visit, the promise of the New Paris was well-established, the friction of the Bonaparte years was smoothed over, and personally Victoria and Louis Napoleon were on highly amicable terms. Baron Haussmann took great pleasure in recalling his role in these achievements and I took great pleasure in recalling my own role in preparing the City of Paris for its transformative international debut.

When it was over, I had expected a lull. It was not to be. Energized by the success of ten days with a Queen, our Baron was a man on fire. In the next months the agenda was not only expanded, it grew ever more complex.

With praise from the Emperor and a fresh circle of admirers, important installations were taking place at prominent locations. Construction of buildings to each side of freshly cut avenues and boulevards was proceeding night and day. City landscaping was forging ahead with wagonloads of mature trees and a wide variety of plants arriving daily from the planting fields at Vincennes. Hundreds of chestnut and lime trees began to line the soon to become famous Paris walkways and along strategic points in the Bois de Boulogne, Gabriel Davioud was supervising the installation of his monumental fountains while Victor Baltard was engineering the flow of water to these masterpieces. For those of us closest to the Paris Project it was a time of great satisfaction as our hard work began to bear fruit, yet pockets of public negativity and criticism continued. Every day, complaints flooded the reception desk at the Hotel de Ville. There was too much dust, too much noise, too much of everything that interrupted life as people had known it and wished it to remain. Overall, though, and in the wake of the Queen's highly successful visit, public curiosity regarding the Haussmann project was at a new high and Parisians from every walk of life, regardless of their opinions, were interested in observing the progress of Haussmann's work on their city. Crowds began to gather at worksites every day. They stood to watch, commenting to one another as the profile and style of Paris changed before their eyes. The children were intrigued when water was turn on for the first time at Davioud's fountains. I often wished Daniel could have been there for those spectacles. He took such pleasure in witnessing the results of our efforts. Towards the end, I could see he was feeling himself to be a genuine part of things, which in every sense he was, but in watching the fountain debuts he would not have been just another forsaken orphan. He would have been an average boy, as mesmerized by fountain magic as any other Paris boy.

The debut process seldom varied and I myself enjoyed sharing in the anticipation with my fellow Parisians. First, there was a hushed silence as all eyes were focused on the fine artwork of the fountain. Then, as a few initial spurts and sputters came dripping slowly out of the mouths of bronze lions, birds, and griffins into vast waiting marble basins, there was the inevitable pause and the long moment of doubt, but when the full force of Victor Baltard's expertly engineered water power was fully unleashed there was wild cheering and applause. These spectacles became causes for public celebration. Entire families soon planned outings to watch and enjoy the show as with Belgrand's expertise and Davioud's artistry, water became one of the most publicly acclaimed features of the New Paris. So noticeable was public interest in this factor that advance notices of dates and times for fountain debuts were published in weekly newspapers. Sundays, when families could spend a full day together, were set aside for the most dramatic of these in the Bois de Boulogne, while at the same time there was no lapse in the overall citywide beautification schedule. As newly created lakes and ponds came to life with dramatic elements, Davioud also began designing and installing what became known as his city furniture. I well remember how this unique enhancement intrigued Daniel as it became one of Davioud's most innovative contributions and a hallmark of his creativity. One summer afternoon, Daniel and I took a brief rest in the shade of a chestnut tree at the northern edge of the Bois de Boulogne. We sat side by side on a newly installed Davioud bench. We leaned back, enjoying the view, and before too long we looked at one another and began to laugh. The novelty of it all, the freedom of being allowed to sit unchallenged on a bench in a beautiful city park delighted us in the same way thousands would be similarly delighted throughout years to come, but benches intended for public use were not to remain unique to public parks and gardens. Soon the entire city was enhanced not only by Davioud's benches, but also by his attractive octagonal kiosks, imposing public lavatories, cleverly concealed trash receptacles, and signature street lanterns which, once again, heightened public interest in the Haussmann Project by inviting people to spend time outdoors both night and day.

"It's working wonders," Count Leclerc said to me at one of The Baron's dinners. "These touches of outdoor seating and night lighting alone could turn the tide of public opinion. I've told the Emperor that people love the idea of round-the-clock city comforts. I'm out all the time. I hear what they're saying. Charles, your team should be proud. You're not only improving the quality of the city, you're providing entertainment. It's a great show and the admission is free!"

Andre Leclerc's assessments were not exaggerated. "I have never enjoyed relieving myself so much," men were whispering to one another upon departing one of the picturesque sidewalk lavatories whose designs Davioud had adapted from the fanciful belvederes, dovecotes, and gazeboes he had admired on the grounds of chateaux in the Loire Valley. Seen as drawings, these urban enhancements were beautiful renderings. In his office, I admired them as works of art. Once built and installed, however, it was their perfection of scale which I found astonishing. Davioud was an artist possessed of great flair. He loved the grandiose touch, but he understood the impact of the balanced whole. Most of all, he loved the sheer, almost childish delight to be found in the unexpected detail: the dramatic flourish of oversized gilded leaves forming the handles of a gate, the pair of gray stone cherubs wearing brass crowns perched on the pediment above a pair of green louvered doors, the intricately carved stone flower garland strewn across a row of dormer windows. Nothing Davioud created was too large or too small. Nothing seemed out of place or inappropriate, not even strategically placed trash receptacles or functioning public lavatories. It must be said here, and quite emphatically, that all members of the inner circle were uniquely creative. They were supremely talented and I admired them enormously, but as I watched the city grow and change, to me it was Davioud's meticulous attention to scale and suitability that inspired and encouraged all to do the same. In his uniquely imaginative way and always with great elegance, the many finishing elements he created so effortlessly contributed greatly to defining the final stunning glamour of Haussmann's functioning Paris.

It was in this dynamic period of late 1855 that the Runner Program was initiated. Throughout the life of the Haussmann Project it was acknowledged as essential to progress and like most of the Project's most successful innovations, it was entirely The Baron's idea.

Daniel was four years old. At the orphanage he and his age group were learning to sing the nursery rhyme song, Alouette.

PART II

THE EXQUISITE PLAN

CHAPTER SEVEN

Past All Endeavor

ALL THE RUNNERS assigned to the Haussmann Project were orphans or runaways and all were boys aged nine to fourteen. For a few centimes each week they carried handwritten notes to and from supervisors at one construction or demolition site to another and to and from The Baron with his updates and notes related to the status and progress of every developing project. The Runners brought a new dimension of efficiency to our work. Many had no idea why they were carrying our messages and didn't care. Others took their responsibilities seriously and concentrated on speed. The classification of Runners as such, would indicate that the boys were expected to race through Paris all day, every day. Of course this was not the case. Although most boys did run, walking was not discouraged. The important thing was delivering the message into the proper hands within a reasonable period of time and promptly returning the reply.

With their wages, most of the boys bought chocolate and sweet biscuits from street vendors. In the spring of 1856 a house was opened for them at the end of Rue de Sospire. It was a large existing single story brown building renovated to suit the basic needs of approximately twenty-five boys. A bed and two daily meals were provided. A woman named Marie Duclos managed the house the boys quickly named Maison Sospire. With the help of two hired servant girls, Marie cooked meals and maintained the house with admirably high standards. It was Marie who sent Daniel to me.

In her own well-organized way Marie contributed greatly to the Haussmann Project. She was tall and wiry, and although she was concerned with behavior and the daily assignments of the boys in her charge, cleanliness was paramount. The dining hall and dormitory rooms constantly smelled of soap and disinfectant. A strict disciplinarian, Marie carried a thin rattan cane more for purposes of intimidation than for actual corporal punishment, but she tolerated no infraction of her strict rules. Bedtime was eight o'clock. Morning bells were rung at four. Bread baked daily in the kitchen ovens was plentiful at both meals of the day, as was the breakfast porridge which was occasionally sweetened with the precious sugar Marie requisitioned, her explanation in acquiring it that a dose of sugar kept the boys' energy high, thus allowing them to work more efficiently.

Marie was not beloved, but she was not exactly hated. I did hear it said that the boys came to believe she had a third eye in the back of her head. Newcomers were warned that it was under the small slit at the back of the white bonnet she constantly wore. "She is a witch with terrible powers!" the more seasoned boys insisted to the wide-eyed uninitiated.

As I came to know her, Marie unquestionably fit the description of 'formidable,' which was a title we all ascribed to her with some degree of respectful affection, but she occasionally displayed a softer side. I saw her embrace and comfort a sobbing ten-year-old whose mother had left him at the Maison Sospire door and vanished. I saw tears streaming down her face as I carried a screaming boy who had fallen into the deep crevice of a debris field on Rue de Marche into her care, blood dripping from his face and both his very obviously broken legs.

As a group, these boys were rescued from the desolation and starvation of the streets, but all was not always peaceful among them. Fights broke out, there was competition and jealousy and plenty of pushing and shoving, but in her inimitable way, Marie Duclos maintained order and always managed to marshal her common sense when dealing with the many issues confronting her each and every day. Clothing and shoes which were quickly outgrown, were a major problem and accusations of theft were common. The hand-me-down system became routine for the younger boys and Marie did her best to fairly distribute the clothing donated by churches and charitable groups to the older boys, but arguments often arose among all, regardless of their ages, when they felt they had been given inferior or ill-fitting items.

It must be said that some boys ran away from Maison Sospire fearing attacks and rejection. Others left and returned to the streets because they were lazy and hated the work. Most knew nothing at all about themselves. They had no idea where or to whom they had been born, but it was generally assumed the majority were the result of what in the past two decades had become an ever-increasing number of out-of-wedlock pregnancies across Paris. Every day, unwanted babies born to destitute or sheltered well-to-do young women were either abandoned on the street soon after birth, or in the case of the more fortunate, left at the doors of churches and orphanages where they were taken in by various orders of nuns. Under the strict supervision of a Mother Superior and raised in the traditions of the Catholic Church, by the time older boys from these institutions came to Marie Duclos as runaways, many were experienced in rebelling against the constraints of religious obedience and took pride in having developed reputations as troublemakers. The vast majority, though, no matter how rebellious they may have felt at times, had experienced enough isolation and hunger to understand how fortunate they were to have the luxuries of daily food and a clean bed in exchange for daily work, and in the event that any boy needed to be reminded of his good fortune, Madame Duclos' evening lectures in the dining hall clearly addressed the blessings for which all were strongly advised to be abundantly thankful, God's unmerciful wrath but a single, small misstep away.

At the beginning, along with the early morning armies of horse drawn scrapers and masses of hammer-wielding laborers, the boys had appeared randomly at worksites, usually just after sunrise, ready to take messages to and from whatever destinations they were told were on the day's agenda.

After a while and to avoid confusion, as did happen when groups of boys repeatedly turned up at the same sites at the same time, Marie Duclos was placed in charge of making daily assignments. A list of the following day's scheduled locations was delivered to her each afternoon, and as the boys filed into the dining hall for breakfast the next morning, she announced assignments. If a boy was working particularly well with one supervisor or facilitator he was placed on that supervisor or facilitator's permanent assignment list. In the years between 1854 and 1863 I had a long series of different Runners. I don't know the number. Some stayed on for a day or two, others for month or two. Many vanished after just a few hours. No Runner had been placed on my permanent assignment list until Daniel Lazare came to my worksite in September of 1863. His registration card listed him as both an orphan and a runaway.

Beyond the abundance of blonde hair which soon came to label him, I well remember that at first meeting Daniel had the same far-away look in his blue eyes I had seen time and again in others boys when I asked where their last homes had been. Despite his vagueness and the reluctant mention of an orphanage, it was his ready smile that from the beginning set him apart. I found him to be surprisingly pleasant and polite, eager to know what was happening to Paris and why. In his first days with me he was more than mildly interested in watching progress, which was a behavior very different from any I had experience with my former Runners. Once he adapted to the range of daily demands, which he did very quickly, he was as reliable as any experienced adult assistant I could have employed. I was impressed by his enthusiasm and quick grasp. Observing the proceedings on any given day, he became very good at anticipating the nature of messages I wished to send to colleagues and facilitators at locations across the city. In no time at all, I felt I had not only gained an excellent Runner, but an assistant in the field.

"Monsieur Fabron, are we ready to order wagons for tomorrow morning?" he asked at the end of the day when barely into his second week with me. "I would say we need three," he had accurately estimated. "I counted five large families who should be ready to leave tomorrow. Shall I go to Monsieur Groganne with your order? I'll be sure to ask for the cleanest wagons he has. I've noticed you do that. Six o'clock?"

Daniel soon came to understand the many subtleties that came with his responsibilities, especially that in working with me he was seeing parts of old Paris for the last time. He was very much aware of the human impact made by the destruction of homes and places of business, and he was likewise aware of the importance of Charles Marville's photography. He kept careful track of when and where Marville's pictures of our next location would be taken. "Tomorrow morning we are to be at Rue d'Alois, he reminded me at one point during a particularly hectic period. "Monsieur Marville says he will be there to photograph just after sunrise, before the pickaxe groups arrive. Monsieur Fabron, I hope you will allow me to watch him take his pictures for a little while. Perhaps I can assist him. For the rest of the day I will run twice as fast with your messages."

Before too long Daniel was making valuable suggestions, and always with his affable smile and natural courtesy. I came to depend on him as another pair of eyes and ears, and as time passed he became dependent on me for encouragement. It was not difficult to encourage Daniel. He asked intelligent questions and made pertinent comments, and although I grew increasingly curious about his background, I was careful not to pry. Experience had taught me that most of the Runners had changed their names not once, but several times. Some had burglarized shops and private homes often enough to be well-acquainted with habits of the police. Others had joined bands of street boys with special talents for picking pockets and running off before disappearing into labyrinths of narrow dark alleyways with remarkable speed. Clever in eluding the law but with a constant fear of being identified, they assumed new names. I couldn't image that Daniel fell into this category, but I never asked. I didn't want to frighten him away. He was becoming too valuable to me.

After a few weeks, during rest periods, we began to talk, and as he became more comfortable with me and his trust grew, I learned that the only home he had ever known was an orphanage run by The Sisters of the Sacred Heart in the village of La Bouille. I had heard of La Bouille. It was about twelve miles south of Rouen. Pauline Caron, my Seine-Maritime housekeeper, had come from La Bouille. She had spoken of the village often and with great fondness. "A beautiful little place set against a wooded hillside along the river," was the way she described it. Although I had only passed through La Bouille on my way to assess municipal projects at Evreux or Infreville, Pauline's description had always left me with illusions of a delightful spot in the countryside which I told myself I must keep in mind for future exploration. Daniel had a very different impression of La Bouille.

"Feeling cold is the first thing I think of whenever I think of La Bouille and Sacred Heart. I will never go back," he stated to me in a flat, hollow voice one day as we talked and waited for a pile of rubble to be cleared. "Even in summer the stone walls of our rooms kept the cold in. Monsieur Fabron, fine people like you don't know what it is like to feel a cold that never goes away."

"But Daniel, surely you were allowed to go outdoors and play in the warm sunshine," I recall being quick to say.

"Oh yes, Monsieur, our fenced-in play yard faced the woods on the hillside. If the weather was good, we were allowed to go out into the yard twice each day for fifteen minutes, once in the morning and again in the afternoon. Most of us stood at the fence and peered out between the slats at the trees and the sky, wondering what the world and the people beyond the trees were like. Once in July and again in August we were taken on picnics in the woods on the hillside. For a whole afternoon we could play games and toss balls in the clearings. We played Pentanque and Bilboquet. I was very good at Billes. It was wonderful. We laughed and ate grapes with delicious biscuits and cheese, and we didn't want to leave once the sun began to set. It was different when autumn came. From the fence in the yard we watched the brown leaves falling from the trees. We knew winter was around the corner and that we would not be playing our games in the hillside clearings until summer came and we could go on picnics again. I don't understand why the orphanage was called Sacred Heart. Strange name for the place, don't you think, Monsieur?"

Several days later we talked again, and once again Daniel found opportunities to emphasize the pervasive cold he remembered as well as he remembered his name.

"Surely in the winter you had warm coats and sweaters and quilts for your beds," I said, attempting to offer some outlet of comfort.

Daniel laughed. "Oh, yes, Monsieur, we were given thin blankets and the outgrown clothes of older boys. One autumn when I was seven I was given a brown coat I outgrew before Christmas came, but last winter I was given a new warm quilt and a very nice green sweater one of the benefactors had brought. I treasured that quilt and sweater. I had never owned anything as nice, but I didn't have them for long. Sister Mary Agnes took them away from me. She said the other boys would be jealous and that we had to remember we were all equal in the sight of God."

"Is that why you ran away and came to Paris, because things like the quilt and sweater were taken away from you?"

"That was part of it, I suppose," he answered, glancing away. "I really decided to run away after I had read a book about a family living in Paris. I loved reading and I loved the books Sister Angelica read to me in the library room next to the chapel. Sister Angelica was my favorite. She taught me to read by teaching me words. Every day, starting when I was about six, she would give me a piece of paper with a word on it. Beginning with the first letter, she showed me where to start the letters of the word and slowly trace over each one with a pencil. I would do the tracing two or three times then I would try to form the letters all by myself on another piece of paper just as I had traced them. Some of the letters were hard to trace and then write, and there were many times when I had to start over. My best letter was "s" and one of the easy words was "baby." I liked words like "baby" or "ball" with two letters that were the same. One day we sat at the table in the library and Sister Angelica opened the first page of a new storybook she said someone had brought to the orphanage. She began reading the words of the story out loud, and as I followed the words on the page, I began to read out loud with her. I recognized many of the words I had traced over and over again. They were words like 'home' and 'family.' I needed more practice, but I knew I was learning to read. Sister Angelica said she was very happy with me. She said I was learning quickly."

"What was the story about?" I asked.

"It was about a family living in Paris. I had never heard of Paris. I had no idea where it was, but the storybook made it a real place to me. There was a mother, a father, and two children. They all lived together in a beautiful house across from a beautiful garden in this place called Paris, which Sister Angelica explained to me was a real city in France. The story told about pretty carpets on the floors and pictures on the walls. The children had a cat. They played with it and gave it bowls of milk. They had nice beds and nice clothes. The family ate their meals together in a special room. They sat on chairs in the special room with flowers painted on the walls. In winter, when it snowed, the family was safe and warm in their house, and in summer when it rained, the roof didn't leak. I asked Sister Angelica if a story like that could be true. She said of course it could be true. She said there were lots of families just like that living in Paris. Starting that day, I thought about Paris and the story about the family all the time. I couldn't get it out of my mind; the beautiful house, the family living in it, the nice beds and clothes, the flowers on the walls. I told myself that someday I would go to Paris and live like the family in the book. I would be the father. I would have a wife, two children and a cat, and we would all live together in a beautiful house with flowers on the walls. I didn't know how I would make all that happen, but I promised myself that when I was fourteen and old enough to leave Sacred Heart I would find my way to Paris and begin to work on my dream. Then, before I could think much more about turning fourteen and leaving Sacred Heart, Sister Mary Agnes announced that in six months the orphanage was closing. The boys ten and older were being sent to Le Havre to work on the docks. The young ones were being sent to an orphanage in Belgium. I was one of the older boys. I asked Sister Angelica if Le Havre was a long way from Paris. She said that yes, it was on the ocean and a very long way from Paris. I did not want to go to Le Havre. Monsieur Fabron, I had my dream and I wanted to start making it real. Le Havre and working on the docks was not part of my plan. One afternoon, when the weather was warm and the leaves on the trees were turning green, we were all outside in the yard. Sister Theresa who had been watching us, was called away. We were left alone. I knew it was my time. One of my friends helped me to climb over the fence and I ran."

"But Daniel!" I commented with a feeling of great sadness in having heard this young orphan's desperate attempt to take matters into his own hands and change his life. "Where did you run to? You were alone. Weren't you afraid? Didn't someone come looking for you?"

"No, Monsieur, I wasn't afraid. I stayed in the woods on the hillside for a few day and nights, I think two or three. I liked it there. It was a pretty place, and warm. There were berries to eat and I found a steam. The water ran clear and clean and tasted very good and I really wasn't worried about anything. I knew no one would come looking for me. Boys had run away before. "One less mouth to feed!" Sister Mary Agnes said each time a runaway was reported to her. I was sure she would be saying the same thing about me, so I wasn't worried at all about being taken back and punished. Besides, I had made up my mind. I would walk to Paris. I had no idea how far it was, or in which direction I should go, but something inside me told me I had to do it. I had the good luck to wander into the village of La Bouille where I asked an apple vendor which way was Paris. He pointed me to the road south, gave me an apple, and I began my journey."

As I write this and remember listening to Daniel that day, I am struck by the same anxiety and compassion I felt then, in those poignant moments when I heard a young boy's unwavering voice expressing his burning desire to free himself from the constraints imposed upon him by others. In truth, the memory of the remarkable courage and determination he revealed that day is always with me, safely treasured in a corner of my heart, the indomitable spirit that possessed him to climb a fence and set out to breathe life into his dream a source of my deepest admiration and affection.

Daniel had walked for days, good luck and resourcefulness his only assets. The apple vendor in La Bouille had told him to follow the road south until he came to railroad tracks. He was to follow the tracks which would eventually lead him to Paris. To assure himself that he was going in the right direction, whenever he came to a station he would ask someone if this was the way to Paris. The answer was always the same. Yes!

At Infreville he approached a woman with his question. She asked where his parents were. "I have no parents," Daniel replied. "I'm alone and on my way to Paris to find a family." The woman took him by the hand and said, "Come with me. I have no family either. I'm Diana Remy. I'll buy you a ticket and we'll go to Paris on the train together. I run a boarding house on Rue Rigaud. You can stay there until you find a family."

While it was true that Diana Remy had rescued Daniel, it was also true that she had escorted him into the Paris world of courtesans and their gentleman visitors. In a protective gesture I have always regarded as profoundly kind, Diana Remy explained to Daniel that her boarding house was a fine establishment for young ladies who were searching for husbands. Of course he believed her, and it was not entirely a lie.

"They all wore beautiful robes," Daniel said, recalling his sojourn on Rue Rigaud, "and they stayed in them all day and all night. During the day, sometimes one or two of the ladies would ask me to sit with them on the fancy red sofas while they were having something to drink in the special pink glasses. The ladies always smelled so nice, like flowers in a garden. I liked sitting with them and they were always nice to me. I wasn't surprised that lots of important looking gentlemen came to visit them. It was my job to take the gentlemen to the rooms on the second floor, the ones with the numbers on the doors. I thought I was being very helpful taking the gentlemen upstairs so the ladies could decide which one they wanted for a husband; this one for number four, that one for number ten. It wasn't until the lady named Apolline was sitting next to me on one of the fancy sofas and began touching me in places no one had ever touched me before, that I began to wonder. When I pulled away she laughed. "Ah, what an adorable little man," she said with a wink. "Soon you will be ready for what I do for all the gentlemen who visit me upstairs. They like it very much and they pay me very well. You must grow up and make lots of money so you can come to visit me too."

Daniel had asked Diana why Apolline had been touching him the way she had and what she had meant about the gentlemen paying her very well for what she did. "Diana closed her eyes and shook her head, explaining as best she could," he remembered. "Here, take this money and go!" she had said to him. "Get your things and go now!" Diana had urged, taking coins from her pocket and handing them to him. "This is not a good place for a nice boy like you. I want you to go to the big brown house at the end of Rue Sospire. You'll be safe there. When you leave this house, keep walking straight ahead until you see the river and the first bridge across the river. Cross the bridge and count three streets. The third street which only goes one way will be Rue de Sospire. Tell the woman in the brown house at the end of Sospire that Diana Remy sent you. Her name is Marie Duclos. She is a good person. She will give you food and a bed and in return you will work as the other boys do. You will be a Runner carrying messages for workers building the new Paris. You may not like it, but it is much better than what you will end up doing here. Now go!"

Confused but grateful, Daniel had reluctantly left Diana Remy and her perfumed ladies of the night. He followed the directions she had given him, finding his way to Rue Sospire and Marie Duclos. He arrived at my Boulevard Saint-Germain worksite the very next morning. For the next three years and under a variety of circumstances he was my shadow.

———✦———

As he wove himself into the ebb and flow of demolition and preparation for construction, Daniel noticed as I did that I was being met by increasingly volatile episodes of confrontation. My name was becoming well known in alleys and lanes, and of course with my dubious fame came mixed feelings regarding not only my reputation for fairness, but the entire point of the restructuring of Paris. I tried to handle every situation and confrontation with as much care as possible. I felt I bore a responsibility to complete often painful tasks and as I was met by tearful women, frightened children, and the anger of men unable to protect their loved ones, the last thing I wanted to convey was pity. I am pleased to say that the avenues of respect and hope were those I chose to travel as I evicted countless families, but I must also admit that under my Haussmann-induced cloak of equanimity, I really did pity those at the mercy of my appraisals. It was a challenge to hide my true feelings when I handed the owner of a dilapidated hovel or the head of a large poverty-stricken family living in a small single room a voucher redeemable at one of the city's exchange booths for the pitifully small sum I had estimated his property and few possessions to be worth. Some situations were beyond any talent of mine to alter with mere words of comfort. Most disturbing were the children and the conditions under which they had been forced to live since birth. Their clothes were in tatters and had long ago lost their colors. Everything in their lives – their food, their beds, their shoes – was gray and shapeless, but it was the sad expression frozen on the smallest, youngest faces that was the grayest of all. Sad or not, too many of the very young had learned to be vulgar and foul-mouthed. Many more were malnourished and sickly and carried with them the pervasive odors of mildew and putrid waste. When not delivering messages, Daniel shared in many of these experiences as he was often at my side observing as I did, the plight of those displaced and dispossessed. As time passed he developed a certain stoicism I admired and although episodes of cursing and shouting directed toward us were unrelenting, he seemed encouraged by the occasional show of optimism regarding the growth of a new Paris. Certainly there was no flood of support for the harsh reality of what was happening around the expropriated, but it wasn't until the spring of 1864 that I was confronted by the threat of actual physical harm.

I had never given much thought to my well-being. I was working under the protection of The Baron and The Empire, but my attitude changed early one April morning at the intersection of Rues Delorme and Soutier when arriving to begin the day, I was confronted by a man carrying a pistol. I have never forgotten the feeling of helplessness that raced through me. As I write about it now, I can easily re-live that rush of sheer terror. The pistol was aimed directly at my head and I recognized the man holding it. It was Bernard Fournier, Simone Villard's rejected fiancé.

"At last, the opportunity I've waited for!" Fournier shouted, his body silhouetted against the white light of breaking dawn flaring up behind him. "Fabron, you have destroyed enough of the old Paris we love. It's time you paid for your willful destruction, but you look very surprised to see me. I cannot imagine why. But ah, they protect you well at the Hotel de Ville, don't they! No one in there knows your schedule, or is that what they have been instructed to say? The street scrapers and sled drivers are not as protective. They talk, and they love to talk to me. One of them told me where you'd be this morning. I must find a way to reward him. What do you think? A bottle of expensive wine? A night with a whore? Suggest someone. I'm sure you've had the best."

I was accustomed to scorn and ridicule, but no weapon had ever been aimed at me. Now, standing before Bernard Fournier, my heart was pounding, yet in spite of my fear I instinctively knew I had to remain calm. I wasn't at all sure I could manage it, but I lowered by voice and did my best to reason with him in the simplest possible terms.

"Bernard, I am doing the work of the Emperor and following the instructions of his Prefect," I said, struggling to maintain my composure as the words came spilling out. "Surely you understand the intention is to create a better life for everyone in Paris, and surely you must also understand that in order to do that, old parts of the past and old ways of doing things must be replaced with the new. You can already see the improvements. Just look to the river. It is cleaner every day."

"Yes, and its historic banks are being vandalized, ravaged by blocks of ostentatious new buildings and fine apartments! Such luxury is for the rich and well-connected, not for those masses of people who live in poverty, or those like me who have educated and elevated themselves only to be caught up in the daily drudgery of tedious, low-wage positions! We live one step, one pay coupon, away from ruin. This tearing down and building up makes no sense to us. We have no place in it, no voice! The neighborhoods we have known all our lives, the houses where our parents and grandparents have lived, are the only security we have! Don't you understand that?"

"Of course, I understand," I replied, "but Bernard, soon fresh opportunity will lie around every corner," I added, aware that my words must be sounding shallow and insincere to someone filled with this much rage. "Bernard, what you see now as only destruction will make sense, and soon," I went on, "and the belief that Paris is being reinvented for an upper class of people must be set aside. It isn't true. Yes, the city will look beautiful to the eye. Yes, it will very likely be more beautiful than any other city in the world, but eventually it will suit all tastes and serve people from every walk of life. By the time the work is completed, the economy of Paris will be infused with the prosperity of a long list of new businesses. Everyone will profit."

I was reaching for words that I myself had only recently come to live by. My hope was to impress those words on this angry, disparaging man standing before me with a pistol.

"Bernard, think of this: soon visitors will be arriving in Paris from every part of the world," I began, trying to make valid sense of what was being seen as evil encroaching on the upstanding and familiar. "They will spend money in our shops, cafes, hotels, and restaurants. They will buy our goods and the work of our artists. Waiters, bakers, and street vendors will enjoy better incomes. In the process, the entire world will see that Paris is comprised of a mobile society made up of all classes of citizens enjoying economic opportunity and unprecedented access to public buildings, public gardens, and a new ease of movement from one point to another thanks to a new system of well-designed roads and railways. Bernard, beautiful parks and gardens are developing throughout the city. Surely you see them. Surely you see the shimmering ponds and magnificent fountains. What do you think they're for? They're for the enjoyment of the people, all the people. The parks and gardens are for promenades, for the pleasure of parents and children, for lovers lost in dreams and dreaming. Bernard, do you really think the Emperor wants all this done to anger the poor and incite the dissatisfied? Do you really believe he wants dissent festering in his capital city? Hasn't Paris had enough of that?"

"You don't fool me with your grand talk!" Fournier interrupted. "Those wide new boulevards and avenues are being built so the Emperor can send his militias to put down citizen protests. Everyone says so. Our old narrow lanes have worked too well for fighting off the bureaucrats who hate us and we intend to hold on to them. Killing you will set a good example. It will send the kind of message that needs to be sent."

"No one hates you, Bernard," I said, realizing these could be my last words. "You have entirely the wrong impression of what is being done in Paris and why."

Bernard shook his head. He hadn't moved and his pistol was still pointed at me. I was failing to convince him that the motives of The Baron and the Emperor were in the best interests of the public, and as I began to face the stark reality that this man was willing to murder me, pay a penalty for his crime, and very likely become a hero of the displaced, it seemed oddly appropriate that the morning sun should have chosen that moment to break forth fully. It was then, as the bright light of day blazed up, that I heard a sharp, cracking sound. I was sure the pistol had fired and that I had been shot, but I was standing. I felt no pain, saw no blood. What I did see was that in the full light of day something or someone had struck Bernard Fournier from behind. He had fallen to the ground and had dropped the pistol. As I ran for the weapon I saw Daniel coming toward me. He was rubbing his hand, a shocked expression frozen on his face.

"I didn't know he was holding a pistol!" he said. "I just saw the look on your face, Monsieur Fabron, and I knew I had to do something! Are you hurt? Have you been shot? Shall I get someone to help?"

"No, Daniel, I'm fine," I answered, stunned by the sound of my own hoarse voice and grateful to the young boy who had very likely saved my life. For months he had been at my side. He had seen the worst of Paris. He had never commented on what he saw or felt, but clearly, he had recognized an overriding danger that for years I had chosen to ignore. In those moments I felt a great surge of gratitude toward this rootless boy and I didn't know how to thank him. "You saved my life," I uttered awkwardly. It was Daniel himself who found words to fill the void. I was grateful for them then and I am grateful for them now.

"It is a life worth saving," he said without hesitation. "Monsieur, you are a good man. Since I became your Runner I have seen your kindness. You want no one to notice, but I see the coins you quickly hand to a child or drop into the apron pocket of a frightened woman, and I have seen the way you lift old people onto the wagons taking them away to places they don't want to go, and always with a smile and word or two of encouragement. Monsieur Fabron, I think you are becoming more welcome in these old lanes and alleys than you know. That must sound strange, but you make the bad news people know you come bearing easier to accept. I see it every day. They hear your calm voice, they see how you listen patiently to their complaints, and more than anything else, they trust you to advise them and do your best for them. You remind me of a man who came to the orphanage now and then.

You look like him. He was tall like you. He always brought books. Those books are how I learned to read."

I was still shaking from my close encounter with death, but I appreciated Daniel's comforting words at a critical moment and I thanked him once again. I would have reason to recall his perceptive observations as time wore on and complications continued to rise one after another, but as I regained my composure during that frightening morning on Rue Delorme, my immediate concern was for Bernard Fournier. Daniel had struck a hard blow to the back of his head. If Fournier was dead we were facing a calamity. At the same time, I couldn't help but admire Daniel's agility and quick thinking. He was tall, and thanks to regular meals at Maison Sospire, he had gained some needed pounds, but he was still a child with a lifetime ahead of him. Trouble like this could change everything for him. Much to my relief, Fournier began to moan, returning to blessed life with a dazed expression on his pale face. Once he was standing I fully expected him to come at me with his fists, but he slowly picked himself up and stalked off, turning to shout out, "Fabron, you have not seen the last of me and those like me!"

In the following days, I tried to put the experience behind me, but Bernard Fournier's attempt to kill me had shaken me into a new reality. From that day forward I was cautiously guarded about my surroundings and suspicious of the excessively disgruntled people I found in them. I met with The Baron and related details of the Fournier experience. He voiced great concern and arranged for me to carry a concealed pistol. I carried it my boot and gave it a name. Gloria. I never told Daniel about Gloria, but in that self-certain way of his, I think he knew we were prepared for any repeat of the Fournier incident. Turning our attention to matters at hand, we resumed our daily routine. It was during this period that I discovered Daniel could read, and not with great struggle or much hesitancy, but with admirable skill and comprehension. His proficiency was to become one of my greatest assets.

He had told me he had learned to read at the orphanage but I had not expected him to be proficient enough to read the messages he carried every day. In most cases it was assumed that the Runners were illiterate, unable to read or write and unwilling to learn. In Daniel's case, his reading ability became immensely valuable as the volume of detail involved in my work was expanded. By that time and as simultaneous demolishing sites were activated across the city, there were several teams of demolishers under my supervision. Transmission of messages became more critical than ever before. I came to rely on Daniel to read to me an arriving message just as I was reviewing yet another set of inventories and appraisals. I would look up and there he would be, slowly reading off a question from a crew supervisor or a directive from The Baron. He liked this aspect of his responsibilities and I saw his skills improve almost daily as new words crept into his vocabulary. The word, 'partout' (everywhere) was one he often read. He confused its usage with 'un peu partout' which meant 'almost everywhere.'

"But how can something such as the rubble be 'everywhere' and then be 'almost everywhere?" he asked with a laugh when I corrected him.

"It depends on the time and the place," I told him. "Let's say you live in a lonely mountain hut in the French Alps. Looking out from your doorway you would say that in winter, snow falls everywhere. Snow is the only thing you can see when you look outside. That's good for the skiing you enjoy on your mountain, but throughout France, which is a large country, during that same winter and at the same time, snow can fall 'almost' everywhere. It may fall in Paris or parts of Rouen, but not in Le Havre, Dieppe, or Calais. For you and me right now, this means that rubble may be piled up 'everywhere' on Rue Sintois, and 'almost everywhere' on Rue de Marchelier."

"I have never skied," Daniel said with the faraway look I had come to recognize in his eyes, the questions of 'partout' and 'un peu partout' suddenly the last things on his mind. "Do you ski, Monsieur Fabron?" he asked. "I imagine it is a wonderful feeling to fly through the air over the snow. Someday I will ski. Will you come with me? Say you will."

"Daniel, I'm not able to see that far ahead," I said impatiently. "For now let's be satisfied with just walking around in Paris without falling into a big hole in the ground!"

Seconds later I regretted those insensitive remarks. I should have encouraged a skiing holiday sometime, somewhere, even if I knew it was never to happen. It would have given a young, disadvantaged boy something wonderful to look forward to. My misgivings were soon replaced by another matter to give me pause when a few days later Daniel appeared at our worksite with a large, curly-haired black dog at his side.

"He followed me from Rue de Sospire," he explained. "He must be lost. He's probably one of the dogs left behind when his family had to leave their home," he announced, his face a mass of concern, his hopeful eyes conveying a message I interpreted all too well.

"Daniel, you cannot keep a dog! I said. "He will not be allowed to stay with you at Maison Sospire, and I see no value in having him with you as you carry your messages. He will be in the way. Please do not take this any further."

"Then what shall we do, Monsieur? Where shall I take him? Look at him. He is a very handsome dog, don't you think? He is so handsome he looks as if his name could be Joli."

I had to admit the dog was handsome and I could plainly see that he had quickly attached himself to Daniel He sat quietly at the boy's side, looking up to him as if he knew that pleas were made in his behalf.

"Monsieur, do you have a dog?" Daniel suddenly asked.

"No," I replied, "and I have no intention of acquiring one today!"

"But Monsieur, if dogs are not allowed at Maison Sospire, perhaps Joli could sleep at your house at night and you could bring him to me at our worksite in the morning."

"Daniel, I have no time for a dog and neither do you! Dogs need walks and attention. They also need food."

"But Monsieur, Joli will run and walk with me all day. He will not need a special walk. I will give him all the attention he needs. I'll talk to him as we run together, but it would be a good thing if you could feed him for me. Please Monsieur."

It was hopeless. Daniel was determined to have this dog and from the look of things I had the distinct feeling the dog was determined to have him.

"A trial period!" I said. "We'll try your plan for one week and if it doesn't work out, Joli will be sent to one of the farms at Montreuil or Sevres, or perhaps to the stables at Neuilly-sur-Seine. And by the way, Joli is a girl's name. Beau is a better name for a handsome dog!"

"I thought of that Monsieur, but I like the name Joli very much. At Sacred Heart, every year when summer came and we looked out to the green grass and trees, we said it was 'tres joli.' For me it was happiest, most beautiful time of year."

I had, of course, made a dreadful error in judgement. The trial period I had suggested was executed without a single flaw. Joli would never see a farm at Montreuil or Sevres, and he would never be sent to stables at Neuilly-sur-Seine. I tried not to like him. I did my best to ignore his impeccable behavior and shows of affection. It was useless. After one week, Daniel and I were sharing a dog. I took Joli home with me at night and returned him to Daniel in the morning. I fed him and went so far as to buy a large bowl for his water. Every night he slept on the floor beside my bed, much as Zoe and Fleur had done at Seine-Maritime-Hill.

The permission I granted for an orphaned boy to have a dog opened a door that could very well have remained closed for the rest of his life. I wish I had seen that more clearly at the time. I would have made more it. What I did see was that with Joli at his side, Daniel was happy. He was more efficient than ever, completing every task, quickly delivering every message, returning promptly with written replies and significant personal observations, and always patting Joli's curly head as with his irrepressible smile he described their daily journeys together though Paris, soon becoming known to supervisors and facilitators alike as the nice boy with the dog.

I now understand that having Joli allowed Daniel to open his heart. Having Joli allowed him to love and for the first time in his life to feel loved in return. With that dog at his side he became a normal boy, and like a normal boy living with a great surge of joy, he also began to feel increasingly comfortable in talking about his young life.

"Monsieur Fabron, you never ask me about myself," he said during a rest period one afternoon as we sat by the side of the road on a pair of badly scarred chairs I had rescued from the vacant house across the street. "You are so kind to me and you don't know a thing about me. All you know is my name and that I am a runaway orphan. Maybe I was a thief or a murderer before we met."

I laughed. "Daniel, you could never be one of those things. I know you to be a very good boy. You work hard and try every day to do the right thing. You have what we call good character. It is enough."

"No, Monsieur, it is not enough," he said, shaking his head as he leaned closer to me, the expression crossing his face as pensive as I had ever seen it. "I want you to know things about me, things I remember about myself, especially the way I feel about the mother and father who didn't want me. Since I have been working with you I see people every day who leave the only homes they have ever known. They are sad to go. The mothers and the children cry. The fathers look lost. I want you to know that I was not sad to leave the only home I ever knew. I did not cry and I did not feel lost when I left Sacred Heart. I was glad to go."

"But the nuns must have been kind to you. You have mentioned Sister Angelica as your favorite. Were there other Sister you liked?"

"No, not really. I was a little afraid of all of them. They were always swishing along the hallways and spying on us in our rooms. They weren't cruel. They were just there. All the time. Every day when we formed a line and walked through the outside corridor to reach the chapel and say our prayers, they folded their hands and walked in a straight line beside us. When I was very little I was terrified of all those black robes swishing next to me."

"Daniel, when you were in the chapel, what did you pray for?" I asked.

"I prayed for warm clothes, a soft bed, and as much food as I could eat, but not bread. We were given a piece of hard bread at every meal. The bread at Maison Sospire is different. It is very good. It is soft. Most of the time it is warm. At Sacred Heart most of the time the bread was dry, like a piece of wood, but we ate it anyway. I promised myself that when I grew up to be a man I would never eat hard bread again. I would eat only soft bread with meat and potatoes and maybe an orange. Mostly though, I prayed for the years to pass quickly so that I would be old enough to leave Sacred Heart. By the time we were fourteen if we hadn't been adopted we were put out to make our own way in the world."

"Did many people come to adopt children?" I asked, almost afraid of the answer I would hear.

"Oh yes, but they only wanted the babies. By the time we were seven or eight, we knew there was no hope for us. I was told that I had been brought to the Sisters when I was a baby, but I suppose I wasn't the kind of baby people were looking for. When I asked Sister Angelica why I hadn't been a good enough baby to be adopted she said I cried more than the other babies."

"You said the boys were put out of the orphanage when they turned fourteen," I stated, desperate to hide my horror in being told of the rejection this young boy had endured. "How were you expected to make your way in the world?" I asked "Were you taught a trade?"

Daniel laughed. "Monsieur Fabron, we were taught to pray and fear God. The rest was up to us. I suppose I was lucky, though. At least I was taught to read. I try not to think of what happened to the boys I knew who were afraid of leaving Sacred Heart when they turned fourteen."

In those moments Daniel's eyes filled with tears. As they rolled down his cheeks there was so much resignation, so much disappointment flooding across his face. I wanted to wipe it away. I wanted to shield him from any further hurt or isolation, but I knew I couldn't. Any show of favoritism would place him in a vulnerable position. That day, though, I vowed I would do all I could to help him develop into a human being who would be able to find some degree of success in life. Beyond that, and despite the demands of our daily work which by its very nature was pessimistic, I told myself I would look for as many positive experiences for Daniel as I possibly could. At first I drew him out by directing his attention to the potential of the world he was now part of. We began to talk about his observations. His perceptions were simple, but focused and well expressed. He understood in clear, simple terms that the City of Paris was undergoing important changes and that they would affect future generations in a positive way. He did not have a vivid picture of what those changes might be, but he was proud of his participation in a multi-faceted event, and whether he watched a row of hovels being demolished or a narrow lane being prepared for widening and paving, he was optimistic at every step of the way. We talked about the buildings rising all around us; their design, their materials, their purpose. After a while he saw himself included in the future of those buildings and the world surrounding them. He had no idea where he would find himself as an adult in the New Paris, but he made no secret of wanting to live in its midst all his life.

As he watched what was developing around him each and every day, he began to see that there was a step-by-step process along which a desired goal could be reached. We talked about the many different facets of that process and the many paths through which a goal could be achieved. As our work continued without pause I encouraged his growing understanding of the importance of making the right choices in life, something I felt I hadn't always done very well myself. At the time I thought I was doing the right thing, that I was helping a struggling child to envision a bright, respectable future. What I didn't realize was that due to my attempts at expanding Daniel's views, there was a sense of immediacy growing in him. He was developing a burning desire to know who he was, who his parents were, and why he had been abandoned as a baby and raised in a remote orphanage. "If good choices are so important, why do you think my mother and father left me at the orphanage?" he asked repeatedly. "They could have kept me. That would have been a good choice."

"Yes, it would have been a very good choice," I said hesitating and doing my best not to sound as disappointed as he was, "but Daniel, sometimes people make poor choices because they can't solve a bad problem and don't know what else to do. From the look on Daniel's face I could tell it was an unsatisfactory answer and that he wondered what that problem could have been with his parents. By then I had no idea that his orphan status was causing him to endure periods of self-doubt and feelings of inadequacy, or that he was becoming aware of his shortcomings as he considered the possibilities of what a future in Paris might hold. A short time later when during another of our rest periods he asked about what the world outside of France must be like, he voiced a fascination for the British. He had seen pictures of England in yet one more book Sister Angelica had shared with him. In seconds I saw an opportunity to expand his world view. It seemed to me that Queen Victoria's visit to Paris was tailor-made for a story-telling approach to a bit of British history he might enjoy. This effort on my part was to remain an illuminating episode for Daniel. It would leave a lasting impression, one he would carry into adulthood and one both he and I would recall repeatedly as the months and years unfolded before us.

When the British Queen arrived in France in the summer of 1855, Daniel was a three-year-old child. It was not until he was nine or ten that through Sister Angelica and books in the Sacred Heart library he became aware of the country called England. Details of the British Monarchy fascinated him and when he realized I had been in Paris during Queen Victoria's visit to Paris, the fascination grew. The fact that I had seen the Queen and Prince Albert in the flesh and that I had attended several dinners and balls at which they were present was an absolute wonder to him. He asked question after question. How had they traveled to France? Was it a very long journey? Had the Queen come in a beautiful carriage? What did it look like? What did she look like? Through his questioning and my answers, Daniel's limited concept of the world began to expand. Until then, France had been his only known world, and as far as he was concerned it stood alone in the middle of a vast ocean. He had seen pictures of England, but he had never heard the English language spoken. Throughout his young life he had heard no language but French. Anxious to satisfy his curiosity and needing little encouragement to relive the grandeur of the British Queen's State Visit, I gladly shared my memories. I can see Daniel's bright eyes as he was transported, listening to me describe the lavishness and fervor of the occasion and how those of us closest to its planning would remember it for the rest of our lives.

What happened when the Queen came?" was the first question. "Did everyone see her? Did she come alone? Is she old and ugly or young and beautiful?"

"The Queen of England is a small woman. She is young and very pretty," I began as Daniel settled himself and listened intently. "She came to Paris with her husband Prince Albert, their children, and a large group of people from her palace in England," I continued to my clearly enchanted audience of one. "I had the pleasure of attending a very fancy supper party the Emperor gave in her honor in The Hall of Mirrors and the Salle de l'Opera at the Palace of Versailles," I went on, describing The Hall of Mirrors, The Salle de l'Opera, and the Palace of Versailles which were places Daniel had never heard of. I told him it was said that in its grandeur the occasion at Versailles was so magnificent that it seemed the old French Monarchy at the height of its excessive opulence had been restored. Of course I explained the meanings of French Monarchy and opulence, but I'm not at all sure I succeeded in doing this very well at all. Since I had been there at Versailles as an invited guest, I did enjoy relating details of that August 25th evening when everything and everyone glittered. Daniel liked that part of the history lesson best of all.

"The beautiful long Hall of Mirrors was lined by rows of tall silver candles in tall, shining holders," I told him, "and one hundred liveried servants carried one hundred matching silver trays of champagne around and through them. The mirrors sparkled, the candlelight glowed, and everyone smiled. It was all like a dream from which no one wanted to awaken."

From my personal point of view, which was one I chose not to share with Daniel, the Queen's visit was, of course, deemed a great success, but apart from its significant diplomatic and social achievements, it had turned out exactly as The Baron had predicted when in January of 1854 he had announced to us that in eighteen months Paris would be ready for an International Exhibition and the visit of a British Queen. Although it pleased me to relate details of Queen Victoria's visit to Daniel, I did fail to add that 'God Save the Queen had been played so many times that at the end of the exhausting ten-day visit I could hum it note for note, from start to finish.

"I will go to England someday," Daniel stated with an assurance I found astounding as he digested my telling of the Queen's State Visit, his young imagination stimulated, his curiosity elevated to heights I could not possibly have fathomed at the time.

CHAPTER EIGHT

The Haussmann World

INTO THE MID 1860's the camaraderie between members of the inner circle continued to grow. Our Tuesday night dinners did a great deal to further social interaction and relieve the increasing pressure under which we were all working. Gabriel Davioud loved these evenings and may have singlehandedly been responsible for turning them into warm, congenial experiences. Apart from his creative talent, Gabriel was fun. He enjoyed a good joke and a funny story and he told both very well. Few people I have ever know enjoyed their work as much as he did, but few also found more corners of humor in everyday life. His good nature shone through at our weekly dinners. So successful were the first few that a weekly tradition was soon established and the Cardon had our table waiting every Tuesday. Understandably, not everyone could be present every Tuesday, and that was fine, but all were included in the standing invitation and the opportunity for informal conversation between colleagues was appreciated by all. Except by reputation and The Baron's initial introduction, we didn't know each other very well. We were kept so busy that except for attending formal evening events hosted by The Baron, socializing between ourselves at the Hotel de Ville was almost non-existent. At the first two or three dinners everyone seemed to be on his best behavior, stiff exchanges limited to inquiries on how the work was going or when we expected to complete a project. One evening Davioud announced that we were making a great mistake in discussing only our work.

"Don't we have anything else to talk about? This is a dinner! The day's work is over and I for one would like a bit of diversion," he stated. "Let me toss this bit of news out to you. Feel free to elaborate. I heard today that Empress Eugenie is with child and that we shall have a Prince or Princess Imperial early in the New Year."

Gabriel's news bulletin was immediately followed by Victor Belgrand's announcement, one in which he displayed the dry sense of humor we would come to appreciate more and more as the years passed. He related a family story. For some unknown reason, the topic of family had never been touched at our dinners. Victor changed that.

"Well, if you live in Paris, I suppose the potential of another Bonaparte is more newsworthy than all the talk I hear about the splendors of the British transatlantic steamships," he offered, taking up his wine glass. "I learned today that in June, my sister and her British husband are traveling from Liverpool to Boston, Massachusetts aboard the Britannia. I'm a bit worried about their voyage to America. It will be twelve days at sea and it's not the Britannia's seaworthiness or the City of Boston's continuing resentment toward the British over the dumping of some tea into their harbor that concerns me. It's my sister's tendency to seasickness. She didn't do at all well on the little sailboat we had as children. Our father would take us out onto the river in that small craft with great enthusiasm, issuing his orders to us like an admiral and before the sails had even caught the wind, poor Aurore had her head over the side."

Between Davioud and Belgrand, the conversational ice was broken and beginning that night, our weekly meetings became occasions for sharing personal experiences, for commenting on Paris life, and best of all, for laughing heartily and enjoying ourselves. Childhood memories came to life as did details concerning more than a few fascinating relationships with a colorful assortment of wives and lovers. Parents were discussed with affection and respect, their health and well-being important to the adult sons who now were assuming increasing responsibility for them as they aged. As a result of this weekly interaction, solid friendships were built, their foundations supported by enormous respect for the talent and professionalism of each individual.

"We should invite The Baron," Alphand suggested one night. "He would enjoy our carrying on here at the Cardon. We don't see his sense of humor very often, but he really does have one, and as we know from attending his Hotel de Ville receptions, he loves good food and wine."

"I don't know," Deschamps interrupted. "We could be crossing boundaries by inviting him. The Baron doesn't like mixing us into his social life if it isn't on his own terms."

"This is different," Baltard said in support of the idea. "He knows we meet here at Cardon's. It's no secret, and I think he would be complimented to be asked to join us for an hour or two over a good dinner at a location that isn't the Hotel de Ville. He may come only once, but it would be kind of us to include him."

"Let's take a vote! Everyone is here," Davioud suggested, signaling to Michel, our affable waiter, requesting he bring paper, pencils and a bread basket.

The paper, pencils, and basket produced, the paper was torn into small fragments, one piece distributed to each man at the table.

"We'll have secret ballots so that later no one can be accused of voting one way or the other," stated Davioud, placing the basket at the center of the table. "Just write a yes or no, nothing more, fold your paper, and place it in the basket. I'll open each ballot and read it aloud when we're ready. Charles, you keep the count as I go."

One by one the votes were unfolded and announced. Out of eight ballots, two were yes. Five were no.

"Fine," smiled Davioud. "We shall continue to enjoy our Tuesday evenings as the jovial group we are. To The Baron!" he concluded, raising his wine glass. "To The Baron!" we joined in unison.

I have never been sure we did the right thing in voting against inviting Baron Haussmann to our dinners, but in the next weeks, something changed. So noticeable was the change that I could not help but wonder if someone had told him about the vote we had taken at the Cardon. If so, he could have taken offense. In any case, we began seeing him more often. Every day, late in the afternoon, he took to strolling the halls of our offices and chatting briefly with any member of the circle who happened to be studying The Calendar or the new Map of Paris which Deschamps was developing as expanded areas of the city, blocks of construction, and new roads were completed. The Baron sometimes walked into an office unannounced, first with a polite or clever greeting, then with a question regarding progress. His efforts at socializing were charming and appreciated, but they were brief and thinly veiled and it was not long before we realized that he was not strolling the halls and issuing polite greetings because he was interested in developing lasting friendships. We were municipal employees living in the strictly structured Haussmann world and as such the Master Builder's niceties were perfunctory introductions to what was really on his mind.

"Ah, what a lovely day," he would announce to stern-faced Jacques Hittorf, this cordial greeting followed by "and when will the drawings on Les Halles be ready? Jacques, I haven't seen order forms for the iron. Be sure to include costs." And to Baltard it was "What of the trees for the Parc Monceau? I've seen no requisitions. Tomorrow would be advisable on those." To Davioud it was," What of your drawings for the Nymphe Marine Fountain and the schedule for ongoing work in the Bois de Boulogne, and what is the status of roofing materials for the kiosks and lavatories on Boulevard des Capucines?"

In my case and with increasing regularity, The Baron began to appear at my demolition sites, his procedure as well regulated as The Calendar posted in the office hallway. Without a word, a smile, or greeting he would step out of his carriage and come to stand beside me. He would watch the activity for a few minutes, make comments, and only then, when he felt equipped with the information he found necessary, would he ask questions, his emphasis always on when I expected the demolition work to be completed.

This pounding focus on exactly when things would be finished and made ready for the next step was an aspect of my work I found exasperating. Daniel noticed my frustration. "Monsieur Fabron, you work hard every day to finish a long list of interviews with people. You supervise demolitions and before you return to the Hotel de Ville at the end of the afternoon you have sent the next day's schedule to facilitators. I know this because I carry the schedules to them. "When will the piles of broken glass be carted away?" Baron Haussmann asks you at almost every site, and "when will the chimney bricks be hauled away to the yards at Vincennes? Have you scheduled the wagons? Those sticks of furniture piled up across the street are of no value. Have you arranged for their removal?"

"I know it is not my place, Monsieur, to say anything," Daniel remarked, with increasing candor, "but even with more assisting field agents you could not do more in one day than you already do."

"I must conform to the schedule," I invariably responded. "I work hard to do so and you, Daniel, are an enormous help." What I did not say in response to Daniel's sensitive observation was that the Baron's relentless inquisition was becoming overwhelming. Keeping up the steady beat of progress and accelerating it whenever he saw fit was his central concern. I understood that, but I also understood that he had little regard for the human toll his unabated insistence was taking. Other than his meetings with the Emperor, he loved nothing more than to see the inner circle inundated with work in their offices or on site with teams of laborers swarming over old Paris, their pickaxes, shovels, and hammers pounding away night and day. More valuable and meaningful to me, were those occasions when he accompanied me into homes as I went about the business of appropriation. At those times I could stand back and watch Baron Haussmann in action as few people ever did. Some occupants of houses scheduled for demolition had absolutely no idea who he was, but for many who did recognize him, his presence inspired a palpable level of awe. Unfortunately, this veneration could quickly disintegrate into the same types of loud, angry bouts of cursing to which I had become immune. Much to his credit, The Baron never once responded with retaliatory comments or negative remarks. Instead, he stood tall and listened stoically, seldom leaving a disgruntled home or business owner without a clearly expressed "thank you for your role in creating the New Paris."

Certainly I appreciated this active participation and support, but I now believe that with first hand experiences in the actual acts of appropriation The Baron gained great insight into the depths of prevailing sentiment. But he was no fool. He expected resistance and criticism. He knew it existed in every quarter and that it emanated from all walks of life, but at my side he saw for what I believe was the first time that poverty-stricken residents of his most resolutely targeted lanes and neighborhoods were of a common mind. He saw that these people shared a common bond and that it was inflexible. To the communities of Old Paris, neighborhoods, no matter how littered, rat-infested, dirty, or crowded, were the one and only fabric of the world that was the real Paris. The homes in them were sacred. In his day Voltaire had decried the city's filth and degradation. A succession of modern writers had continued to expound on his criticism, but in the hearts of the poor and dispossessed, change for the sake of change was creating no relatable or tangible path to a better future.

"We must work every day to convince these unyielding hearts that the new city is for them," The Baron said to me on many occasions when we were being met by shouts of protest and streams of insults. "We must do all we can to keep the hope of those promises alive until people see the New Paris emerging for themselves and find their places in it as I am convinced they will. Until then if we must exaggerate, we will do so!"

In theory I shared The Baron's hopes for an inclusive Paris and I had come to see myself as aiding in the achievement of that goal, but I vowed I would not allow myself to resort to blatant exaggeration. I too wanted the future to appear bright and filled with opportunity for all. At the same time I doubted that the dark memories of those souls who were being summarily disenfranchised would ever be erased. I feared that grudges would be carried for many years to come. Memories might fade, broken spirits might be healed, but under the restorative tenets of time I strongly suspected that an uneasy cloud of resentment would hover over the New Paris for a long time to come. The Baron was aware of my feelings. We discussed the issue of resentment many times, and although he sympathized with my view of conditions and prospects, his position remained rock solid and he repeated the often sung song:

"When completed, the transformed Paris will win over hearts and minds. I know I am right! It will happen. Don't worry, Charles. At the end everyone will see that no sacrifice has been too great, no act too small to affect the magnificent result we will achieve."

Of course The Baron's unfailing optimism was supported by that of the Emperor. To the Hotel de Ville staff it was abundantly clear that both The Baron and The Emperor wanted the Paris project to succeed not sufficiently or adequately, but heroically and on a massive scale. A few pretty parks and a collection of newly paved avenues lined with attractive apartment buildings and mirrored cafes did not fully conform to their completed vision of the new Paris. Far from it. The success they had in mind and yearned for was far greater than anyone beyond the doors of the Hotel de Ville imagined. The primary goal was, of course, to transform the look of Paris and address its sanitation problems. That much was a given, but the ultimate goal was to affect the international soul; to affect international social ideals and influence international opinions to the extent that Paris would set the world standard for what a powerful city could and should be. All factions of life would be affected as with its exterior stylishly rebuilt, Paris alone in all the world would be in a position to reflect the very best to be found in architecture, interior design, fashion, food, music and art. The City by the Seine would lead by example and set the world standard for all that contributed to a life of quality and good health. No other city would compare.

Egotistical? Arrogant? Yes, but not impossible, not with the vision of a wildly ambitious Emperor and the immense ego of a tireless Baron named Haussmann. As sections of the city began to reveal a defining architectural flair and the planting of thousands of carefully selected specimen trees began to enhance and further beautify the soon to become iconic urban landscape, the Haussmann staff was under greater pressure than ever to produce. We too were ambitious and energized by evidence of what was happening around us. We too had egos and aspirations, but the constant undercurrent clearly implied that no matter how hard we worked or how well we adhered to the schedule that we could always do more, go farther, move faster. We were constantly being pushed, constantly being watched, and as if the limits of our patience weren't being stretched thinly enough, there were The Baron's daily notes and memorandums. Most were repetitious requests for confirmation of completion dates and numbers of laborers required for one project or another, but here again the sequential order demanded of destruction and subsequent construction was always paramount. When something old came down, something new must go up. It was that simple, the chain of related procedures in reaching the intended goal a constant challenge and genuine worry to all of us. He may have been an administrative genius, but Georges-Eugene Haussmann could be as annoying as a pair of tight boots. He had no time to discuss complications, delays, or changes in work orders. Those problems were ours to solve. To outsiders, supportive or not, he was establishing a reputation for efficiency and remarkable productivity. To us, functioning as his production company, he was a demanding taskmaster. The pressure had become so unrelenting that I believed then as I do now, that an invitation to our Cardon dinners would have sabotaged the camaraderie the inner circle was building, ultimately affecting the outcome of the Paris project overall. Evidence of The Baron's punishing behavior toward us became most apparent when we began witnessing his frequent outbursts which were manifested in embarrassing episodes of contentious anger during weekly meetings, but in all fairness it must be remembered that The Baron had his own pressures to deal with. In the final analysis the Emperor was not only determining the agenda, he was in charge of the clock, and he was in a hurry. Empirical impatience was Baron Haussmann's true driving force. It was our worst enemy.

"Do not bring me half-finished work!" he exploded on one occasion as we met around our table in the Throne Room. "I thought I had made it clear during our first meeting that I was not interested in fantasies that reside only in your own heads! I know you are talented and creative! I know you have experience. You would not be here if you were not all those things, but I have no time for your vague probabilities. I am building a city! Put your proposals and intended procedures for completion on paper! Make them real! Monsieur Hittorff, I especially want to see clarity from you, not the mere prospect of intentions that float about in the rarified air you alone seem to breathe. When you submit a drawing or a proposal to me, please have it completed on time, and please have your facts and figures ready and correct when we meet for discussion! And Monsieur Davioud, please know your intended locations. Do not imagine where they are! Go to them with your ethereal imagination! See them! Examine and study them before you start dreaming and drawing in that secluded cocoon of an office I have allowed you to have!"

It was at this point that Davioud rose from his chair, collected his notes, and stormed out of the room. He had said not a word as he headed for the door, but his face was flaming. I knew what he must be feeling, his process challenged, his fragile creative flair diminished by the belittling, embarrassing commands and comments of his employer.

"I will not be insulted this way!" Hittorff shouted out, pounding on the table and facing The Baron directly. "I am not some amateur you can prey upon and order about like a weak know-nothing! I was creating masterpieces in Paris while you, Georges Haussmann, were nothing more than a flailing Prefect's Deputy playing up to your superiors in some minor Prefecture! I insist on an apology, and one thing more. No one conforms to the schedule better than I do! Do not chastise me again on timeliness or I may find myself forced to go the Emperor! He should know how you are treating your staff! We are not your slaves! Perhaps I would do better myself at managing the transformation of Paris! I will suggest it!"

No one ever knew how or when the flare-up between The Baron and Hittorf was resolved, but since both men stayed on in their respective positions, we could only assume that somehow, somewhere, there had been a meeting of the minds. In the following weeks I saw the two in frequent conversation and all seemed calm and friendly enough, but Gabriel Davioud had cleared his office and without a word had left Paris for Deauville. We had no idea when, or if he would return.

He wrote to me, his letters expressing no animosity toward Baron Haussmann, only the personal realization that the love he had always felt for his creative work had been jeopardized by the pressures of an overly rigid schedule. I read Gabriel's letters with great regret. I missed him as a friend and supporter, but I also understood his need to free himself. I often felt the need for that same freedom. Somehow, though, I stayed the course as did my colleagues, and in retrospect I'm glad we did. Overall, the rough places were eventually smoothed over, our dinners at the Cardon were held every Tuesday, and Baron Haussmann continued to exert his influence on what had become a circle of seven who took his talent for over-reach with polite silence. To the world beyond the walls of the Hotel de Ville all appeared to be moving along in an efficient manner. To that same outside world it must also have appeared that Baron Georges-Eugene Haussmann was leading an idyllic life which, in truth, he was.

His mornings were spent not with laborers and tar merchants, but in palaces meeting with the Emperor of France, the two putting their heads together under one gloriously painted ceiling after another at Saint-Cloud, the Elysees Palace, the Tuileries, Versailles, the Grand Trianon, or the Petit Trianon, as with little regard for costs they discussed plans for a golden city. Afternoons were taken up with a review of plans, supervision of staff, and a rigid survey of progress from the comfort of one of his luxurious carriages, his evenings an endless stream of glamorous soirees, dinners, and receptions.

With a penchant for associating with the upper classes, The Baron was often invited to attend private functions in the company of the most influential men and women of the time, but the invitations did not pour in because Georges Haussmann was attractive or gifted, which indeed he was. They poured in because he was powerful. He had the ear of the Emperor and with full control over the re-building of Paris there were those who knew that fortunes and valuable alliances could be made in his company. This is not to imply that Georges Haussmann was a shallow individual lacking in social skill or intelligence. Quite the contrary. He could tip-toe around any topic and deflate any suggestion of criticism with an erudition that many sought to emulate and never did. Of course, the intelligentsia wanted to ignore him, but invitations to his fetes at the Hotel de Ville were irresistible. He loved a good party and no one but the Emperor hosted a better one. In a very short time all Paris knew two things about Georges

Haussmann: that he had mastered the art of entertaining, and that the Hotel de Ville provided him with an unparalleled stage. Both being quite correct, it was there, in his official setting which it must be remembered, was his home as well as his place of business that in highly creative ways The Baron exercised his love of superabundance. He directed the execution of his magnificent formal balls and countless dinners in spectacular rooms whose potentials he understood better than anyone. Nothing escaped his attention. He planned the décor, usually with a theme in mind. He chose the furniture and designed its arrangement. He selected the flowers, the music and the menus, all of which were breathtaking. Fine wines were personally selected and usually from the best chateau vintages of the Bordeaux. His own private cellars of fine Bordeaux wines were extensive and nurtured through the years at his country house in Cestas, the lush vineyards of local Bordeaux winemakers he befriended providing countless occasions for tastings and exclusive purchases.

Why, at this time, in addition to being recognized for his administrative skills, he was not also becoming known as a man of culture and taste remains a mystery to me. He was turning the long neglected French capital city into a world treasure brimming over with outstanding examples of classic architecture. The new monuments, parks, and gardens were works of art. He worked tirelessly. He was methodical and calculating. His energy level was unsurpassed. Following an evening of luxurious entertainment, he returned to his office to review all the reports of the day. He did not sleep until he had completed reading each submission and noting applicable comments. It wasn't enough. Perhaps it was his domineering personality. Perhaps it was his insatiable appetite for status and popularity. Whatever the reason, the public in general regarded him as a crass, tasteless individual and to put it bluntly, a man ill-suited to directing the beautification of a city as prestigious as Paris.

"People with nothing better to do need something to criticize," he would say with his broad smile and a quick thrust of his imposing chin when negative, often hurtful comments appeared in newspaper articles and scathing letters poured in by the dozen. The Baron may have wished to take complaints and barbs in his stride, but as the years unfolded, words such as common, unsophisticated, and upstart were often associated with him. Like every man, Georges Haussmann had his faults, but he was not at all common or uncultured. He knew history and philosophy. He could discuss Voltaire and Rene Descartes at length. He loved music. He had made life-long noble connections. At his school, the Lycee Henri IV, among his boyhood friends and subsequent adult companions were the Duc de Chartres, the Duc d'Orleans, and the Duc de Nemours, all sons of King Louis-Phillipe. Every year they invited him to the Musee vivant du Cheval Event at their magnificent Chateau de Chantilly. The Baron's Hotel de Ville Musicales became famous, the Lenten Concerts of The Prefect of the Seine one of the city's most well-attended musical events of the year. He played the cello, and very well, as I had discovered while awaiting my first interview. He had attended the Paris Conservatory where he studied both organ and cello. He and Hector Berlioz, another life-long friend, met there and studied Counterpoint with Cherubini. Opera was a particular favorite musical interest and for many years The Baron subscribed to a box at the Paris Opera. It was there that he became acquainted with the young ballet dancer, Francine Cellier, and despite having a wife and two daughters, it was with her that his already delicate public reputation acquired its further tarnish.

The Ballet as a performing art had been born in seventeenth-century Paris and had become an integral part of performances at the Theatre Imperial de l'Opera. The beautiful young female dancers attracted the attention of many prominent men who appeared at performances in splendid evening attire and seated themselves in the Imperial's luxurious boxes, trying not to appear overly anxious as they peered through their powerful opera glasses, pretending to enjoy the singing and dancing and not the sensual movements of the beautiful young dancers. Emperor Louis Napoleon himself was not immune. He attended the Opera so often and with such close attention to the young dancers that he kept a room backstage. The Baron did not keep a room, but his affair with Francine Augustine Cellier, one of the principal dancers and a young woman thirty years his junior was, in addition to the ever-present criticism regarding the upheaval in Paris, the talk of the town. I saw them together in his carriage on a number of occasions. Their relationship continued for many years and with The Baron as her benefactor the lithe and lovely Madame Cellier lived and entertained lavishly in a series of expensive apartments on elegant Boulevard Malesherbes. It was no secret that in 1859 she bore The Baron a daughter. The child was named Francine Eugenie Cellier, her middle name chosen in homage to the Empress. But for the flood of gossip it engendered, I have no particular opinion to share concerning this liaison. Sexual intrigues were part and parcel of the glamorous ballet world and as such were accepted and integrated into the Paris personality as readily as wine and baguettes. Adding to the ballet's intrigue however, it bears repeating the widely circulated rumor that the most successful of the courtesan ballerinas were said to satisfy three lovers at a time: one for prestige, one for money, and one for love.

This then, was the state of things as the decade of the 1860's evolved. Little could I have imagined how seriously these demanding years would affect my future, but the great wheels of Haussmannization were spinning ahead and turning not only against the nameless and unknown but now against the most familiar names and faces in my life.

CHAPTER NINE

Cross Currents

IN ORDER TO STAY one step ahead of construction progress and as had become my habit, every afternoon I consulted The Calendar. In meetings with Deschamps I concentrated on studying long-range plans for neighborhoods on the Left Bank, in particular at this time, demolition and redistricting of one specific area surrounding a section of Boulevard Saint-Germain. It was with increasing concern that I noticed Rue de l'Eperon's intersection with Boulevard Saint-Germain at issue again and again. On one day The Calendar showed l'Eperon and its surrounding area scheduled to be totally demolished, the next all was to remain. Such indecision was highly unusual. I began to worry, and with good reason. Rue de l'Eperon was but a short walk from the Rohan Courtyards. It intersected Boulevard Saint-Germain. I travelled it every day. If plans called for the demolition of l'Eperon's entire general area, beginning at its intersection with Saint-Germain, my home, the Villard home, their bookstore, and the Rohan

Courtyards themselves could be leveled. Quite innocently, Jean Barillet-Deschamps clarified the situation for me.

"Charles, a section of Boulevard Saint-Germain is to be extended at some points and widened and re-routed at others," he informed me as we reviewed demolition orders for the coming month. Final details are being worked out now. The problem is Rue l'Eperon and whether it should be widened or done away with altogether. That has yet to be decided, but if l'Eperon is indeed done away with, one of the neighborhoods which will require the most extensive demolition is located very near to the Boulevard's intersection with l'Eperon. It's along an odd narrow street which from what I can see on my map, ends in a cul de sac. Charles, you'll have your work cut out for you there. As it stands now, The Baron's plans call for direct access from Boulevard Saint-Germain at its junction with l'Eperon all the way through that little street and its cul de sac to Rue Saint-Andre des Arts just beyond it. Once cleared, the plan is for Saint-Andre to be widened and landscaped, perhaps a park added. He is talking to Belgrand about a water feature for the park today. Charles, don't you live in that area?"

There it was, the sinking feeling, the terrible fear that once again something I cared for was about to be snatched away. "Yes, my house is in the Rohan Courtyards," I managed to reply. "The only access is from what you call that 'odd' little street. It's Rue du Jardinet. The Rohan Courtyards are at the end of Jardinet and of course have no outlet. They form the cul-de-sac you say stands to be demolished and cut through. Rue Saint-Andre des Arts is on the other side of the cul-de-sac's farthest bordering wall which protects all three Rohan Courtyards."

"Oh Charles!" Deschamps said, putting his hand up to his forehead. "I'm so sorry! This is terrible, but constant upheaval drives the Paris we live in now, doesn't it? I wish I could do something, but you know better than most of us how things are now. Once The Baron makes up his mind, there is no further discussion."

From the start, Barillet-Deschamps had been a sympathetic colleague, expressing concern whenever he knew I was about to destroy a particularly large swath of Old Paris. He knew the city well and often shared interesting recollections about the people who had lived in a particular area or neighborhood targeted for destruction. He would become uncharacteristically animated, and it was at these times that I realized he dealt with concerns very similar to mine as he prepared The Calendar and Map. Working closely with The Baron, he knew well in advance of all of us what was coming and the areas about to be affected. A thoughtful, organized man, Deschamps was one of the inner circle's members most concerned about his aging parents and what might lie ahead for them as Paris underwent its transformation. He had brought them to visit the Hotel de Ville on several occasions, delighted in gaining permission from The Baron to give them a tour, take them into his office and allow them a view of their son's daily working environment.

"My parents live near Rue de Richeline and one of these days I expect they will receive the same sort of news you could be about to deal with," he shared with me. "It's coming. It will be heartbreaking for them, but for a long time I've wanted them to move away from that part of Paris. I've done everything I can think of to encourage them to leave. I've offered to help them pay for a home in a better area, but you know how it is. For years they've lived in the same house on the same street. As their age the last thing they want is change. Their oldest friends are close by and the old habits are deeply ingrained. They all go to the same butcher, the same boulangerie, and the same church. Unfortunately, in the process of buying food and visiting with God they don't see the gloss on the cobblestones."

Here, once again, I must digress and briefly set aside the sharing of my personal concerns regarding the fate of the Rohan Courtyards which were, by any measure, considerable, for in recalling Deschamps' parental narrative I am reminded of the most pressing, most difficult public issue to have faced The Baron and the vision he shared with the Emperor. It had nothing to do with the creation of impressive buildings or grand boulevards. It had to do with improvements to public health and the eradication of epidemics of disease which had swept through Paris repeatedly through the ages and continued to do so without interruption.

We were all aware of the fact that through the passage of countless centuries, deposits of human urine had applied a coating of polish to many of the old cobbled streets. I smile when I realize how durable a human product it was. Once it had settled in comfortably and layered itself repeatedly throughout the course of years, the heaviest rains and deepest snows did nothing to wash the gloss away. It was the most remarkable thing. The fiercest downpours and deepest snowfalls seemed only to enhance the glow. Today, as the world begins to understand the nature and origin of serious infection, I can only imagine what impact was made every day by moist, disease-causing agents left to fester on street surfaces, horse hooves, on dogs, cats, shoes, boots, and ground-trailing dresses. Every day and without the slightest concern, men relieved themselves in the streets and every day, also without concern, pots of family waste were added to the mix. These were the unassailable habits of a populace held in the grip of its past and it was in addressing issues of sanitation and health raised by habits such as these that what I believe to be The Baron's greatest success was achieved.

The choice of Victor Belgrand to design and implement an efficient sewer system as well as a water delivery system capable of efficiently distributing clean, potable household water had been a stroke of genius. He masterfully devised a system which provided clean running water to most of the population. Adding to this heroic accomplishment and with a gift for ignoring a wide range of daily pressures, he brought his experience and the practical application of his extensive geological studies to bear on his work, excelling beyond all expectations in re-orienting the city's sewage miles away and holding true to his early pronouncement that one day the sewers of Paris would be a great source of pride to a city known for its stench and outbreaks of disease. Sadly, adjustments in human behavior supporting the scope of Belgrand's achievements were not immediate. For some time following the completion of his work and ignoring the advent of indoor plumbing, men would continue to urinate in the streets and pots of family waste would continue to be dumped both onto the streets and into the River Seine as the routines of long centuries remained unchanged regardless of the wonders made possible by scientific progress and modern ingenuity. That the nature of this human frailty was understood from the start speaks well of both The Baron's foresight and Victor Belgrand's patience. Fortunately, Belgrand's brilliant work would stand the test of time and eventually, as deaths resulting from cholera and dysentery diminished and cleaner, healthier lifestyles became the norm rather than the exception, the population of Paris would come to understand the importance of its own daily responsibilities in matters of sanitation, gradually learning to implement the tools readily placed at their disposal.

Returning now to the dilemma I faced as prospects for annihilation of the Courtyards confronted me, I decided to turn to Henri Villard for advice and perhaps some solace. He had lived in the Courtyards for many years and was as familiar with its surrounding areas as anyone. He was also intelligent and reliable. I admit to having faced the prospect of our discussion with trepidation. The news I would be delivering was hardly pleasant, but I felt I had to talk to someone and I had to start somewhere. I arranged to meet Henri one morning for a walk through the neighborhood. While my courage was at its peak I came directly to the point.

"Henri, I must confide in someone and I can't think of anyone I trust as much as I trust you," I began. "I have serious concerns about the Rue du Jardinet area which I know you will share."

Henri stopped walking and faced me. "I knew something must be on your mind, Charles. You have a very solemn look on your face. Is it the Courtyards? Have we been placed on a list of potential casualties? Claire and I have discussed this possibility many times in recent weeks. Has our turn really arrived? "

"It's likely," I said. "I hate to bear this news, Henri, but you should know that as things stand now, Rue du Jardinet, The Rohan Courtyards, and all the cross streets north of Rue de l'Eperon are marked for potential demolition. Nothing is firmly scheduled as yet, but it soon may be. I felt you should know."

I had never seen fear in Henri Villard's eyes. He was the most affable, most positive thinking human being I had ever known, but there it was in those dark, intelligent eyes; fear in the cloud of helpless anxiety, fear in the unfathomable prospect of being torn away from his home, his beloved bookstore, and fear of being separated from every familiar fragment of life as he knew it.

"What can we do?" he asked, the look of concern on his face elevating my own. "There must be some way to stop this. Charles, surely you can do something."

"Henri, I'm not sure I can. I have rules to follow and directives to carry out. I shouldn't be doing anything about this at all, but I've gone ahead and tested a few possibilities and I've designed a prospective plan for re-directing Boulevard Saint-Germain where it intersects with Rue de l'Eperon. Complicating my best efforts, though, I discovered just yesterday that there is currently an official plan developing for a major new sewer network of complex conduits and drains just under l'Eperon's junction with Saint-Germain. At that location I'm told there is to be a major central drain where a series of large pipes will handle a considerable volume of area waste, sending it miles away. As is to be the case with the city's entire underground sewer and water delivery system, accessibility for necessary maintenance and cleaning will be from utility stairways at several points on the land nearby and down to underground concrete tunnels large enough for a human being to walk through. I've studied the terrain where l'Eperon meets the boulevard. I do have a surveyor's background, and using a model I found successful at Evreux when the new roadway was being laid out there, I saw that I was dealing with a natural incline. A similar incline confronted us here in Paris where Boulevard des Italiens meets Boulevard des Capucines. Have you ever wondered about the sudden jog as the two avenues meet at Rue Scribe? Originally, a monument with enough space for carriages to pass at each side was to separate and clearly define the two boulevards. We were not prepared for the underground stone formations we found close to the incline's surface where the boulevards were to meet, but rapid progress being paramount, the underground plan and the design for the monument were quickly abandoned. The surface above ground was quickly scraped and prepared, gravel and tar were applied, the surfaces were smoothly raked, and the odd jog where the two boulevards meet at Rue Scribe was created. If the incline at l'Eperon is found to extend for more than thirty feet underground and a complex of ancient stone is found, the proposed sewer design may require considerable alteration or at the very least, re-direction. That would take too much time. Under those circumstances, The Baron could decide to re-route the project or abandon it altogether. Of course that would be the best scenario we could hope for."

"All that sounds reasonable," Henri said. "But what if there is no stone? What if the incline can be eliminated?"

"I don't know," I helplessly stated, but I had to tell you. Surely you understand I cannot go directly to Baron Haussmann and ask for favoritism because I live here. He frowns on that sort of thing. It has come up a number of times. He sees favoritism as a form of corruption, which I suppose it is. But Henri, the Calendar for next three months is almost finished. I saw a draft of it a few days ago, and of course once it's finalized there's no going back. Henri, we must face facts. The Baron wants to clear our entire area and re-develop it so that from Boulevard Saint-Germain, the Rue de l'Eperon is widened to cut straight through this Rue du Jardinet we are walking on right now. The demolition and widening will eliminate the narrow cross streets and continue through our Rohan Courtyards which will also be demolished, leaving l'Eperon to open onto a new commercial area at Rue Saint-Andre des Arts complete with shops and a public park."

Henri stopped walking again. "Our cul de sac will be demolished, cut through, and opened onto a commercial area on Saint-Andre des Arts? I cannot picture it. We live in an historic enclave. The Courtyards date back to the fifteenth century. They should be protected. Paris Bishops created them as their center. For centuries they lived here in secluded safety much as we do now. King Henri the Second built a house here for Diane de Poitiers. It still stands and is occupied today. Do the tenets of history reach Baron Haussmann at all? Does he understand that places like this should remain as they are? And what of my bookstore and the shops of my friends on Rue du Jardinet? Where are we to go? How are we to make a living? Who can I see at The Hotel de Ville to straighten this out? I will go right now, today!"

Henri's passion was not unlike my own, but I had to tell him that dozens of requests for historic preservations were being presented and denied every day. They had become little more than tiresome details. At the same time I began to realize that I needed to meet with someone who could influence the Rue l'Eperon situation and present The Baron with a convincing alternative to demolition. If the plan to eradicate our homes and the neighborhood was to change, our solution would have to come not from me, but from an influential person whose opinions The Baron respected. Henri seemed to read my mind.

"Charles, if you feel you cannot talk to Baron Haussmann, you must talk to someone else. That person must be someone who can look at the situation from a distance in a rational, sensible way, someone capable of presenting a very good argument for preserving this part of Old Paris. And Charles, if plans exist for our homes and businesses to disappear, you are the best possible advocate for us. I don't like the news you bear but I appreciate your confidence in me. I know your efforts cannot be obvious, but you must find a way out. Please do your best for us. I will help you in any way I can, but this must be solved. The thought of a commercial district replacing our little gated heaven is beyond my comprehension. I won't say a word to Claire, not yet, and neither should you."

We had reached the Courtyards gate when Henri said, "Charles, perhaps what you need is not so much a new design, but a good idea; an idea to present to that influential person you will talk to; yes, a better idea than the one Baron Haussmann is proposing for re-development here. Yes, that could be it, and not only must it be a better idea, it must be irresistible. It would require an important focus, perhaps something to please the public, something to enhance Haussmann's reputation and make him appear sensitive to the historic importance of certain areas of this city, an affirmation he could use right now. But what could it be? A new church? A school to be built behind the Courtyards instead of a new commercial district? Whatever the solution may be, our rear wall must remain in tact and protected or we are done for."

My mind was racing. "There are enough churches in the area," I said, "but I do like the idea of something for children, perhaps a school, but not another potential Sorbonne, or Ecole des Beaux-Arts; perhaps a school for very young children, not one affiliated with The Church but a non-denominational public school totally funded by the government and open to all area children more or less between the ages of five and ten. I know it's a wild thought, but it's a good idea. I think people would love the idea of being able to offer their youngest children a good start in their educations. Of course funding would be a big issue, but it's worth a try."

Henri was smiling. "You could have something there, Charles. A unique school open to the public without charge could be very appealing, but you're right, finding the money would surely present a big hurdle. Try to find a way around that. Put that good brain of yours to work and explore a few approaches, but now, about the person you should talk to concerning all this. During your time in Paris you've made influential friends. Choose someone from that influential group to talk to. Have a friendly conversation, perhaps over a luncheon or dinner. I wouldn't advise this person be someone you work with at the Hotel de Ville. You could risk being thrown into the rumor mill and Baron Haussmann has enough of that on his hands. And, if during your luncheon or dinner meeting you feel the idea of a school is not striking an immediate chord, you should have an equally appealing alternative ready, perhaps an idea for an unusual public building or garden. Well, perhaps that's a silly idea. Whatever it is, you'll think of the right thing. In any case, the person you meet with must be an individual of intelligence and sensitivity, and it would be an added advantage if he has The Baron's ear and The Emperor's as well. Is that asking too much?"

"No, I don't think it's asking too much at all," I replied slowly, my brain still racing. "Henri, you've given me more direction than I was hoping for. I believe I know exactly the person I should meet with and I'm happy to say he fits all our requirements."

The person I had in mind was, just as Henri had suggested, intelligent and sensitive and had the ear of The Baron as well as that of The Emperor. The next day I sent an invitation by courier to my distinguished friend, Count Andre Leclerc, suggesting we meet for luncheon at Le Grand Verger. It would be expensive, but this was important. Once the date and time were set I would pre-order the famed roast duckling with caviar and foie gras and worry about the damage to my bank balance later. A response was waiting for me when I returned to the Hotel de Ville the next afternoon. It had been left with Secretary Merruau. The Count was accepting my invitation to luncheon, but he preferred I join him at his home in the Marais. He wrote: "Charles, how nice it will be to enjoy your company at luncheon. I like Grand Verger very much, but we will have privacy here at my home and we can discuss any topic you like. Come to the Marais. The Verger will be waiting for us another time."

——•◉•——

What can I say about the Marais? I had been to Adele Alessandri's impressive house on Place des Vosges any number of times, but always at night. The daytime view of the Marais conveyed a very different magic. In the light of afternoon it was a grand but wistful place, beautiful in its architecture, much of it having successfully resisted the impatience of time, its sturdy seventeenth-century timber-framed houses well kept, the old paned windows once overlooking bucolic fields and pastures now viewing a mysterious new world of noisy street vendors and the idly curious who found a great deal to admire. Many of the original front doors were armed with their original carved depictions of growling lion heads and fierce Medusas, some amusing to the passer-by who couldn't help but point out missing bits of a nose or eye to a companion. By contrast, a collection of splendid eighteenth-century mansions faced the square of Place des Vosges, these, like Adele Alessandri's, the city chateaux of wealthy merchants, bankers, and rich aristocrats who willingly sacrificed the luxury of rolling country acres for a fine house on a small piece of land in close proximity to the attractions and conveniences of the city. Count Leclerc's was one of the most impressive of these, its brick and limestone façade discreetly protected from street traffic by a tall thick hedge, its heavy wooden courtyard gates standing open as my carriage approached. The Count was waiting in the doorway as I stepped out onto the drive.

"I knew you'd be prompt, Charles," he greeted with an extended hand and his engaging smile. "It's become a way of life for you I imagine. Wonderful to see you. Come in."

I was led across a stone floored hall and into a large room overlooking a terrace and a garden. A small table and two chairs waited in the alcove at the window.

"Earlier this morning I thought we might enjoy our lunch on the terrace," the Count said, "but its clouding up out there. My aches and pains tell me it could rain, so I had everything set up in here. We'll have an aperitif before Annette announces luncheon. Alcohol always makes me feel better. When you get to be my age it will do the same for you."

The Count poured two glasses of Dubonnet from a sideboard decanter and gestured me to the long sofa facing the fireplace. The portrait of a woman standing before what looked to be the same fireplace stared down at us. The Count was silent for a moment or two.

"My wife," he said. "She died twenty years ago. It still feels like yesterday. Charles, you can't know what a loss like that is like. It tears your heart out and tries to break you."

I sipped at my glass of Dubonnet as it was a life raft. I could feel my fingers holding on to the delicate crystal too tightly. Afraid it would break, I put it down on the small table beside me and stared into the fireplace where no flames leaped out and only dry logs lay awaited the first cool morning of autumn. Leclerc was voicing feelings I knew and understood too well. I wanted to tell him to stop, but he went on, expressing the same anxieties I had shared with no one in Paris but Adele.

"When you lose someone dear to you, if you let yourself falter under the pain and let yourself be broken, you're done for," he went on. "I was a soldier, trained to fight. I watched comrades suffer and die. I lost close friends in battle, even my two brothers. Those were ugly things in my life, but losing Nadia was much worst. I suffered for a long time. It may surprise you to know that Adele Alessandri rescued me. Yes, she put me together again. The night I met you I mentioned that one day I'd tell you about my feelings for Adele and this is as good a time as any. Now, don't get the wrong idea. There was never a great, undying amour between us then and there isn't now. It was just an affair, a brief dalliance, but it was a lovely, healing time. Simply put, Adele was there, having luncheon or dinner with me, talking about the opera, telling me about her own late husband, listening to me talk about Nadia, and describing her house in the country. It was somewhere in Bordeaux, she said, by a lovely pond. We would go there together in the summer, she said. We would wear old hats and old shoes. We would walk in the meadow and fill baskets with wild daisies. We never did go. We never wore old hats and old shoes and we never picked the wild daisies, but isn't it a beautiful thought? The idea of it all intrigued me. It gave me something lovely and alive to think about. I suppose the romantic aspect of the whole thing made me fall in love with Adele. What man worthy of the name wouldn't fall at least a little in love with a woman like beautiful Adele? I think if she had stayed in Paris instead of running off to Italy the way she did I would have become hopelessly devoted to her."

I said nothing about Louisa, our twin sons, or my own feelings of loss; nothing about the ways I had locked away the past in my heart so it would always be there, safe and untouched. I said nothing to the Count about Adele Alessandri and our brief liaison and I said nothing about the invitation I too had received to visit the house by the pond in Bordeaux and pick the wild daisies, but I knew exactly what Leclerc was doing. He was telling me that he knew all about my suffering. Someone had told him, and with carefully chosen words he was conveying his understanding. So much went unsaid between us, but so much was clearly understood. Annette came to announce luncheon and like a pair of wayfarers who had paused during a sad journey we silently seated ourselves at the table by the window. The consomme was served and as I watched my host slowly unfold his napkin I wanted to ask who could have shared the tragedy and pain of my loss with him. It is another of my regrets that I sacrificed a significant moment for what, at the time, seemed a greater goal. Talk of deceased wives and daisies in the country were not what I had in mind when I arranged to see Andre Leclerc, so I let the matter pass, but on a warm spring afternoon in the Marais as I sat at a table and looked out to a garden I was tortured once again by the memory of trees just waiting for swings and climbing and the way life might   have been at a lovely house on a faraway hill.

"Now, Charles, what is it we are to discuss today?" my host asked, leaning back in his chair as I tore myself away from impossible images. "Whatever it is, I shall advise or assist you in any way I can, and as you can see we have complete privacy."

With those words I began to wonder if Count Leclerc had purposely arranged for our luncheon not at a restaurant, but at his home where we could be totally alone and where a portrait over a fireplace could provoke an ambiguous conversation. Was it the nature of our personal losses and the coincidence of our mutual concerns that he thought I had come to discuss? Was this the reason for his friendly suggestion that we meet in the seclusion of his home, and was I there to benefit from his sympathy and wise counsel? These considerations aside, I wasn't sure how to proceed in explaining the true nature of my visit, but with a glass of wine in hand I decided to go ahead and state my case. I began by saying I knew I was being selfish in using my access to information with an advantage my despairing victims would never be given.

To this day, I cringe just thinking about those moments. In baring my soul and laying out my ideas to Andre Leclerc I was betraying every person whose property I had summarily appropriated with words of encouragement. At the same time I was exposing myself to all sorts of personal guilt and professional jeopardy. If Leclerc went to his powerful friend, The Baron, or worst, his yet more powerful friend, The Emperor, and word of this meeting was shared with either one of them I could be sacrificing my self-esteem, my Paris career, and my only source of income, but did I listen to the voice of higher calling? Did I even consider abandoning my course of action? Of course not. I had come to love my Paris home too much. I loved my garden, my neighborhood and my neighbors. I was wrapped in an abundance of comfort and safety and like those I displaced I was being driven by the fear of losing it all. The most wretched aspects of Haussmannization had found me.

As I had hoped, and with no further discussion of houses in the Bordeaux, Count Leclerc was sympathetic to my problem, my personal considerations, and the solutions I presented. Sipping his wine and gazing out to his garden, he listened to me with the attention of a man who had traveled a similarly complicated path many times before. Not too surprisingly, he addressed my concerns with a quick grasp and an abundance of basic common sense.

"Don't make this so difficult, Charles," he said. "You're focusing on all the wrong things. You're afraid of losing your home, your feelings of self-worth, and possibly your career as a result of your actions. I understand all that, but as you worry about these things you're losing sight of the prize, and there is always a prize to consider in situations like this. Charles, understand this: the prize is not you and your wishes. The prize is not the maintenance of your present way of life and the present lives of your neighbors. The prize is greater than yourself. It always is and must be if it is to be won. Napoleon Bonaparte taught me that lesson when I served on his General Staff. For all his eccentricities and self-aggrandizement, he knew he was nothing unless he kept his eye on the prize. And whether it was a military battle or a political fight, he disciplined himself and put France first. France was the prize; its heart, its pride was everything. He was the most patriotic man I've ever known. He loved Josephine deeply but he loved France more. He wanted to leave it in the hands of an heir, a son who would carry on with his same spirit and ambition. Of course it didn't end as he wished and he was captured, but his defeat and exile had nothing to do with his abilities as a military leader or Emperor, and he didn't die at Saint-Helena because he lost at Waterloo. Waterloo was just a consequence. Napoleon died at Saint-Helena because he had let his guard down. He had put himself and his exhausted military in the wrong place at the wrong time and fearing he might lose to the great Wellington he lost sight of the prize. Wellington became the prize. The idea of defeating the great English warrior defeated him. He was intimidated, challenged by his own personal fears. Charles, let that be a lesson to you. Don't let your personal fears about losing houses in charming courtyards stand in the way of your thought process or like Napoleon, you too will be defeated. You can achieve your goal. It's possible, but first you must clearly identify your prize and most important of all you must be able to show its benefits for the greater good not only well, but brilliantly. Concentrate on that. It will be difficult but it is the only way."

"Count Andre, you have given me a great deal to think about," I remember saying, "but what is the prize? A school? A church? A park? What would do the most public good and at the same time save my home and the homes of my neighbors? How would I approach it? Who would support my efforts? Where would the money come from?"

"I like the idea of a school," Leclerc offered. "Strange as it may sound I also like Haussmann's idea of a commercial area and a public garden in that section of Saint-Germaine. Don't forget that money-making ventures appeal to him. There are plenty of churches in the area, so you should forget that. A school has merit, but I have tried it myself. Money for public education is a big hurdle. Of course people do love to see their names on monuments and buildings. Who knows? Haussmann himself might like to see his name emblazoned across the gates to a park or school. He may not be terribly wealthy, but he's clever enough to convince someone else to provide the funds so that he enjoys the benefits. And there is always that loud-mouthed ogre, Maurice Bessette. He holds a secondary seat on the Council and keeps presenting manifestos demanding Haussmann save his favorite parts of Old Paris. An hour later he's in a café gathering a crowd and spreading venom about Haussmann as he decries the whole transformation project. It could be that if he were given one or two successes, he would keep his mouth shut. The man is vicious but he has money to burn and could easily fund your whole project, whatever it turns out to be. You may have to court him and appeal to his ego which I admit is bigger than mine, but I can help with that. Armand Laurent could handle the formal presentation for the plan of a school. He's a member of the Academy and has a well-known interest in public education. Laurent knows how to present an argument to the Council. He's a good debater and I have no doubt he could get a school approved on its merits. For the garden you may have to deal with Adele Alessandri, especially when it gets to the point where the Emperor hears about the project, which he will. He'll want her to design and supervise the planting of the garden. You look surprised, but you should know that even from Italy, Adele continued to create small, choice gardens for His Imperial Majesty and other close, shall we say, friends. At our first meeting I told you she had involvements. They are all kept quiet, very 'entre nous,' but Adele is very talented. She enjoys creating beautiful gardens for people she thinks are special. It's the reason she gave up her career and spent so much time in Florence. She was studying horticulture and landscape design at the Boboli Gardens. Gardens really are her first love. You're looking out at the one she did for me long before she left Paris for life among the garden-loving Italians. Have you heard? She's back in Paris. I saw her just last night. We had dinner here. She plans to live in Paris permanently now. I'm happy about that. She'll be just two doors away."

I tried not to show my surprise. I tried to ignore the image of Adele in Paris again but I couldn't. In a rush of tempting images I could see her entertaining again, greeting guests in the hallway of her house, extending her hand and spending time with elegant Andre Leclerc, a man I was certain she could seriously consider marrying. I looked out to the garden. Of course. The Alessandri stamp was everywhere and Count Leclerc had a view of it every day. He must see the garden as I did; like Adele herself, a fragment of heaven on earth, a romantic vision of nature, the parterre she had created a tableau of color as green as her eyes, the stately allee of trees in the distance meant like her, to be seen and admired, the carefully planted beds of brilliantly colored flowers a joy to behold, their natural grace also like hers, vulnerable and short-lived. For a few minutes I was lost in my dangerous reverie, but I wisely recovered my senses and ideas were soon flying again. Count Leclerc was beaming. "This is wonderful!" he said with a broad smile. I'm so glad you've come today, Charles. All this is doing me a world of good."

"I'm the grateful one," I said. "Count Leclerc, your views and experience will guide my thinking. Even if nothing at all comes of my efforts, I shall always remember your advice, but I know I've been indiscreet. I hope you understand."

"Understand? If I were in the same position and this house and those around it were being threatened with demolition I would fight the whole process to the death. Don't worry, my boy. You are reacting like a normal human being with a heart.

The Count walked out onto the drive with me and as I stepped into the carriage taking me back to the Hotel de Ville, he said, "Charles, here's a thought: Why not do all three? There are good arguments to be made for a school as well as a controlled commercial area complete with a garden, or better yet a park," he said. "And keep in mind that with a few concessions, preservation of the historic parts of the area such as your courtyards could satisfy that rich ogre, Bessette. The Diane de Poitiers house you describe may appeal to him. He could even try to buy it. If he likes the whole idea, your money worries are over."

I left the Marais feeling drained. Leclerc had been helpful in suggesting solutions to my dilemma concerning the Courtyards, but at the same time he had implied a knowledge of my private life that I found invasive and unsettling. My past difficulties were my business. Leclerc had been clever in coloring the details of his own personal loss and what was obviously an ongoing affair with Adele, even going so far as to say that our mutual 'friend,' Adele Alessandri had saved him, but his intentions were clear. He was sending me a message, one that said someone had told him about the difficulties in my past and my reasons for coming to Paris, but who could that have been? Who would care anything at all about a grieving widower and the opportunity he had been given for a fresh start and a new life? My musings ending in senseless conclusions, once again I decided to put the entire matter aside. I told myself I was placing far too much emphasis on a trivial incident and foolishly reading into things. I went so far as to convince myself that there was absolutely no good reason for Count Leclerc to have told me about a country house in the Bordeaux where he had been invited to stroll in the meadow and pick the wild daisies. It was a conversation. Nothing more.

CHAPTER TEN

The Boy With Yellow Hair

IN THE FOLLOWING DAYS I went about my scheduled assignments as usual, but I was preoccupied by solutions to the problems confronting Rue du Jardinet and the Rohan Courtyards. Worried and entirely too self-absorbed, I was unaware of the extra pressures being placed on Daniel. I should have watched him more closely, supervised him with a firmer hand, but my own pressures were mounting and with his customary efficiency he seemed equal to every situation. With Joli as his constant companion, he had settled into what he said was "a fine life for a boy like me." He seemed content and I saw no reason to worry about him. He fulfilled his daily duties efficiently, he maintained good relationships with the boys at Maison Sospire, and although some may have envied him the companionship of a dog, I was aware of no serious incidents. Having Joli with me each night served to protect both Daniel and the dog from prospective mischief-makers and although I didn't admit it, I enjoyed having Joli. At the same time I knew I was growing overly protective of Daniel and entirely too content with his place in my life. Outwardly, I did my best to maintain an objective attitude, but under my impartial façade I wanted to do whatever I could to help him rise above his circumstances. He was industrious and serious-minded. He was even-tempered, and he had proven his trustworthiness time and time again. I was convinced that with positive experiences and a decent education his future could l ook bright. Beyond my own evaluation, supervisors and contractors recognized Daniel as an asset not only to me, but to them. "Such a fine boy, that one with the yellow hair, always prompt and polite," I heard time and time again. I had begun demolition of Rue Marmousets when things changed. I blamed myself then. I still do.

Unknown to me at the time, advantage was being taken of Daniel's good nature. In addition to his Runner responsibilities, he was being asked to run extra errands by several supervisors and contractors. As for myself, I was once again facing stacks of appropriation-related paperwork which added to my daily responsibilities at several demolition sites often left me exhausted. I was grateful when The Baron recommended Marc Basse, Gabriel Davioud's former drafting assistant, to assist me with appropriations. With Davioud now in Deauville, The Baron wanted to reassign Basse.

I found Marc Basse to be an engaging sort. He went out of his way to make friends and was highly enthusiastic about the Haussmann Project. He wasn't terribly remarkable in appearance; of average height and medium build, but always well turned out, his suits and boots of high quality, his face clean shaven, his black hair wavy and thick and carefully pomaded every day. The first time I met him I recalled that Davioud had complained about him. "He loves to talk! Too much! His mouth is like The Baron's whole body: on the move from morning until night! I can't get my work done!"

At a point when Marc's incessant prattle became unbearable, Davioud had asked The Baron to re-assign him. As always, his words were chosen carefully. "Monsieur Haussmann, Marc Basse is a fine draftsman," he told me he had announced to The Baron. "He is technically accurate and painstaking in his work, but as was the case with our colleague, the photographer,

Charles Marville, once again our creative needs find us outgrowing our present office space. Marc has acquired a new drafting table, an impressive collection of yardsticks and protractors, and along with our two desks and assorted materials, we find ourselves squeezed into too small a space."

Once again, The Baron was immediately accommodating. He promptly assigned Marc Basse to the spacious office of part-time architects, leaving Davioud blissfully alone to create his masterpieces quietly and free of interruption until the day ultimately came when he could no longer tolerate The Baron's demands. In the meantime, making rounds with me, The Baron could see for himself that I was being consumed by a myriad of simultaneous demands myself, all driven by the succession of one process feeding on the other in what in theory would seem to be a simple procedure, but which in practice did not always go smoothly.

At times, houses and shops were not cleared of their furnishings or even of their occupants before my pick-axe and hammer crews appeared to begin their destruction. Complications were endless. More and more often, wagons were not arriving on time to drive property owners away. Piles of uncollected debris and glass stood in the middle of a roadway blocking the expected delivery of construction materials. A horse had gone lame. A wagon wheel had been damaged. Essential tools and materials not been delivered to distribution points as scheduled. Stonemasons and carpenters had arrived on the wrong street at the wrong time. Tempers flared, mine included. Hours were wasted. I know I have made similar comments before, but I cannot overstate my admiration for the rapidity with which, in spite of human error and unpredictable delays, The Baron's massive projects were begun and completed. Sometimes I stood back and shook my head in awe. On one morning a neighborhood was in complete chaos, by afternoon it was leveled, the next day a park was emerging, trees were being planted, and structural foundations for fountains were being constructed. With admirable foresight, Baron Haussmann saw when potential gaps were likely to occur and when they did occur he addressed them promptly. I believe it was with this pervasive aversion to delays that he arranged for Marc Basse to join me.

The understanding was that if after accompanying me for a week or two and gaining insight into procedures, Marc could be seen as capable of managing both the personalities of those being expropriated and the expropriations themselves, he would become my Supervisory Field Assistant. Expropriation, or the eviction of inhabitants and the follow-up of appropriation of property, were serious business and the most time-consuming part of my responsibilities. In developing a system of procedures for this important work I had seen the position of Supervisory Field Assistant as one requiring a working knowledge of fair property values based on classifications which The Baron had himself painstakingly formulated.

He had divided the city into sections, each assigned a general value for estimates of household items, utensils, furnishings, clothing, and the overall property itself depending on location, age, condition, and appearance. The process never changed. At each property targeted for demolition, forms made up of columns for the recording of monetary values in each category were filled out and totaled, corresponding vouchers were presented to property owners, the completed forms submitted to Secretary Merruau for final review by The Baron. Although on the surface this procedure would appear orderly and accountable, in fact there were always subtleties to be considered. A modest property in a clean, well-maintained area would be assessed at a greater value than a hovel at the side of a garbage-littered lane. A fine property in a wealthy area would, of course, be assessed at the highest value permitted but no property's assessed value could exceed or fall below established limits at both ends of the spectrum. The subtleties came with assessment of furniture and household goods. Surprisingly, some dilapidated houses badly in need of repair contained pieces of fine, valuable furniture. Many once comfortable families who, during hard times, had found themselves forced to abandon their houses, had managed to hold on to one or two lovely desks, chairs, tables, porcelains or paintings which, although covered in layers of dust, had, over time, increased in value. By contrast, houses of the wealthy could contain furnishings and household decorations of little or no value. These very real situations could change the total amount of an owner's voucher and it was left to the decision of the supervisor in charge to determine all voucher amounts as he saw fit.

I recognized good quality in the contents of a house or shop when I saw it. I had been raised in a home furnished with more than a few things of value. There were French landscape paintings on our walls. Our tables, carpets, and desks came from reputable Paris shops, and the pieces which satisfied my mother's insistence on a well-set table were Sevres and Rouen blue and white porcelain. Marc Basse's background was even broader. He came from a family of Paris antique dealers who had made good money if not fortunes in the months directly following the Revolution when magnificent French furniture and decorative pieces were pillaged from palaces and chateaux only to be quickly grasped at low prices and sold at outrageously high prices by clever tradesmen to a hungry European network of discriminating dealers, wealthy collectors, and more than a few royal families. The Basse family had done very well in this lucrative, unregulated market, so much so that in one generation its senior members had prospered enough to elevate the family image from that of pushcart tradesman to prestigious antiques dealer, plying their profitable trade from three sumptuous Paris galleries. Until a few illegal financial irregularities in bookkeeping were discovered by suspicious customs officials, they had also polished their social standing, enjoying the company of a wide circle of rich clients and admirers, including Baron Haussmann. Unfortunately, it had ended badly and the Basse family was left bankrupt and socially isolated from the circle of well-to-do Parisians they had successfully cultivated. Fortunately, Marc had completed his education by the time the public prosecutor was pounding on the Basse doors, and having been nothing more than an innocent university student with a modest allowance as his father and uncles were counting their money and maneuvering through international trade laws, he had distanced himself from the upsetting turmoil, proceeding to make his adult living as an architectural   draftsman of considerable ability. Baron Haussmann had found him through Count Andre Leclerc who was among those well-to-do Parisians the Basses had befriended in better days.

It all worked out. Marc took to the process of appropriation quickly and well. I was glad to have him. He was on his own in two weeks, his gift for talking and dealing with people a great asset when confronted by the verbal assaults and streams of cursing which by now I had come to consider routine. I tried to prepare Marc for the onslaught, but he was one step ahead of me.

"Ah, Madame, you seem far too intelligent to be using such foul language," I heard him calmly reply to an offensive young mother with the vocabulary of a pirate. "I remember when my Cousin Emile used those words in my mother's house, "he added. "She opened the front door and pushed him out into the street. Of course, I have no intention of doing such a thing to you, Madame, but respect and cooperation could mean a great deal as I estimate the value of your property and decide the worth of your furniture. Is that a Boulle chest I see under the window? Lovely. Was it in your mother's family? Perhaps your father's?"

The ensuing conversation could quickly turn to fond memories, a few tears, and the recollection of pleasant family experiences. When all was said and done I knew I had acquired a competent Supervisory Field Assistant. Our relationship worked beautifully for several months until one late afternoon when Daniel failed to meet me at the end of the day.

I had waited. A half hour passed, then another. It was growing dark and I began to wonder if he had misunderstood the location of the last site I had sent him to. Perhaps he was lost. It often happened to Runners as sites once familiar became strangely alien once demolition was fully away and mountains of debris changed the look of things, but Daniel had never lost his way. He had an excellent sense of direction. Perhaps he had thought I was attending a meeting at the Hotel de Ville. I couldn't remember having told him I was doing such a thing, but whenever I was returning to the Hotel de Ville for a meeting or to complete paper work, he did know it was a simple matter for me to go only slightly out of my way to take Joli to my house where he stayed until I returned for the night. To clarify Daniel's whereabouts at the end of the day I decided I would try to find the crew supervisor who would have received the last message Daniel would have delivered. Perhaps he knew something. It occurred to me that Marc Basse had been in the same area that day. If the crew supervisor had no information, I would try to find Marc. I did not have far to go, but I was just in time. Franco Lessage, the supervisor in charge that day at Rue Delambre, was turning over his report to the night supervisor.

"Ah, Monsieur Fabron! Yes, the boy with yellow hair was here. Such a fine boy! He took my reply to your message the way he always does and then he talked to Monsieur Basse for a few minutes before leaving. I went back to my work and when the night man arrived and I came for my tools, the boy and his dog were gone. There's no trouble is there?"

"No, of course not, but did Daniel leave this site with Monsieur Basse?"

"No, they didn't leave together. Monsieur Basse is still talking to people on the street. I will go to ask him if he knows anything about Daniel. I'm sure it's just a small thing. You know how boys are. He's probably under a tree somewhere enjoying a vendor's delicious warm biscuits with that wonderful dog of his."

"Thank you Franco. I'll find Monsieur Basse myself."

Certain that Daniel would never keep me waiting at the end of the day to enjoy a vendor's warm biscuit while sitting under a tree somewhere, I walked quickly along Rue Delambre and saw Marc standing in the middle of the street.

"Well, Charles, what a surprise!" he said as I neared the group he had collected around him. "These fine people and I were just discussing procedures for tomorrow's departures to Montreuil, and Courbevoie. I've been telling them about employment opportunities in the new factories there. Today I learned there's a new piano factory being built at Clichy. I should think that would be an interesting place to work."

"I'd like a word with you, Marc," I said, nodding my head in pleasant agreement as I stepped away. Marc quickly came to my side and as we walked I asked him about Daniel.

"I hope you don't mind Charles," he said to me, "but I asked him to do a small personal favor for me this afternoon. I didn't have time to do it myself. It was nothing important, just a note I had written to a friend of mine. He's an engraver and has a shop not far from here. I didn't think it would take Daniel more than a few minutes to hand off the note before he got back to you. He's such a nice boy, so trustworthy. Is there a problem?"

"I don't know, but Daniel never did get back to me. It's not like him. He always meets me at the end of the day. I'm a little worried. Who is the friend of yours? I'd like to check with him."

Marc directed me to Samuel Navier's shop at the corner of Rue Lenoir. Navier was just closing for the night when I arrived. "No, Monsieur, I received no message from someone named Marc Basse today," he said when I inquired about Daniel, "and no messenger boy was here. I certainly would have seen him."

"The boy would have had a dog with him, a black dog," I pressed. "Monsieur Navier, did you leave the shop at all this afternoon, even for a few minutes? Please look to see if a note was left somewhere for you while you were gone."

"Monsieur, I have been working inside here for the entire afternoon without so much as a moment to relieve myself in the back alley," came Navier's reply. "I had a lot of customers. It's a good thing I have a strong constitution, but I will look on the counters and in the message box there by the door. Monsieur, anyone can see the box if I'm not here. And Monsieur, anyone can see it's a message box!" he said, clearly exasperated with me.

There was nothing in the prominently labeled message box by the door and no note was found anywhere in Navier's shop. I didn't know what to do next. It was too late to go back to the Hotel de Ville where it was only remotely possible that Daniel waited for me. I decided to go home. What I really hoped was that by some miracle Daniel would be waiting for me at the Rohan Courtyards gate, Joli at his side. He had never been to the Courtyards and I had never invited him, but I remembered that on more than one occasion I had talked to him about the cul de sac they formed in the Saint-Germain area. I comforted myself by remembering that he and Joli had been to nearby Boulevard Saint-Germain with me on several occasions as I mapped out future demolition areas and I had spoken of the area as my neighborhood. On my way to Rue du Jardinet, worry took over and I told myself I was being silly to think Daniel would be waiting for me. Something terrible had happened to him. A hundred possibilities ran through my brain. He was probably hurt and lying in a ditch somewhere. Maybe he had been threatened by one of the older boys, or worst yet, perhaps someone I had expropriated that day had decided to take out their vengeance on him. Yes, that had to be it. In the morning we had been on Rue Sellier and I had talked to five families, all of them particularly resentful. I decided that if Daniel wasn't at the Courtyards gate I would go back to Rue Sellier and question everyone there. Someone had to know something. Turning from Rue l'Eperon, I raced along Rue du Jardinet. I looked into doorways and peered into shop windows. There was no sign of a boy and a dog, but as I looked ahead, in the distance I could see a dark mass at the Courtyards gate. I ran closer. It was Joli. He was alone. My heart sank. When he saw me he began to bark and wag his tail. I reached to pat his head and he quickly ran from me and onto Rue du Jardinet, circling back to where I stood and barking just as Zoe and Fleur had done at Seine-Maritime Hill when they were ready to return home.

For months, when Daniel had left me at the end of the day to return to Maison Sospire, Joli had ridden beside me in my carriage to the Hotel de Ville complex where each afternoon I returned the carriage to the stable yards and then delivered the day's inventories to Secretary Merruau while Joli waited outside. These final daily obligations completed, in good weather Joli and I took the pleasant stroll together from the Right Bank, across the footbridge to the Left Bank and Boulevard Saint-Germain, and to the turn from Rue l'Eperon to Rue du Jardinet. We had walked along the same route and made the same turns every day for months. In the colder weather and when it rained, I took Joli with me into a for-hire carriage, a treat he seemed to enjoy very much, seated proudly and looking out through the small circular windows as if he were a paying passenger. He always knew when we turned onto Rue du Jardinet. He grew animated and came to sit closer to me. Joli was an intelligent creature and now watching him as he circled on Rue du Jardinet I understood what he was doing. He loved Daniel. He was devoted to him. He knew where he was and he had come to take me to him.

With an altogether admirable ability, Joli led me along the same route we had traveled together many times. I followed, struggling to keep up as he raced ahead and occasionally looked back to be sure I was there, his dedication and strength of purpose as we rushed along a true marvel to me and one I can never forget. What a sight we must have been, a man chasing after a large black dog, crossing over a bridge and past the Cathedral of Notre Dame, running as fast as they could.

Breathless and feeling my heart would burst, it began to look as if Joli was leading me to the Hotel de Ville stable yards where he had waited for me every day. I was not entirely wrong. Once we reached the Right Bank, he led me beyond the Hotel de Ville and to the building backing onto the stable yards. It was the Police Station. Panting and whimpering, he paced back and forth at the door. Daniel had to be there. I opened the door and Joli followed me inside only to be immediately turned away by a uniformed officer. "No dogs allowed!" he said, pointing to the sign beside the door. I nodded and took Joli outside. I patted him on the head, knowing he would wait for as long as it took me to bring Daniel out to him, all night if necessary. Returning inside, I went to the Commissaire on duty and asked if a boy named Daniel Lazare was being detained.

"Yes, a boy named Daniel Lazare is here," came the response.

"I am his employer. My name is Charles Fabron," I stated.

"Daniel Lazare is in considerable trouble, Monsieur Fabron," the Commissaire stated. "There has been a theft of money and the boy is accused of stealing it. The amount is fifty francs."

"And who has filed the complaint?" I asked. The Commissaire looked through the papers on his desk.

"A Madame Lydia Roussel filed the complaint. She is a biscuit vendor," came the reply. "All is appropriately signed and witnessed."

"I would like to see the boy," I said. "Since I am his employer, I wish to question him about this matter."

A guard led me along a narrow hall and to a door which he unlocked as I waited. Daniel was seated on a wooden bench in a small windowless room. He stood when he saw me and tears began to stream down his cheeks. I went to him and hugged him close. He sobbed in my arms. "Oh, Daniel, what happened? Tell me everything."

"Monsieur Fabron. I have broken your trust in me!" he blurted out. "I know you may never forgive me, but I swear I did not steal the money they say I stole. Please say you believe me."

"Of course I believe you, Daniel, "and I know you will tell me the truth," I said as I sat on the bench beside him. "You are a good boy. I trust you and I will do all I can to help, but you must tell me exactly what happened."

Daniel's voice was shaking as he began to relate details, but despite his anxiety, his first concern was for his dog.

"What will happen to Joli if I must stay here? When the police took me away I couldn't give him one last pat on the head the way I always do at the end of the day. I heard him barking when the doors closed behind me. Where do you think he is now?"

How pleased I was to tell this young boy that his dog deserved his loyalty; that he had known something was very wrong and that I was the one who would help. "When you left him," I explained, "Joli decided to find his way to the Rohan Courtyards where I live and where, as you know, he stays every night. He waited for me at the entrance gate and when I arrived he barked and circled again and again. He was telling me something and I knew exactly what it was. He wanted to take me to you and here I am. Joli is waiting for you outside right now," I said. "Maybe you'll be able to see him in a little while. I'll have a talk with the Commissaire and try to work something out, but Daniel, first you must tell me exactly what happened."

Clearly, Daniel was relieved to know that Joli was waiting nearby, but he was also eager to show his gratitude to me. "Monsieur, I have never had anyone speak for me," he said. Thank you for coming here to help me. You are a busy man and this is a lot of trouble, but I want to tell you everything so that no matter what happens, at least you will know the truth."

I assured Daniel that I would stand by him and do whatever I could to help him. With his typical attention to detail, he proceeded to tell me what had happened.

"I had taken your last message of the day to Franco Lessage, the supervisor on Rue Delambre and I waited while he wrote his answer. Monsieur Basse was there talking to the people on the street. You know how he is about that. Monsieur Lessage wrote his reply at the bottom of the note you had sent him, he gave it to me, and said good-bye. Just then Monsieur Basse waved and started to walk toward me. He was very nice, the way he always is, smiling and pleasant, and he gave me an envelope. He said there was a note inside. He asked if I would do him a favor and take it to Navier's Engraving Shop on the corner of Rue Lenoir. He said I was to give it to Monsieur Navier and wait for him to write an answer. I was to return the note in the envelope to Monsieur Basse on Rue Delambre and then go to meet you with the last message as I always do at the end of the day. I know now that I should never have said I would take his envelope, but Monsieur Basse is a friend of yours. He helps you. I thought I was doing the right thing. Also, Rue Lenoir wasn't so far, just two streets away, and I was sure you would approve. Did I do the wrong thing, Monsieur Fabron?"

"I don't know yet, Daniel," I answered. "Just tell me what happened next."

"I put Monsieur Basse's envelope in my trouser pocket. When I put it there, I remembered that I had been paid my Runner wages that morning. I had twenty centimes at the bottom of my pocket. I put the envelope Monsieur Basse had given me on top of my money and set off for Rue Lenoir. It didn't take long to get to Navier's. I looked at some of the engravings in the shop while I waited for Monsieur Navier to read Monsieur Basse's note and write a reply. When he had finished his reply, I put the envelope he handed me in my pocket and on my way back to Monsieur Basse I passed the biscuit vendor on Avenue d'Aubert. The pralines looked so good. I decided to buy two, one for me and one for Joli. When I reached into my pocket for two centimes to pay the vendor, I had to take out Monsieur Basse's envelope first, so I put the pralines the vendor had handed me on the edge of the cart and held the envelope in one hand while I reached for my money with the other. The vendor asked me what was in the envelope. I told her I didn't know. I was just doing a favor for a friend. "Let's see what it is!" she said, and she snatched the envelope out of my hand. She quickly tore it open and looked inside. She laughed and began to run. I ran after her. I didn't know what she had seen in the envelope, but whatever it was, I had to get it back and bring it to Monsieur Basse. Joli was running beside me and barking. People were staring. The vendor was shouting that my dog and I were chasing her because I was trying to rob her. She was waving the envelope high up into the air for everyone to see. It was only then that I realized the envelope I had been carrying from Monsieur Navier's must contain money. "Police! Police!" The woman was shouting. The police did not come right away. The woman turned into the dark alley behind Rue Sellier. She thought she could hide there, but I know that alley. You and I had worked near there the day before and I knew where she would be. I found her. She was hiding behind a big pile of rubble. I saw the envelope in her hand. I snatched it away from her the way she had snatched it away from me and I began to run. I thought I had saved the money or whatever was in the envelope for Monsieur Basse, but the police came and caught me. They held me by my collar. Joli was growling at them and showing his teeth. One of the policemen took out his bat and was about to strike Joli. I told Joli to run. He did, and maybe that's when he ran to your house, Monsieur Fabron.

"What questions did the police have for you after Joli ran off?" I asked. "Did you tell them about being in Navier's shop? Tell me exactly what happened with the police."

"There were two policemen," Daniel replied. "One of them asked me why I had stolen the money. I told him I did not steal any money. I also said I didn't know that there was money in the envelope, only a note I was supposed to take to Monsieur Basse. I said that the woman who sold me the pralines had snatched the envelope out of my hand and that when she saw money in it, she ran. I also said that when I found her hiding on Rue Sellier I snatched the envelope with the money back and began to run away from her. The money and the envelope were not hers. She had robbed them from me. When I began to run, the woman chased me, calling me a thief and shouting for the police. When they came, she told them I had stolen the money from her. I tried to explain it wasn't true, that she was lying, and that she had stolen from me, but the police didn't believe me. They believed her. Before I was brought to this room the second policeman asked me where I lived and the names of my parents. I told them I had no parents and that I lived at Maison Sospire. The policeman smiled and left me alone here. Monsieur Fabron, I promise you, I did not steal the money. I have never stolen anything in my life. What will happen to me now? I'm afraid. Why didn't the police believe me? Is it because I'm an orphan?"

"Of course you're afraid, Daniel," I said. "I would be afraid too if I had been accused of stealing and the police had chased me, but being an orphan shouldn't matter. I will do all I can to straighten this out. It may take a while. In the meantime I want you to stay calm. Try to rest. I'll see about a cot and some blankets. One more thing, Daniel. Was anyone else in Samuel

Navier's shop when you arrived there, perhaps one or two customers who could tell the police they saw you?"

"No, Monsieur, no customers were in the shop. Only Monsieur Navier."

My first thought was that Samuel Navier had lied. He had told me that no boy fitting Daniel's description had been to his shop that day. He had also told me there were so many customers in his shop that afternoon that he had no time to relieve himself in the alley. Daniel had said no one was in the shop but Navier. I believed that he had indeed been to Navier's with a note from Marc Basse. Marc himself had said he had asked Daniel to deliver a note. From what Daniel had told me and there being an issue of fifty francs, I also believed that Navier had very likely placed that sum of money in the envelope which Daniel was to return to Basse on Rue Delambre. But why? Why was Samuel Navier sending fifty francs to Marc Basse? And why was he lying about it?

I left Daniel and went to talk to the Commissaire on duty. I explained the circumstances and requested an immediate release. The Commissaire was not favorably inclined. From behind his desk he told me that unless a bond was posted and a qualified French citizen assumed responsibility for a juvenile like Daniel, he was to be held until the hearing date which was a full two weeks away. I said I would post the bond and that I would assume full responsibility for the boy. I was told that if my request was granted I must keep him in my supervised custody until the date of the hearing. With Baron Haussmann as my reference I showed my impressive Hotel de Ville credentials signed by Baron Georges- Eugene Haussmann, Prefect of the Seine. The necessary paper work took more than an hour, but after paying the bond of 100 francs with a bank note I was given full custody of Daniel. Only one barrier stood in the way. Daniel would not be allowed to pursue employment of any kind until he was cleared, which meant that he could no longer function as my Runner. What was I to do with him? I had daily responsibilities. He would be at home with me at night. That was fine, but I couldn't leave him alone all day with nothing to do while I was working, and I couldn't expect my neighbors Claire or Henri Villard to look after him. They had a store to run and a life of their own. Once again, though, and with unfailing understanding, the Villards were there for me.

Over time I had talked about Daniel with them. They knew that of all the Runners I had employed that he was the most reliable and effective. They were also aware of my regard for Daniel, but by then, of course, they knew exactly who Daniel was and like all the others, they said nothing to me.

I never asked Claire or Henri when they had learned the truth about Daniel, but I was living in a world of expertly executed deception, its confidential boundaries so artfully constructed that there was never the slightest lapse or error. In my heart I know now that those involved thought they were doing the right thing. Loyalty and love were at the heart of it all, but the circumstances, the timing, the opportunities presented to me could not have been planned any better. It was a masterful scheme: Baron Haussmann's letter enticing me to Paris, Claire meeting me at the station, talking nonstop and racing through the Gare du Nord, giving me no opportunity whatsoever to tell her I had changed my mind about Paris and that I wanted to return to Rouen on the very next train. Then there was her consummate skill in rushing me through the crowd and out to the carriage, all the while chatting about Baron Haussmann's fine plans as I struggled to keep up with her. And there was Henri waiting in the carriage, ready to signal the driver to immediately pull away as soon as my luggage was secured and I was seated beside him. I remembered having thought at the time that it had felt like a kidnapping, which indeed it was, every detail carefully thought through; every possibility explored in order to do one thing: keep me in Paris.

It would be months before I put all the pieces together, but as Daniel faced his legal challenges, more of life itself had yet to be lived and I remained blissfully ignorant. I realize now that knowing the truth would have changed our lives radically just then, Daniel's and mine. Fortunately, for the time being it was Claire who solved the daytime problem I faced with Daniel.

"I could use a little vacation," she said in the charm of her dining room as I explained my daytime dilemma concerning Daniel. "I'll look after him during the day. It's only two weeks until the hearing. Henri and Simone can handle the store and Lily will help after school. Charles, don't worry about a thing. We'll manage very well. I'll give Daniel all my attention. We'll read and talk and have lunch together every day. I can teach him some card games and although I've never played backgammon, we can learn it together. We have a backgammon table at the store. I'll take Daniel there and ask one of the students who comes in and plays almost every day to come and tutor us. It will be fun. Plan on coming here to dinner often for the next two weeks. We'll all make the best of a difficult situation. Lily will help. Don't worry. It will be fine, and in case Daniel wants to rest or just be alone for a while in the afternoon, I think I'll make up the small bedroom next to ours. The third floor rooms you were in are too far removed from the household's daily life for a young boy. I don't want him to feel lonely. He has enough to deal with."

Enough to deal with indeed! Daniel certainly had his cross to bear, but Claire could have been referring to me. Most days I hardly knew which way to turn. The fate of the Rohan Courtyards hung in the balance, despite Marc Basse's assistance my daily work continued ever more demanding, Daniel was in legal trouble and depending on me, I wasn't sure how to handle his situation with Baron Haussmann or my colleagues, and a new individual had come into my life. Inspector Hugo Valois was investigating Daniel's alleged crime. He visited us on the evening following Daniel's release into my care. He spent more than an hour asking question after question and by the time he had left there was no doubt in my mind. We needed a lawyer. Inspector Valois had listened to Daniel's story with close attention, but at the conclusion of his visit, as I showed him to the door, he said, "Monsieur Fabron, these orphan boys are all the same. They can't be trusted. I've been dealing with them for years. They learn to lie and steal at an early age and it becomes a way of life. This boy is fortunate to have you on his side. I'm sorry to say it will not make a difference. He may not have had much of an identity before all this happened, but he'll have one by the time his hearing is over."

"But Inspector Valois," I insisted, "Daniel Lazare has been nothing but reliable and honest as my Runner. We spend a great deal of time together. There have been no missteps, no breaches of trust. I can give you a list of supervisors who will provide glowing references. Everyone likes him and trusts him. Right now he may not have much of an identity as you say, but he has the potential to make an honest one for himself. I wish you would at least try to see that potential in him. "

"Monsieur Fabron, it's nice to see someone taking an interest in a troubled boy. It's a fine thing you're doing, taking him into your home and supporting him, but unless you can produce solid evidence that he did not steal the money at issue here, he's headed for a prison term."

"That's exactly it, Inspector," I continued to insist. "There is convincing evidence. Samuel Navier told me the same thing he must have told you: that he did not see a boy in his shop on the day in question and that he received no note from Marc Basse. There's a message box in his store. If he steps out for a while, messages can be left there. He says he was so busy with customers that he didn't step out of his shop at all that day, not even to relieve himself in the alley. He insists that the message box remained empty and that no boy delivered a note to him from Marc Basse. Inspector, Navier is lying. Daniel insists no one came into the shop while he was there, but the fifty francs you found in Daniel's hands had to come from somewhere. If not from Navier, where would the boy have gotten it? And where would the vendor, Lydia Roussel, get fifty francs? The biscuit vendor business must be very good. Perhaps I should look into it myself. Inspector, it is entirely possible that Samuel Navier did put money and a replying note into the envelope for Daniel to return to Marc Basse. It is also entirely possible, as Daniel says, that when he stopped to buy two of her pralines, Lydia Roussel snatched the envelope away from him, saw the money inside, decided to keep it for herself and ran, shouting "Thief, Thief," just as the boy says. Don't you see? Lydia Roussell is the thief, not Daniel Lazare!"

"No, Monsieur Fabron, I'm afraid I don't see," Valois said. "What I do see is a boy who has told a good story. Monsieur, consider this: Daniel Lazare may not have stolen the money from Samuel Navier at all. He may have stolen it from someone else. I agree with you that it is a goodly amount of money. Perhaps the boy is a talented pickpocket. That's a common thing with these orphans. We see it all the time. Some of them are fine actors too. When we catch up with them they put on the most innocent, angelic faces while telling their sad stories. They should be on the stage. Now, Monsieur Fabron, I must be going. My wife is making a tarte-tatin for me and she will not like it if I'm not at home to enjoy it. You understand. She makes a really delicious tarte-tatin. The apples are from La-Roche-Guyon. They're really delicious. It's that apple region near Gisor. I love the cider they make there."

Later that evening, when we were alone in the study, Daniel expressed concern for the future. "I'll never be able to go back to Maison Sospire," he said. "Even if I'm cleared at the hearing there will be suspicious boys who will taunt me, attack me, and try to force me out. Madame Duclos is kind but even she may wonder about me."

The days passed interminably, and although my work continued at its usual pace my thoughts were with Daniel and the approaching hearing. Providing the only comfort was Claire Villard who was handling the daytime hours with Daniel very well. He seemed to like the routine and everyone in the Villard family. Lily and he had become good friends, and in the late afternoons as I arrived home I often saw them walking through the Courtyards with Joli. Not too surprisingly, it was Lily who always seemed to be the one doing the talking.

———◈———

There were as many lawyers in Paris as there were bankers. I didn't know where to start in finding someone to help Daniel. I couldn't seek the advice of The Baron or my colleagues at the Hotel de Ville. I had taken on personal responsibility for a Runner, a young orphan boy who should have been treated with the same cool detachment as any of his fellow Runners. I had let things go too far with Daniel and now I was left with the consequences. I needed the advice of someone I could trust. Several options explored and quickly discounted, I decided to call on the only lawyer I knew. He was someone I trusted implicitly. He didn't live in Paris, but he had known me since birth. I sent a message to my father in Rouen. He was in his late fifties. He was healthy and robust and he still practiced law.

I met his train at the Gare de Lazare, impressed as I always was by his appearance. Stepping onto the platform with the confident air of the intelligent, distinguished gentleman he was, a black leather briefcase clutched tightly under his arm, his dark suit was impeccably tailored, his shoes glistening, the crown of his black felt hat creased straight down the middle, in the current fashionable style. I had forgotten how tall he was, but I hadn't forgotten his warmth and the love I knew he held for me.

"My son, you look very well," he said as he hugged me. "Don't worry. We'll straighten everything out. I'll just need some time to review things and decide how to proceed. First, I want to know how everything is going in Paris with you these days. I want to hear every small detail. Have you been enjoying the theater? The opera?"

Father had just arrived and I didn't have the heart to explain that I had precious little time for evening entertainments and that I was lucky to make it to the weekly dinners at Cardon's. I simply smiled and nodded and saw to his luggage.

I had prepared one of the upstairs bedrooms for him. He seemed pleased with the arrangements and especially with the assistance of indispensable Natalia. She unpacked for him, shared the more colorful historic details about the Rohan Courtyards, and made it clear that he must tell her which cheeses, fruits and vegetables were his favorites and whether he preferred duckling to rabbit.

Daniel had been with me for four days when Father joined the household. I couldn't help but notice that at first meeting Daniel was visibly tense. He stepped back and stared at Father when I introduced him. I thought that was odd. I had never seen Daniel uncomfortable when meeting new people but he knew exactly why Father was there with us and I attributed his unusual behavior to his understanding that if a lawyer was advising us, he was in serious trouble. As I might have expected, Father was his usual professional but disarming self. By the time the three of us were seated together in the study he was engaging Daniel in casual conversation.

"I understand you have a fine dog there," Father remarked, lighting a cigarette and smiling to Joli who sat at Daniel's side. "Charles has always liked dogs. We always had them when he was growing up and I'm sure he's told you about the two spaniels he had at his home in Rouen. They were the most energetic dogs you can imagine, always wanting to go for walks and run through the woods. It's hard to keep up with dogs like that. I like quieter dogs, more like Joli. Of course he must get lots of exercise keeping up with you all day. I imagine he just wants to sit or go to sleep when he's in the house here."

Daniel laughed and soon relaxed, affectionately patting Joli on the head as he told his story. When Father questioned him on particular details he remained remarkably calm, but of course Father was an expert at immediately getting to the heart of things.

"I wish you could be spared the exposure of a hearing," he said as Daniel finished telling his story. "You're just a boy, but the law must be followed and unfortunately the amount of money involved makes the incident serious. A theft of less than fifty francs is considered a petty theft in France. The slightly more than fifty francs at issue in this case establishes a higher level of criminality. Fortunately, the hearing process is simple enough and Daniel, keep in mind, this is not a trial and no penalties have been set. It is just a hearing, an inquiry to determine what happened, who was involved, and whether the evidence supports moving on to a trial. After you state your name and take the oath to tell the truth you will be asked to tell your entire story. Take your time and tell what happened just as you've told it to me. Following that, a few questions may be asked. Remember that I will be there to support you at every step of the way and that I will speak out to the presiding justice if and when I feel you are being misdirected. I may also be allowed to call witnesses. I don't think it will take very long. On our side it's just a matter of getting Samuel Navier to admit that he placed the money in the envelope and gave it to you. Perhaps he just forgot, or perhaps he believes you came in on another day, not the one in question. Busy shopkeepers can be confused from time to time. There is always so much to do. Then we must get Lydia Roussel, the vendor who signed the complaint against you, to admit she snatched the envelope out of your hand, saw the money in it, and ran, attracting attention to you by shouting that she had been robbed when in fact she had done the robbing. That will be the hard part. Daniel, you say a Monsieur Marc Basse started all this when he asked you to deliver a note to Samuel Navier? I'll want to talk to Monsieur Basse. Do you know him well?"

"Monsieur Basse is Monsieur Fabron's field assistant," Daniel answered. "There is so much to be completed every day that Monsieur Basse was brought in to help. Most times he takes one side of the street and Monsieur Fabron takes the other."

I explained to Father that Marc assisted me with expropriations. Realizing that he wished to pursue specific details concerning Marc's authority, I suggested to Daniel that he take Joli out to the garden for a while.

"I have a book to return to Lily Villard," he said. "It's about America. Lily says she wants to go to America someday."

Lily Villard had been bringing books from the store to Daniel. I had overheard bits of their conversations regarding a character or two of particular interest. There was Jean-Maurice in Heart of Stone, the story of a lonely boy with no friends. There was Isabella in The House of My Aunt, the comical tale of a dreadfully forgetful aunt and her seven cats, and there was what had sounded like a favorite: Life in America, an Illustrated Panorama of America and the Lives of its Early Settlers. As Father and I began to discuss Daniel's dilemma, it pleased me to know that Lily was encouraging Daniel's reading skills. Of course I had no doubt that she would be taking on the role of tutor and that Daniel would profit greatly from her maddening but well-intended attention to detail. With Daniel safely occupied, Father was, as usual, eager to get on with things.

"Does Marc Basse handle money?" he asked as soon as we heard the garden door being closed.

"No, he doesn't. He estimates values of a property and its contents and he writes a voucher which he gives to the property owner for the amount he has estimated. The voucher can be cashed in for its full amount at any one of a number of city exchange booths across the city."

"Then do I understand correctly that it is entirely up to him to determine what a house and its contents are worth?"

"Yes, that's correct. There are guidelines and laws to follow, of course, but Marc is well-qualified to determine values, especially when it comes to household contents. I trust him. He comes from a family who bought and sold high quality furniture, paintings, and decorative items such as clocks and porcelains. For a time they did a healthy business at several locations here in Paris. Marc knows what he's doing. He's been a great asset to me."

Father rose from his chair and walked toward the window. I went to stand beside him.

"It's a fine day, Charles," he said looking out to the garden. "Not a cloud in the sky. What was the weather like on the day all this bad business started? Do you remember?"

"Cloudy, rain showers off and on all day, a bit cool," I answered. "I remember because as Joli and I arrived at the Police Station there was a sudden downpour. Joli quickly found a dry place under a corner of the overhang and I was glad to get inside. Why do you ask?"

"Oh, I was just wondering," came the reply as Father clasped his hands and tapped his index fingers, one against the other. "People can do odd things when they're caught in the rain, but I'm also wondering what happened to the note Marc Basse says he wrote to Navier. Daniel was instructed to return it to Marc in its original envelope and the boy says he waited while Navier wrote his answer. So much is being made of the money but right now I'm more interested in the note Basse wrote and the reply he was expecting. Did Inspector Valois say anything about the note to you? Did you ask if he had found it? Did he ask if you had found it or if Daniel still had it?"

"No, Valois didn't mention the note and I didn't mention it either, but I must tell you about something that troubles me. At the Police Station in the room where he was being held, Daniel told me there were no customers in Navier's shop while he was there. He maintains that he and Navier were alone, yet when I went to see Samuel Navier, he said his shop was so busy that he had not had time to relieve himself in the alley. Father, I refuse to believe that Daniel is lying but I do think Navier has something to hide. Daniel is an honest boy. He has a good life now. He can see a good future ahead. Why would he jeopardize his chances?"

"Well now, isn't this getting interesting?" Father chuckled. "Four corners of the same piece of cloth, each corner a different color. This is why I love the practice of law! We have the accused, the accuser, the man in the middle, and the note writer, each with a variation on the same central theme. This situation gets stranger by the minute and now, the conflicting statements of whether or not there were customers in Navier's only complicates matters. If there really were one or two customers in Navier's who remember having seen Daniel handing the note to Navier and waiting for his reply we would be getting closer to the truth. With that mop of blonde hair, Daniel stands out even in the largest crowd and of course there's the dog. If Navier is telling the truth, someone in his shop that day has to remember seeing the boy. I'll talk to Samuel Navier myself and try to jostle his memory."

Father became pensive as he considered his approach. "All this could change the boy," he suddenly said to me in a near whisper. "He seems so decent. I can see you're fond him. Perhaps too fond. Charles, you don't know anything about him, where he came from, who his mother or father were. All you know is that he's an orphan. He could be.........."

"Father, please," I interrupted. "I don't care where Daniel came from or who his parents may or may not have been. It's not important to me. The boy is in trouble and I'm all he has. Now please, just help us to get through this. I'm relying on you."

"Be careful, Charles," Father warned, turning to face me. "You could end up being hurt. When this is over, if things go our way perhaps you should have Daniel assigned to someone else, or perhaps he should be sent away. Think about it."

"Sent away? No, I won't have him assigned to someone else and I won't send him away! I want him with me. He's turning fourteen this year. Runners are dismissed at that age. Some good ones have the opportunity to work as assistants to supervisors. I'm recommending Daniel for that position with me. When this is over he'll need my support more than ever. Now let's put an end to what I should and shouldn't do and attend to the matter at hand."

The next day was Sunday. When I came down to breakfast, Father was seated at the dining room table, sipping his coffee. "Good morning," he said. "The croissants are delicious. This is my second one, and the strawberry jam is perfect on them. Natalia certainly knows how to do things."

I helped myself to one of Natalia's croissants and added some sliced pears to my plate. Seated across from my father at the table, I poured a cup of coffee from the pot on the tray.

"Marc Basse kept me awake last night," Father announced, helping himself to a generous serving of Sorbonne butter. "You say his family bought and sold antiques for a time. Are they still in business?'

"No, they're not," I answered. "The way I understand it, several family members including Marc's father were involved in a scandal a few years back. Their Paris antiques business had become so successful that they expanded the company into exporting and importing. It was all going well until they were found to be dealing in illegal financial transactions across Europe. Something to do with customs misrepresentation and bank fraud. Marc was still away at school when everything went wrong."

"Could Marc's background explain why he would be sending a note to a man running an engraver's shop? Does he collect engravings? Is he an art lover?"

"I don't know, but I've thought of that too. You can ask him when you meet him. I can take you with me to Rue Taranne tomorrow morning. He'll be there."

"No, I don't want to meet him where he works. Do you know where Marc lives? We could pay him a visit. Perhaps later today. What does he usually do on Sunday afternoons? Do you know?"

I did know what Marc did on Sunday afternoons. He had told me that every Sunday afternoon he took his lady friend to see the latest developments in the New Paris. On this particular Sunday, water in the monumental Saint-Michel Fountain was being turned on for the first time. I knew Marc and his lady friend would be there. It was an auspicious occasion. Notices alerting the public had appeared in newspapers and pamphlets. A large crowd was expected to fill the square in Boulevard Sebastopol.

After a long absence and at The Baron's request, all had been forgiven and Gabriel Davioud had returned to Paris to design the Saint-Michel Fountain and facades of the new buildings around it. His work had lived up to expectation. It had required the work of several sculptors to create the commanding bronze figures, but when finished, Haussmann's New Paris had one of its most spectacular artistic achievements. I was thrilled for Davioud. The Saint-Michel was the last of the monumental wall fountains created in the Haussmann years and it dazzled with heretofore unincorporated materials in a variety of colors, its heroic Corinthian columns of stunning rose marble, its scale once again in keeping with Davioud's talent for proportion, its location concealing the end of an unsightly building hardly a challenge for the prodigal son's return to the Hotel de Ville's creative fold. The Saint-Michel is another of the Paris landmarks I must visit whenever I am in the city. I stand in the square, awed by the unfailing impact made by the powerful composition, the bronze statue of the comely, winged Saint-Michel standing triumphant over the conquered Devil who writhes at his feet. I smile, thinking that the depiction is perhaps not too far-fetched a reflection of what Davioud's triumphant return to The Baron's circle may have felt like.

Marc Basse was there at the Saint-Michel debut. He and his lady friend had arrived early enough to be standing at the front of the crowd. I spotted them but they were difficult to reach. People were squeezed close together and protective of their places in the unusually large crowd. I didn't want to risk the probability of sharp words or quite possibly a fight, which was known to occasionally happen. Not everyone who attended the fountain debuts looked favorably on their addition to the Paris scene.

It was not until the fountain had successfully established itself as fully operational that the crowd began to disperse and I was able to see Marc and his pretty companion coming our way. "Well, what a nice surprise!" he said as the pair approached us. We made introductions all around and apparently pleased with the company, Marc suggested we go to the Café Gibert for refreshments. Compliments abounded on Gabriel Davioud's Saint-Michel masterpiece and so detailed was the conversation that I made no mention of the reason for my father's visit.

"Sadly, Patrice must leave us to visit her mother," Marc said as the attractive Patrice squeezed his arm and said good-bye. "She's an only child and a devoted daughter," Marc said, watching her disappear into the Sunday afternoon throng on the boulevard. Seeing Patrice readily absorbed into the city's activity I couldn't help but notice that the Paris citizenry was out and about in greater and greater numbers every Sunday. It was spring, after all, but habits were changing. More than ever before, people were enjoying the outdoors. Traditional indoor Sunday luncheons were becoming family outings in the parks. By spring of 1865 picnic baskets were a common sight. Ladies were wearing wide-brimmed hats covered with colorful flowers and feathers. Children laughed and played games in the parks. They fed the pigeons and ate red and white striped peppermint sticks while the sun shone and street musicians played festive tunes. It was a forward-thinking, optimistic time and in spite of my concern for Daniel I was gratified in knowing I was part of what was making it all possible.

Father wasted no time in getting to the point with Marc once we were seated at our table in the Gibert. Marc was surprised to hear what had happened to Daniel. He was even more surprised to learn that Father was a lawyer representing him.

"I can't believe it!" he said. "Daniel accused of stealing money? That nice boy? He's so trustworthy and reliable."

Marc's disbelief was understandable. In recent days, instead of working in the same general area with me, he had begun appropriations on distant Rue Saint-Benoit. There had been no opportunity for us to discuss what had happened to Daniel and Marc would not have noticed his absence, but on the day of the incident he would have been waiting for Daniel to return to him with Navier's note along with whatever was inside the envelope. I said nothing, but I was sure that Father had not missed Marc's clear omission of that fact.

"It's a bad situation for the boy," he began, addressing Marc as our coffee and biscuits were served. "What troubles me most is that Samuel Navier told Charles that he has no recollection of Daniel coming to his shop. Don't you find that odd? I do. I can't understand it, can you?"

"It could be that Daniel is lying," Marc offered. "He could have stolen the money. Perhaps he picked the pocket of an unsuspecting tourist on the street. I know that must sound completely out of character, but we don't know what's in the minds of these orphans and runaways. They're used to life alone on the street. They have no one to answer to, no one to set a good example. Their goal is self-preservation and when it comes to survival they know how to grasp an opportunity. It could be that Daniel has done exactly that."

I bristled at Marc's assessment. Daniel had been nothing but friendly and helpful to him and he wouldn't have found himself in this situation if

Marc had not asked him for a personal favor. Father saw my sudden dismay and skillfully changed the direction of the conversation, turning Marc's attention to the issue that bothered him most: the note he had given Daniel.

"Marc, as I understand it, you gave a note to Daniel to be delivered to Samuel Navier. I don't want to intrude on your affairs, but a good boy is in trouble. We should help him, don't you agree? Did you give Daniel a note for Navier, and did you expect him to return both the note and some money to you?"

"Yes, I did," Marc answered, looking directly into Father's eyes. "In my note I asked Navier for a refund on an engraving I had purchased from him. It had turned out to be a fraud. I had it appraised and was told it was worthless. I not only asked Navier for a refund, I asked for a note of explanation which I expected Daniel would bring to me. Can you imagine the nerve of people trying to cheat good customers?"

"The world certainly is changing," Father confirmed in agreement. "In my day, a man's word was everything. For me it still is. I'm glad to hear the same is true of you, and as I've said to Charles, don't worry. We'll work all this out for Daniel and I know you'll want to help."

The three of us sat in the Café Gibert, our conversation touching on a variety of topics, Marc smoking cigarettes, Father and I smoking pipes, my thoughts not too far away at all from a troubled boy and a man named Marc Basse whose loyalties I now doubted, but at least Marc had supported part of Daniel's story. He said he had indeed sent a note to Samuel Navier through Daniel, but now the question loomed as to why Samuel Navier had hidden the fact that Marc was requesting a refund for an engraving. There was nothing nefarious about a request for a refund on an engraving. Why would Navier lie about it? And what had happened to the return note Marc had been expecting from Navier?

The dreaded morning finally arrived. We were due in the Police Station hearing room at ten o'clock. It was a Wednesday. As usual I was awake early. Dawn was just beginning to break. I thought to look in on Daniel. I hoped he was still asleep. It would be a difficult day for him. There was no telling what he would be going through. Father would be there and I would be there, but so would Inspector Valois and likely Samuel Navier and Lydia Roussel. Daniel would need to be relaxed and well rested. He had told his story over and over again. If he told it as well as I had heard it, he would sound convincing and sincere. I slowly opened the door to his room and looked inside, toward the bed. The light was dim, but bright enough for me to see that the sheets and blankets were neatly arranged and that Daniel was not lying under them. Joli was not curled up asleep on the floor beside him. I walked into the room and quickly glancing around me I saw that the dresser was cleared of the few personal items it had recently held: a hair brush, a bar of soap, a towel and a box of nougats. I opened the drawers. They were empty. I had bought some clothes for Daniel, a few shirts, a jacket and sweater, and two pairs of trousers. Everything was gone. There was nothing to indicate that a boy and his dog had occupied the room at the end of the hall for several days. My heart started to pound. I could feel the blood pulsating through my veins. I had to sit down. I reached the edge of the bed and sat there like a stone. It was like re-living the terrible hours I had spent in the room where Louisa had died. It was the same feeling of emptiness; the same feeling of loss, but this was the loss of a real, breathing boy. Daniel was alive somewhere but he was afraid, so afraid that he had run away, so afraid that even my support wasn't enough. I tried to imagine where he might have gone but my mind was a blur. I thought to search the rest of the house but I knew it was useless. Daniel was gone. He had dreaded the hearing. He had feared he would not be believed and he was probably right. Even if he was cleared, he had known what a return to Maison Sospire might mean. Suspicion and attacks would follow him and make his life miserable. I clenched my fists, took deep breaths, rose to my feet, and walked to Father's room. The door was ajar. He was already awake, seated at the desk by the window in his robe, reading through his notes. One look at me told him what had happened.

"Oh, Charles. Its Daniel, isn't it. Is he gone? I worried that something like this could happen," he said as I nodded my head. "I didn't want to mention it to you but I could see it was all getting to be too much for the boy. You probably saw it too. He was withdrawing more and more into himself every day. I'm so sorry."

There it was again. Someone telling me he was sorry when sorry wasn't enough. Doctor Mercier's words were ringing in my ears just as they had in Rouen when he had calmly said, "these things happen."

"We must go immediately to the Commissaire and inform him," Father said quietly. "Be prepared. He will set the wheels in motion for a search. This house will be searched from top to bottom, as will every other house here in the Rohan Courtyards. And Charles, you assumed full responsibility for the boy. The authorities will believe you assisted Daniel in his escape. Fortunately there are those of us who can at least try to convince the authorities that you and Daniel were here all night. Last evening I was here in the house, Natalia was here, and the Villards came for a visit at about eight o'clock. They didn't stay long, but you and I were in Daniel's company all evening, offering whatever encouragement we could. He seemed resigned and well prepared by the time he said good-night. We agreed on that. One more thing, though: you may be watched for a while, but I don't think anything more will come of it. These situations have a way of fading quickly. Daniel's alleged crime involves a fair amount of money but certainly not enough to arouse much public attention."

It was exactly as Father had said it would be: the house searches, the suspicion, the questioning, the label of guilt attached to me and to a boy who had fled rather than face the ordeal of a hearing and very likely a trial and imprisonment. I apologized to my neighbors. I cooperated with every interview and maintained my position in having no knowledge of Daniel's whereabouts, but in my heart I was glad he had run away, glad he had been wise enough to realize the odds were against him. I prayed for him. I fell to my knees and bowed my head in La Madeleine, in Notre Dame, in Saint-Sulpice. I lit candles in the Church of Saint-Germain des Pres. Watching them flame up I prayed Daniel would be strong. I prayed he would elude the authorities. I prayed he would find a place where he could be safe and face the future without fear. I prayed that Joli would protect him and warn him of danger. I prayed that one day I would find him. Daniel was fourteen years old. He had been with me for three years.

Time passed; days, weeks, a month. Daniel was not found and he did not return. Inspector Valois came to see me once more, watching me closely as I answered his questions, testing me again and again to assure himself that I had not engineered Daniel's escape. Every day many people connected to the Haussmann project kindly asked about the boy with yellow hair. "Is he ill? Where is he? I haven't seen him in days." Every day I tried to imagine where he could have gone. I considered dozens of possibilities. He had been fascinated by my talk of England. Perhaps he had made his way to the Normandy coast and had found a place for himself as a cabin boy on a packet ship crossing the Channel to Dover. Once on English soil, perhaps he had been able to make his way to London where he could disappear into the anonymous swirling crowds. But no, the language barrier would make life too difficult. He was somewhere in France. He had to be. Perhaps he had changed his name and found work. He was resourceful and strong. And so it went, my musings endless, my admiration for Daniel's courage a cause for secret rejoicing.

Father stayed on for another week. He accompanied me to several demolition sites and was especially interested in the process of appropriation. He was fascinated by the fact that efforts were made to re-settle the dispossessed. I was rather proud to say that as hundreds of square miles were added to the city's geography, creating new suburban towns and villages, the dispossessed were encouraged to begin new lives in them, the many factories manufacturing a wide variety of goods providing numerous employment opportunities. I enjoyed my father's company during the time we spent together. Our love and regard for one another was reinforced in the simplest range of activity. As my time allowed, we strolled through new parts of the city, Father marveling at the blocks of apartment buildings and landscaped parks and sharing in the public's delight at the inauguration of several fountain dedications. We both avoided talking about Daniel, but like any concerned parent Father found occasions on which to offer me assurances. His words changed with each iteration, but they always meant the same thing.

"It's for the best," he said repeatedly. "Charles, you were too attached to the boy. I could see it. Now he's gone and you shouldn't worry about him. He's intelligent and self-reliant. He'll find his way. You must forget this episode and you must forget him. It's in your best interest."

In the next months I didn't forget Daniel. I couldn't, but I also couldn't allow myself to fall victim to despair again. I knew all too well what it could do to me. Slowly, but surely, I fought my way through and added Daniel to the place deep down where I kept my memories safe and uncompromised. I applied myself to my work with fresh determination, always hoping that by some miracle Daniel would appear at one of my worksites, Joli at his side. I attended the Cardon dinners every Tuesday without fail. I acquired a series of new Runners. I never talked to them at length, never cared about them. They were Runners. Nothing more.

Daniel had been gone for three months when during one of the Cardon dinners our waiter brought me a note. I excused myself and quickly glanced at it. The name Diana was written across the folded sheet of paper, and an address. 44 Rue Rigaud. I placed the note in my breast pocket and continued at dinner. Later, I said good-night to my companions, hailed a carriage, and directed the driver to 44 Rue Rigaud. It was a longer drive than I had expected. Crossing the Seine to the Right Bank, we continued along Rue Saint Gervais and finally turned onto a cobblestone street. It was a neighborhood of modest but large houses. Gas lanterns lined the streets. At Number 44 we stopped at a three-story house set farther back from the street than its neighbors. Candlelight shone out from all the windows on the first floor. I paid the driver and as I stepped onto the narrow walk I heard voices. It sounded as if a celebration of some kind was in progress. Answering my knock, the door was opened by an attractive, dark-haired woman. I introduced myself. The woman smiled, nodded her head and said, "I have been expecting you, Monsieur Fabron. I am Diana. Please come in."

I was led inside through a hall and into a large room where, as I had surmised, a party or gathering of considerable size was in progress. Clusters of men and women held glasses of champagne. They chatted and occasionally nuzzled one another. Some kissed and embraced. Some climbed the stairs arm in arm. The air smelled of gardenias and cigarette smoke. Diana took my arm and gestured to a sofa in a quiet corner. "I have something to show you, Monsieur," she said. "Excuse me for just a moment."

She disappeared through a draped doorway and in the background I heard a dog barking. I knew that bark. I had heard it many times before. In seconds, through the draped doorway came a large curly-haired black dog.

He ran toward me, his tail wagging. He jumped up on the sofa and licked my cheek again and again in a great show of affection.

"Ah, I see you and Joli are old friends," Diana said, smiling. "It's just as Daniel said it would be if you came," she added, opening a gold case and offering me a cigarette before taking one herself.

"Is he here?" I asked as I struck a match and lit our cigarettes, Joli watching my every move. "If Joli is here, Daniel must be here too. I want to see him. I have been so worried about him."

"No, Monsieur, Daniel is far away from here," Diana said slowly blowing a puff of smoke into the air, "but he wanted you to know he is alright. He told me you would be at The Cardon on a Tuesday evening. He asked me to contact you there. He hoped you would take Joli and care for him. He could not take the dog with him. I confess I have taken a liking to the creature, but he has not taken a liking to me or to this house. He's restless during the day and he whimpers at night. He disturbs our guests. You understand."

"Yes, of course, but where has Daniel gone? Surely you know. Please tell me."

"Monsieur Fabron, Daniel does not want to be found. He was here until last week but when he left he made me me promise not to tell you or anyone else where he was going. I myself am not sure where he is exactly, but I do know that this is no place for a boy like him. I was glad he came to me when he needed a safe place. I was happy to help him, but you can see what this house is. Monsieur Fabron, I earn a good living here. I take good care of my people and I have a good life, but I wanted Daniel to leave as soon as possible. He's an intelligent boy with ideas and an imagination. He will make something of himself. I have no doubt of it. Since I can see you are concerned about him, I will tell you this: I made arrangements for him with a fine gentleman who is a frequent guest here. He comes to Paris three or four times a year to buy paintings and he spends many of his evenings here. Please do not ask me what those arrangements are or who the gentleman is. I promised Daniel I would keep his confidence and I will keep that promise. Just know that the boy is safe and well. He has clothes and money with him. I saw to that, but it might interest you to know that before he left, I cut his hair. He looked into my mirror and said he liked what I had done. I thought he looked very handsome. Monsieur Fabron, I have never had a son of my own, but if I had, I would want him to be exactly like Daniel."

Diana smiled the smile of a kindly, loyal friend and I realized this was the same woman named Diana who Daniel had said he had met in a train station on his way to Paris just after he had run away from the orphanage. He had followed the train tracks from La Bouille, intending to walk all the way to Paris. I reminded myself that waiting in one of the stations, the woman he called Diana had struck up a conversation with him. She had bought him a ticket to Paris and had taken him to what she called her boarding house.

"But is Daniel still in Paris?" I asked, anxious for any word at all. "Tell me at least that."

"No, Monsieur, he is not in Paris. That much I can tell you, but as I said, I myself am not sure of his exact whereabouts. He has not written to me and I don't expect him to, but I have every confidence that all is well. He is with someone you would approve of. Don't worry."

"Did he leave a message for me?"

"No Monsieur, no message other than that he hoped you would look after Joli. I really think he wants you and me and everyone else he knew here in Paris to forget about him, and perhaps that is best."

"Daniel told me about you, Diana," I said, recalling Daniel's burning desire to somehow get to Paris, even if he had to walk all the way. "He told me a nice woman named Diana bought him a ticket to Paris and that after spending a few weeks at her boarding house she sent him to Marie Duclos at Maison Sospire. Why did you do send him there, Diana? Do you know Marie Duclos?"

"Monsieur, some things are best left unsaid. Let us just say that I was happy to be able to have a place where I could send Daniel just then. The situation here was inappropriate for him. Now, would you like to stay a bit longer? Perhaps a glass of sherry or champagne and some charming company? Michelle is the girl sitting alone there in the blue chair. She's lovely."

I had to agree that Michelle in the Blue Chair was indeed lovely, but I was not in the mood for female company, at least not that evening. "Thank you, Diana," I said, "but I must go. I have an early start in the morning. Thank you very much for taking care of Daniel and helping him. If you ever change your mind and decide to tell me who he is with or where he could be, please don't hesitate to do so. We never know what the future holds. Here is my card."

Over time I returned often to Number 44 Rue Rigaud. Lovely Michelle in the Blue Chair became a close friend and Diana continued to keep the promise she had made to Daniel. She was a strong-willed woman. On an occasional evening we discussed many of the day's issues as we smoked cigarette after cigarette, and no matter how cleverly I thought I was guiding the conversation toward gaining information on Daniel, she just as cleverly avoided any topic concerning his possible whereabouts.

For a time Joli seemed happy to be at home with me. He was in familiar surroundings and he was accustomed to my routine. He was with Natalia during the day as she went about her household tasks and tended the garden. She said he enjoyed chasing the rabbits and barking at the red squirrels who scampered up the trees to the highest branches, but as weeks passed, we both noticed he was growing restless. He took to waiting by the front door, hoping, we both felt, that Daniel would come through at any moment. I occasionally took him to my worksites, but he was always searching, looking, waiting. By summer his appetite for food and water began to fade. I spent extra time with him. I took him for evening walks and visits to the Villards, but I was well aware that no amount of attention could fill the great void in his life. One morning Natalia found him lying motionless by the front door where for weeks he had patiently waited for Daniel. We buried him in the garden.

Daniel turned fifteen that year. He was living more than 300 miles away from Paris.

The Basse-Navier incident and Daniel's involvement in it had faded, but its loose ends continued to nag at me. The question of what had happened to the note Navier was to have sent back to Marc Basse remained unanswered as did the mystery of the whereabouts of the last message of the day Daniel was to have returned to me which was from Franco Lessage. I assumed that neither one had been found. And there was something else to challenge my imagination. My father had asked me about the weather that day. "It was rainy and cool, showers off and on," I had told him, neglecting at the time to ask why he wanted to know about the day's weather. I wrote him a letter asking him to clarify the question. He answered by writing back that in a sudden shower people might have found Navier's shop full of engravings an interesting temporary shelter, in which case, Daniel might have been lying when he said that he and Navier were alone.

"Charles," he wrote further, "You must put this matter aside. The boy is gone and nothing will change that. Forget him. You have a good life in Paris. Pay attention to the important things and enjoy yourself. It is what your mother and I want for you. And if you're seeing an interesting woman, so much the better. If not, find one."

Any attempt I might have made to put the matter of Daniel aside as my father recommended was forgotten when Inspector Valois arrived at my door one evening with a a delicious-looking pastry in his hands.

I brought you one of my wife's famous tarte-tatins," he announced. "It comes with some interesting news."

I was quick to express my thanks for the fine dessert as I invited the Inspector in, but the suggestion of interesting news surpassed any feelings of gratitude for his gift.

"I've come with information I want to share with you," he began once we were seated in my study. "Monsieur Fabron, it appears that I was wrong about Daniel Lazare. A few days ago it was discovered that a bit of corruption has been accompanying the Haussmann Project. Your field assistant, Marc Basse has been stealing from the people he appropriates. Samuel Navier has been his accomplice. It's been going on for months. Daniel Lazare was used as an innocent messenger. It seems that Marc Basse and Samuel Navier were operating a scheme whereby vouchers from displaced property owners were being cashed in at a number of the city's exchange booths for large amounts of money. The scenario goes something like this: Marc Basse tells an appropriated property owner that he himself will be happy to cash in the voucher he has prepared, thus making the difficulty of adjusting and relocating less challenging, he says. "One less thing to do," he tells the disgruntled owner, "and I will see to it that the money is in your hands today." With his friend Samuel Navier's assistance, vouchers for much more money than the property owner will ever see are promptly cashed in at the city's exchange booths, the small amount Basse has allotted the property owner delivered back usually within hours and arousing no suspicion. Apparently, Basse was in the middle of one of his more complicated voucher transactions at the end of the day when Daniel conveniently appeared and innocently agreed to save him some time by taking an envelope to Samuel Navier on Rue Lenoir. All along Basse said he had sent a note requesting a refund on some engravings. There was no such note and there were no engravings. Daniel unknowingly delivered an envelope full of fresh vouchers to Navier who placed money he had collected on that morning's vouchers in the envelope Daniel was to return to Basse. Apparently, Navier acted in Basse's behalf at a number of different exchange booths throughout the city, helping himself to a percentage of each transaction as the two had agreed. Unfortunately, once leaving Navier's not with the note he had been told he would be returning to Basse, but with Basse's money, Daniel made the mistake of stopping at the biscuit vendor's cart to buy pralines. His problems began right there. The boy was telling the truth all along and I feel badly that my suspicions led to his disappearance, but I must add that Basse and Navier thought they were very clever. They weren't. They were careful, though, not to frequent the same booths too often, and in a few cases booth attendants themselves were in on the scheme, quickly pocketing a handy bit of cash for themselves on a regular basis, but it was one of the District Exchange Directors who brought the situation to our attention. He was noticing unusual excesses in his account columns and he asked us to look into the matter. We arranged for several of our inspectors to pose as property owners and several others to pose as booth attendants. It wasn't long before we saw that the amounts on the vouchers both Navier and Basse were presenting to our booth attendants didn't match up with the amounts Basse had quoted to the supposed property owners. They were for considerably more. We repeated the process several times. It didn't take long for the truth to emerge. The threat of prison does the most remarkable things to people."

"And what of Lydia Roussel, the biscuit vendor?" I asked. "Doesn't she bear at least some responsibility for Daniel's problems?"

"Technically she does," Inspector Valois admitted, "but we can't find her. Believe me, we've tried, and the trouble there, Monsieur Fabron, is that even if we did find her there really is no one to press charges. No one has come forward to say he or she witnessed what happened and that's what we would need. Lydia has not been at her usual corner location since the incident occurred, and of course other vendors in the area say they know nothing about her. She has probably moved on to another city or town where no one knows about her or the incident. I want you to know that this aspect of Daniel's problem has bothered me a great deal, but there is still another interesting consideration and in some ways it has made me feel better. If it were not for Lydia Roussel's actions in snatching away the envelope Daniel had in his hand and running with it, we might never have discovered the Basse-Navier scheme, but it's true that Lydia's confessed or witnessed actions along with the District Exchange Director's testimony would have created even more conclusive evidence than we already have."

I thanked Inspector Valois for his attention to Daniel's issues. I felt he had pursued things as thoroughly as he could.

"Does Baron Haussmann know about this?" I asked as we walked toward the front door.

"Oh, yes. He was informed just this morning."

"The Baron was very good to Marc Basse," I recalled aloud. "I'm sorry to know his best intentions were misplaced, but I must tell you I knew all along that Daniel was incapable of having committed any crime. He's a good boy with a good heart. Being an orphan placed him in an untenable position. I wish I knew where he was right now. I wish I could tell him what you have just told me. He has paid a terrible price for his position in life. What will happen to Marc Basse and Samuel Navier?"

"Along with their circle of accomplices whose numbers seem to grow by the hour, the law will be applied as it should," Inspector Valois replied. "Right now they are being held by the authorities. A hearing will take place next week. I expect the whole business will end in a trial. When it's over they will receive long prison terms. We're collecting solid evidence against them every day."

"Marc was very good in the field," I found myself saying. "He had so much potential. I'm sorry he has done this to himself."

"Well, Monsieur Fabron, human weakness is what I deal with every day. Theft, murder, abandonment. I sometimes wonder why I chose this line of work. It certainly isn't making me rich. Every now and then, though, I'm able to put the pieces together and find the right answers. That makes me feel good. In this case, I'm especially pleased I could come to you with a little good news."

I said good-bye to Inspector Valois with a heavy heart. He had cleared Daniel's name. I was grateful for that, but it was difficult to accept the fact that Daniel would very likely never know his story was finally believed. That evening I had no appetite for tarte-tatin. Beautiful as it was, it sat in the kitchen until the next morning and even then, it held no appeal. To this day, I will not eat tarte-tatin.

———◉———

I was called as a witness to the Basse-Navier hearings. Seeing Marc and Samuel Navier in the flesh, a mere few feet away from me was disturbing to say the least. Of course I was asked if I had known about the corruption they had fostered and the amounts of money they had pocketed. I said no, that I had no idea they were conducting a money-making scheme at the expense of people who were surrendering their property. When asked why I had accepted Marc Basse as my field assistant I knew I was adding to the evidence against him when I said that from the day of his arrival at my worksite I had found him to be exceptionally adept at dealing with those he was sent to expropriate.

At the end, both Basse and Navier were found guilty of conspiracy and theft and sentenced to long prison terms. I was left with an immense level of disappointment in myself for having allowed Marc Basse's activity to go unsupervised and I was furious with myself for having placed Daniel in a position so threatening that he had run away. It was many weeks before I could put the matter aside, but with The Baron's approval I did create a new system whereby vouchers could be cashed only with identification and at only five certified exchange booths in the city. Their managers were former bank clerks who were required to present weekly reports directly to me and following review I, in turn, submitted them to the accounting department at the Hotel de Ville. Unfortunately, even under these strict rules and with the best accounting policies possible, we could not be absolutely sure that those people presenting vouchers at certified locations were the rightful recipients of funds. The new procedures added to my responsibilities but I felt I was doing what I could to protect those persons most seriously affected by the drumbeat of progress. I may have been a poor choice for Supervisor of Demolition during the Haussmann years, but I was determined to proceed with as much integrity as possible.

In the course of several meetings and as details of Daniel's problems emerged, The Baron reassured me that I had done the right thing in supporting my Runner. His confidence in my decisions meant a great deal. "You have a reputation for being a kind person," he said during one such meeting. "I'm not at all surprised that you handled matters as you did." Thoroughly disappointed in the actions of Marc Basse, however, he memorably said, "Charles, unfortunately, the more successful our project becomes, the more opportunities we create for corruption. Tar merchants are becoming rich as our new boulevards take on their glistening surfaces. Tool makers are enjoying unprecedented prosperity as the need for more and more equipment arises, but should we arrest some of the fine craftsmen and laborers we have? Should we imprison the Italian stonecutters who are the best in the world? Should we report our suspicions at every turn?"

Corruption remained a dilemma we could not always control and we were aware of its existence in many quarters. As time passed, ever more clever schemes were devised for making money on the transformation of Paris and I can only imagine what vast amounts were secretly passed from hand to hand as the City by the Seine was perfected and beautified.

CHAPTER ELEVEN

Chambers Of Truth

1867

DANIEL HAD BEEN GONE for more than six months. I thought about him every day. He had ingrained himself so completely into my routine and for so long a time that it was impossible not to miss him. It was especially difficult not to compare each of my new Runners to him. This one was too slow. That one was too sullen. This one talked too much. That one didn't talk at all. The boys came and went, one after the other as the New Paris continued to emerge and I forced myself to concentrate on the unrelenting business of appropriation and demolition. Adding some small comfort to my ever demanding schedule, I was now working close to home, quite near the area surrounding the Abbey of Saint-Germain-des-Pres where I continued to strip away long rows of houses and shops to make way for Boulevard Saint-Germain's ongoing reconstruction. At every turn I was haunted by unknown prospects for Rue du Jardinet and the Courtyards. To complicate matters, I could not help but be reminded that it was on the Boulevard Saint-Germain and across from the blue doors of the Abbey, that Daniel had appeared at my worksite three years earlier. With a myriad of personal concerns confronting me, the Saint-Germain project became a worksite I did not look forward to facing every morning. "Plans are still developing," Deschamps said to me at one point when my patience regarding the fate of the Courtyards had reached a breaking point. "It's becoming too complicated," he added in a near whisper. "I don't like it. Now there are new issues to consider. As if we needed new issues! Charles, The Baron is not pleased, and that is an understatement. You know how he can be. First of all, Belgand wants to re-orient the whole Rue l'Eperon area for the sake of placing his underground tunnels and sewer pipes in a direct line with the main drains already in place on the boulevard at its intersection at Rue Jacob. That makes sense, but it will take weeks if not months to complete. Then there is the Emperor who has stepped in demanding a public garden in the area. Although not opposed to a garden, The Baron tells me he himself wants a commercial area with direct access from l'Eperon straight through what you know as the Rohan Courtyards which, if he has his way, will be completely cut through and destroyed. He likes the idea of a money-making project no matter the consequences, and of course he sees an opportunity for advancing another magnificent example of our architectural and landscaping expertise. He's waiting for Belgrand's plans for water distribution right now. If you hear cello music being played later today, you'll know that our Baron is still waiting and thinking and that matters have not yet been resolved. Poor Johann Sebastian Bach. He could be getting a real going over today! Charles, it's all a big muddle. I'm sorry, but that's all I can tell you. Boulevard Saint-Germain has become an enigma. I get nervous at the mere mention of its name. It's been giving me terrible headaches."

I watched Deschamps as he strolled down the hallway. Midway along he turned and said, "Of course I'll let you know as soon as I know anything new! And don't forget to listen for the music. It could be an encouraging sign."

I nodded appreciatively, disappointed by the indecision and at the same time hopeful. The Courtyards would survive for at least another day.

Along with extensions at Rue Rivoli, the Boulevard Saint-Germain was unquestionably the most important, most complicated project of the 1860's. It had been in planning stages from the beginning. Running close to the Seine and named after the Church of Saint-Germain-des-Pres, it was to extend east to west for two and one-half miles, traversed at its mid-point by Boulevard Saint-Michel and Davioud's fountain. New buildings which would line long stretches of the roadway were being designed, the area constantly surveyed and studied by a team of architects hired specifically to supervise the project. As was the case all along, the great challenge was the everyday traffic which continued to use the boulevard as a necessary thoroughfare, thus interfering with demolition and construction progress. It was one thing to efficiently clear a narrow lane in a neighborhood where traffic was limited to the occasional horse and wagon. It was quite another to deal with a daily melee of horse-drawn carriages, milk wagons, dumpcarts, and pedestrians.

The boulevard being mere minutes away from Rue du Jardinet, I was working close enough to home to be constantly reminded, as I summarily displaced scores of families, that soon I could be one of them. I had begun to think about where I would live if worst came to worst. My choices were limited. Of course, apartments were available in the new Haussmann buildings but most of them were expensive, and apart from their cost, The Baron had determined it to be inappropriate for a member of the Haussmann staff to reside in a Haussmann building. Second, the city was in such overall disarray that finding housing in a well-located existing or older apartment building that wasn't about to be torn down was next to impossible. Once again I considered going home to Rouen and re-establishing my architectural practice. In Paris I had worked hard. I had proven myself, but The Baron had never offered me an architectural opportunity and I relished the idea of designing and drawing again. I still owned the house on Seine-Maritime Hill. The lease with my tenants could be re-negotiated. I could make the hill my home again. Paris had worked its charm on me and the years had softened the pain of the past. Thoughts of Louisa and my sons no longer haunted me, and as much as I knew I would regret leaving everything I had worked so hard to accept and accomplish in Paris, a return to my native city and its familiarity held considerable appeal.

I needn't have worried about moving. I heard The Baron's distracting cello music being played only once, but I still laugh when I remember the afternoon when, as Deschamps passed me in the hall, he said not a word, but raised his eyebrows high into his forehead as loud strains of a Bach cello suite filled the potent air. Encouraging us however, a short time later organizational plans became clear. The cello music stopped and I received orders to level the area behind the farthest Courtyard walls in preparation for construction of a new commercial area and a park on Saint-Andres-des Arts. Much to my relief, no mention was made of The Rohan Courtyards. There were no instructions to begin their demolition or cut through the protective far wall to Saint-Andre des Arts. Every day I checked, and every day the Rohan Courtyards remained absent from both the Calendar and the Schedule. Deschamps provided the final stroke of encouragement when he came to me with The Baron's final decision.

"The Baron says he has no time to worry about three old courtyards and some houses at the end of an old street. He's in a hurry again," he reported with a broad smile," but his plans for a commercial area as well as what is being called The Emperor's Park behind the Courtyard walls are moving ahead, and quickly. Belgrand is creating a water system for the park and Baltard is ordering hundreds of plants and trees for a woman who has been put in charge of supervising the park's design and planting. I have no idea who she is, but as chief landscape designer on the Haussmann project, Baltard is insulted. He says this woman, whoever she is, shocked him by wearing men's trousers and tall boots at their first meeting, but he also admitted that she was ordering outstanding specimen plants. That should be an interesting relationship. I'll let you know what develops. In any case, it appears your courtyards are saved, Charles. Shall we meet later at Voisin's and celebrate?

The news was exactly what I had hoped for, but to hear it directly from Deschamps who held sway over the almighty Calendar left no doubt that three old courtyards at the end of an unimportant old street would remain untouched. I was elated. The fact that a woman in trousers had been put in charge of planning The Emperor's Park was another matter entirely. Deschamps had said he had no idea who the woman was, but of course I did. There was no question in my mind that under the auspices of the Emperor, Adele Alessandri had been assigned to create a landscaped jewel. I could only pray that as my demolition work on the area behind The Courtyards began I would not meet up with her. My prayers went unanswered. Adele was at the worksite on the very morning I arrived to plan the schedule. The former opera star who had worn an endless array of magnificent gowns and jewels was wearing brown trousers, a white shirt, boots, and a wide-brimmed brown hat. She looked stunningly beautiful.

"I hoped I would see you this morning, Charles," she called out, coming toward me with her memorable smile. "I've prepared a set of drawings showing what I want to see here in the park I'm designing. I'd like to have you look them over. You won't mind, will you? We can discuss them tonight. Come for dinner. Eight o'clock. You remember the address."

Dear Adele. It was as if no time had passed and nothing had changed. More than ten years after our affair the diva was as presumptuous as ever. I didn't take the drawings she tried to hand me. "Adele, I have plans for this evening," I said. "It's Tuesday, and every Tuesday I meet with a group of friends for dinner. I'm also married," I lied, as I had learned to do in a number of situations where a statement of marital attachment rescued me from unwanted entanglements. "Now, if you will excuse me, I have work to do. I'm sure your drawings are quite perfect. I would expect nothing less."

"Ah! Married! And who is the bride? Do I know her?" Adele persisted.

"No, you wouldn't know her. She doesn't travel in your circles!" I snapped.

"I imagine she's lovely, wise, and endlessly attentive too?"

"Adele, yes, my wife is all those things and I will not discuss my private life with you. Now, is there anything else?"

I wanted to get away, far away from reminders and feelings I didn't trust, but there was no escaping those riveting emerald green eyes. "Don't put me off, Charles," she said, coming closer, her smile quickly vanished.

"Your marriage has nothing to do with this project. I want things to go well here and you can help me with the necessary survey of available land. Baron Haussmann himself suggested I talk to you about it."

"I'll be happy to conduct a survey," I said, unable to avoid facing her. "It's usually a requirement of my assignment once demolition is completed, so it will be no trouble at all."

"Wonderful!" she said, "but I'll need to have you review your findings with me. Surely you agree that before planting begins I should be informed of any irregularities in the land. I've ordered some exotic plants. They'll require special placement."

"I don't foresee any insurmountable irregularities," I interrupted, "but I'll be here every morning for at least the next week. If you decide to come and study the site, any questions you might have can be answered right here, right then."

The old jousting had begun. I recognized it. I could feel it. The long-quieted confrontational air had been stirred up between us. Despite the years that had passed between us, Adele Alessandri was prepared to raise the dust and have it settle her way.

"I know what you're doing, Charles," she said, her voice just above a whisper, "and I don't blame you for treating me this way. I behaved very badly that last night we were together. Wasn't it shortly before Christmas, just after my farewell concert? Whenever it was, you have every right to be as cold and distant with me as you are right now, but all that that was a long time ago. I'd like to have the chance to explain. And aren't you the least bit interested in what I've been doing with myself in all this time? Do come to dinner tonight. Your wife will understand. She must know how important your work is to you and I promise to be on my best behavior. You'll find I've changed. I'm rather surprised at myself. Really I am."

I repeated my earlier statement about my Tuesday night dinner plans and all the while I saw the old contentious fire in the green eyes I had known so well. It was still there, the light and heat of it as vivid and mesmerizing as I remembered.

"Adele," I said with a sincerity that truly surprised me, "whatever happened between us has been over for a long time. We've each gone on with our lives. I appreciate your attempt at an explanation, but there's no need for one. You are who you are, and I am who I am and that's all there is to it. Now, it will be best for both of us if we go about our work here and concentrate on nothing but doing our best."

The words came so easily. As they spilled out they sounded so very noble and high-minded. "Yes," I stated like a seasoned philosopher, "let's go about our work and concentrate on nothing but doing our best."

I laugh aloud when I think how foolish I was to even suggest such a directive could be followed. Adele and I parted that day on less than amicable terms, but exactly as in the past she had found the opportunity to have the last word and provide a required opening for the next.

"Of course you're absolutely right, Charles," she said. "You always did know how to do things, and it will be exactly as you say. We will do our best," she added as she turned to leave, "but if you think about me later, which I know you will, and decide to change your mind, you know where I live. Eight o'clock. Count Leclerc will be there. Charles, I hope you don't mind, but at a dinner he and I shared a short time ago I told him about the deaths of your late wife and children. Since he experienced a similar loss, I thought he could offer you the comfort I couldn't. Although I secluded myself for a time after his death, my husband Didier's passing was not a heartbreaking loss."

"The Count has touched on the subject with me," I said, quickly thinking back to our luncheon together when the portrait of his late wife had led to veiled comments I hadn't understood. "It was good of you to consider my feelings, but Adele, I have healed. I'm fine."

"Do you still waltz at The Baron's receptions?" she called out over her shoulder as she walked away. "I remember you were very good at waltzing............for a turtle, that is."

I attended the Tuesday night dinner at Cardon's. I ordered baked turbot in white wine and butter sauce. I joined in the conversation, enjoyed my food, and drank the wine. I laughed at the jokes and I thought about the woman with the emerald green eyes who in spite of the undercurrent between us had managed to make me feel like an admirable old foe with a score to settle. Turtle indeed!

My demolition work on the land behind The Courtyards began with the elimination of a field of neglected trees. Adele appeared as the last of them were being sawed into small limbs, stacked, and loaded onto waiting wagons.

"I hate to see old trees come down," she remarked, her hands in the pockets of her trousers as she watched. "Don't you find it sad to put an end to such beautiful works of nature? On second thought I suppose you don't. It's all just cut, crush, and cart away for you, isn't it?"

"These trees will be put to good use," I shot back without looking away from the loading process. "Firewood is in short supply for the poor, but of course you wouldn't know anything about that."

"Still on the attack I see!" came the counteroffensive I should have expected. "Still ready for a fight! I love it, but Charles, it's not the attitude I'd expect from a happily married man. I must say, though, it really is fun."

"Why are you so annoying Adele?" I asked. "Aren't you getting too old for this?"

"Too old? Hardly. And if you would accept my invitation to dinner you'd find that to be true for yourself. I have the constitution of a woman half my age and, I might add, the same hearty appetites. I'm sure you remember."

"Adele, stop this! I have work to do here. You're interfering. Now please do what you came here to do and leave!"

"Well, unfortunately, I seem to have lost my touch with you, Charles Fabron! All right. I know when I've been outplayed, and by the way, I don't believe you're married. You never did manage avoiding the truth with much conviction. I know you too well. Something changes in you when you exaggerate. It's in the way you suddenly look away and blink too many times, at least five or six. I've counted those blinks. There's something sweet about them, but it's alright. I know what you were trying to do with that little white lie, and don't worry. I won't bother you again. I'll work on my own here and you won't hear a peep out of me. I'll finish this garden without your advice, but remember this: I was the woman who brought you out of that shell you were living under when you arrived in Paris. And I was very good at liberating you, wasn't I? Look at you now. Strong and impervious, even with me!"

Demolition on Saint-Andres-des Arts was completed in four days, not in the full week I had planned on. Construction of the existing commercial district was likewise completed in a remarkably short time and in short order Adele's garden for the Emperor was heralded as one of the loveliest in Paris. After that I saw her at several of The Baron's grand evening receptions, including events held for a number of State visitors. We didn't speak or acknowledge one another, and as the decade of the 1860's came to a close both Adele's appearances at The Baron's grand receptions and the receptions themselves became fewer and farther between. Reasons for the decline in these well-staged Hotel de Ville events were as yet unknown, but as the final months of 1869 and the early days of 1870 progressed, it would become abundantly clear that matters far more pressing than entertainments were on The Baron's mind. In the meantime, I was celebrating the decision to preserve The Rohan Courtyards and I was not alone. When I delivered the good news, Henri Villard may have been the happiest man in Paris.

"I'm so glad I didn't tell Claire a word about any of this!" he stammered out. "I was tempted a few times," he admitted. "I don't keep anything from Claire, but when I realized she would make herself sick with worry I stopped myself. Charles, I haven't slept well at all since you told me we were in danger of losing our home and very likely our business. Tonight will be very different. Thank you."

When I went on to explain the final official plan for the area just behind the Courtyards, Henri listened with a broad, contented smile frozen on his face. "It's all wonderful," he said. "A park and a commercial area will give us a little more activity behind the wall, maybe more noise, but at least we'll be staying in our precious corner of the world. It's a small price to pay. How long will it take?"

"Not long. A few months," I said to him. "Baron Haussmann has put extra workmen on the project. He wants it finished as soon as possible. There seems to be a great need for added haste right now, more than ever before. I really don't understand it," I added, completely unaware of the reasons for the excessive haste at the site of every project in Paris and the real reasons behind the decision to turn attention away from our precious old courtyards. My first hint that trouble could be brewing came from Henri himself when he shared his concern for another matter that would affect not only our neighborhood, but eventually all France.

"Charles, your news quiets my heart, and I'm grateful for it," he said, "but something else is happening that doesn't. I'm not sure what it means, but students from the Ecole and the Sorbonne who over a long period of time have been interested mainly in books on French history and French art have been requesting books and materials on Prussian and Austrian history; maps and graphs, that sort of thing. At first I thought it was a passing notion, something a professor had suggested as historically interesting or related in some way to a topic of current or coordinated study, but lately requests for almost anything on Prussia have been so numerous that I've been placing large catalogue orders with publishers in Hamburg and Berlin. When the books arrive and we place them out on the floor, they fairly fly off the shelves. Claire has her hands full. Of course there's a nice increase in our income, but Prussia? It's a German state."

I reminded myself that Prussia was on the southeastern coast of the Baltic Sea and that although the area had been annexed to Germany, it had retained its Prussian name. I also reminded myself that Left Bank bookstores were largely supported by needs of the surrounding Left Bank's vibrant educational community and that Henri and Claire saw these businesses as community barometers of sorts. Henri was sensitive to the movements of these barometers and he saw something happening.

On several occasions he had mentioned to me that whenever student and professor requests for textbooks and maps veered away from customary patterns, the changes were seen as suspect. It could mean that new laws or regulations were being considered or that an author or journalist had appeared on the scene with wildly popular or equally unpopular ideas or techniques. It didn't happen very often, he said, and norms were usually quickly re-established he emphasized, but both he and Claire were in agreement that to the proprietors of Left Bank bookshops, extended irregularities in sales were always signals of change. In view of this revelation I myself became aware that in recent months there had been one irregularity after another at the Hotel de Ville. Most noticeably, that staff meetings were being cancelled at a moment's notice, Secretary Merruau announcing to us by way of explanation that Baron Haussmann had been called upon "to attend the Emperor." I was also reminded that there had also been an overwhelming succession of State Visits which in just a few months had made the Hotel de Ville's grand halls and reception rooms bustling centers of Empirical activity.

As had become customary, a State Visit's social events were planned under the direction of Baron Haussmann and demanded huge blocks of his time to prepare. In rapid succession, from 1867 through the winter of 1870, Tsar Alexander of Russia had come to Paris, as had the King and Queen of Belgium, the Sultan of Turkey, the King and Queen of Portugal, Alexander, King of Greece and in October of 1867 the Prussian Kaiser, Franz-Joseph of Germany and Austria. The Kaiser and his Chancellor, Otto von Bismarck, had arrived with an imposing entourage, one much larger than we had seen attending former State visitors. 1867 was the year of the International Exhibition in Paris and official word circulated that the Kaiser and Bismarck had come to see its many marvels. Unofficial word circulated that they had really come to see the results of Baron Haussmann's long Paris labors. The latter indeed being the case, the Prussian visitors, as we were instructed to refer to them, were suitably impressed. Paris was sparkling. In addition to its blocks of beautifully uniform, romantically balconied new apartment buildings and miles of immaculate new roadways, there were new buildings at The Louvre, there was a racetrack in the Bois, the public was freely enjoying hundreds of acres of greenspace, the city's twelve arrondissements had been increased to twenty, and the source of Baron Haussmann's greatest pride, the Arc de Triomphe's twelve avenues radiated out to all parts of the city. The Prussian visitors were suitably impressed. It was the beginning of the end.

I remember seeing the Kaiser and Bismarck at the Exhibition. Kaiser Franz Joseph was an imposing figure in his elegant State Uniforms as he reviewed only a fraction of the 50,000 exhibits displayed on more than 100 acres of the Champs de Mar, but he was outshone by Chancellor Bismarck, an enormous hulking man whose heavily decorated white uniforms and gleaming silver helmets attracted a great deal of attention. For a full week, his girth and the conspicuous array of medals adorning it were everywhere. In full regalia, he was constantly admiring, inspecting, and evaluating, but he was not the only extravagantly decorated public figure attracting attention. By this time The Baron had accumulated his own collection of impressive medals and he knew how and when to use them. At the several State events to which I was invited I was proud to see that he was not outdone by Bismarck. The Baron's decorations virtually covered the impeccably tailored tunic of his Prefect Uniform and included the Grand Cross of the Legion d'Honneur, Eight Commonwealth and Foreign Orders, and countless Empirical Honors bestowed by the Emperor. However successfully competitive The Baron may have appeared to be with or without his medals, it was the extended stay of the Kaiser and his Chancellor in Paris that gave rise to speculation that difficulties with Prussia could be brewing on the horizon.

Many people chose to ignore the whispers, confining them to idle gossip and pure conjecture, but there was a definite instability in the air and it came from several quarters. From my vantage point, and because I spent so much time there, irregularities were most evident at the Hotel de Ville where the city's municipal business was conducted. The typically well-organized business day had descended into a haphazard set of confusing hours consisting of cancelled appointments and endlessly long lines of people waiting for license renewals and business permits, as well as those who chose to present an endless litany of personal complaints. Signs of ambivalence were growing daily as elements of doubt and supposition were also finding their way into the city's most readily available gathering places. The city's cafes had always been sounding boards for the latest gossip and rumor but now, behind the beveled glass windows of every popular café and restaurant there was talk of potential war with Prussia and it grew more heated by the day. The disbelievers held their ground. "Impossible! Mais non!" individual voices were head to cry out. "This is France! We are the French people! We have our cultural integrity, our national pride, our unrivalled position in Europe! No jealous outsider, regardless of title or due, would dare to insult us and intrude on our borders!"

It was a loyal, assiduous position to take, but few could have counted on the ambitions of Otto von Bismarck, and fewer yet could have been aware of the fertile, emotional seeds he had been planting across his country for months.

Unification of Germany's 300 distinctly separate and individually governed states which for hundreds of years had been entities unto themselves, had become Bismarck's most passionate mission. Until his arrival on the scene in 1862, Germany was a country unified only by language. Now, according to Bismarck's edict and with the Kaiser's complete approval, every corner of the country which included Prussia, was to be governed under one set of laws and one leader. In addition to quickly promoting his plans for nationalization and the raising of armies, Bismarck applied the power of what he clearly understood to be the ultimate emotional weapon at his disposal. It was free of charge and more powerful than the law itself. It was patriotism, and in all its infectious passion it spread like wildfire. A national anthem and a national flag were created as tangible symbols of a land unified by pride and devotion. Rallies and assemblies were held and in no time at all Bismarck had his country solidly behind him as he set his sights on domination of Europe. Paris, unfortunately, was his first target, Emperor Louis Napoleon his early prey. By January of 1869 the hunt had begun. War was declared on July 19, 1870.

The nearest history book will tell the story of the Franco-Prussian War and its origins in scholarly detail. Those of us living in Paris at the time needed no explanation or study guides. We understood the war's origins with great clarity. Its sour roots had been planted and sowed in a lethal confluence of human failings, on one side a driving hunger for status and power, on the other a desire for peace and a reluctance to act.

But for Alexander and the Roman Caesars, few men in history had exhibited a hunger for status and power more aggressively than Otto von Bismarck. With the full support of Kaiser Franz Joseph, his intention was not only to unify the fragmented German states, but to create a great German Empire as the new major power in Europe, it territories extending from the westernmost borders of France and Spain, through Germany and

Poland, and across Russia's six thousand square miles. He began with a march into glittering, irresistible Paris. The first Prussian troops arrived on September 19th, Bismarck in his white Cuirassier uniform and plumed helmet leading them through the majestic Arc de Triomphe. With that act The Siege of Paris had begun.

It was a nightmare. All of it: the concept, the purpose, and the speed with which the unthinkable became harsh reality. Worst of all, too few people in Paris were emotionally or physically prepared to be under siege. And exactly how does the populace of a city prepare for a siege? What exactly is it? What are its guidelines? Who is in charge? What is to be believed? Who is to be believed? What are the enforceable rules? I couldn't answer those questions then and I cannot answer them now. I only know what I saw and how I felt, but the question I asked then and the same question I ask now is why wasn't Bismarck stopped? Why was France unable to prevail over his very clearly transmitted intentions? What of diplomatic efforts? What of the good relationships between France and its European neighbors, particularly nearby Spain, the respected close ally who when called upon failed to offer aid. In the final analysis, the answer which satisfies me best has to do with Emperor Louis Napoleon himself and the devastating coincidence of total upheaval in his own government.

He was, of course, surrounded by ministers, councils, and a parliamentary system, but Louis Napoleon III had not met the moment. He had pursued his own policies behind the backs of his advisors. Determined to single-handedly dominate foreign affairs without delays and interference, he made countless diplomatic attempts aimed at continuing to enhance the reputation of his country and prevent domination by competing European powers. As a result he stretched the limits of his emotional and physical health. He traveled constantly and entertained hourly. He studied, lectured, and wrote treatise after treatise. It was too much. By 1870 his health was failing and he had lost interest in everything, even the Paris Project. The energetic Bonaparte responses he had been famous for were gone. For seventeen years and with his natural gravitas, he had held the famous Napoleonic drive and ambition in the palm of his hand, but he had lost irretrievable ground when and where it mattered most. I could accuse any number of men in high places of playing a role in weakening Louis Napoleon's position and setting the stage for the Franco-Prussian War. It is true that these prestigious political figures held countless diplomatic meetings in an effort to maintain national stability and it is true that they exchanged hundreds of messages in the hopes of avoiding war, but from my point of view and simply put, as Bismarck made the war appear necessary and corrective, Louis Napoleon made the war seem inevitable. In the blink of an eye and prepared or not, Bismarck became master of all we possessed and Paris was indeed a city under siege.

We had been warned. At least there was that, but the definition of the word 'Siege' remained vague to the majority of Paris citizens. "What does it really mean?" was the question being asked repeatedly throughout the city.

"It means that the Prussians will occupy Paris and eventually all France, cutting us off from the rest of Europe," was the answer The Baron gave to the question raised during one of our hastily called staff meetings. It was as devastating a statement as I had ever hear him make. Each man's face took on an expression it pains me to recall as we heard from our most reliable source that our lives and our city were about to be challenged by this evil condition called war.

"There will be food shortages, curfews, and martial law. Prepare yourselves and your families," he added with a thrust of his intimidating chin. "I must announce regretfully today that our work on the city may be interrupted, but I also hasten to add that I am confident we will return to our responsibilities after only a brief pause. Do not worry. The Prussians will be quickly defeated, and make no mistake. You and I will resume our work on Paris. All will return to normal and be restored promptly and exactly as it was. Until further notice, continue on with your designs and plans and schedule your meetings with me as is our established pattern here at the Hotel de Ville. Demolition and construction projects may be temporarily delayed or rescheduled, but do not lose heart. Be prepared to resume work at locations posted on the Calendar at a moment's notice."

At first, confident in the government and the French military to successfully and quickly address the situation, people continued on with their lives with few, if any concerns. Denial came easily. It was a safe and comforting state of mind. The true gravity of what lay ahead gained credulity when livestock began arriving in the Bois de Boulogne.

"I was turned away from my morning ride in the Bois!" shocked frequenters of the bucolic riding paths were heard to complain. "Farm animals were actually being herded along my customary route and I was scolded for interfering! Why is this happening?"

The Bois; the royal hunting grounds of a series of French kings and more recently the two-thousand acre jewel in the Haussmann crown was being readied to serve as headquarters for the Paris food supply. Hundreds of cows, goats, sheep, and horses were herded along the manicured walkways and riding paths of the Bois de Boulogne and enclosed in quickly erected stalls and fenced yards. Wagonloads of pigs, chickens, geese, and ducks were penned in large tree-bordered areas with views to arguably the most picturesque ponds, fountains, and monumental statuary in the world. Eugene Baltard, chief architect of the Bois, was deeply disturbed by the invasive scene.

"For years I have struggled to create a landscape of unparalleled beauty," he announced in anther hastily called staff meeting, "and now I must contend with the droppings of livestock and the rank odor of cow and horse manure! What was it all for? Is there to be no end to the travails befalling Paris?"

Belgrand joined in. "I have finally succeeding in cleaning the once foul-smelling River Seine. I have devised an efficient system for sending human waste miles away from Paris. Is it to be my responsibility now to do the same with horse and cow manure?"

Like the angry flames of a fire, once the spiral began, there was no stopping it. With the arrival of the first Prussian troops a nine o'clock curfew was imposed, all imports and exports ceased, and in the midst of a disbelieving Europe, Paris became an island unto itself. I never thought I would live to see people leaving Paris in droves, but I did. Anticipating the Prussian advance and fearing the worst, as early as April many left their homes and businesses for the safety of distant cities and towns throughout Europe. London was the most popular destination. The greatest exodus began in June as over-crowded trains headed for the Normandy Coast and the seven-hour journey across the English Channel in packet boats departing Calais, Caen, and Le Havre became a common sight.

At another hastily called meeting, The Baron advised us to leave Paris. His originally optimistic attitude had been altered by his first hand view of rapidly unraveling events. As Prefect he was supervising municipal preparations for the Prussian Occupation, everything from advising and organizing medical centers and city maintenance workers to arranging for protection of buildings and monuments. Now there was no optimism, no question in his mind that Paris was about to be a city compromised by invaders. "Fires may be set," he warned, "our parks utilized as military camps." In keeping with what we knew of him, it was no surprise that the lack of a known time-frame annoyed him most. This was to be the last time we were together as the Haussmann team.

"There is no telling how long the siege will last," he announced as he concluded his remarks. "Sadly, we will find ourselves under the control of an enemy for an unknown period of time. Daily life will not be pleasant. Evening activity will be cut short by curfews. Theaters will be closed, as will the opera and many restaurants and cafes. Be aware that people seen on the streets after curfew will be in danger of arrest or worst, and of course our work will cease. Keep in mind that we are dealing with a dangerous adversary. As of today, anyone employed at the Hotel de Ville who wishes to leave the city for safer parts of Europe is free to do so. Remain in Paris if you wish. I plan to stay."

Of course unanswerable questions loomed, hundreds of them, all our most passionate issues fixed on the potential fate of Paris. How would the invading Prussians treat the city we had worked so hard to improve? Would they deliberately destroy its most beautiful assets or were they so taken with the Capital City's beauty that they would respect it and tread lightly? What of our sixteen thousand miles of newly paved streets, boulevards, and avenues? What of our six hundred thousand trees, five thousand acres of parks, and twenty-four new squares totaling a breathtaking one million square feet?

I was not the only man to leave that last meeting with tears in my eyes. Lives, loves, and futures were at stake and we finally knew there was no hope of stemming the tide of evil. But the central question loomed. Why had it come to this? Why had the ugliness not been stopped while there was still time for resolution? Why had the Emperor not taken a strong stand? Hadn't he held the power to do so?

The widely circulated fact was that as Emperor, Louis Napoleon had always wanted a peaceful relationship with all his European neighbors. At the same time it was common knowledge that he was first and foremost a soldier, and a soldier in his Uncle Napoleon Bonaparte's aggressive mold. But what had happened to that Bonaparte aggression? A love of battle was in Bonaparte blood. It was admitted to on many occasions, and rightly so. Louis Napoleon could look with pride to his military role in the Crimean War. His perseverance at Boulgne-sur-mer had become legend enough for heroic paintings to have been created of his arrival at Boulogne's rocky shores, and there was the revolt at Strasbourg and the Battle at Austerlitz, all these experiences evidence of his capable military leadership, but now with threats coming from across the Rhine, Louis Napoleon was a deeply conflicted warrior. This condition was at the heart of the dilemma the country now faced.

On the outside, the Emperor appeared to welcome the potential of facing Bismarck and his Prussian armies, but the inner man was neither prepared nor eager to engage an enemy on the battlefield. Not yet. Not now. Why? Because behind the palace walls he was dealing with serious difficulties at the highest level. Prussian timing could not have been worst. Most pressing, as Bismarck's armies were organizing and preparing, were the demands of The French Municipal Council who were challenging Louis Napoleon's decisions and authority in every area of government, most vigorously his support of Baron Haussmann and the wildly expensive Paris Project which at its astronomical cost of more than two billion francs they insisted was about to bankrupt the country and place the affordability of a war in jeopardy. The fragility of the empire Louis Napoleon had solidly nurtured with visions of greatness for himself and all France was teetering on the edge of destruction.

Basically, it was being argued, and with powerful attention, that the municipal administration of Paris and its finances under Haussmann as

Prefect had been largely ignored while with the Emperor's endorsement Haussmann went about his long, unbridled transformation of Paris, cost be damned. Determined to bring down both Haussmann and the Emperor and ignoring the reality of a Prussian onslaught as it gathered at the doorstep, Ministry officials took every opportunity in this highly critical period to attack Louis Napoleon's ignorance of facts and The Baron's lack of financial experience and economic understanding. Fierce arguments ensued, accusations, attacks and counter attacks converged into a melee, and the inevitable crumbling began. Holding firm, The Baron did not take the accusations hurtled toward him lightly. He could reflect on a long list of proud achievements and he did so, repeatedly. He also saw himself as a public official more popular and more highly respected than any other, a position which to those against him only highlighted his arrogance.

With the success of the 1867 Exhibition attended by the Kaiser and Bismarck, it was all too obvious to the opposition that The Baron had enjoyed an overall rise in popularity. And why not? In addition to planning and hosting social aspects of the State visit, he had applied all his powers to the Exhibition itself which was, by every count, a euphoric event. There were custom-designed booths and stalls overrun with foods and beverages from around the world. Each country represented opened its own fully equipped, uniquely designed restaurant. Characteristic houses were erected: an English Country Cottage, an Egyptian Temple, a Chinese Pagoda, a Tyrolean Hut. On the heels of praise and congratulatory letters from around the world, in December the powerhouse behind this overwhelming success confidently appeared before the Municipal Council and presented his 1868 budget complete with his customary memorandum, expecting immediate approval. The Municipal Council was not impressed, not with Haussmann's numbers, not with the success of the Exhibition, and most of all, not with Haussmann himself. The most influential Council members had hated him and his project from the start, and as the Prussians polished their weapons and trained their eyes on Paris, tempers flared, accusations were hurtled, and the battle behind Louis Napoleon's palace walls was no longer a mere incident.

In the first round of attacks The Baron was accused by the Council of disguising a short-term loan between the city and the financial institution, Credit Foncier. They said he had converted short-term Public Works Fund Bonds into an undisclosed long-term loan, arranging for its conversion with Credit Foncier in secret. When challenged, The Baron denied that the bonds constituted a disguised loan. He called it a small matter and a commonly implemented administrative procedure. Unmoved, the Council continued on, calling out the Prefect's Balance Sheet as a false document intended to keep the Council, The Emperor, and the public in the dark. Had he been blind to the reality of the critical financial situation he was creating they asked? Did he realize that to date he had spent more than two billion francs on his Paris Project? Was he lacking in foresight, or did he know exactly what he was doing in perpetuating the disguised loan with Credit Foncier, part of which was surely destined for his own pockets? And were there other loans, other secret transactions? An investigation was called for.

The victim of growing alienation and acutely aware that he was being accused of corruption, The Baron proposed that the loan in question be consolidated, the agreement between the City and Credit Foncier arranged openly and received with the approval of Parliament. It was a fatal mistake to suggest involving Parliament. The Council found the recommendation highly agreeable and for the first time in seventeen years Baron Haussmann was called upon to appear in person and submit his proposal and budget to Parliament, a demand which on its face was a motion of censure.

How it came to be that The Baron fell out of favor so suddenly and that he experienced a loss of confidence at the highest levels of French Government so totally remains to me a lasting mystery. That he may have been found abusing his access to the Emperor and their shared vision with excessive, careless, or undisclosed spending is of course, the first conclusion to which any rational mind familiar with conditions would come, but I myself have never come to terms with this assumption. The State was involved all along. Senators, Councils, and Ministers had been skeptical of Haussmann and the entire Paris Project from the start. If they were watching closely and concerned about his spending they could have investigated his process, gathered their majority, and stepped in to stop him. If they were so offended, so concerned, why didn't they do something?

At the risk of oversimplification, it is important to realize that technically the renovations of Paris were managed by the State and financed with loans backed by the State. How The Baron maneuvered through these technicalities came down to a matter of trust and the only trust that mattered to him was that of the Emperor. The fact that the two men shared the same vision for Paris must not be overlooked. With rare exception and for seventeen years they had met every morning to perfect their mutual vision. I will never believe that The Baron would have deliberately attempted to deceive or mislead his Emperor. Baron Haussmann loved his country and the City of Paris. He was as loyal a French patriot and supporter of Emperor Louis Napoleon as could be found and like the Emperor he too was a staunch Bonaparte militarist in the old style. He thrived on old-fashioned court formalities and I never for a moment knew him to depart from the strict behavioral boundaries traditionally imposed between Emperor and Prefect. These were formal parameters which he understood very well and which by his behavior he exemplified far better than many who also enjoyed easy access to the Emperor. What I did see was that the same officials who eagerly rose to denounce the man who had freed their city from its medieval imprisonment were the same officials who just as eagerly had accepted invitations to his elegant balls and receptions, very much enjoying the access to power and privilege his position provided them. Nonetheless and despite The Baron's talents and allegiances, financial matters confronting him remained paramount and in question.

The modernization of Paris had begun not by raising taxes, but by selling city bonds to small investors. At the beginning, so well had the public message been conceived and presented by The Baron and The Emperor that a bond issue of sixty million francs was sold out in one day. At the end, however, over two billion francs had not been enough to pay for destruction of more than 20,000 buildings, the construction of 30,000 new buildings, and in all, the rebuilding of over sixty percent of Paris. A long list of private investors, bankers, and speculators had played their roles in financing Baron Haussmann's project as he quietly and creatively went about the business of creating the New Paris, transferring funds from one project to another, from one entrepreneur to another, and confidently presenting his budgets year after year. It couldn't continue. Rumors swirled, once loyal bankers and investors who feared being named and fatally involved, turned against him, and by autumn of 1869 he was accused of having deliberately falsified his budgets. He was publicly humiliated, his name uttered with contempt throughout Paris, and by the fifth day of January in 1870 it was over. On that date, Louis Napoleon, unable to tolerate the harsh public and administrative criticism any longer, abandoned his loyal Prefect and Master Builder, placing all blame for the ills befalling Paris on his shoulders and using him as a scapegoat in rationalizing his own inadequacies. As final preparations were being made for war and siege, Louis Napoleon was on his way to the garrison town of Metz. Disgraced and I believe, heartbroken, Baron Haussmann, abandoned by his Emperor and stripped of every shred of power, left Paris to take refuge at his house in Cestas. Feeling very much alone and abandoned myself, I was forced to change the plans I had made to leave for London. There was trouble in Rouen. In late May, I received a cable from my father informing me that my mother was seriously ill. He advised me to come to Rouen as soon as possible. I left Paris on the afternoon train. I was too late.

CHAPTER TWELVE

In My Father's House

May 1870

"IT WAS SO SUDDEN," Pauline sobbed when I arrived at the house my parents had shared for more than thirty years. "She was perfectly well until a few days ago. I had come from Seine-Maritime Hill to visit her. I tried to come every Thursday. She told me she was having bad headaches, but she seemed to be managing very well. In the morning we talked and walked in the garden together, but by afternoon I could tell she wasn't herself. I should have put her to bed, but she said since it was such a beautiful day that she wanted to go to the park across the street to watch as the gardeners put in the fresh border of begonias around the pond. You know how she enjoyed the spring planting here in Rouen. Oh, this is terrible! Your father will tell you the whole story Monsieur Charles, but it all happened so quickly. One day she was wasn't feeling well and the next she was gone. I can't believe it. I've been staying on to help where I can. The family living at Seine-Maritime Hill know how I feel about you and your parents. They agreed that I should stay on here as long as I'm needed."

Father was standing in the hall, his face ashen, his eyes red and swollen. We embraced and both dissolved into tears.

"For about four days she had been having headaches," Father said, confirming Pauline's explanation, his voice unsteady as we walked into his study," but you know how your mother was. "She didn't give in to sickness easily. She expected to feel wonderfully well every day of her life. When I saw the headaches were continuing I urged her to see Doctor Mercier, but she said she was sure it would all pass. Two nights ago she collapsed in the upstairs hall. I was here in this room when I heard a loud thump overhead. I ran up the stairs. Mother was lying on the floor. She was very still, but she was breathing. I carried her to her bed and waited for her to regain consciousness. I was sure she had just fainted. She had fainted twice before in recent months but she had always awakened quickly. I prayed it would be the same this time. I rubbed her hands and called her name. Pauline applied warm compresses to her forehead, but Mother didn't respond. I sent Pauline for Doctor Mercier. He came immediately but he was very direct and said her heart beat was weak. He held out little hope. It went on for two days and nights. I sat in the chair beside the bed and called her name again and again. Doctor Mercier came in twice a day. I prayed for a miracle. I prayed hard, but Mother never awakened. Doctor Mercier was here when she died this morning. He said her heart had finally failed. Pauline did all the preparation. Your mother is lying in her bed. She looks as if she's just taking a nap. I'll come upstairs with you."

"No, Father. I'll go alone," I said. "I want to."

I climbed the stairs slowly, feeling like a stranger in the house I had known all my life. I had always thought of it as a lively, happy place. Mother had made it that way. With her lighthearted, thoughtful ways she had made her house a joyous, welcoming home not only for my father and me but for every relative and visitor who appeared at the door. Now, without her cheerful presence, a quiet sadness clouded every corner. I stopped midway up the stairs and sat on one of the steps remembering the day when I was about ten how she had watched me taking the stairs, two at a time. "I'd like to try that!" she said with a laugh. And there, in the downstairs hall, she lifted her long skirt, took a running start, and proceeded to amaze me by racing up the stairs just as I had, two at a time. When she reached the top of the stairs where I waited she was breathless, but she held me close and we sat on the top step laughing and hugging each other.

An enormous lump formed in my throat as I reached her room and walked toward the bed where she was lying motionless and pale. Her favorite yellow flowered quilt had been placed over her body. Her hands were folded at her waist. The tears rolled down my cheeks as I sat at the edge of the bed and studied her face. She was beautiful in death, at peace, and exactly like the young mother I remembered from my childhood; the loving mother who had played with me in the snow in winter and named the flowers in the park with me in spring. I buried my head against her and let the tears flow.

The funeral took place two days later. A Mass was held in the Rouen Cathedral. There were flowers and candles and scores of friends and relatives. Mother was buried not far from Louisa and our sons in the cemetery behind the church bell tower.

I stayed on for a week. Father remained distraught and except for bringing flowers to the cemetery every day and making an appearance at dinner, he kept to his room. I spent most of the time by myself, walking in the nearby park and thinking back through my childhood and what I knew of Mother's life. I remembered the many times I had been told that she had been born in Paris and that Claire Villard was her closest childhood friend. I tried to imagine what those two must have been like as young girls, playing games and sharing secrets. When Mother was twelve, the family left Paris and moved to Rouen. Her father was a lawyer and had taken a position with a respected Rouen legal firm. My own father had joined that same firm shortly after he and Mother were married. When he became managing partner, they bought the house on Rue Epreville where they had lived throughout their married life and where I had been born. It was a spacious house with a wide terrace and a garden, its rhythms and habits not unlike those of any other professional family living in Rouen. It would be different now. The house would lose its meaning. It would stand solid and strong, as it always had, but nothing about the life inside its walls would be the same, not as I had known it when Mother was alive.

This was the last time I would feel like a child of the house. In the future when I came to visit my father, the rooms would look the same and smell the same, but the void in them would never be filled. On the last day I had intended to remain in Rouen I decided to walk through the house and enter each of the rooms with one last image of the past as I wanted to remember it. I saved Mother's sitting room for last. The door had remained closed since the day of her funeral. I turned the knob slowly and stepped inside. It was as if she had left only moments before. The gentle tuberose scent she favored perfumed the air. Her books and writing papers were neatly arranged on the desk by the windows facing the garden. Notes and small booklets were stacked to one side. Across the room at her dressing table, a vase of fresh yellow roses had been placed beside a small glass jar of hairpins. I was sure Father had brought the flowers. I sat in the chair facing the dressing table mirror, my eyes slowly scanning over the tray of brushes and combs and bottles of scent. I opened one of the deep side drawers. In it were handkerchiefs embroidered with her initials and some colorful silk scarves. I would keep these as personal mementos, I decided. It was when I had placed the handkerchiefs and scarves on the dressing table and had begun to close the drawer that I noticed something lying at the bottom. It was a brown leather notebook. Inside, on its pages, were poems Mother had been developing, one on her garden, another on my house at Seine-Maritime Hill, a house she described as the prettiest in Rouen. The lyrical phrases flowed one into the next so beautifully that I felt I was intruding on thoughts too personal to be shared, but here, in my mother's handwriting, were observations she had made, thoughts she had shared with no one, and poetic phrases she had applied to paper with a heartfelt sincerity quite obviously intended for no one's eyes but her own. I turned the pages and read the well-cadenced lines, admiring my mother's talent with great pride. I decided I would tell Father that along with the handkerchiefs and scarves I also wanted to keep the book of Mother's poems. I placed it on the dressing table surface and was about to close the drawer one final time when I noticed another notebook lying at the bottom of the deep drawer, this one smaller than the first, its black leather cover worn and scratched. Taking it in hand and opening its pages, I found it was a calendar, a diary of sorts covering several years past in which Mother had noted her appointments and engagements and where she had written occasional reminders and jotted remarks about places she had been and people she had seen or met. I crossed the room and sat in one of the yellow flowered chairs by the fireplace, leafing through the pages. Mother may have been a free spirit and very different from my highly organized Father, but for a time the mother I knew as oblivious to the discipline of calendars and daily schedules had kept a diary and it revealed another side of her. The entries were dated and although they were not daily entries, they covered a span of several years which interested me. 1850 caught my attention. It was the year I had met and married Louisa.

April 4, 1850: The center of old Rouen is undergoing a great renovation. Charles is very much involved. I am proud of my son and his dedication to our city. He tells me he has met a young lady. He is bringing her to dinner tomorrow night.

April 5: Her name is Louisa. She is lovely. She likes gardens and music. I hope she is the one.

May 4: They are engaged. The past month has been a whirlwind, but a very pleasant one. Charles is so very happy. I know Louisa is right for him. They will have a wonderful life.

June 30: The wedding in the Rouen Cathedral was beautiful. Louisa was the loveliest bride I have ever seen. Afterwards, a garden party at home of her parents. They are a very handsome couple and so happy. Off to Nice for wedding trip.

1851: New Year's Day. They have joined Andre Rousseau and his bride at Lyons-en-foret for the New Year celebration.

August 1851: Have been to visit with L. Such a fine girl. C is a lucky young man. I am as excited as they are about the coming baby in December. Christmas will be very special this year. L. tells me they are trying to decide on a name for the child.

December 2, 1851: It is a wonderful time for my family. We may have our grandchild by Christmas Day. I have prepared a layette. Every piece looks so very small. Today I finished the knitting on the white christening shawl.

January 5, 1852: We grieve. My dear son grieves. It is the most terrible thing. With Louisa and the babies gone he is distraught and adrift in a sad, lonely world. I don't know what to do for him. I feel helpless. I pray.

Entries for the remaining months of 1852 were sparse and unrelated, but three were unusual. I didn't understand.

October: 1852: Have been to LB and the lovely church. It is not very far away but every time I go there I feel as if I am in another world. P says my visits to LB make me sad. She says she will go in my place. I must talk to her about taking warm clothes. Winter is coming. The boys are in need of coats and sweaters.

December 1855: He is four years old.

June 1856: He is a beautiful child, full of energy and curiosity.

December 1856: SA has nursed him through three days of fever. I thank God he has recovered.

The letter P was not difficult to understand. I was sure it stood for Pauline, but the letters LB and SA were a puzzle. Downstairs, I found Pauline in the kitchen and I asked if she knew what the letters might stand for. She shook her head. "No, Monsieur Charles," she answered. "Why do you ask?"

"I found a diary Mother kept. One of the entries refers to LB. "Have been to LB again," Mother wrote. "It is not very far but every time I go there it feels as if I am in another world."

"It is not very far must means a place close to Rouen," I assumed to Pauline, "but what could my mother have meant by writing that she felt sad and as if she was in another world when she went there? Do you know where Mother went that made her sad, Pauline? And who is SA?"

"Ah, she must have meant La Bouille. Monsieur Charles, your mother visited the church and the orphanage there. You know how she loved children. She would bring them clothes. Your father went with her sometimes. He brought books and one Christmas he brought a rocking horse. When I went one Christmas I brought a little wooden horse my brother had carved."

An orphanage. La Bouille. Daniel had talked to me about La Bouille. His orphanage was located there and if that was the orphanage Pauline referred to, something about it had bothered Mother. She and Father apparently visited there not once, but regularly. Why? What was it about La Bouille and the orphanage there that could have impacted my parents? I couldn't get the questions out of my mind. Later, at dinner that evening I asked Father about La Bouille.

"It's a village not far from here, about twelve miles. You've probably passed it dozens of times. Pretty little place. Very small. Pauline grew up there. Why do you ask?"

"I found a diary Mother kept. In it she refers to LB. Pauline believes the letters LB stand for La Bouille. Daniel talked about La Bouille. He told me his orphanage was there."

A shadow came over Father's face. "I didn't know your Mother kept a diary!" he remarked, his voice stern and tense. "She never mentioned it to me. Where did you find it? Diaries are private things, Charles. You shouldn't have read a single page of it! I wish you hadn't! You should have given it to me!"

I cancelled my plans to return to Paris. The next morning I hired a carriage and set out for La Bouille. It was, just as I had been led to expect, a beautiful little village set along the river, exactly twelve miles from Rouen. The picturesque Church of Sainte Madeleine perched at the river's edge was its centerpiece. In her diary, Mother had mentioned a church at LB. It had to be this church. I would start there. I had to know what it was about this place that made my mother repeatedly sad and I had to know if Daniel Lazare had told me the truth when he said he had lived at the Sacred Heart Orphanage in La Bouille. I found a priest alone in the sanctuary. He was lighting candles for the noonday Mass. When I approached him he introduced himself as Father Nicholas. I told him my name and asked if there was an orphanage nearby. He said there was no orphanage in La Bouille at present, but that there had been a boys' orphanage once.

"Was it called Sacred Heart?" I asked. "I need to know. My mother visited there."

"Yes, there was an orphanage, and yes, it was called Sacred Heart." Father Nicholas confirmed. "Usually there were about twenty-five boys living there. Shortly after it closed there was a terrible fire. It destroyed everything. Thank God there was no one inside. What is it you seek, my son?" he asked. "I see you are troubled."

I made no pretense of exchanging pleasantries with Father Nicholas. Since my concern was obvious to him I did not hesitate to ask the questions that nagged at me. I had to know more about my mother's visits to La Bouille and I had to know if Daniel Lazare had lived at Sacred Heart.

"Father Nicholas, is it possible there are records of the boys who lived at the orphanage? Could those records have survived the fire? " I asked. "And if there are records, do you know where they would be kept?"

Father Nicholas looked at me with the expressive patience a cleric conveys so effortlessly when he accurately interprets the intensity in a stranger's request.

"We have many records in our Chancellery offices, my son," he said, nodding his head and leaning closer to me. "Some are from Sacred Heart, and I hope God will forgive me for telling you this, but they are not filed very well at all. Even more embarrassing, I must also confess that they are incomplete. I have intended to get to them. The Lord knows my heart has been in the right place, but whenever I've thought about attacking those boxes, the task has seemed hopeless and so, time has passed and here we are."

I couldn't help but smile as Father Nicholas apologized for his poorly organized records. His approach was a bit discouraging, but determined as I was to search for any helpful information at all, I said I would be happy to go through the records myself.

"I will help," he said. "Father Benedict can take over the noonday Mass. Come, I'll take you to the Chancellery. I've been attached to this parish for many years. Perhaps as we look through the boxes I will see something or remember something that will be helpful to you. I had just arrived here at La Bouille from Calais when I was appointed director of the Boys Choir at the orphanage. The building was there next door to the church through the open passageway you may have noticed when you arrived. It's just a meadow now, but pheasant and deer often come out of the woods to eat the wild grasses and nibble at the young bracken fern. I like to watch them. I was so sorry when it all ended so quickly at the orphanage," Father Nicholas continued, folding his hands. "I liked the Boys Choir assignment very much," he added, "and we were doing very well. Some of the boys were excellent singers. We were preparing a special program for the Bishop's birthday when I was told the orphanage was closing. After the announcement was made, everything happened very quickly. It seemed that overnight the boys were gone, the older ones sent off to Le Havre, the younger ones scattered to several orphanages in Belgium. I didn't have a chance to say good-bye to them. It still saddens me to remember that confusing time, but I tell myself it was God's will. Now, if you tell me which years you are interested in knowing about, I will be happy to help you find whatever exists of those records. You are looking for one of the boys, aren't you, my son? He must be a special boy for you to come here and take the time to search. What was his name?"

"The years would be from 1851 to 1863," I said as we walked through a side door, into an anteroom, and finally into the Chancellery. "His name was Daniel Lazare and when the orphanage closed he would have been one of the older boys. I don't think he was sent to Le Havre or to another orphanage in Belgium. He may have run away to Paris."

"How sad it is to think about those boys and what may have happened to them, but here you are, wanting to know about one of them. I have been here since 1848 and to my knowledge no one has ever inquired about Sacred Heart's orphans. I don't understand it. No one cares. We must pray for the negligent souls among us."

Father Nicholas bowed his head, folded his hands, and closed his eyes. I wanted to join him in praying for the negligent among us, but instead I prayed that on this day, in this place, I would find the answers I was searching for.

———◦((◦))◦———

The Chancellery was beautifully paneled. Its oak floor was polished to a high gleam, its ceiling moldings beautifully carved. Impressive as it was, the Chancellery was not in good order. Items were scattered everywhere.

Father Nicholas' desk was piled high with stacks of paper, an empty wine glass stood next to the dusty inkwell, and the files in question were stored haphazardly on the floor around the room in old wooden crates of various sizes.

"Now, our first task will be to locate the years in question. 1851 to 1863 you say?" Father Nicholas shook his head. "I hope the Holy Mother has granted you the gift of patience, Monsieur Fabron" he said with a frown. "This could take time."

Nothing was properly labelled. Nothing was categorized. One after another we opened the boxes and rifled through. Most of the records related in some way to the church itself, but occasionally we came across a record from the Sacred Heart Orphanage. Names and where possible, birth dates were recorded, but for the most part the creased sheets of paper dealt with the arrival and departure dates of nuns and a succession of Mothers Superior. Father Nicolas' arrival in 1848 and his work with the Boys' Choir was duly noted with words of praise and appreciation from a Sister named Maria Fiore.

"Well, look at that. Isn't that nice?" he occasionally said, enjoying the journey through history as he rifled through sheet after sheet of yellowed paper. "Ah, here's something on Sister Angelica!" he exclaimed. You would have liked her. She was young and wonderful with the children. She kept the library, small as it was. As I remember, she was teaching one of the boys to read. It looks as if she was at Sacred Heart during the period of time we're looking for."

Daniel had talked about a Sister Angelica. She was his favorite of the Sacred Heart nuns. He had said she had taught him to read. It was a story they had read together that had ignited his desire to run away to Paris.

Seated on the floor, Father Nicholas and I must have looked through the contents of a dozen boxes. It was tedious work, and tiring, but by late that afternoon I had not only found answers to the nagging questions raised in my mother's diary, I had uncovered an astonishing truth.

"Here, I think I've found something!" Father Nicolas called out just as I was about to give up. He handed me a page of yellowed paper. Written in faded blue ink it read: December 19, 1851. Male Infant brought to The

Charitable Order of Sisters of the Sacred Heart, Village of La Bouille, France. Name: Daniel Lazare. Born: December 19, 1851. Not expected to survive.

December 19, 1851. That was the night Louisa and our babies had died. It was the night that had changed my life. But how was it that a baby named Daniel Lazare had been brought to the nuns of Sacred Heart on that same date? Was it a co-incidence? Was it possible? My stomach was churning. I could feel my heart pounding as the reality of what I now could be facing became all too clear. Could it be that one of my twin sons had survived? Of course. That had to be it. The baby the Sisters of the Sacred Heart had not expected to live had survived. He had been born on the 19th day of December in 1851. He had lived and breathed and he had remained at Sacred Heart until he had reached the age of eleven. He had run away just before the orphanage had closed. He had run to Paris. He was the boy I had known as Daniel Lazare and he was my son. I must have cried out in some terrible, painful way. The next thing I knew, Father Nicholas was at my side, patting my shoulder. "I found this at the bottom of the box," he said as he handed me a little hand-carved wooden horse with the letters DL scratched onto its head. Only hours before, Pauline had told me that one Christmas her brother had carved a small wooden horse she had taken to the orphanage.

"You have found more than you expected, haven't you, my son?" Father Nicholas said, watching me closely. "I had a feeling it would be this way. I will pray for you."

I was too stunned to speak. I remember sitting on the floor for what seemed an eternity, holding the yellowed sheet of paper in one hand, the wooden horse in the other, tears rolling down my cheeks. "I have found my son," I finally said. "I have found my little boy. He didn't die at birth. He lived and I have seen him. He is tall. He smiles a lot, his hair is blonde, and his eyes are blue, just like his mother's."

I had a son. I was stunned by what that short sentence meant. My son's mother and his twin brother had died but he had lived. Why, though, was his name changed from Fabron to Lazare and why was he raised in an orphanage? I was just twelve miles away. I was his father. He could have lived with me in the house on the Seine-Maritime Hill. He could have gone to good schools, made good friends. He could have had good influences in his life. He need not have lived the life of an orphan. How had all this happened? Why? I thought of my mother's diary. She had written that it made her sad to visit the orphanage at La Bouille. Of course. A grandmother would be very sad to see her grandson growing up in an orphanage, secretly hidden away and disconnected from her and all the love and advantages she could have showered on him. That was it. And my father had been to Sacred Heart with Mother. Pauline had told me he brought books and that one Christmas he had brought a rocking horse. Daniel had told me that a tall man who looked like me brought books to the orphanage. That man was my father. It had to be. Father knew about Daniel. He had to know, and Daniel had recognized him when all the trouble began and Father came from Rouen to help. He had to have recognized Daniel at my house. He had been seeing him at the orphanage for eleven years! And Daniel had remembered him from the orphanage. He had become uncomfortable when I introduced Father to him as the lawyer who would help us. In a room of my own house, he had stepped back, clearly surprised, but like Father, he had said nothing. Of course. Everything was fitting together: the birth date of December 19, 1851, the announced closing of the orphanage in 1863 just as Daniel had said. It was the year he had run away, the same year he had appeared at my Boulevard Saint-Germain worksite to become my Runner.

I returned to Rouen like a wild man and stormed into my father's house. I found him in his study. I knew my face was flaming. My blood felt as if was boiling.

"I've been to La Bouille!" I shouted. "I've seen the records! Both my sons didn't die, did they! One of them survived! I have the document! Daniel Lazare is my son, isn't he! For some reason his name was changed from Fabron to Lazare, but he is my flesh and blood! You visited his orphanage again and again over the course of eleven years. Why didn't you tell me? Why didn't my mother, my dear, loving mother tell me? Why did you do this to me? Why did you do this to your own grandson?"

"It was for the best!" father stormed back at me, sitting upright in his chair. "I won't deny it. I thought the baby would die. He lived but he was weak. And do not chastise me! You were young! Being left a widower with a baby to raise was not what I wanted for you. I wanted you to pursue a prosperous career and live your life without the responsibility of a sickly child, free to live life on your own terms, not held back by a needy baby. Don't you see? Charles, you were special. From the day you were born you were our golden child, your mother's and mine. We had lost our little daughter. We never recovered. When you were born we wanted to protect you, give you the best of everything: a good home, a good education, a good view of life, and you did not disappoint us. You were intelligent. You did well in school. You had personality, vitality, and good looks. Please try to understand. When Louisa died, your mother and I saw what your grief was doing to you. I knew I had to step in. You were wasting away, dying before our eyes. And the baby in the orphanage? Yes, I arranged that. Just after the two babies were finally delivered, Doctor Mercier pronounced both of them dead along with Louisa. Pauline was there. She had been there all night assisting the doctor. When everything was over she took the two babies and put them in the basket beside Louisa. Doctor Mercier came downstairs to tell you what had happened while upstairs Pauline noticed a little hand moving in the basket. By the time she hurried downstairs to tell Doctor Mercier what she had seen, he had left. You were beside yourself, so she took me aside and told me that one of the babies was very weak, but alive. He would surely be dead by morning, she added. I went upstairs to see the baby for myself. The baby was indeed alive but I had to agree that he was very small and weak. He hardly moved. I told Pauline to say nothing to you about what she had seen. When I said I wanted the child taken away to spare you further pain when he finally did die, Pauline said she would take him to Sacred Heart where the nuns there would take care of final arrangements. You will remember Pauline is from La Bouille. She had known Sacred Heart from earliest childhood. We were both sure the baby would die at the orphanage, but two days later, when I sent her back to La Bouille to obtain the child's death certificate, she found he was alive and doing well. The nuns had called on a wet nurse from the village to nurse him. He began to thrive. When Pauline returned to me with the news, I decided it would be best to leave the child with the nuns. He would very likely be unhealthy and a burden to you. Time passed and you were fading before my eyes. Watching you grieve was unbearable. I couldn't allow it. I couldn't allow you to destroy yourself. I felt I had made the right decision. I wanted you to continue to explore all the potential I had seen in you from the time you were a young boy. A sickly baby did not fit into the plan!"

"Fit into the plan? What plan?" I interrupted. "There was no plan! I was a grieving man who would have done much better overcoming the loss of his wife with the responsibility and companionship of one of his children regardless of his health. Did you ever think of that?"

"Yes I thought of that. I thought of it many times. When your mother and I saw what was happening to you and how you were wasting away, we wanted to tell you everything, but the baby was settling into the orphanage. The nuns doted on him. He was a beautiful baby and he was doing well. It was too late. Too much time had passed. Your mother said, "Charles will hate us for even considering such a cruel thing. We cannot have that. We lost our daughter. He is all we have. Nothing will be the same if we tell him we placed his son in an orphanage, expecting him to die."

When I pressed Father for further explanation he elaborated on the desperate action he had taken. "I decided it would be best for you to leave Rouen and get as far away as possible from circumstances that at one time or another might reveal the truth and hurt you," he said as if defending a client in a courtroom. "I found a solution when I heard that Baron Haussmann was undertaking the transformation of Paris," he continued. "I went to see him. I thought he would need an architect like you. We were classmates for a while at the Paris Conservatory. He remembered me very well. He played cello in the orchestra and for the one year I spent at the Conservatory, I was the orchestra's concert pianist. We became friends and had a wonderful time performing in any number of concerts, then celebrating our successes later at a café, but I left the Conservatory to tour the continent. As you also know, I quickly found that I didn't like the concert lifestyle. I decided to become a lawyer and earned my credentials at the University at Lille. Baron Haussmann remembered that I was unusually talented. We had a very pleasant visit at the Hotel de Ville. We reminisced for a while, and when I explained what had happened to you and that you were an experienced architect in need of a change of scenery and a new life, he assured me he would find something for you in his Offices of City Planning. He was in the process of hiring architects, engineers, and landscape designers for the rebuilding of Paris. My timing was absolutely perfect and a position in faraway Paris seemed exactly the right thing for you and the child."

I listened, paralyzed by what I was being told. For the best? The timing was perfect? A position in Paris exactly the right thing for me and my child? I couldn't hold myself together.

"Father, you saw Daniel!" I exploded. "You were there in Paris! You were in my home for several weeks! You knew who he was. You had seen him at the orphanage on countless occasions. For eleven years he lived as an abandoned, unloved boy. In my house, under my roof, you saw how compromised he was, how ill-prepared for life he was! Was that for the best? Is Daniel's life better because of your decision? Is mine? I don't even know where he is now. Is that for the best? I console myself with the fact that at least he can read."

"Oh yes, and about that," Father said. "How do you think Daniel learned to read? I was the one who brought books to the orphanage! I made generous contributions to the Charitable Order of the Sacred Heart so that Sister Angelica would be assigned to teach that boy to read. Your mother brought clothes and quilts. We thought it was the least we could do. Now I see it was a waste of time and money!"

"A waste of time and money?" I felt ill. My stomach was lurching. My head was pounding. It was as if every vein and artery in my body was about to burst. This was my father, the man who had raised me. I had loved and admired him. I had lived in his house. All my life I had conformed to his every demand. I don't know how I managed to ask him my next questions. I just knew there was more.

"Well now Father, tell me, who exactly is buried with Louisa?" I asked, struggling to keep the tears back. "There were two babies. Is Daniel's brother lying buried with his mother or was he found to be alive and did you arrange for his disappearance too? And why was Daniel's last name changed to Lazare?"

"Daniel's brother was born dead. He is buried with Louisa," Father said, tears finally flooding his eyes, "and Pauline put some small blankets together to look like the covered body of a dead infant so that in Louisa's open coffin before the funeral, it would appear there were two identical babies lying beside their mother. Charles, I'm sorry. I thought I was doing the right thing. It was all for your sake. I did all I could to set you on the right path and I succeeded. I would do it all over again! You are part of an historic event! You will live in the most beautiful city in the world! You should be proud of that! And Pauline chose the name Daniel Lazare. It was her grandfather's name and the first one she thought of when she was asked what the baby's name was. She was trying to protect all of us so that when he died no one would connect the baby to our family and all would be forgotten."

Given the nature of all I had heard, my next question could not have come as a surprise. I faced my father directly and asked, "Did you advise Daniel to run away? Tell me the truth! Did you frighten him and tell him he was about to be found guilty of a serious crime and sent to prison?"

"Yes! Yes! I am guilty of that too! Charles, I saw what your son had become. He was a dirty, devious boy who had worked his way into your affections in order to gain favor! And how well he succeeded! I saw that winsome expression he could put on his face when it suited his purposes! And that long yellow hair! It gave him an identity that set him apart, made him special and angelically dear, as if he had been born with a halo. And look at what you did for him! You took him into your home, supported him at every turn, bought him clothes, fed him, even tolerated his dog, and when he got into trouble you engaged a very good lawyer to defend him! Yes! Face it! He committed a crime! Charles, you know as well as I do that he stole the money. He is not worthy of being your son or my grandson! That miserable wretch would never have done anything to make us proud of being Fabrons! I went to his room late that night before the hearing. I woke him up and told him he was damaging your position with Baron Haussmann by remaining in Paris. I told him there was no solution to his problem and that he must leave your house and escape from Paris immediately if he expected to avoid going to prison for a very long time."

I fell into a chair, dumbfounded. "You are a terrible man!" I called out. "I am ashamed to call you my father! You are ruthless and vicious! I am your son and you have made my life and your grandson's life a living hell!"

"Don't talk to me about ruthless and vicious!" the paternal voice I now could not silence called out. "I am wise! I make decisions! I do what's best! I have built my reputation on confronting difficult issues with strength and determination! I am a problem solver. I solved a problem for you! I saved you from yourself! You were too weak, too slow, too wrapped up in that luxury of self-pity you have a habit of falling into! And I will add that Baron Haussmann saw nothing wrong with my decisions!"

"Do you mean to tell me he knows about all this?"

"Yes, he knows! Of course! He's known all along! When I went to him in Paris and told him about your long bereavement and explained that I felt it would be best for you to leave Rouen for a while, I also told him that as a grieving young widower you were in a fragile place in life and that I hoped he would find an appropriate position for you, a demanding one that would strengthen your resolve and invigorate you, give you purpose and restore your determination. He recommended Supervisor of Demolition. It was a stroke of genius!"

A stroke of genius! Of course. Demolition! How appropriate a position for a man on the verge of a breakdown! Now I was beginning to see how the great puzzle had been assembled, its first piece my meeting with The Baron in his sumptuously impressive Hotel de Ville offices, the second his insistence when I voiced concerns about the position of Demolition Supervisor that I return the following day, the third and final magnificently well-conceived puzzle piece my inclusion with members of the inner circle, that small band of extraordinarily talented colleagues who impressed me and made me feel part of things and not the outsider that despite their best efforts I felt I had remained through all the wasted years. I was a good architect. I had come to Paris with credentials and an impressive portfolio. Given the slightest chance I would have met the high bar The Baron set, but I was tolerated, marginalized, left to brace myself and learn my lessons in the outside world of destruction where I was expected to gain experience in becoming a stronger, more worthy human being.

I hope there are not too many people in the world who learn to hate their fathers as I learned to hate mine; not too many whose fathers, like mine, assume such a degree of secretive, powerful control over the lives of their children that they slowly but surely become gods unto themselves, elevated instruments of their own vanities and perpetrators of hateful but brilliantly conceived indiscretions.

The breach between Father and me was never healed. After May of 1870 we never saw each other again. We didn't write. We didn't care. When Father died five years later I felt relieved of a great burden. I attended the funeral and watched as he was buried beside Mother, not far from Louisa and one of our sons. That same day I was on a train back to Paris with one pressing issue on my mind. Within hours of my arrival I made an appointment to see Baron Haussmann. The time had come to place a proper frame around the puzzle. I had to know how my son Daniel had come to be placed with me as my Runner.

Greeting me in his offices, The Baron was in his customary good form, welcoming and pleasant, but direct and anxious to get to the point of my visit. Once he understood my purpose his demeanor changed. He became sympathetic and more understanding than I had ever seen him. By now I was well-acquainted with his intrinsic desire for brevity no matter the situation and I wasted no time in telling him about the discoveries I had made at La Bouille and the conclusions I had drawn. He listened intently, surprised, he said, by most of my revelations but aware of several conditions that had led to Daniel's plight as an orphan. He was open and candid in describing his role in the actions which had led me to a prominent position on his staff, and he was clear in letting me know exactly how Daniel came to be placed as my Runner. This is our conversation as I have remembered it through the years and as I will remember it to the end of my days:

"Your father was a good man," he began, seated in a chair very similar to the one he had settled into during our first meeting seventeen years before. "He wanted only the best for you," he added as I settled myself into the chair closest to him. "When he came to see me seventeen years ago I was happy to be in a position to help a former classmate. You must know your father and I were friends at the Paris Conservatory. He was a talented pianist, a fine musician really. He could have made a great career for himself. I'm sorry he didn't."

There was an unusual warmth in his voice as he referred to his friendship with my father and recalled the passion they had shared for music, but I could feel my blood running cold as in proceeding to tell me what had happened, he painted a dark, overwhelming picture.

"Your father came to see me shortly after I was appointed by the Emperor. He told me about you, about your architectural background, the loss of your lovely young wife, and the son who had survived his difficult birth. He saw the child as a hindrance to your future. He said that without your knowledge he had made arrangements for him. He said those arrangements were for the best and that when I met you and saw the type of kind, considerate person you were, I would see how the responsibility of a sickly child would have pointed your life in the wrong direction. He said he wanted you to make something special out of your life and to take advantage of every available opportunity. He wanted you to come to Paris, take a position with me on the Paris Project, and above all, he wanted you to make your permanent home here in Paris with no knowledge of the child. He was very clear on the importance of your being away from Rouen. I agreed that a new life and involvement in my exciting new project would serve you well and more than likely set you on the road to recovery. What I didn't understand was why he felt your child would be a hindrance to you. I have gentlemen friends, widowers who have lost their wives under similar circumstances. They keep their children and arrange for someone to live in the home and look after them. Charles, I now see I should have questioned the situation immediately, but there was a great driving urgency in your father at the time, a genuine desperation about him, and he was my old school friend. I wanted to help him. I set my doubts aside and assured him that I would find something for you. Charles, I want you to understand that until recent circumstances required me to become more involved, which I will explain in a moment, I had no idea your infant son had been sent to an orphanage. My understanding as explained to me by your father was that as an infant your child had been placed in wonderful situation not far from Rouen where a woman took unwanted babies into her home and with a small staff looked after them until she could find proper homes for them. My further understanding was that babies who, for one reason or another were not taken into homes by the time they were a year old, were sent to the Sisters of Charity at the nearby Catholic School where they would live and receive fine educations. "

I could stand it no longer. "A school?" I shouted. "A woman who took in unwanted babies until she could find proper homes for them? Lies! All lies! Baron Haussmann, my infant son was taken in by no benevolent woman. He received no fine education! He was raised in the Sacred Heart Orphanage just twelve miles from my home, the home that should have been his! I have been to the village of La Bouille where he was raised. I met with the priest at the local church. He had directed the Boys' Choir at the Sacred Heart Orphanage. It burned down a few years ago but some of the records were saved. He helped me to find documented proof that my son was brought to the Sacred Heart Orphanage in secret, taken there on the day of his birth and not expected to live! I carry that document with me every day. Well, what a surprise it must have been! The baby survived, and instead of being raised in the loving home he could have had with me, he became one of twenty-five boys who lived in cold rooms and wore threadbare clothes until they were old enough to be sent out into the streets to make their own way in life!"

The Baron rose from his chair and poured two glasses of cognac. I took my glass and eagerly drank down its entire contents, my memory jostled to an incident that had haunted me for years.

"Baron Haussmann," I said, "At this moment I am reminded of the day I left Rouen for Paris, anticipating my meeting with you seventeen years ago. Along with my mother, my father saw me off at the train station and only now, all these years later, do I understand why I have carried the mental image of how oddly triumphant he looked as the train departed Rouen and he waved and smiled approvingly. Now I know how delighted he must have been with himself. His plan was working out perfectly. He knew you would convince me to accept a position no matter what it was or how reluctant I might be to accept it. Best of all, I was moving out of the way, miles from Rouen and any hint of a son in an orphanage."

For some reason I suddenly thought of Pauline and the vase of roses she had placed on my hall table along with The Baron's letter the day it arrived at Seine-Maritime Hill. She knew what Father had arranged with Baron Haussmann. Father had told her to expect the letter from Paris and he wanted her to do all she could to make its arrival seem special. Pauline, my trusted housekeeper and beloved childhood confidant had been part of the great scheme to send me away from Rouen, far away from my own son and off to Paris.

The Baron returned to his chair. "Charles, you have a difficult burden to bear," he said, "and now, I do as well. It's quite remarkable and I hesitate to say this, but for a long time everything was going according to plan. Then something happened and it all changed. Your father came to see me again. He said the school he had told me about, which I learned only from you now was in truth an orphanage, was about to close. He hadn't expected that. I could see how the news had unsettled him, but he told me that your child, who by then was an eleven-year old boy named Daniel Lazare, was about to be sent to Le Havre where he would be forced to work on the docks. He had heard about my Runner Program and asked if I could find a place for the boy. It would be a temporary measure, he assured me, only until he could find a suitable place for him. He took great pains to insist that I not reveal Daniel Lazare's identity to anyone, not under any circumstances, and especially not to you. Charles, I was completely frank in telling your father that I did not wish to be involved in a family situation like this. I made it clear that I had a great deal to contend with every day and that my every hour was spoken for. I had no time for outside dilemmas. Nonetheless, I agreed to find a place for the boy as a Runner. In my heart I felt that the truth would come out somehow. It had to. Circumstances were too coincidental, their final outcome too inevitable. With that assurance in mind, I decided there could be no better place for Daniel Lazare than with his own father, and of course, that was you, Charles. It seemed an ideal situation and I was rather delighted with myself for having thought of it. I knew you as a kind, thoughtful man and I knew you would treat the boy well. Furthermore, I was convinced once the truth emerged, which I was sure it quickly would, that there would be a happy ending. Until then the boy would be safe. As far as I was concerned, that was the important thing. I went ahead and arranged with your father for Daniel to be taken from the orphanage and put on a train to Paris. On the appointed day, Marie Duclos was to meet him at the Paris station, take him to Maison Sospire, and assign him as your Runner. The very next morning, she was to give him directions to your worksite. Everything was in place. It seemed a perfect plan until two days before he was to board the train bound for Paris I received word that Daniel had run away from his so-called school. Of course, once again, that changed everything.

Charles, the fact that the boy eventually found his way to Paris on his own is a miracle. I don't know how or why he arrived at the door of Maison Sospire. Perhaps you do. I've thought he could have met up with another orphan on the street who told him about the Runners, but I believe that once he did arrive at Maison Sospire's door and told Marie Duclos he was Daniel Lazare, that she remembered his name from the message I had sent to her concerning the assignment I had requested for him. She is a very astute woman. It was Marie who, with no idea that you were the boy's father, went ahead and assigned him to you as she had been originally instructed to do. Much to her credit, she promptly sent me a message informing me of all this. If memory serves, she went so far as to write that she had sent the boy to your exact worksite on Boulevard Saint-Germain.

Charles, I hope you know it was never my intention to hurt you or the boy. I wanted to help your father. He was an old friend and I was happy to be in a position to be able to give him some peace of mind. I never imagined he would lie to me. I suppose I didn't look far enough ahead or ask the right questions. Perhaps you will always think I didn't do the right thing, but you must remember that I didn't know the truth. I'm very sorry about my role in all this and I hope you can forgive me, but like your father I wanted you to heal, find happiness, and establish a good life here in Paris. I would have wanted nothing less for a child of mine."

It was the last time I saw Baron Haussmann in Paris. We would meet again in a different place and under different circumstances, but not until a series of events conspired to affect us in similar ways. Two months later, War with Prussia was declared and my life in Paris came to a close. It was a bittersweet period, one that in its powerfully conflicted way resolved the most pressing issues of my life. In an ironic turn of events, I learned by letter from my father's legal counsel that at his death my father had left me nothing. He left his house in Rouen to Pauline. I later learned she had sold it and returned to La Bouille to live with a cousin. As his will directed, Father's bank accounts and considerable financial assets were dissolved, their balances distributed to orphanages in and around Rouen and Paris.

CHAPTER THIRTEEN

A Slant of Light

1870. JULY. The Prussian were on their way to France. I left Paris on one of the last trains to the Normandy Coast. From Calais I crossed the Channel aboard a crowded packet boat and seven hours later stepped onto English soil. Like many of my countrymen I had left the shores of France with pangs of guilt. There were those of us who could afford to escape the Prussian Siege and take care of ourselves for a while without worrying about money, but there were those who could not. The stalwart souls who stayed behind with limited resources faced the unknown with little more than faith and courage. Still others who could have left with ease and financial security simply chose not to. The Villards were one such family. I did all I could to convince them to join me in London, but both Henri and Claire held their ground and insisted on remaining in Paris. Until the last minute Lily made every attempt to change her parents' minds, but her arguments were not convincing, and in fact were met with stern reprimands. Dutiful daughter she was, she stayed on with them. While in London I thought of

Henri, Claire and Lily every day. I wrote letters, anxious for news. They responded when mail out of Paris was permitted. Unfortunately, much of it was censured and they could not always present an accurate picture of what was actually happening around them. The uncertainty was maddening. On the whole, my stay in London was fraught with constant worry about the Villards, my Hotel de Ville colleagues, my house, and Paris itself. As was the case with all of us who had left, I had no idea what I would or would not find when I returned home, but like a favorite aunt with a lovely large house in a park, cosmopolitan London succeeded in providing the temporary comfort I sought.

At first I was overwhelmed by its size. The city was immense, the largest in the world, but once I had settled into comfortable rooms at the Charing Cross Hotel, I discovered I had chosen a highly manageable location for my London stay. The Charing Cross was in the City of Westminster which I learned was a city within the city, a situation which I was certain bore historical significance but which, as far as I was concerned, only enhanced my easy access to The Strand, Trafalgar Square, and Whitehall. Adding to my satisfaction with conditions in my temporary home was the fact that as a result of the mass exodus from Paris there was a large French speaking population throughout London. Many restaurants and shops were patronized by my French countrymen and as I began to find my way around it was reassuring to hear my home language being spoken. Like flocks of birds ending a long migration we gathered and eagerly made new friends, doing all we could to help each other adapt to the new norms in our lives. We met for luncheons and dinners, we practiced our conversational English, and we spent many afternoons browsing the shops. Essentially, we did what we could to make the best of life in London. Some did better than others. There were love affairs, dalliances, and quite a few marriages, but every French heart taking refuge in Paris was heavy and more than anything, we wanted to return home.

Once I settled into a semblance of routine, the London art galleries became my favorite distractions. Of course I loyally maintained that the Paris art world was in a class by itself what with the treasures of The Louvre, the annual Salon Exhibition, and a never ending series of gallery shows and exhibitions, but the London art scene was lively enough to attract my attention. I frequented the British Museum, the Victoria and Albert, and the National Gallery. I found the Clarke Gallery one afternoon. It was small and inviting to the browser and every painting displayed on its red damask walls was available for sale. So conducive was the Clarke's welcoming atmosphere that I became interested in the possibility of acquiring a painting or two. With his charm and patience, the Clarke's proprietor provided further incentive. Not too surprisingly, that charming, patient man was Monsieur Clarke himself.

Mason J. Clarke was a highly personable individual who, having made frequent trips to Paris to buy paintings for his London gallery, had become fairly comfortable with the French language. His place of business being visited by an increasing number of Parisians who provided further opportunity for him to exercise his French language skills, he was able to handle transactions with relative ease. My own progress with the English language was not as advanced, but I welcomed every opportunity to at least attempt English phrases and sentences I had heard at the hotel or practiced with my new British friends. My progress was, in a word, slow. During my first encounter with Mister Clarke and eager to impress him with my English, I launched into what I thought was an intelligent observation on a landscape I liked. Although I stumbled and hesitated, searching for words, I felt I was being understood perfectly. Mister Clarke must have thought otherwise, for he tapped my shoulder with a sympathetic smile and in French said, "Let me call on the language skills of my assistant. He has all the information on the landscape you seem to like and he is from Paris. He speaks fluent French and excellent English. He will be able to help you. His name is Charles Lazare."

In a matter of minutes I was introduced to a tall, flaxen-haired young man who extended his hand with a familiar smile. I had to catch my breath. I had seen that smile many times before. As the voice behind it politely said, "it is a pleasure to have you visit our galleries, Monsieur Fabron," my heart was racing. I knew exactly who this young man was and I knew he recognized me. He may have assumed the name of Charles Lazare, but one look at him told me that he was the boy I had known in Paris as Daniel

Lazare. He had been my Runner. He was the son I thought had died at birth. I wanted to shout it out, all of it. I wanted this handsome young man who had grown to look exactly like his beautiful mother to know right then and there that I was his father and that had I known the truth I would gladly have spared him the troubling years he had spent in an orphanage. Any instinct I may have had to reveal the truth of our relationship in a blur of explanation was held in check when with the self-certainty I had admired in him at the tender age of eleven, this Charles Lazare said smoothly, and in precise French, "Monsieur Fabron, the landscape Monsieur Clarke tells me you are interested in is one of our choice canvases this season. It was painted by a talented young woman who lives in Staffordshire. She brings us all her work. It sells very well. You have good taste."

"And what is the price?" I asked, playing the game like the novice I quickly realized I was being asked to portray.

"The artist is flexible," was the unruffled answer to my question," but we can discuss the price of the painting and other matters at greater length if you like. There is a very nice tea room just two doors down. I have a delivery to make this afternoon, but we can meet there later. Shall we say five o'clock?"

I thought five o'clock would never come. I wandered around for what seemed hours. I strolled through Hyde Park. I admired the well-tended gardens. I bought a bag of bread crumbs, sat on a bench, and fed the pigeons. I admired the fine house granted by Queen Victoria and a grateful nation to the Duke of Wellington following his victory over Napoleon. At last the hands of my pocket-watch reached 4:45. In fifteen minutes I would be meeting with my son. My heart was racing again. This would be the most gratifying experience of my life. My son would finally have the answer to the question of who he really was and I would have my child. We would make up for all the lost years. I would tell him about Father Nicholas at La Bouille and how we had scoured through Sacred Heart's old records. Together we would marvel at the proof I had found, proof that a baby named Daniel had been born in Rouen and that he had been taken on the exact date of his birth to the Sacred Heart Orphanage with low expectations for survival.

I would tell him that Pauline Caron had presented him as being named Daniel Lazare, not Daniel Fabron. As of this day his name would finally be my name.

He was late, or perhaps I was early. I don't remember. I do remember that I sat at one of the tables facing the door so I would be sure to see my son as soon as he arrived. I ordered tea, a tray of sweets, and two glasses of sherry. I watched every person who came through the door until at last there he was, walking in long, even strides, smiling when he saw me and extending his hand which I took in mine, delighting in the mere touch of my son.

"Ah, Monsieur!" he said, seating himself across from me. "I was so surprised to see you in the gallery today. I couldn't believe my eyes. I've thought about you all afternoon. I hope you understand why I could not be warmer in welcoming you at the gallery. I wasn't sure how you would feel about seeing me again. I know I disappointed you by running away from Paris, but I had no choice."

"Oh, I understand," I lied, attempting to hide my anxiety, "and you never disappointed me Daniel. I just worried about you, but things seems to be working out very well for you here. I'm glad."

"Yes, they are working out well," he said, "but Monsieur, we have so much to talk about. I'm happy to see you've come to London. It must be a terrible time in Paris. We hear there are food shortages and that children are dying. It's a horrible thought. As soon as I heard the news about the Prussian march into Paris I thought of you and Baron Haussmann and all the others I knew. You must be worried about what could happen to all your work on the city. I'm so sorry."

"Yes, I'm very worried about conditions in Paris. It is a terrible time for the French people," I answered, sharing what little I knew as I sipped at my tea and took in every detail of my son's cultivated British appearance: his immaculate black suit and crisp white-collared shirt, the gray striped silk cravat perfectly knotted, the matching gray silk handkerchief peering out of his breast pocket in four perfectly folded points.

"Those of us who could leave Paris feel safe here in London," I added, "but we have no idea what we'll find when the war is over and we return home. News out of Paris is sparse. Right now, though, I'm interested in you, Daniel. From what I saw today in the gallery, you have found a good place for yourself."

"Yes, I have, Monsieur. I could not be happier. I love my work."

As we discussed his gallery duties I watched his every move; the way he used his hands to emphasize a point, the thoughtful way he tilted his head when I asked a question. The easy banter continued until at last I found the opportunity to say what was in my heart.

"Daniel, and I hope you understand that I feel I must call you Daniel, I never thought I'd see you again. Ever since you left Paris. I've wondered where you could be. Your friends on the Paris Project have asked about you again and again. We have missed you, all of us, but it pleases me to see you have found a good situation here in London. It suits you. I'm just curious to know why you changed your first name to Charles."

There was a long pause as Daniel looked into my eyes. "We recognized each other immediately in the gallery, didn't we, Monsieur Fabron," he said, pausing once again. "Why did I change my name? The answer is simple. You will remember that I was in trouble in Paris. There was too much debris associated with the name of Daniel Lazare, too much for me to fear, and once people from Paris began arriving here in London by the hundreds I couldn't take the chance that someone from the past would recognize me or my name. I didn't mind when Mr. Clarke introduced me to his British and American clients as having come from Paris, but beyond that I couldn't take the chance that the good reputation I was building with him could be affected. Mr. Clarke agreed. He knows all about my difficulties in Paris and my reasons for changing my name. He says my past doesn't matter and that I should concentrate on doing my best in the present, but yes, things are, as you say, working out well, and thankfully in the few years that have passed since I came to London, my appearance has changed. I've grown taller. My frame has filled out. I keep my hair cut short. I know it's still very blonde, but I don't think I look at all like the Daniel Lazare of my Paris years, do you?"

I smiled, and although in the gallery I had recognized him immediately as the Daniel Lazare of his Paris years, I nodded my head in agreement and as I listened and watched my son, my love for him knew no bounds. I saw that he was proud of his maturity and his transformation, and rightly so. He had grown strong and decisive. The intelligence and hunger to learn I had observed in him as an eleven -year-old had blossomed. His natural curiosity was serving him well. He was a young man nearing twenty, but in those moments at a table in a London tea room, to me he was still the eleven-year-old boy with yellow hair who on a September day appeared at my worksite on a boulevard in central Paris and from that day forward made my work less burdensome and infinitely more tolerable. I thought of my Father when in his rage he had said, "I saved you from yourself!"

My Father had not saved me from myself. It was Daniel who had saved me from myself. It was Daniel who from his compromised position in life had seen what I had not seen as I displaced people and tore down their homes. It was Daniel who smiled at mothers who cried and shook hands with fathers whose anger subsided when he assured them, as I had, that all would be well and that they were fortunate to be together as a family. "It is the most important thing in life. Someday I will have a family," I heard him say repeatedly.

"You haven't answered my question," I persisted, facing my son and forcing myself to turn away from matters that continued to haunt me. "Why did you change your name from Daniel to Charles? I want to know. It's important to me."

"It was your name, Monsieur Fabron," came the answer. "The name of Charles was connected to everything I learned to admire about you: your manner, your position in life, your polished ways. I wanted to be just like you. You may not have noticed, but in Paris I watched you all the time. In my bed at night I would pull the covers over my head and practice the phrases and tone of voice I heard you use with people. "This may be difficult now, but you are on your way to a better life," I heard you tell people very confidently as they climbed onto the wagons taking them to strange new villages where overnight they were expected to lead new lives. "Be assured I shall do my best to see you receive the full amount you are due," you would tell a man who lived with his large family in a worthless tin-roofed hovel no bigger than a shed. I loved copying your words and your manner.

Monsieur, having your name makes me feel secure and important, kind too, and still connected to you in some way. I like that. Whenever I'm in doubt, or when something goes wrong with a client I think of how you would handle the situation. You have no idea how helpful you have been to me and how grateful I am for all you did for me. I want to apologize for leaving you the way I did, and Monsieur Fabron, I want you to know that I did not steal the money I was accused of stealing, not from anyone; not from the street vendor and not from Samuel Navier. I did not pick the pockets of a passer-by as your father accused me of doing the night I ran away, and I was not trying to run away from the police as he also said. I was trying to do the right thing, but I was not important enough to be thought of as innocent. I was just another worthless orphan in a big city. You must know I was afraid I would be sent to prison, but I have never forgotten the way you tried to help me and the good days you and I had together. Of course, Monsieur Clarke is a good man too. He saved me. He brought me to London during a bad time and as I have said, he knows all about my so-called Paris crime. Once I explained what had happened and told him I was innocent, he said we would never speak of it again and we haven't. I will always be grateful for that. He and his wife are very good to me. They have given me a good home and a reason to hold my head up even though I was raised as a discarded human being and accused of being a thief."

"Daniel, I always believed you. From the beginning I knew you had not stolen the money in question. I'm happy to be able to tell you that a few weeks after your disappearance, Inspector Valois uncovered a corrupt scheme that proved your innocence. You are in no danger. You could return to Paris at any time. Your name is cleared."

I proceeded to tell Daniel about the circle of corruption Marc Basse and Samuel Navier had conducted. Although pleased to know his name had been cleared, he was shocked to learn that Marc Basse could have masterminded such a devious plan. To my surprise, he did not choose to dwell for long on details, relieved, I assumed, by the overall outcome of events and the liberating feeling brought on by his complete exoneration. He soon turned the conversation to his work in the gallery and the Clarkes. He was clearly fond of them. I tried not to, but I found myself resenting the protective parental role they had come to play in his life. Listening to his flattery and compliments I told myself that I should have been the parent who was there when he was afraid and in need of protection. I hated the idea that with the Clarkes, Daniel was finding the happiness and security I had not had the opportunity to provide.

"From the very first day, the Clarkes made me feel as if I belonged with them," he told me with an affectionate smile. "They have a fine house in a fine part of London. I have a nice room of my own. The bed is soft. I have warm blankets and a view of the park across the street. There are servants. There is a terrace and a garden and lovely people come to dinner, but the Clarkes have no children of their own, no sons to care about them or take over the gallery someday. I want to take it over. Monsieur Clarke wants me to. He has drawn up legal papers that will allow me to own the Clarke Galleries one day. I love the work. I love the atmosphere. Right now I work very hard. I'm learning all the time. I organize our exhibitions, I supervise the hanging of paintings, and I am doing all I can to learn about the artists who bring us their work and the many who hold important places in the history of art. I will be called an expert someday. I intend to prove myself."

"I listened to my son as he gazed into his future with complete confidence. I remembered his interest in Charles Marville's photographs and Gabriel Davioud's artistry. His interest in a career in the art world made perfect sense but it was what he said in the next moments that I would remember and deeply regret for the rest of my life.

"Monsieur Fabron, I know I am still young but someday I want to be known as having the best art gallery in London," he said, leaning forward in his chair. "I want to be so successful, so prosperous, that I can forget I was an orphan. I want to become so happy that I can forget about the mother and father who didn't want me. I want to become so rich that I can stop wondering every day who those hateful people were and why they didn't love me enough to keep me. When I was your Runner in Paris I saw poor families every day, mothers and fathers with nothing to their names, but they were good mothers and fathers who loved their children enough to keep them and take care of them as best they could, no matter the circumstances. To this day I think of them."

I had to look away. I heard the harsh rancor in my son's voice. I saw the bitter rage flaring in his sensitive blue eyes. It was too late. I was too late. There would be no joyous reunion between a father and his son, no answers to questions an orphan had asked all his life, no making up for the lost years. Revelations and apologies would never be enough to heal this wounded child of mine. His injuries were too deep. The truth would not heal them. The truth would hurt him. Confessions would lead to more rage, more rancor. I would inflict further harm on this splendid child of mine by telling him he belonged to me and that he had disappeared by the time I had discovered that fact. My parents would be vilified as perpetrators of unspeakable cruelty. The grandson they had made an orphan would come to know his grandparents as people who visited his orphanage for eleven years and saw him, watched him, and brought books and clothes to somehow make up for their sin. Their preference for my happiness over his would never be understood, never be forgiven. The contempt for past offenses had festered for too long. It had been part of the boy. Now it was part of the man. It would be ingrained in him for all time. We had been cheated.

Our meeting in a London tea room ended when we agreed on a price for the landscape. I was heartsick as we made arrangements for its delivery to the Charing Cross Hotel, but before we parted ways the subject of Joli was raised.

"Diana Remy contacted me," I said, answering the inquiry in as steady a voice as I could. "I went to see her. She had sent a note to me at Cardon's where you had told her she would find me on a Tuesday evening. She was looking after Joli for you but when she said she couldn't keep him any longer, I was happy to take him. He seemed content enough for a while, but when I took him to worksites with me he waited and watched for you at every corner and intersection of Paris, always alert for any sign of you, always ready to resume his tasks with you. At my house he slept every night on the rug by the front door, waiting there, hoping you would come. One night, still waiting for you by the front door, he decided to die. Joli is buried in my garden at the Rohan Courtyards."

I saw Daniel in London on many occasions after that, and each time it pleased me to know that he had cleared the air with Mason Clarke by telling him about being my Runner in Paris. How he had explained our mutual ambivalence during my first visit to the gallery was never fully understood, but Mason Clarke appeared to have taken no offense. I could see he was very fond of Daniel and that he would have forgiven any indiscretion. During my frequent visits to his gallery he remained cordial, and whenever we referred to Daniel I was struck by the way he spoke of him; with great respect and pride, as if he was his father.

At first it was difficult to be in Daniel's company. I walked a fine line. I wanted to tell him everything and on a few occasions I almost did, but fearing the hurt and pain I would be inflicting and unwilling to risk the likelihood of his total rejection, I couldn't. I couldn't tolerate the thought of having him hate me and everyone connected to the limitations imposed on his childhood. I loved him and I wanted him to know nothing but happiness. He deserved nothing less. Of course I wanted to be with him, to see him, to watch him as a grown man, but it became a balancing act. When I saw him at the gallery I didn't want to appear overly encouraging or protective. I also didn't want to appear disinterested or distant. Thankfully, with each visit I became more comfortable being Daniel's friend and not his father. I repeatedly told myself that at least I had influenced him in positive ways during the short time we had worked side by side, the way a father should. He invited me to all the exhibitions at the Clarke Gallery. He was becoming interested in the work of a group of French painters, artists who had left Paris and had come to London for the same reasons I had and were eager to return home. He was very proud to show me evidence of his knowledge and rapidly developing popularity with the London art crowd. He introduced me as a childhood friend. The first time I heard those words I cringed, but witnessing the enthusiastic following he was enjoying and the encouraging surroundings in which he was becoming a star I was immensely proud of him. It was fine, I told myself. My son was on his way and I was becoming an art collector, the walls of my rooms at the Charing Cross rather nicely decorated with an ever-expanding collection of landscapes.

As a frequent client, I was eventually invited to dinner at Mason Clarke's home. I was pleased to receive the invitation, but I couldn't bring myself to accept. I made up an excuse about a scheduled dinner with friends. The truth was that I was afraid. I was afraid I would see the fine house where my son was living. I was afraid to meet the fine woman who had assumed the role of his mother. I was afraid I would be in a position to watch the affectionate interaction between the residents of the Clarke household. More than any fear, I knew I would be putting myself in a position to once again be disappointed in myself, in my parents, and in anyone who had played a role in this debacle that had become my life, even Baron Haussmann.

As I might have expected, Mason Clarke was not a man to extend merely one invitation to a loyal client. After a second attempt to invite me to dinner, I had no choice but to accept. I dreaded the thought of it. I dreaded the idea of close proximity to my son's home environment and the comparisons I knew I would make to Seine-Maritime Hill and the life we could have lived together there. With all this in mind, I accepted the invitation into the Clarkes' private world, mindful of the fact that Mason Clarke must be the gentleman and client Diana Remy had told me had saved Daniel by taking him away from Paris. I reminded myself that whenever she and I had talked during my subsequent visits and the subject turned to Daniel, that she was never clear on his exact whereabouts, and although she had never revealed his name, I now knew that Mason Clarke had to be the client who she told me visited Paris several times each year to purchase paintings for his London gallery and spend evenings in her company.

I left the Charing Cross and was driven by carriage to the Clarke address. It was Wilton Crescent in Belgravia, an area of large white stucco houses built in a contiguous crescent shape. Daniel had not overstated the quality of the Clarke house. It was indeed, fine. To my mind it was grand.

Mason Clarke and his wife, Anne, were delightful people. Their home, its elegant furnishings and art reflected their family backgrounds in upper class British society, but they carried no airs or affectations. I was immediately put at ease by their casual humor, their facility with the French language, and fulfilling my expectations, Daniel appeared to be completely comfortable in this setting and with them. He was an integral part of the conversation throughout the evening and instead of feeling hurt as I had expected to be, I was happy to see him so well-adjusted. The evening turned out to be one of several I enjoyed with Daniel and the Clarkes during my London stay. I cannot say that despite their good company I came to think of Mason and Anne Clarke as close friends. I didn't. I couldn't. Under my projected good manners I continued to resent their roles in Daniel's life. I couldn't help myself, but my son was happy. He was prospering. His future looked very bright. He was everything I would have wanted him to be had he grown up at my side as my son.

———— ·《Ø》· ————

I left London and returned to Paris in November of 1871. The rubble of war was everywhere. I could not blame the Prussians entirely. No one could. France had been damaged to an alarming degree by the Prussian Occupation as battles between the warring forces had raged at Beaune-la-Rolande, Amiens, Villers-Bretonneau and countless strategic locations throughout the country, but the greater damage to Paris had been inflicted by a protesting group of disgruntled Paris students and workers who directly after the Armistice was signed, formed a Revolutionary Government. They called themselves The Paris Commune.

As the war ended in defeat for France and humiliation with the Treaty of Versailles, this Empire-weary group of protesting Parisians rose up on March 18th of 1871 and took its revenge. The Second Republic had not protected them or their city, they cried out in unison as they marched. The Emperor had not stood up to the enemy. He had not lived up to expectations. He had allowed his people to suffer the travails of starvation and disease. Meat-loving Parisians had eaten dogs and cats, rats, and horses. When the livestock supply in the Bois de Boulogne had been depleted, hungry Parisians had raided the zoo. Castor and Pollux, the zoo's elephants, were first to be shot, their butchering and human consumption followed by a long list of exotic animals who met a similar fate along with two of Louis Napoleon's favorite horses. Restaurant menus featured innovative dishes such as kangaroo roast and leg of wolf with kitten sauce. No animal, wild or domesticated was safe in the besieged Paris of abandonment and suffering.

I felt guilty in the face of these violations. As Paris had suffered unspeakable horrors, I had been in a safe city. I had eaten good food. I had lived in a fine hotel. Like similarly transplanted Parisians I had suspected poor conditions existed in Paris, but as the city began its return to some semblance of normalcy and tales of deprivation began to circulate, the harsh truth emerged in grim detail. I had enjoyed the company of friends. I had explored the beauty of parks and squares. I had begun to collect paintings. I had spent time with my son. My guilt at having done these things was real but short-lived. It turned to anger when I saw what the Commune had done to the city I had come to love. Massive destruction, the worst in the city's long history had taken place as torch-bearing insurrectionist mobs descended along Baron Haussmann's wide boulevards, shouting out their themes of protest and resentment. To them, Haussmann's grand new Paris was an exploitation of cheap labor and reviled capitalism. In all its beauty and gentrification, it stood as the ultimate example of the diabolical tyranny inherent in Empire. The Second Republic must be dissolved, the Bonaparte Emperor sent into exile or better yet, executed, was the loudest cry. The French military had responded to the Commune with admirable force but when the fighting and killing was over more than 20,000 had been slaughtered. The idyllic setting of the Parc Monceau seen through Gabriel Davioud's magnificent gates had been the site of the Commune's bloody end as its last leaders were assassinated in the tree-shaded elegance of the Monceau's romantic landscape.

It was over, but in the space of mere days, the Place de la Concorde and each of Baron Haussmann's great avenues radiating from the Arc de Triomphe were bloodied and battered. The Chateau of Saint-Cloud was overrun, set afire, and virtually destroyed. Napoleon's Column in the Place Vendome was toppled and crumbled as great clouds of black smoke engulfed the city and in a final stroke the Hotel de Ville was set ablaze, its spectacular architecture badly damaged, its historic files and records destroyed, most significant to me, those of the seventeen Haussmann years and the historic plans for Paris which Napoleon Bonaparte himself had drawn and which I had seen in The Baron's office during my earliest hours in Paris.

I was told that for three full days a wild storm of ash and fragments of scorched paper had floated down from the windows of the flaming Hotel de Ville. I could not imagine the extent of what was lost. What I could imagine, and very clearly, was that my Paris life was over. There was nothing to keep me there; no career, no family, no future. My friends and colleagues had scattered to all parts of France. The Baron himself was gone. He had intended to stay. He had said as much, but as the Prussian shadow had lengthened and darkened and his own position as Prefect and Master Builder of Paris grew untenable, he had fled. It was at his home in the quiet of the Bordeaux countryside that he came to terms with reality, but it was difficult to face the fact that he had become an intensely hated man. Criticism had always rolled off him like a sheet of water. This was different. Now, everything was at stake: his career, his finances, and the French Empire itself. Most crushing of all was his abandonment by the Emperor who had no heart for contending with the barrage of accusations and ultimatums hurled at him by the French Council, the Senate, and the public. Weakened and sickened, shortly after the outbreak of war, he had been taken prisoner at Sedan. This humiliation compounded the symptoms of his failing health and he became as much a victim of the war as any critically wounded soldier.

The Villards had remained in Paris throughout the Seige. There was no damage to houses in the Courtyards, but the Villards themselves were damaged. Henri had lost much of the affability I had early on come to identify with him. He had seen too much. Claire was thin and fragile, the light gone from her blue eyes, her resolute spirit suppressed, but not altogether vanished.

"We will make the best of it," she stalwartly declared, wiping away tears during my first return visit with her. "Things will improve, the country will recover, and before too long Henri and I will be in the book business again. Education will continue and students from the Ecole and the Sorbonne will come to us as they have in the past. It will be as if nothing happened."

The old determination was there, the old fire perhaps an ember for now, but with a bit of fuel the old Claire would be back and she would bring Henri and Lily along with her. I was sure of it. They would mourn the loss of Simone for the rest of their lives, as I have, but along with the entire population of Paris they would repair and restore. Life in Paris would be good again. I had no doubt of it.

My own house in the Courtyards had been maintained by Natalia. I had offered to take her to London with me but she insisted on staying. She had relatives nearby, and like most Parisians she thought the Siege would be brief. Her predictions failing, she had suffered from hunger and fear, but like Claire, she now stoically predicted better days. Having been away for more than a year, I walked through the well-tended rooms of my house grateful for Natalia's devoted care, but always with the increasing conviction that my days as a resident of The Courtyards were over. There was nothing to keep me there. Somehow the affection I had felt for the house and the area had died and I decided I would sell or perhaps rent the Courtyards house and return to Rouen. The time had come for one more change. I was packing books and personal items when a solicitor appeared at my door.

"Monsieur Charles Fabron?" he asked, seeking affirmation. "Yes, I am Charles Fabron," I responded.

"Monsieur, you have inherited property at Claremont, a village in the outskirts of Bordeaux. I have been instructed to deliver this deed of ownership which the late benefactor's will requires I present to you. It is signed and certified and is accompanied by a personal letter and directions to the property from the Claremont train station. Please sign here."

"Monsieur, you must be mistaken," I said, quite certain the solicitor had the wrong address. "May I ask what address you were given?"

"The first of the Rohan Courtyards, the house at the end, the home of Monsieur Charles Fabron," came the answer.

I invited the solicitor in. Standing in the hallway I opened the envelope he had handed me and read the letter it contained in disbelief. It was from Adele Alessandri. "Charles, I am leaving you my house in Bordeaux. When I am gone I want you to live in it and enjoy it as I have. It will suit you and the way you are now, free of your turtle shell. Please leave the meadow as it is. The wild daisies bloom there every summer, and although we never wore old shoes and hats and enjoyed them together, their faces will be something to remind you of my love. I played many games with many men over the course of the years, but you alone took possession of my heart."

CHAPTER FOURTEEN

Glimmers of Sun

IT TOOK TIME FOR ME to grasp the idea that Adele had died and that she had left me anything at all, let alone her country house. We had been lovers so long ago that I was sure the gloss of our romance had faded into nothing more than a dull shadow, especially after our last contentious encounter in Paris.

At first I wasn't sure how to handle things. Having been left a house is not at all the same as being left a nice piece of furniture or a subscription to the opera. A house is a significant gift. Certainly, I appreciated Adele's generosity and her tender note, but my first thought was to sell. Of course first I would find out how and when she had died, but I didn't want or need a country house. I had a house in Paris and I had made plans to return to Rouen and Seine-Maritime Hill which I had continued to own throughout my Paris years. Another house was the last thing I needed. I decided to visit the village of Claremont, take a quick look around, and then proceed to make whatever local arrangements were necessary to sell. I packed a few things in a suitcase, boarded the overnight train, and three hundred miles later I was in the legendary Bordeaux wine-producing area of France. That advantage aside, I was discouraged by the great distance from Paris and Rouen. Then and there I decided I had no choice but to sell. Confident in my decision, I engaged a carriage at the Claremont station and handed the driver the directions Adele had left for me. I had to admit the drive was pleasant enough, lovely really. It was late-autumn and the Bordeaux countryside was glowing in a burst of fiery color. About three miles from the station the carriage turned onto an unmarked dirt road, then quickly made another turn onto a narrow gravel drive lined on both sides by a procession of old plane trees. The house stood waiting at its end. Approaching closer, I was taken aback by the good condition of the property. I couldn't imagine that Adele had been there often enough to have supervised its maintenance, especially during the war, but everything was attended to. Windows shone, box hedges were clipped, and the gravel drive looked freshly raked. I paid the driver and arranged for him to return for me the next day. Retrieving my suitcase, and walking up to the door of the house which I now owned. I took the key the solicitor had given me out of my pocket and turned it in the lock. Once again, as was the case the first time I walked into my house in the Courtyards, I fell in love at the door. On the outskirts of Bordeaux I had walked into an enchanting house at the edge of a pond. All thoughts of selling vanished in an instant.

<hr />

My house is a rambling, slate-roofed cottage built of stone. I have no idea how old it is, but the respectable aura of age exists in every room. The ceilings are low and beamed and the walls are paneled in pine that has turned golden with the passing of nameless years. There are wide plank floors, fireplaces in every room, and at the top of the stairs a loft with a window overlooks Adele's meadow. The furnishings are rustic and simple. A piano sits in a corner of the center room and the air smells gently and constantly of chestnut and pine. There is a barn where I keep my horse, and at the edge of the pond I keep a small blue boat. All is exactly as a house in the country should be: quiet, comfortable, and unfettered. Adele had named it Le Calme. I found the green porcelain nameplate by the front door when I arrived. I also met the caretaker that same day, Jacques Amboise. He came walking up the drive as I stood outside, marveling at the beauty of my inheritance.

"I worked here for Madame Alessandri for more than ten years," he explained. "I live with my mother in the house across the pond," he said, pointing to a small white house framed by tall trees along the banks of the gentle waters. "Madame did not come here during the war, but I knew that someday she would come back, so I kept taking care of things for her. One day, when the war was over, a man named Count Leclerc came. He said Madame had often told him about the house and the meadow and that he had come to see it for himself. Madame invited many friends to Le Calme, but I had never seen him before. He didn't stay long, but when he told me Madame had died he asked me to stay on and look after things exactly as I had while she was alive. I receive a payment from him every month. Madame loved this place. I love it too, especially the meadow. I came today to trim the boxwood. Madame was fussy about the hedges."

Adele's sensitivity to the character of the house shone through to me from the very first hour I spent in its peaceful atmosphere. I had no trouble understanding her fondness for it. She had found a haven where she could rest and let go of her fears and doubts. Le Calme was an island where nothing mattered but living quietly day to day, close to the natural world she respected and nurtured.

I have lived the year round in that world for more than a dozen years now. I sold the house in the Rohan Courtyards, and although for about a year I divided my time between Rouen and Bordeaux, I soon found that Seine-Maritime Hill had lost its meaning. I didn't need it anymore. I didn't need Rouen, I didn't need architectural offices on Rue de Vicomte, and although I would never forget them, I was no longer haunted by thoughts of the dead in a cemetery behind a church tower. I was also financially independent. Through my years with Baron Haussmann I had spent and saved wisely, and with profits from the sale of two houses I took great comfort in the knowledge that I could live without worry for the rest of my life. It had taken years, but at last I was free; free to be myself and free to make my own choices. The realization was euphoric as the house called Le Calme became for me the home and haven it had been for Adele.

The meadow she loved is a wide expanse of natural beauty blessed with a border of fine old trees along the edge of the pond and an abundance of seasonal wildflowers. In every season of the year it is a joy to the eye and a garden unto itself. Through spring the bluebells and mauve-colored betony abound. The lavender mallow and white mayweed follow, and through summer the appearance of Adele's beloved yellow-faced wild daisies makes my Bordeaux world the only place I wish to be. One summer I placed wooden benches under several of the trees. I painted them with the same blue paint I had used on the little boat. Adele wouldn't mind. She would find the benches convenient places from which to enjoy the view which requires no human effort to maintain, no horticulturalist's expertise to explain. Nature takes care of it all and does a fine job of things indeed. There is, however, a garden to tend. To one side of the house a short path leads to a stone wall and an arched wooden gate so old that it creaks and groans whenever I open it. At one point I thought to oil the hinges, but I changed my mind. I like the creaking and groaning. It's as if I'm being announced to the grasses and plants. "Here he comes! You know how he is! Put your best face forward!"

Once through that lamentable gate I enter what at one time was an abandoned garden. When I found it during my first visit, it was a gray, lifeless ghost of what I was sure had once been a lovely bit of earth. Jacques told me that Adele had insisted on tending it by herself and that when she died Andre Leclerc had instructed him to leave it to nature. Loyal Jacques had followed the Count's instructions all too carefully. Gnarled branches littered the ground, tall nameless weeds prospered alongside tangles of thorny brambles, and ugly twisted roots encroached like horrific black fingers on the paths. In its day it had surely thrived under Adele's expert hand, but time and war had taken their toll and left to its own devices, but for its overgrown boxwood and cypress hedge, it had fallen fallow and like Adele, had died. I decided I would restore it as a tribute to her. I'm glad I did. Adele's garden has developed into a special world for me, one I created myself as she did, with no help, and one I now nurture by myself and with great affection.

Until I came to Bordeaux I never had a garden of my own. My mother had her garden in Rouen. At Seine-Maritime Hill I paid a gardener to take care of my landscape, and in Paris, Natalia tended the roses. I had never given a thought to keeping a garden. Here, though, in the quiet of the countryside and with ample time for consideration, it felt like something I should do. I wish Adele could see it, but of course she would want to tear the whole thing up and start all over again. Nonetheless, under all her bluster I believe she would approve of what I've done. I certainly had enough experience watching the gardens of Paris come to life. Of course my garden is nothing at all like those masterpieces. It is a manageable piece of country ground where I plant and sow and cut and reap and walk and enjoy the simplicity of being close to the natural world.

I've learned a great deal from my garden. The lessons have often been difficult. First of all, I've learned that a garden is like life. It never turns out quite the way you want it to. You can plan and plant and water and cultivate, but you are not the emperor of the garden. By yourself and through your most heroic, backbreaking efforts you alone and with the mere wave of a hand do not determine success or failure. There is a cast of players eager to step onto the waiting stage, their roles and the entire production intricate and incredibly time consuming. First of all, the sun and the shade and the moon and the seasons direct everything. Adding to the mix, from day to day the rain and temperature play their capricious games, and they are devious. Those two irrational elements can fool you into thinking they are friendly and warm. You begin to trust them, but overnight, with a little assistance from precocious winds, they can turn wet and icy cold and destroy everything you've worked on and worried about for weeks. Then there are the weeds. And the rabbits. And the aphids, the cabbage worms, and the caterpillars who are the hungriest of all the vicious little beasts of the garden. It is a veritable war, but it is a war which to a very large extent I have waged well and won. After a long period of frustrating trial and error and despite Bordeaux' acidic soil which is ideal for wine growers but not for all plants, every summer I now successfully grow several varieties of roses which, shortly after beginning work on my patch of earth I was told by my nearest neighbor, are at the heart of every French garden worthy of the name. Recalling the beauty of my Paris rose garden and fulfilling what my neighbor regards as my patriotic duty, every summer, in addition to roses, I presently also produce neat rows of healthy cabbages, onions, peppers, and carrots, and I am an absolute authority on protecting strawberries and a little delicacy I like called pitahaya rouge which I grow only in the sunniest, warmest part of the garden. All through summer, bouquets of fragrant roses adorn the tables in the house, but the quantity of produce I grow is too much for one person to consume or store in the cellars for winter. Jacques is welcome to take whatever he and his mother can use and I take baskets of my treasured bounty to the local church and to Baron Haussmann who lives not far away.

His estate is at Cestas, like mine also on the outskirts of Bordeaux. He has lived there since the onset of the war in 1870. It is an impressive property. The house sits on more than one hundred acres of land, most of it wooded. I see him often, especially in summer when I bring him samples of my latest garden experiments. I tried cantaloupe melon this year. It did well. Yesterday we sat on his terrace and enjoyed slices of it together while watching the birds fly back and forth between the oak trees until it was time for him to tend the orchids which he does every afternoon at three o'clock. The orchids have saved him. They need his care and nurturing. He needs their beauty and strength.

I watch him in the greenhouse as he fusses over the regal Cattleyas and I see myself in him. Something very dear to him has died and he grieves as I once grieved. He goes through all the motions of living as for years I did. He entertains at dinners in his beautiful dining room, he takes long walks in the woods, and he communicates with friends and colleagues of the past, but he is as I was: a creature of habit, a lover of safe routine, a man not exactly sad, but never entirely happy. What I know pains him most is his inability to restore his place in the beloved world of Empire which no longer exists. It is this disturbing condition, this end of aristocratic life as he knew it, to which he cannot adjust. We no longer have an Emperor. The Baron no longer has an all-powerful friend and ally in the nearest palace. Empirical edicts no longer become immediate law. They mean nothing. France has a President now and laws have been established to prevent there ever again being a Bourbon or Bonaparte ruling France. Finality came with the news that Emperor Louis Napoleon had died. His passing came barely two years after the war with Prussia ended. The Emperor who had arrived in France in 1852 with an ambitious agenda and a burning desire to transform neglected Paris, took his last breath in 1873 in England, at Chiselhurst, Kent.

For a time after the war, the fiery yearning for position and recognition had burned brightly in Baron Haussmann's Bonaparte-loving heart. The mastermind who had lived and fought and succeeded beyond expectation had lost all support, all influence, and yet in September of 1871, four months after the end of the war, he was named a Director of Credit Mobilier. In 1873 he was promoted to Administrator. Considering the flood of ruinous accusations once hurtled at him regarding serious financial malfeasance I could not fully comprehend the wisdom of this association with a prestigious Paris financial institution. Be that as it may, in 1877 and aware of its ironic twist, the Baron Haussmann of Second Empire dreams managed to astonish me once again when he was elected to a two-year term as Bonapartist Deputy for Ajaccio, Corsica, birthplace of Napoleon. It took several days for me to recover from this remarkable turn of events. When Louis Napoleon died, The Baron did not attend his funeral. He could not forgive the man he had faithfully and tirelessly served as a devoted public servant for abandoning him at the end, but every year he attends the Emperor's Annual Memorial Service at Notre Dame, appearing magnificently turned out in his formal Prefect Uniform and Decorations.

It was upon his return to Cestas from Corsica that I noticed the change in him. He became introspective, turning his daily attention to writing his memoirs, playing his cello, and tending the orchids. I believe it was the insulting negligence of the new government that cast the final blow. Baron Haussmann, Prefect and Master Builder was not asked to assess the ravaging damage to Paris after the War or the destruction wrought by the Commune, nor was he asked to supervise repairs to the city whose infrastructure and design he knew better than anyone. Adding considerable insult to injury, last year an attempt was made to rename the boulevard that bears his name. Thankfully, at the last minute the attempt failed and Boulevard Haussmann remains an important thoroughfare in the heart of modern Paris.

Time passes slowly for him as today he arranges matters of his daily life at Cestas, but that is not to say his flamboyant personality has diminished entirely or that he has turned away from the interests of his Bordeaux community. The art of Municipal Administration is engraved into his being. It is who he is. Unable to resist, he readily offers advice to members of the Town Council when he hears about a new municipal project, but the 'scandal' as it is called, of the Paris years follows him. In matters of local Bordeaux governance his reputation remains tarnished. His opinions are politely heard, taken lightly, and passed over. His interest in Bordeaux wines and the Maison de Vin promote more sincere, somewhat less complicated associations.

The Maison de Vin is a large building in the center of the City of Bordeaux. It attracts locals and tourists alike. I've heard it said it is this building that inspired the Haussmann architectural style. Bordeaux was The Baron's last Prefect assignment before he met with the Emperor in Paris and his life took on its famed direction. He knows Bordeaux well and I must admit that architecturally The Maison de Vin does bear a strong stylistic resemblance to the distinctive rectilinear Haussmann buildings of Paris. In any case, it serves as the major sales and distribution point for the wines of Bordeaux and its existence now nurtures The Baron's social life as at the same time it helps to maintain his extensive wine collection. The Maison hosts wine tastings and sponsors tours through many Bordeaux vineyards. Best of all, it is a popular meeting place for the many local growers and collectors who have been The Baron's friends for years and care not at all about his Paris difficulties. They are, in fact, great admirers of his accomplishments as Prefect and Master Builder. As a group they are intrigued by his tales of demolition and construction, and on several occasions they have enjoyed excursions into Paris, their guide none other than The Baron himself who enjoys leading these forays into the world of past glories as no one else possibly could. During our last visit, I told him that I myself wish to join the group he will be escorting through Paris next month. He tells me he will be careful not to exaggerate since I know what is true and what is not.

I am perfectly comfortable with The Baron. I enjoy his company during our visits and I especially enjoy the opportunity to re-live the many hours we shared as Paris became Paris. I do not hold him responsible for errors or disappointments of the past. He acted as a friend to my father and a mentor to me. I understand the difficult position in which he found himself as he weighed fact and fiction, but I am grateful to him for having sent Daniel to work at my side. At least we had that time together.

This then, is the state of things as I welcome spring of 1885. I live content in a quiet world far from city life and my Rouen roots. Jacques Amboise continues to look after Le Calme for me as he did for Adele. He makes repairs as needed. He clips the hedges and keeps the gravel drive raked. When I wrote to Andre Leclerc to tell him I had inherited Adele's house and that I would be living there and taking over maintenance payments to Jacques, he acknowledged my letter and wrote back to tell me that Adele had died in his house. I was glad to hear that she had not died alone. She had developed a fever and never recovered. Her house in the Marais had been requisitioned by the Prussians during the Siege and she had been staying with her dear old friend. Digesting the news, I sat for long hours on one of the blue benches under the trees in the meadow. I couldn't imagine Adele removed from the world. She was so passionate about its endless possibilities, so desperate to mold them to her liking, forever fighting its twists and turns as if she could control them all by her complicated self. I often pray that in death God has granted her the peace that eluded her in life and I thank Him for the gift of her presence in mine.

The time I now have to myself brings me great satisfaction, and lest I leave the impression that I am totally alone here in the country, I must clearly state that this is hardly the case. I have visitors and friendly neighbors. They invite me to lovely dinners and casual visits and I return their invitations with pleasure. I have a housekeeper who is a fine cook. Dorette comes in every morning to look after me and my country cottage. She is married to the Claremont stationmaster. Over her delicious meals in my charming dining room my new friends ask about my time in Paris and I enjoy telling them about the city as I knew it. On the third Wednesday of every month

I receive the greenhouse catalogues from the planting fields at Vincennes. I have learned to look ahead to the growing season well in advance of its arrival and like my country neighbors, I order my cuttings and seed packets early and prepare accordingly. Occasionally I travel to Paris. I stay with Henri Villard and Lily at their house in the Rohan Courtyards. Lily never married. She came close once or twice, but she has remained devoted to Henri and to life in the familiarity of the Courtyards. She is the same strongly opinionated person she was as a young girl and the Courtyards are as secluded and insulated as they were in my day. Of course, few of the Courtyard residents I knew now live behind the protective gate at the end of Rue du Jardinet. Most have either moved away or died. I am happy to say that Henri is in good health, but Claire died three years ago. She took ill with a winter cold. It developed into an infection from which she never recovered. Henri misses her terribly, but he goes on as best he can. He continues to run the bookstore with Lily. He tells me he hopes to die there one day, slumped over a stack of books. The third floor of the Villard house is still my domain, exactly as it was years ago when I arrived in Paris, struggling to adjust to a new life. The ceiling at the end of the sitting room continues to be the same sloping challenge it was then, and during my last visit I bumped my head against it just as I had in the past. Strange as it seems, there was something comforting about that painful bump. It gave me a sense of being welcomed into a familiar world where once, and when I needed it most, I had been loved and made to feel I belonged.

I do regret never having lived up to the agreement my good friend Andre Rousseau and I made as young men to meet every year at Jacotin Pond and jump in stark naked no matter how old or fat we became. In letters he sent over the years he reminded me of my great negligence in this matter, and always with his memorable friendly sarcasm. Andre was killed during the war. He had joined the French effort and lost his life at the Battle of Bellevue.

Here at Le Calme, what I treasure most is time to call my own. That freedom has provided me with a splendid peace of mind. I sometimes think Adele knew this would happen to me here; that I would find the center of myself in her favorite place in all the world, and that here I would find the better part of her as well. Did she hope I would learn to love her here at La Calme? I think so. And I have; not as the eager, passionate lover she once knew, but as a good friend; as a close ally and confidant with an understanding heart. Adele was difficult and could be terribly foolish, but despite her demands and contradictory moods I believe she knew what she meant to me. I confess to missing her. I think of her more often than I care to admit, but in a fleeting moment when I am in the garden or sitting in my chair by the fireplace I will suddenly remember the sound of her beautiful singing voice, the lilt of her laughter, and the comforting touch of her lovely hand. It is as if a part of her remains alive for me alone.

Daniel and I exchange letters now. I treasure each one I receive from him. I save them in the top drawer of my desk. The letters I write to him are addressed to Monsieur Charles Lazare, but in the body of the letter itself I always begin with Dear Daniel. When he last wrote, he suggested that I at least try to refer to him as Charles. This will never happen. To me he will always be Daniel, and in my next letter I must remind him of that fact. He lives in America now, in New York City. He owns and operates the Clarke Galleries on an avenue he tells me is called Madison. I am proud to say that his client list is long and impressive. He is well-connected and successful. And he is married! To a niece of the Clarkes. Her name is Elizabeth. I am very happy for them. They have two children. A third is on the way. I am a grandfather.

⎯⎯⎯ ⎯⎯⎯

As I reflect on what I have written across these pages, I am confronted by measures of pleasure and pain and not just a little doubt. Part of the pleasure comes in knowing I contributed to the transformation of a city that is loved and revered throughout the world, but greater pleasure comes with the knowledge that my son Daniel is living a happy, productive life. He has met his goals with hard work and constant study. Best of all he is blessed with what he has always wanted: a family of his own. This, more than any other milestone or success in his life makes me happy, but I do often think of those three years we spent together. They are precious to me. In those moments when I have received his letter from New York and hold it in my hands, I find myself thinking back to one incident or another we shared long ago and I pray that at the time I was setting a good example; saying the right thing, doing the right thing. The pain always comes with the knowledge that Daniel and I have never known the loving relationship a father and son should know. I suppose many people live their lives under similarly unpleasant circumstances, at some point taking comfort in apologies and empty promises, but it takes time to process through the pain. Once he reads this memoir, I hope Daniel will experience very little, if any, pain. There is no reason for him to be hurt by learning the truth about himself with anything but pride. He started life at a great disadvantage, but through all his challenges, and there have been many, he has triumphed. I thought long and hard about placing this new burden on his shoulders but I cannot take this secret to my grave.

Daniel, my son, the time is right to tell you everything as I have here. I am encouraged by the fact that you are at a solid stage in life. You have your own family to love and care for and having spent as much time with you as I did in London, and from what you tell me in your letters from New York, I have no doubt whatsoever that you will handle what you learn from these pages as you have handled all the unforeseen circumstances you have faced: with your natural optimism and uncommon grace. You are after all, and will always be to me, the boy who appeared on a Paris boulevard one September morning, the splendid boy who moved like the wind, his cheeks flushed, his flaxen hair a ready foil for the bright glimmer of sun that seemed so eager to follow him.

THE END

AFTERWORD

In preparation for the writing of **BUILD ME A CITY** my research and inspiration were drawn from many sources, both written and personal. I would like in particular to name *The Works of Voltaire: Essays on Literature, Philosophy, Art, History* (John Morley), *Thomas Jefferson's Enlightenment: Paris 1785* (James C. Thompson), *Walks Through Lost Paris* (Leonard Pitt), *Americans in Paris* (Brian N. Morton), *Napoleon III and His Regime* (David Baguley), *Napoleon III and His Carnival Empire* (John Bierman), *A Duel of Giants* (David Wetzel), *Napoleon III — A Life* (Fenton Bresler), *Haussmann, His Life and Times* (Michel Carmona), *Transforming Paris* (David P. Jordan), *Marville* (Sarah Kennel), *Charles Marville: Photographs of Paris, 1852- 1878* (Alliance Francaise, Jacqueline Chambord, Editor), *Baron Haussmann* (J.M and Brian Chapman), *Literary Cafes of Paris* (Noel Riley Fitch), *Elegant Wits and Grand Horizontals* (Cornelia Otis Skinner), *The Fall of Paris* (Alistair Horne), *Chantilly, The Conde Nast Museum* (Raymond Gazelles, Curator of The Collection), *A History of Private Life* (Philippe Aries and Georges Duby, General Editors), *The Piano Shop on the Left Bank* (Thad Carhart).

For facilitating the production of this book I extend thanks to Christopher Caspers and Nile Graphics. I wish to thank Barbara Feighner for her book cover design. I am grateful for the interest of friends Eva Maria and Didier Ernotte who graciously offered me access to their rare Volumes of French History and introduced me to Josette Levrivain-Comte who I thank for her photographs of Chateau Haussmann at Cestas as it exists today.

Nancy Joaquim